Original Intent

a novel by
Drew Nelson

ISBN: 1475289464
ISBN 13: 9781475289466

A Note on Characters

for Laine

The only real security of liberty, in any country, is the jealousy and circumspection of the people themselves. Let them be watchful over their rulers. Should they find a combination against their liberties, and all other methods appear insufficient to preserve them, they have, thank God, an ultimate remedy.

JAMES IREDELL

North Carolina, July 1778

Prologue

Paris, France
April 7, 1783

She crossed the worn threshold of the tavern and slithered through the cracks in the sea of coattails, her pale petticoat breaching the brown mass as she moved toward the American. Strands of her midnight hair had pulled free and were swinging loosely around her shoulders. They swayed left, then left again as she effortlessly brushed away a few stray looks and an unwelcome hand.

In her wake, the patrons whispered, "La femme fatale."

The American saw only potential.

A beautiful creature, he thought as he watched her approach. *More than enough to turn the head of the Ambassador*. Benjamin Franklin's interest in the women of Paris was legendary. His hands were as relentless as his mind. The curved hips of the French woman, the American knew, would be irresistible.

It took only a single introduction to begin the affair.

༄

The American sidestepped a carriage, plunging the sole of his left boot deep into the slop of the thoroughfare. As he crossed the street, he checked the reflection in the dirty glass of the shop windows. He saw no glimpse of Thomas.

He reached the sputtering lamps of the tavern and glanced back once more into the fading light of the evening. The American had been in Paris for months now, and these late strolls had become more than a habit. Many evenings he would allow his young son to accompany him. Other nights he would walk alone. Yet even then, he would catch glimpses of Thomas, or at least a shadow shaped like the curious twelve-year-old, dancing in and out of the lamplight and trailing him. Reprimanding the child seemed to have little effect. Thomas, like the city around him, was developing a taste for rebellion.

The formal name of the tavern was engraved on the door in front of him: *La Grande Taverne de Toussaint*. Standing three blocks south of the American Ambassadorial Residence, its location perfectly suited the needs of the American. Yet, despite the lofty location, at this tavern, formality ended at the door. On the streets of Paris it was known simply as the *la tavern grande*. And in that scornful accent only a Parisian can summon, the word *grande* was often accompanied by a mocking tone.

It was here that he had first met the French woman. And it was here that they had met roughly every fourth or fifth night since – as they would again tonight.

While he waited, he studied the crowd shifting in front of his splintered table. It was the standard mix of working-class Frenchmen and merchants. A wagon wheel dangled above the gathering, hanging parallel to the floor from its four rusty chains. The chandelier it replaced had been sold years ago. It hung motionless, the melting candles affixed to its edge periodically dripping wax onto the shuffling crowd at the bar below.

"You've brought the notes?" the American quietly asked, as he helped the French woman into her seat. He tossed his right hand toward the bar, signaling for another glass of what passed for wine in the Grande Taverne. He admired her clothing as he returned to his chair. She had made substantial changes to her attire since their first meal. Likewise, he had adjusted his etiquette. The changes had allowed them to blend with the surrounding tables.

"Yes. Ambassador Franklin has been a charming host," she replied in heavily accented English, the slightest hint of a sarcastic smile floating over her lips. From below the table, her hands produced a small set of loosely bound notes. "He had discarded them. Just as you thought."

His hand reached for the notes while his eyes watched the other tables. There was no response from the crowd, no lingering looks of interest. As he had planned, the months of dining had dulled the attention of the tavern's faithful patrons. *We have simply become part of the backdrop*, he thought. *Just another table. Another empty bottle of wine and half-eaten loaf of bread.*

The American smiled as he received the bound notes. "You've done well. Exceptionally well." He quickly thumbed through the pages. It would take weeks, and men with a far-different skill set than his, to understand their meaning and apply their science. His task had been to relieve Ambassador Franklin of these particular notes. Or to confirm that the rumors reaching the American shores had been false.

He had done the former. His fellow members would be pleased.

As he rose from the table, he pulled his overcoat across his shoulders and slipped the notes into an interior pocket, exchanging them with the envelope of francs he had been carrying. The money bulged against the brown paper and the frayed strands of twine barely holding the package closed. Moving carefully so as to not attract attention, the American slipped the stuffed envelope onto the wooden table. With his other hand he lifted the remainder of his wine.

"Thank you, Monsieur Augusteel," the French woman responded, as she retracted the envelope onto her lap.

"No names, please."

"But, it is over," she replied, the money now concealed by her crossed arms.

The American could read the relief on her face. He had wondered how long she could continue to fool the great Franklin. *Long enough*, he thought, smiling. *Long enough. That is all that mattered.*

"Indeed, it is over, mademoiselle," he replied, his calculating, ice-blue eyes studying the contours of her chin and the bend of her flawless neck. His arm remained suspended above the table. He tilted the rim of his raised wine glass toward the French woman.

"To the Republic," the American said quietly, offering a departing toast as his eyes continued examining the woman's neck. Emptying his glass, the American turned to leave the Grande Taverne for the last time.

∽

Eleven steps from the threshold of the tavern the French woman ducked into the entrance of a darkened alley. Her feet balanced along the tops of the mud-drenched, uneven stones of the old path. It was finished, finally finished. The game had exhausted her. The charade had depleted her. Franklin had been easy to seduce, but difficult to deceive. She knew the Ambassador had grown suspicious.

She clung tightly to the bound lump of francs, hidden and nestled, cradled in her arms like a child. The package felt like a safety blanket in the Paris night. The lamps, stationed along the street she had just left, flickered over her hunched shoulders. In the dying light, she glanced downward once more as she navigated the alley's rounded, slick stones. It was her money. Not her father's. Not a token gift from some suitor in the King's court. *Her money.* It was money to run, to shake loose the shackles of society, to disappear into the revolutionary mist gathering in the far corners of the country. It was money to . . .

Before she could register the movement, the glove whipped around her mouth; the grip was steel, stifling. Her involuntary scream never left the leather hand. She flailed against the iron arm. The blade of the American flashed against the soft white of her throat. The envelope of francs spilled over the wet stones, the thin paper absorbing, first, the watery mud of the alley, and then the blood of the French woman.

The American cautiously stepped over her body and made his way back toward the mouth of the dim passage. Looking up, his blue eyes met the wide eyes of Thomas Augusteel. The twelve-year-old boy was frozen on the edge of the thoroughfare, again a shadow against the glare of the Paris street lamps. The unanticipated appearance of his son made the American hesitate.

Thomas followed me to the tavern.

Then the feeling passed, and was replaced by a different sentiment.

It was time he learned, the American thought, his leather-gloved fingers unconsciously patting the pages of notes folded into the interior pocket of his overcoat. Failed though it might be in the eyes of the great statesman, Franklin's work had immense value. The inventor may not appreciate the invention. The man who forges a sword does not necessarily wield it best.

Jefferson, Adams, Hamilton, the others; they all squabbled over their competing ideas – but it was men like the American, men like those within the league, that would determine the course of American development. There was a war being waged for the infant soul of America. And the Augusteel family was bringing a new weapon to her shores.

Chapter One

Twenty days before the execution of Parker Brown

Judge William Iredell glanced past the shoulder of his tailored, charcoal suit. His left hand gripped the handle of the unmarked door. Above him, the summer night stretched like a carnival tent, draping the skyline of government and professional buildings in downtown DC. Down the alley and across K Street, his fellow judge offered a final wave. A town car cut between them. The sound of its passing engine drowned out the other man's voice. *Had he offered another parting "congratulations" – or was it simply good-bye?*

Iredell returned the wave with his available hand. He shuffled his feet as he waited for the signal to enter.

Loose pebbles scattered like ants fleeing the hard soles of his dress shoes. A security camera, bolted to the nondescript side-wall of the office building, angled down toward the judge. The lens spun, the mechanical pupil narrowing until it focused on the late visitor. With a near-silent click, the magnetic lock released the door. William Iredell twisted the metal lever, spilling light from the well-lit lobby onto the gravelly rear entrance of the Lexington League's Washington office.

Iredell took one more look down the alley before stepping onto the marble floor. He was in the heart of the American power structure. Stationed on the corner of K Street and 14th, the office stood only a few blocks from the White House and a few more from the U.S. Capitol. From this central location, the conservative organization had functioned as a primary player in every political or legal movement since the early 1990s.

While its K Street address physically positioned the Lexington League near the center of conservative political power, figuratively, it had gradually become the center. No significant issue moved without Lexington League investigation, no debate without its influence. Most importantly, no conservative judicial candidate moved without its endorsement. Its growth had been astounding. Within five years of its establishment, judicial candidates wielded its support as a weapon in the political wars. Within ten years, the Lexington League welcomed its first Supreme Court Justice to its ranks.

And with the confirmation of Judge William Iredell, the Lexington League was poised to control – for the first time – a majority on the Supreme Court of the United States.

"I'm here to see . . . ," Judge Iredell started, crossing the empty, marble floor and walking toward the intense stare of the armed guard. Yet, before he could finish, the guard cocked his head toward the open elevator doors to Iredell's right. The judge hesitated; then he realized that the guard had been expecting him. In the brief moment of quiet, he heard the magnetic lock reseal the external door behind him.

Iredell pivoted toward the open elevator. *These people supported me from the start*, he thought. His seat on the Supreme Court had been a foregone conclusion by the time the Lexington League had finished laying the groundwork. His confirmation – first by the Senate Judiciary Committee and then, only a few hours ago, by the Senate as a whole – had never been in doubt.

Judge Iredell's background was perfect. He was a former prosecutor and had served the last twelve years on the federal appellate bench. His academic credentials left no room to question his competence, and his scholarship on traditional conservative issues left no room to question his commitment.

The icing on the cake was his blood-line. William Iredell was a direct descendant of James Iredell, a Founding Father from North Carolina and one of the first men appointed to the Supreme Court. With this sort of lineage, William Iredell's background was easily distilled into a compelling narrative for the evening news broadcasts.

The Lexington League had endorsed him. The President had nominated him. And the Senate had confirmed him earlier that evening. In three days he would be sworn in as the next United States Supreme Court Justice

As he stepped onto the polished wood of the elevator, Iredell felt the three pages of the letter rustle in the interior pocket of his suit. His ascent to the Court had been well-planned, well-oiled, and well-executed from the beginning. He hoped it would stay that way after tonight.

❧

Like an ornate curtain, the elevator doors parted and Judge William Iredell entered the penthouse conference room. He was of average height, with a thick stock of brown hair and an air about him that bordered on regal. Even outside his judicial robe, Iredell carried himself with the controlled assertiveness of one in charge of his surroundings.

As Iredell entered the room, his host rose from one of the room's five leather seats. A taller man than Iredell, he rounded the oaken table in the center and strode toward the judge. "Judge – or should I say Justice – Iredell," he said, his hand extended and his smile broadening. "Congratulations on your confirmation to the Supreme Court."

Below the two men, the eight floors of offices were empty. Hours ago, the attorneys and staff of the Lexington League had exited into the Washington streets. William Iredell reached for the extended hand of his host as he replied. "I appreciate you meeting me at this hour. And I am pleased that we've been able to find a quiet place to talk. In all the times I've visited your offices, I don't think I've come in the back door. And I'm fairly certain I've never seen this room."

As his hand grasped the palm of his host, Iredell examined the five-sided table in the center of the conference room. It had been the first aspect of the room to catch his eye – as it usually was for the few people who had visited the room. Other than the table, there was nothing particularly impressive about the space. It was a standard, executive conference room, constructed above the office levels and reachable only by an elevator dedicated exclusively to the room. Access was carefully controlled by the guard on the ground floor.

Besides the unique table and its surrounding five chairs, the simply decorated room held a small, but rather ornamental, wet bar. A large flat-screen television was attached to the wall opposite the elevator doors. Below the television sat a small table, holding the room's communication equipment and other electronic devices. To Iredell's right, a bank of windows looked out onto the Washington night. To his left, a portrait of James Madison hung on the otherwise empty wall.

"His first Inaugural, 1809," his host offered, turning toward the picture.

"To prefer in all cases amicable discussion and reasonable accommodation of differences to a decision of them by an appeal to arms," quoted Iredell, his eyes failing to leave Madison's face.

"I should have expected you'd know the speech." His host laughed and pulled one of the five chairs away from the conference table. "Please have a seat, judge. You know, I read a great deal of your writing over the last few months; a lot of people in this building did," he noted as he took his own seat toward the far end of the table. "We look forward to having your pen on our side of the Court."

Iredell let his gaze linger a moment longer on the Madison portrait before he acknowledged his host's comment with a slight nod of his head. "We do indeed see eye-to-eye on a series of issues. And I want to personally thank you for your support, and the Lexington League's endorsement."

"If memory serves," his host responded, "you've been a member since your days at Yale. In fact, I just read one of your law review articles from back then. A beautifully argued defense of states' rights in the face of an overbearing federal government," the host continued, touching on a cornerstone of conservative judicial philosophy. "Amen to that. And I'd think you'd get an 'amen' from Mr. Madison, up there, too."

"Maybe so," Iredell replied. "Of course, it is always difficult to nail down exactly what they thought back then."

His host rose from his leather chair and strolled toward the broad panel of windows. The lights below were dispersed unevenly across the capitol city, dotting the dark landscape like spilled marbles. "Thankfully though, we have their writing," the taller man offered. *The Federalist Papers*, the notes from the ratification debates, and in Madison's case, the Constitution itself. They point us toward a better understanding of what our forefathers were thinking.

"Your work on the federal bench has been a testament to this idea," the host continued. "You want to know what the Constitution means? You want to know how to interpret it? How to understand its sometimes vague and complex language? Look to the people that wrote it; look to their work. Look to the original intent: the Constitution means what the Framers meant it to mean. We follow their lead."

Iredell remained seated, but rotated toward his host. His head tracked the taller man as he moved through the conference room, observing every step he took, just as the Lexington League's security camera had tracked Iredell only moments before. "You'll get an 'amen' from me on that," the judge responded.

His back still turned to the judge, the host raised his hands in mock surrender while his eyes focused on the distant light rotating at the top of the Washington Monument. Like a ruler towering over his servants he surveyed the streets below. "I'm sorry, judge. We get so used to defending 'originalism' around here that sometimes I forget my audience.

You, of all people, certainly don't need a lecture from me on the intent of the Founding Fathers.

"But I will tell you this," the host continued, spinning toward Iredell. "There are a lot of people in this building – in this country – that are excited about you taking your seat on the Court. The fifth vote; a majority of the nine! We've never had that before."

Iredell's gaze finally broke from his host. The judge reached for the three folded sheets of paper stored in the breast pocket of his suit. Straightening them on the conference table, he noticed the pause in his host's speech. Iredell had the man's attention.

The judge could feel his blood pressure rising. He hadn't known it would be here, in this room, but he had known this moment would eventually come. Without looking away from the papers, he spoke, his voice taking on the tone of a professor offering a question to his class of first-year law students. "What if the intent of the Founding Fathers was for us to disregard their intent?"

Iredell raised his eyes and looked toward his host. The taller man seemed to be frozen in contemplation. Reaching forward across the table, the judge gently pushed the folded paper toward the other man.

"What is that?" His host was advancing now, moving around the conference table toward the documents.

"Some words from a Founding Father, or at least a copy."

The host picked up the papers and pulled out the nearest chair, scanning the date at the top of the first page. He read the first paragraph and then quickly flipped to the last page, searching for a signature. Turning back to the first page, the host stared at Judge Iredell as though the man had just handed him some sort of bomb. "Is this real?"

"Yes."

"You said this was a copy?"

"It is. But I have the original. Safely stored, of course."

Iredell continued to speak as his host read through the three-page document. "As you know, the process judicial nominees are put through is, shall we say, vigorous. Maybe 'intrusive' would be the better word. I wanted to be prepared for anything that the liberals could dig up, so I conducted my own search. I knew that if I dug deeper, and searched harder, I would be ready."

Iredell tapped the top of the page his host was reading. "My research yielded the original version of this letter."

The host froze, his eyes lifting from the third page where some notes had been made in the margin. He stopped reading and locked on Judge Iredell. "Where is the original?"

"I wanted to show you this copy before I showed anyone else. I felt I owed you that after your endorsement."

"So no one else knows about this? No one else has read it?" asked the host, having finished the final page and double-checked the signature. He dropped the letter back on the conference table, rose, and stepped toward the windows. Even over the short distance, a new unsteadiness was apparent in his stride.

"No. Not yet," William Iredell responded.

The beacon on top of the Washington Monument was shining in the distance, hovering over the rest of the city. The lights of the White House were visible – the windows were dark, but the surrounding grounds were lit with the dull glow of flood lights. The host could see the reflection of the conference room in the glass. The wet bar. The elevator doors. Madison, seemingly staring straight ahead, sharing the view of the Washington night.

Behind him, Iredell collected the three pages of the letter and returned them to his suit pocket.

The host wheeled toward the conference table, turning in place and then stepping toward the wet bar. "Judge, I'd like to hear your thoughts on that letter," he said, his steps accelerating as he walked toward the bar. "It is a lot to take in, a lot to consider. I'm still trying to digest its meaning. You think you can slip your judicial robe back on and help me out?" the host asked, desperate to keep Iredell and the letter in the room.

Iredell hesitated. "Well, I would have considered it pretty self-explanatory."

"Judge, you know we invested a lot in your nomination and confirmation – and I'm not just talking about the Lexington League. There's a mountain of conservative activists in this town that picked up an oar for you, not to mention all the people across the country emailing and calling their senators in support."

Iredell's host had reached the wet bar and was unlocking the cabinet beneath. Kneeling, he called back toward the opposite side of the room. "I'm not asking you to abandon your principles, but I'm going to have to answer to all of those people."

The host rose to his feet, unfolding his tall frame. His back was to the conference table, but Iredell could see the man's hand reach for one of the bottles behind the bar. He could hear the splash of liquid hitting empty glass.

"Judge," the host continued, turning toward Iredell, a drink in each hand, "I've got to tell those people something. I backed you. You're our fifth vote. You were going to help us turn back the tide." The host strolled back toward the conference table. "In three days the President is going to

swear you in. Once word of this letter is out, every conservative activist in this country is going to unleash their political
attack-dogs."

The host neared Iredell's seat and offered the drink in his
left hand to Iredell. "Scotch, unless I'm mistaken.

"They'll do everything they can to keep you off the
Court," the host continued. "But it is like you said: 'To prefer
in all cases amicable discussion and reasonable accommodation of differences to a decision of them by an appeal to arms.'
I think we should talk about that letter before you show anyone the original version."

The host raised the glass of scotch that remained in his
right hand. "To the Republic."

Iredell accepted the glass, raised it, and tipped the glass
toward his host. "Indeed," he answered. The judge pulled a
long sip of the scotch as he stood to leave. "However, I'm not
sure there is much to discuss."

"Fair enough," the host answered. "It's your letter and
your confirmation. We'll play it according to your rules." He
extended a hand toward the departing judge.

Iredell reached for it, but suddenly felt a flush of heat
come over him. His outstretched hand reached for the corner
of the conference table. He guided himself back into his seat.

"Mr. Iredell." His host remained standing, slightly leaning over the collapsed judge. "The copy that is in your pocket,
is that the only one?"

Judge Iredell pushed his chair back from the table. He
fought to stand. "It is," he heard himself saying. It felt like
the answer had come from outside his body, like he was
standing behind himself and watching another man answer.
He staggered back toward the elevator, searching for the call
button.

His host stepped closer to him. "Where is the original version of this letter?"

Iredell had reached the elevator doors, but couldn't find the call button. His vision beginning to narrow, he steadied himself with one hand on the elevator door. "No," he coughed, fighting the urge to respond.

His host advanced another step, preparing to catch the judge. The substance had been used before, but the host had never seen it in person. The judge would eventually be incapacitated; that much was known. But the guidance that had been passed down over the years indicated that each recipient would react at a different pace, and in a different way.

"Judge, where is the original version of the letter?"

Iredell leaned against the elevator doors, fighting to focus on anything in the room. His eyes landed on the portrait of Madison — his writing had built the American government; now it would change it. Hands pressed against his chest, he instinctively protected the copied pages in his coat pocket. William Iredell locked eyes with his host, summoning every ounce of self-control he could gather.

It was not enough.

"Edenton. My family's house," Judge Iredell released, one hand reaching out to the elevator frame to prop himself upright.

The taller man had what he needed. Advancing toward the communication table on the opposite side of the room, the host offered only a quiet, sarcastic reply: "thank you, Judge," and pressed the button to call the elevator.

Iredell could feel the soft rumbling of the elevator as it climbed the eight floors. His eyes closed, he remained leaning against the ornate interior doors of the elevator. His labored breathing filled the otherwise silent conference room.

With a ring, the elevator doors opened. Judge William Iredell tumbled backwards into the chamber, landing with his legs extending over the threshold and stretching back into the room.

His host crossed to the elevator, collecting both glasses of scotch on the way. He stood over the collapsed judge. For a brief second, he watched the judge writhe at his feet. Then he tipped the two glasses of scotch. The liquid, dribbling at first, but then pouring forth, spilled onto the chest of William Iredell. With a foot, the host unceremoniously pushed the legs of the man expected to become the next United States Supreme Court Justice into the small elevator. "Thank you, Judge," the host repeated.

෨

His first phone call was to the private guard at the base of the elevator. "Judge Iredell may have had a little too much to drink this evening," the host instructed the guard. "Please help him – *quietly* – find a hotel room for the night."

Iredell was no longer the main concern; as far as the Lexington League knew no person had lasted more than a day after a dose of the powdered substance. Most had lasted less.

The contents of the letter were what mattered now. A copy could be easily dismissed, but the original version was a real threat. Its validity could be established, and if made public, it could disrupt most of what the Lexington League had worked for.

Putting a foot on one of the curved legs of conference table, the host withdrew a cell phone and reclined to make his second phone call.

"Yes," Gloria Augusteel answered.

"Gloria, it's me. I need you to go to Edenton, North Carolina. I'll need your brother, too."

Chapter Two

Edenton, North Carolina
August 20, 1798

*T*he old man sat sullen; his white hair, unruly and cascading down the back slope of his rounded head like a rolling snowdrift. His glasses were in his hands. The wrinkled fingers held the wiry frames as though they intended to clean the lenses, but had paused midway through, having realized that nothing in this prison would ever be clean.

Thomas Augusteel's eager, blue eyes watched the white-haired man from across the holding room. Augusteel silently rehearsed his story. *Gambling debts*, the young man reminded himself. *Unpaid gambling debts. That is why I'm here.*

The debtors' prison was dirty. And the daily holding room was no exception. In some places the floor had rotted through to the soil below. Six benches stretched across the open, roughly square enclosure. The wooden seats were maybe half full this morning, as some of the men had congregated in the corners of the large cell. Others milled about, pacing along the cracks in the worn-out, plank floor. The holding area had a door on one end through which the prisoners would trudge back to their cells at night. On the other side, the iron bars of a large gate divided the men inside from the handful of clerks and guards in the front room. Sunlight passed through four barred windows along the single exterior wall. The room held the men during the day, like a cage, a dumping ground for the shamefully indebted.

Augusteel rose from his seat, passed the benches between himself and the old man, and worked through the crowd. It was calm today. Sometimes things could get out of hand; debtors' prison was unpredictable – or so he had been told by other members of the league. It took all kinds: from the common drunk, to the deckhand, to the upper crust of the cultured class – hell, even an Indian or two had passed through these filthy walls. It was anyone and everyone in the great state of New Jersey who found himself without the means to pay his debt. It could be a combustible mixture. *Even him*, Thomas considered, rounding the final bench and eyeing the old man. *Even one of the great minds of our nation is locked in here.*

Augusteel gathered his final thoughts as he took a seat opposite the old man. He was now just feet from his target. "Justice Wilson?" he asked, his blond-haired head tilting toward his shoulder as he spoke, trying to catch the eyes of the man across from him. Augusteel's voice was low, well-buried under the din of the packed holding room.

There was no response.

Behind Augusteel, a prisoner began pounding against the iron gate. The thudding noise rebounded into the room. He raised his voice, eclipsed the racquet, and tried again. "Justice Wilson? I'm Thomas Augusteel. I believe we met in Charleston last year," he lied.

A grunt. The old man looked away as he returned his glasses to his eyes.

There is still some fire in him, Augusteel thought, as Wilson's eyes briefly passed into, and then out of, sight. *He hasn't been entirely broken yet.* The ghosts of failed, speculative investments had trailed Wilson for years. And the connections and "gentlemen's agreements" he had earned from his central role at the Constitutional Convention had finally run out. His heavy debt had landed this sitting Justice of the United States Supreme Court in this confined holding room. More importantly for Thomas Augusteel, the Justice's debt had given the Lexington League an opening.

"Justice Wilson," Augusteel continued, undeterred by the silence from the opposite bench. "What sort of misunderstanding has placed you here, sir? What sort of man would bring a claim against you? It seems entirely uncalled for – a man of your stature, sir, locked in a place like this. Certainly there has been some error."

This earned little more than a second grunt from the Justice.

Augusteel studied his target, examining the older man for any sign of acknowledgement. The league had placed Thomas Augusteel here. But he was not here simply to look. He was not here to watch or to learn. The league had already taken those steps. Augusteel was here to engage. Before him was James Wilson, whose name appeared on the Declaration of American Independence, who received one of General Washington's original appointments to the newly formed Supreme Court of the United States, who led men in revolutionary battle. Yet, here Wilson sat, surrounded by his brothers in debt, like a stubborn, aging turtle with little reason to move – a fixture on this broken and creaking bench, instead of the gleaming wood of some courthouse bench.

"Justice Wilson." Augusteel inched closer as he spoke, leaning between the two men to narrow the distance. "Let me help you, sir." This was the moment. "My father will arrive soon. I – how shall I put this? – wagered, and sadly lost, more than I had with me yesterday evening. Let my family put an end to whatever dispute has landed you here. Let us pay your debt."

For the first time, Associate Justice James Wilson raised his tired head and acknowledged Thomas Augusteel. He hesitated before answering, pausing as if he was pondering the offer. It was a deliberate move that was to be expected from a man with his illustrious background. Pride was often the last wall to crumble.

Yet, both Thomas Augusteel and James Wilson knew the old man had already made his decision. He had only one way out of the holding cell.

After the false hesitation, Wilson accepted – and made an offer of his own: would the young man consider becoming his personal clerk?

The blue eyes of Thomas Augusteel sparkled in the hazy light of the prison.

∽

Over the year that followed, Augusteel was nothing short of a loyal and dutiful clerk for the Pennsylvanian. However, as he served, he scrutinized James Wilson. He studied the aging Justice: the forswearing of speculation, the redoubling of his effort on the judicial circuit, the subtle twitch in his hands and pause in his speech prior to his abrupt denial of every new investment opportunity in the West.

But over their time together, he noticed another of Wilson's desires, the desire for which Augusteel had been sent to watch, the reason the Lexington League had worked to place Thomas Augusteel in the same prison as James Wilson: James Wilson longed to return to a more prestigious role in the new republic. The few cases heard by the new Supreme Court were failing to create the sort of grandeur worthy of a mind like James Wilson's.

Sensing his opening, Augusteel moved quickly to exploit Wilson's ambitions. Initially, it was simply questions about General Washington and comments on the wealth being accumulated by speculators in southern real estate. Then it was the upcoming election. *Could Adams repel the Jefferson charge? Did Justice Wilson miss the give-and-take of politics? Did he feel stifled by his seat on the Court?* He nurtured the seed of speculation, knowing that the prospect of quick wealth was never far from Wilson's mind: *Would the Justice like Augusteel to introduce him to investors in North Carolina?* He stoked the fires of glory:

Was Justice Wilson ready to, again, fight for the American cause?

◌

Augusteel's plot came together. Step by step, he nudged Wilson closer to the edge. Late August brought the unrelenting heat of the summer and the final stage of the plan: it was time to pull back the curtain. Augusteel's task had been to plant the seed and work the soil; introducing Wilson to the men in the upper levels of the Lexington League should bring forth the fruit.

They left Pennsylvania and traveled south. By the time they crossed from Virginia into North Carolina everything had been arranged. Augusteel delivered Wilson to the prearranged location and then retreated to the rooms he had rented in Wilson's name.

He paced as he waited, retracing the same floorboard as he traveled the length of the short room. Augusteel checked his pocketwatch. The hours crawled slowly, but time nevertheless was passing. The sun set. Night fell. Augusteel waited.

Wilson's room was next to his, but he had heard nothing through the thin wood of the connecting door. He reclined on the rented bed. The tattered mattress was torn around three of the edges, but comfortable after the long ride south.

❦

"I want to leave with first light, Augusteel." James Wilson roused his clerk from sleep. His grip conveyed the same quiet urgency as his voice. "I want the horses prepared and our belongings packed."

Rubbing his eyes and reaching for his clothes, Augusteel tried to fight through the confusion. The room slowly came into focus, and he realized that Wilson had either already dressed or never undressed from the evening before.

Augusteel's pocketwatch was resting on his chest. He caught it as he rose from the bed. *The sun will rise within the hour.*

"Prepare the coach, Augusteel, and tell no-one of our plans, save those who must know," Wilson said over his shoulder as he walked into the adjoining room. Augusteel could hear him shuffling papers and clasping his small traveling trunk. "I shall meet you at the stables at sunrise," Wilson called back in the general direction of his clerk. "Offer the inn keeper whatever it takes to hire his driver."

Pulled between the adrenaline of sudden confusion and the leftover daze of sleep, Augusteel found the inn keeper already awake, talking quietly with a man Augusteel recognized from the evening's recruitment meeting. "Thomas Augusteel?" the man asked, extending his hand. Augusteel nodded in response, as he observed that this man, like James Wilson, remained in his formal dining attire from the night before.

He could see the man's hard eyes. They locked with his own.

"There is no time for formalities, Augusteel. We have friends in common. Do you understand?"

"I do," Augusteel replied, meeting the man's gaze.

"Our efforts with Wilson have failed."

Augusteel started to interrupt. Certainly with more time, he could bring Wilson around to their cause. The man waved for silence and continued. "Yet, it is worse than that. The notes from Franklin are missing."

Augusteel stole a glance at the clock over the man's shoulder as he spoke. Sunrise approached.

"Mr. Augusteel, Justice Wilson's interactions this evening were coordinated to keep him only in the company of dedicated members. We organized our recruitment so that it could easily be dismissed as idle political conversation should

Wilson choose to discuss our efforts in public, but if he has somehow learned about Franklin's notes – moreover, if he has the notes themselves – he can end us."

The man gestured toward the inn keeper. "He spotted Wilson briefly, but says he's left the inn. Is that true?"

"It is, sir. I'm to meet him at the stables. We're to leave at sunrise. Should I delay our departure?"

"No," the man responded. "If he's trusting you to leave with him, he must not know you're with us. Leave as planned. However . . . ." He paused, his hand disappearing into the side pocket of his overcoat. "Your assignment has changed."

꩜

Their rented stagecoach thundered across the jutted and muddy trails twelve miles north of Edenton. Roughly one day had passed since the recruitment had failed, but the absence of sleep and the ragged road beneath the wheels of the coach made it feel much longer.

They had crossed the northern finger of the Chowan River near midnight. If a trap had been set, Augusteel assumed it would have been at the bridge. He had searched the shadowed tree-line as they passed, but they crossed without incident. The coach had then turned south toward Edenton, sticking to the old Virginia road – the only trail toward Edenton that offered any chance of safe passage by night.

The gathering storm had followed them across eastern North Carolina. Initially every strike of lightning had snapped James Wilson's head toward the rear opening of the

27

coach. If the old man managed to see anything in the brief moment, it was only broken road and overhanging trees, and darkness beyond. No torches, no riders. By the time they had turned south, the storm had caught them.

Of the five lanterns Thomas Augusteel had purchased at the swing station, only two remained lit. Wilson had commanded that one be hooked to each corner of the coach and one left with the driver. The driving rain had extinguished two and one had rattled off as they pounded over the Chowan River bridge. The driver's light remained, shielded under the canvas canopy that kept the worst of the rain off his perch.

The fifth lantern, now hanging inside, on the wall of the cabin, was steadied by Augusteel's hand, its dwindling light reflecting off the pool of water lapping at the sides of their boots.

"Again, Augusteel," Wilson commanded his clerk as he turned toward the rear opening of the coach.

"Justice Wilson, I'm not certain we'll . . . ." He trailed off.

"Again. Now."

Augusteel's left hand found his lantern's handle while his right checked the two small vials secured in his traveling coat's pocket. He heaved open the plank covering the window of the coach and extended the lantern as far toward the rear as possible, silently praying that his final source of light would survive yet another excursion into the dark.

For a moment, the cabin was plunged into near blackness, and filled with the sounds of rain pounding the side of the coach and horses pounding over the muddy ground. They had acquired a new team of four at Tarborough. Justice

Wilson had hoped to drive them hard enough to reach Edenton by morning.

Outside, the light of the lantern did little to illuminate the road, and Augusteel quickly drew back the lantern as more rainwater splashed onto the cabin's floor.

As Augusteel struggled to slide the wooden window covering back into place, Wilson pulled his eyes away from the rear opening and turned to face across the cabin. He took another healthy sip of wine and wedged his cup back between his seat and the side door. "They're back there, Augusteel. They are coming for me. They know I took them," he said, his eyes darting around the corners of a cabin that seemed to be growing smaller by the mile.

The rented coach was far from waterproof and the intensity of the storm had discovered more inadequacies in its roof. The rainwater was rising in the floor, splashing over the toes of their boots and against the cabin walls, as the wooden cabin rocked with each new rut. Augusteel decided to give it one last effort. "Justice Wilson, I see no one behind us. I've seen no one since Tarborough."

"I've taken something from them, those men I met with. Something that can be traded. My ticket, Augusteel. My ticket back. Once we reach Edenton, it – and I – will be safe," Wilson yelled back over his shoulder, as he turned again toward the rear opening.

Augusteel sank back and pulled the lantern from the hook next to his seat. He had hoped to reason with Wilson, to convince him to return to Hillsborough, to the men from whom he fled. Yet, Thomas Augusteel had failed. He had hoped their coach would be overtaken or stopped along the way, but if the league had given chase, it had also failed. Edenton was only a few miles away and his options had been narrowed to one.

Placing the lantern on the floor of the cabin, he removed his traveling coat. Augusteel briefly turned his back to Wilson. Shielding his hands, he removed one of the two vials, and then hung his traveling coat on the hook that had been holding the lantern.

Augusteel had been given strict instructions: *Find out whether he has the notes. Take them back if he does. Allow Wilson to discuss this with no-one.*

He glanced at Wilson, double-checking that the Justice continued to stare into the darkness. Then he quickly reached across the cabin and emptied the contents of the vial into Wilson's wine cup. The white powder dissolved instantly, a dying cloud fading into the blood-red liquid.

"Justice Wilson, perhaps if I try the lamp again . . . ," he shouted over the storm.

"No. It does nothing," Wilson responded, waving off Augusteel with the back of his hand. He wheeled back into the cabin. "It makes no matter now. We're within a few miles."

Wilson stood into a half-crouch and crossed toward Augusteel. Reaching past his clerk, he opened the upper window into the driver's seat. Attempting to overpower the sound of the driving storm on the canvas cover, he called toward the driver. "When we get to Edenton, you're to go directly to Justice Iredell's. Do you know the house?"

"Yes, sir. I've taken men there before."

Wilson slammed the panel closed and fell back into his seat, reflexively reaching for his cup of wine. "Augusteel, they say that the darkest hour always comes before the dawn." He raised his cup, his outstretched arm swinging with the movement of the coach. "Lord, I hope they are right," he quietly mumbled, and then finished the cup in one swallow.

Wilson could instantly feel something. His joints were battered and numb from the ride, but now he felt a new sensation: a gentle tingling. No, pain. He adjusted himself in his seat and tried to stretch his arms.

"Sir." Augusteel had been told he needed to act fast. "Did you take Ambassador Franklin's notes when we were in Hillsborough?"

Stretching was not helping the pain. Wilson turned toward Augusteel. "What did you say? Can you help me out of this damned coat?!"

"Did you take Ambassador Franklin's notes when we were in Hillsborough?"

This time Wilson heard the question. It felt like the answer was climbing out of him, involuntarily pushing toward the surface, like lava rising toward the tip of a volcano. He no longer heard the storm or felt the rain sputtering through holes in the roof or saw the light from the lantern playing off the pooling water on the cabin floor. He felt the dull pain and the answer – moving, up. And then, out.

"Yes." It was true, but it felt confusing. He felt confused.

Augusteel's face moved in the foreground. "Sir, where are those notes now?"

"They are here." Again the answer seemed to simply rise from him. Wilson's hand reached to the side and rested on the clasp of the travelling trunk that sat next to him. "They are in my trunk." His head was swinging freely. He fought to keep it upright, to keep his eyes open. The pain grew within his chest.

Augusteel watched the older man. With a suddenness that surprised him, he saw Wilson's head fall to his chest. His body toppled toward the open space between the two coach seats. Augusteel lunged to grab the lapels of Wilson's coat, but could only grip his left arm. The right side of Wilson's body fell forward, toward the cabin floor; his knees splashed into the collected rainwater.

Thomas Augusteel saw it before it happened: Wilson's free right arm swung wildly to his side, driven by the momentum from the fall. His body separated Augusteel from the outstretched arm. Wilson's arm flailed freely in the open space of the cabin, and then circled downward. It crashed into the lantern at Augusteel's feet, shattering the glass.

The flash of the ignited oil lit the cabin like a sunburst. The flare fought off the encircling darkness for a brief second, but then gave way. The pooled water surged to the side and swallowed the remnants of the lantern just as the darkness of the hour surged into the cabin and swallowed Thomas Augusteel.

Chapter Three

Washington, DC
June 11, 2010

Nineteen days before the execution of Parker Brown

Chief Aaron Evanston adjusted his dark-blue dress uniform, pushed through the crowd of journalists, and climbed the three steps toward the wooden briefing podium. His 285-pound frame still technically fit into the uniform, but his midsection had reached an intolerable level of tightness over his twenty-three years on the Force. The steps bowed under his weight as he heaved himself up the short climb. The blue of his suit and his graying mustache left the reporters before him with the distinct impression of a grandfatherly seal lurching up an ice shelf. Reaching the podium, Evanston straightened his tie, smoothed his mustache, and tugged at the sides of his dress coat. He stole one last, deep breath before the show started.

The small briefing room at the U.S. Capitol Police's Public Information Office was not set up for this type of overflow crowd. Its worn blue carpet had been here longer than Chief Evanston and of its thirty seats – arranged in six rows of five and climbing toward a rack of stage lights in the rear – at least three could no longer safely support the weight of the typical DC journalist.

Evanston could see camera crews from the national networks lining the back of the room. Silhouetted against the cameras' lights, Evanston's public information officer scrambled in and out of the stenciled, glass door along the left wall, weaving her way through the throng of reporters and then weaving her way back out into the neighboring hall. *She's in over her head*, Evanston thought as he watched her try to hold seats open for the Capitol correspondents from the major media outlets and simultaneously try to usher in as many local cameramen as could fit along the side walls. *We're all in over our head on this one.*

"Good evening," he started, gently leaning into the bank of microphones haphazardly clipped to the podium. Glancing down, he hoped those microphones would hide both his notes and the slightly shaking right hand that held them. "I am Chief Aaron Evanston, with the U.S. Capitol Police." Each camera now flashed a red light. *We're live*, he thought. And, not for the first time that day, prayed he was making the right decision.

An excited restlessness surrounded him in the room. The raised platform felt like an island in a boiling sea of whispered comments. Against the hushed voices of the reporters, his voice sounded clipped, overly formal. "I am going to make a brief statement and then I will take questions. At the outset, let me state that I am not in a position to provide any information concerning any ongoing investigations by the U.S. Capitol Police or the FBI." Evanston turned toward the younger man standing slightly behind him at the podium. "To my left is Dr. Samuel Ortiz, a deputy chief medical examiner in the District's medical examiner's office. He is here to handle any medical questions to the extent that they can be answered at this point."

Evanston's eyes scanned the reporters in the front rows. Their heads were buried in their small notebooks, their hands flipping pages and scratching notes. He could tell the difference between the television reporters and those from the newspapers. The television reporters – or in some cases, *personalities* – were well-dressed, each hair in its styled place and ready to "go live" as soon as the press conference ended. The newspaper reporters had the luxury of working off-camera. No tie matched the dress shirt beneath. He couldn't see a dress coat on the back of any of their seats. Of course, he couldn't blame them. It was DC in the summer, after all.

His public information officer was still ushering some of the late arrivals into their reserved seats. Evanston continued. "We'll be joined momentarily by Carol Cushing, the United States Attorney for DC. My understanding is that she is finishing up a press conference concerning the Parker Brown sentencing hearing that was held this afternoon. Her office has jurisdiction over all crimes committed on Capitol property."

Four heads from the front rows popped up; their note-taking stalled.

Chief Evanston didn't need their eyes to tell him he had made his first mistake. *Why did I say "crime"? We agreed that I would not call this a crime.* He considered a course-correction, but decided that would just dig a deeper hole. He pressed on, referring to his prepared notes, and assuming as much of a matter-of-fact tone as he could muster. His nervous words chopped into the tense air. "At approximately 2:15 this afternoon, officers from the U.S. Capitol Police were notified that an apparently non-responsive individual was discovered in a vehicle parked in the second level of the basement parking garage underneath the Dirksen Senate Office Building. Two Capitol Police officers responded to the scene, and located the vehicle and individual in question.

"After briefly attempting to rouse the individual, the officers unlocked the car door and removed the man from the vehicle. One officer immediately began to provide CPR; the other contacted the Capitol Police central dispatcher, and requested an ambulance and medical support."

To his left, Evanston could see U.S. Attorney Carol Cushing entering the room through the glass door and making her way toward the podium, her well-tailored gray suit standing out amongst the disheveled assemblage of the press. *Get through the facts*, he told himself. *Get through the facts and then hand this to the lawyer. Get away from these cameras.* A handful of reporters trailed Cushing into the briefing room, and pressed their way into the front row, filling the remaining seats.

Evanston smoothed his mustache again, paused, and scanned the sea of reporters. "The central dispatcher reported that the vehicle was registered to William Iredell, Washington, D.C. An officer then located the individual's driver license within the vehicle and confirmed that the individual in question was, in fact, Judge William Iredell."

The briefing room erupted into action. Each reporter was shouting unintelligible questions. They seemed to swell as a mass, pushing toward the podium.

Evanston took a step back. He could hear only jumbled phrases and words: ". . . condition . . . where is the . . ." A female voice from somewhere in the middle rows: "Has the President been notified? Has he issued a response?!" A voice, shouting from the back: "Is this connected to the Parker Brown sentencing?"

The Chief's eyes swept the room. The seal of the Capitol police on the back wall. His information officer's blonde hair. Cushing, to his left, beginning to look uncomfortable. The cameras. The red lights. He raised his hands toward the shouting mass of reporters. "Please. If you will hold your questions until the conclusion of my statement . . . ."

Glancing down again at his notes, he restarted, well aware that with each passing moment more and more viewers were tuning into the broadcast. The word was spreading. People on the east coast were just returning from work. Turning on their televisions, expecting to see their local news broadcast, they were instead provided with this press conference. The nation was turning toward Chief Evanston on this Friday evening, whether he liked it or not.

"I was contacted at approximately 2:20 p.m., after the identity of the individual was determined. I immediately contacted the FBI and DC police, and issued an order to seal the Dirksen parking structure. We believe that the structure was almost immediately sealed."

Evanston was regaining control of the briefing, but he knew it was only temporary.

"At approximately 2:25 – ten minutes after Judge Iredell was discovered – the ambulance arrived," he continued. Evanston's knowledge of constitutional law didn't extend much past the *"Miranda* Warning Card" he was required to read every time he made an arrest, but he knew William

Iredell's confirmation to the Supreme Court had been critical. He was set to become the fifth conservative on the court, and five votes out of nine was a majority. The *Washington Post* coverage had been predicting all summer that Iredell's nomination would turn the Court in a conservative direction for the first time in a generation. Affirmative action, abortion rights, civil liberties – everything was on the table now.

He paused. Dead silence in the room. The red lights, unblinking. "Judge William Iredell was declared dead at the scene."

This time there was no stopping the onslaught. Evanston singled out a middle-aged man in the front row. "Michael Owens, *LA Times*," the man announced as the other journalists quieted down, their hands remaining in the air. "Chief, are you considering this a murder?"

Evanston knew this one was coming. "At this point, we – along with the other agencies – are working through the preliminary stages of our investigation. We are not prepared, at this time, to state that any crime has been committed."

A reporter from the second row jumped in, a younger woman that Evanston didn't recognize. "Is there any explanation for his death other than homicide? Could this be a suicide?"

"I can't provide evidence pointing toward any conclusion. Investigators from our office are working alongside agents from the FBI. Our investigation is in the early stages."

Voices rose immediately from the sea of hands, trying to draw his attention. Evanston pointed toward a reporter near the back, who rose to ask his question, partially blocking one of the cameras along the back wall. "Are there any conclusions about the cause of death?"

"Let me again introduce Dr. Oritz. I believe he can speak to that question."

From the Chief's left, Sam Ortiz approached the podium as Evanston stepped to the side to make room for the young physician. U.S. Attorney Cushing climbed onto the stage, assuming Ortiz's position flanking the podium. Evanston met her eyes. As the only other two people in the room who knew what Dr. Ortiz was about to announce, neither of them smiled.

The long, white coat lent Ortiz an air of authority. He was thirty-eight, yet had the appearance of a younger man. His thick black hair and athletic build would let him pass for someone much closer to thirty, given the right context. Sandwiched between the solemn face of Carol Cushing and the sagging face of Aaron Evanston was exactly such a context. Sounding slightly uncomfortable, Ortiz rushed through his memorized opening. "The Office of the Chief Medical Examiner is currently conducting an autopsy. The results, when they are available, will be released or retained according to the protocol of the primary investigating agency. However, there are a few preliminary results that are available at this point."

He drew a note card from the large side pocket of his white coat and continued. "The initial examination of Judge Iredell revealed moderate contusions on his occiput – that is, bruising to the back of his head." While he held his notes with his left hand, Ortiz moved his right along the back of his scalp, slightly turning his head to demonstrate the area of the bruising. "The remainder of the initial physical examination failed to reveal any additional characteristics inconsistent with a deceased male of Judge Iredell's age."

A journalist from the third row raised his hand, his arm floating like a buoy above the sea of reporters. Both Ortiz and Evanston recognized him as Joshua Michaels, the *Washington Times* crime reporter, one of the few in the room that had been there before. Michaels had turned his attention in recent years to corporate crime, but his background was more on-the-beat than in-the-boardroom. "Is the bruising the cause of death, or related to the cause of death?" Michaels asked.

"At this point, we have no reason to believe the bruising is related to the cause of death," the physician responded.

"Follow up." Michaels again, jumping at the opportunity before the other journalists could elbow in a question. Ortiz nodded toward him. "Can you ballpark the time of death?"

Ortiz looked down at his card again, paused, and looked sidelong at Cushing. She subtlety nodded her head. Ortiz turned back to his prepared remarks. "Our office puts the time of death between ten and eleven a.m., approximately."

The heads of the reporters returned to their notes – all except Joshua Michaels's. His eyes remained on the podium, shifting from Ortiz to Cushing. Then back to Ortiz. "Dr. Ortiz," he started, his speech slowing slightly. A few other reporters turned toward him. The other dogs in the pack were sensing that one of their number had found the scent. Some lowered their hands.

"If . . . ." Another pause. He restarted. "Doctor, if he was found around two fifteen, identified, and immediately taken to your office, that puts him on the table at about three fifteen? Assuming the office was fully staffed on a Friday afternoon. Even later if people had to be called in?" Michaels had the attention of the room now.

"This press conference started around five thirty. How is it that your office has been able to make such a quick, and confident, determination on time of death?"

The question had to be answered at some point. Cushing had decided that Ortiz should answer it if it was asked, but not offer the information in his initial statement. He again checked with the attorney and again received an affirmative sign. "In some cases, particular signs of death appear on an individual's body shortly after death. One such sign is hypostasis, or what is commonly referred to as livor mortis. It is the process by which the blood, once the heart stops pumping, collects at the lower points of the body."

Chief Evanston was looking at the red lights. Cushing was staring at her notes. Every other eye was on Ortiz. "It was immediately apparent from our office's examination that the individual's red blood cells had congealed in his capillaries, but not in his soft tissue. From this evidence we can call the time of death as being between ten and eleven o'clock this morning."

More hands dropped down, heads turning deferentially to Joshua Michaels. The reporter seemed deep in thought. Finally, he raised his eyes back toward the podium. "Still, Dr. Ortiz, that was a rather quick assessment, wasn't it? My recollection is that it normally takes your office a day, at least, to examine the capil . . . ." Michaels stopped, his train of thought changing tracks.

"Dr. Ortiz, what color were Judge Iredell's feet?"

Ortiz ran his hand through his dark hair. He knew the decision to release this information was made by someone above his pay-grade. Maybe his boss. Maybe Cushing. Maybe *her* boss. He would have handled this differently, but deputy medical examiners don't get to make the calls when a soon-to-be Supreme Court Justice turns up dead in a parking garage. "The initial physical examination revealed Judge Iredell's feet to be a pinkish color, consistent with the pooling of blood near the lowest point of his body. This would be expected when an individual dies in a generally upright, sitting position."

Michaels did not care about the upright, sitting position. And he was no longer on the scent. He had trapped his prey. "Doesn't livor mortis normally produce a red appearance?"

Michaels didn't wait for an answer. "Dr. Ortiz, what is suggested by the pinkish appearance at the collection point of Judge Iredell's blood?"

Ortiz didn't need to check his notes; the answer was not there. He, along with every first-year medical student watching this press conference, immediately knew the answer: "The appearance of a pink color as a result of hypostasis can be expected in a person that has died as the result of the ingestion of a toxic substance."

For the third time, the room exploded. Involuntarily, Ortiz backed away, seemingly pushed from the podium by the shouted questions. Chief Evanston stepped into the opening, again raising his palms toward the mass of outstretched arms from the crowd. "Please. If you will hold . . . ," he started, but it was of little use against thirty-plus insistent voices.

From the corner of his eye he saw his public affairs aide approaching from the left. She had a note in her outstretched hand. Turning toward her, he noticed a familiar face quietly entering through the glass door along the side wall, all but lost in the fray of the shouted questions and completely ignored by the cameras and journalists. *What in God's name is he doing here?* Evanston thought, taking the note from his aide.

Evanston had never seen the man in person before, but his face, hair, image, were unmistakable: salt-and-pepper hair, with more salt at the temples; the healthy tan of a person who managed to spend his weekends outside his office; lips poised to break into his trademark smile. His eyes: welcoming, but without the slightest hint of weakness or wavering. *He looks just like a politician ought to look*, he thought. *And just like that headshot plastered all over the FBI offices.*

He began again, returning to the bank of microphones after quickly reading the note from his aide. "Um, we are, at this point, prepared to announce that our office and the FBI have contacted and questioned Mr. Luke Lyford, of Washington, DC, in association with this event." Evanston was now looking directly at the cameras along the back. "Luke Lyford has not been arrested and we are not – let me repeat that – *not* prepared to call Mr. Lyford a suspect at this time."

"Why was he questioned," called one of the reporters that had trailed Cushing into the room. "How is he involved?"

The note disappeared into the dark-blue pants pocket of Evanston's uniform. "Evidence gathered at the scene indicates that he may have been one of the last persons to see Judge Iredell alive. He has been contacted simply in an effort to establish a timeline."

The same reporter. "So, would you call him a person of interest? What was the conversation with Mr. Lyford about?"

"We believe that he can provide information concerning the events leading up to the discovery of Judge Iredell's body. So, yes – we are calling him a person of interest at this point. As to the nature of the conversation with Mr. Lyford: I am not going to go into the substance of an ongoing investigation," he answered with an attempt at finality. Chief Evanston started to straighten his notes. "One more question," he announced, recognizing an attractive female reporter. Might as well keep the locals happy.

She stood. *They know when the cameras are on, don't they*, Evanston thought.

"Kelly Addison, NBC15. Has there been any evidence, any theory, anything that links Judge Iredell's death to today's sentencing hearing for Parker Brown?"

"No." Evanston liked the easy ones. He could see movement to his left. Ortiz stepping away from the podium, he assumed. He could already see that Cushing had moved off the stage, back down the steps. "Thank you for your time. Our office will . . . ." Other reporters were now raising their hands. *They never quit*, he thought. "We will provide additional information as it becomes avail . . . ."

Kelly Addison remained on her feet, raising her voice to be heard over the crowd. "Is there anything linking Iredell's death to the Brown case?" She was no longer looking at Chief Evanston. Instead, she was following movement to his left.

As he traced her gaze, he felt a firm hand land on the striped shoulder-strap of his dress uniform. Turning, he caught the reflection of the stage lights bouncing off the metal clasps of his own shoulder straps, and off the flat, silver surfaces of the other man's watch and ring. He nearly stepped directly into that trademark smile.

"I'll handle that question," replied United States Attorney General Edwin Carter, as he stepped toward the bank of microphones.

Chapter Four

Whispering Pines, North Carolina
June 11, 2010

Nineteen days before the execution of Parker Brown

Tears streaked down the face of his fourth Pabst Blue Ribbon of the evening.

In the setting sun the colors of the deck were less distinguishable than they had been when he opened his first can of beer. The few remaining spots of unblemished white paint, less-assaulting once the sun dropped below the line of surrounding pines, were joining the other dominant colors: the soft grays of the dirt-stained paint and the brownish old wood revealed by the peeling.

Eventually, he knew, he was going to have to pull himself off the canvas straps of the deck chair. Reason one: he had only thrown four beers in the cooler. Reason two, and of much less importance to Mark Ellis: two of his three sources of light were dwindling. The sun was beating its retreat into the West and the coals in the grill to his right were virtually done. The Stinger UVB45 40 Watt 1-Acre Ultra Bug Zapper hanging over his head had been passing out justice all evening; however, it was all but worthless as a reading light.

Ellis put the count at twelve and a half to three. The Stinger had claimed at least eight victims that he had noticed. Four mosquitoes had ventured from the nearby woods to make their move toward his uncovered lower legs, but ended up losing the battle to his right hand. He felt certain that his dog had snagged one about an hour ago, so he was giving himself half a credit for that one. He decided that three mosquito bites – one to the neck and two around his left ankle – over three hours was tolerable.

That is what ought to happen in this case, he thought, eyeing a Motion to Continue filed earlier that Friday by the opposing counsel in a local contract dispute. *A swift, clean result. No motions, no delay.* The key witness against Ellis's client had apparently decided to take a summer vacation and the trial scheduled for next week would, according to the other side, need to be postponed. Again.

Briefly, he thought about putting up a fight. He thought about going into court on Monday morning, pounding the table, and calling forth the great William Gladstone: justice delayed is justice denied. But he knew he would lose; just like he would eventually lose the trial.

Then Mark Ellis had a better thought: more beer. He flipped the Motion back onto the stack of unread documents he had brought home from his office that afternoon. The legal filing slid over the top of the stack, its corner coming to rest in a puddle of ketchup left on the plate next to the papers.

Rising from his chair, he tried to balance the now-empty fourth can on the mountain of other bottles and cans filling his green recycling container, which, along with The Stinger and Roscoe, his dog, kept him company most nights. It didn't work. The red, white, and blue of the PBR can slipped from its position on the mountaintop and clanged onto the paneled deck. Roscoe stirred, watched the can roll to a stop against the metal frame of the deck chair, and went back to sleep.

By the time the can hit the chair leg, Ellis had passed through the sliding-glass door and onto the floor of the kitchen, its linoleum cool to his bare feet. Staring into a refrigerator that looked like it somehow might be older than his rental house, he assessed his options: grab the two Bud Lights that had been cohabitating with some potatoes in the bottom of the vegetable drawer for the better part of the month, or take a ride down Pine Ridge Drive to the Exxon station before he had too many more.

Ellis grabbed the Bud Lights with his right hand. *Two in the hand were worth more than six at the Exxon.* With his left he reached for a wall switch, turning on a flood light that partially lit the back deck. Through the glass door he could see a couple of mosquitoes dancing in and out of the twirl of smoke rising from the dying coals – drawn to the lingering smoke, the smell of grilled hamburger it carried, and the electric lights, bright against the nine o'clock sky.

The Stinger glowed a soft white; the aged flood light a dull yellow. Ellis could clearly see one mosquito now, poised on the black plastic grate encasing the bug zapper's core. From the small, black ledge maybe it considered its options; maybe it stood in the smoke, confused. Maybe the mosquito believed it was making the right decision, the intentions of its tiny soul, pure and purposeful.

The sound of the Stinger was final, swift. *Thirteen and a half to three*, Ellis thought.

Ellis retrieved the Motion he had thrown aside, smearing the ketchup back onto the plate. The mark left on the document's corner mirrored the red stain on his khaki shorts, the remainder of one of the four intruders he had conquered earlier. Above the khaki shorts, he was wearing the same light-blue polo shirt he had worn to his office that day. The polo shirt covered a body that most would describe as being of average size. His weight tilted toward the heavier end of average, thanks in part to his nightly meetings with a handful of PBR cans, but he nevertheless remained well within the range of typical. His brown hair was unkempt and somewhat overdue for a haircut. His skin was tanned from the North Carolina summer. Mark Ellis flicked the final piece of leftover burger to the dog and fell back into the deck chair.

The second mosquito was weaving between the flood light and the bug zapper, passing through the shifting finger of smoke.

Ellis turned the pages of the Motion to Continue, his mind wandering to his client: a Hispanic day laborer from nearby Taylortown.

He watched as the mosquito landed on the black grate of The Stinger, occupying virtually the same position as its former compatriot. The lure of the smoke and light was strong. As its instinct commanded, the mosquito edged toward the light.

The used truck his client had purchased from a local dealer had been "marked down" for an End of the Month Sale and had broken down within a week. The dealer didn't care; the day labor didn't speak English. Two years of saved money for three days of transportation.

The electric buzz of The Stinger – this time lingering for a few seconds until the second mosquito detached from the core and fell seven feet into the mountain of cans overflowing the recycling bin.

Ellis looked at the name on the top of the document in his hands: Julio Flores, Plaintiff. *Sometimes you're the mosquito*, he thought, considering the very likely defeat headed toward Mr. Flores's lawsuit. *You follow your natural instinct and your good intentions straight into a dead end.*

∽

Forty-five minutes, and one and a half beers later, Mark Ellis still had his feet on the railing of his deck when his cell phone jolted him out of his half-sleep. The Motion to Continue had been thrown again to the side and rested with the other unread documents Ellis had intended to review. His dinner plate remained in the same place on the patio table. Roscoe opened a lazy eye at the sound of the phone.

"You've got to be kidding me," he said, looking down at the face of his phone and smiling for the first time that evening. He answered the call. "Lyford. Shouldn't a big-city lawyer like you be tucked away with some deposition transcript or something on a Friday night?" His friend didn't laugh at the light-hearted insult.

"Mark." The voice on the other end sounded rushed, panicked. "I need your help."

So much for the friendly call, Ellis thought.

"Did you see the press conference today?" Luke Lyford asked, barely taking a breath between the sentences.

"No. What press conference?"

Luke Lyford launched into an explanation, catching Mark up on Judge William Iredell's death and the spectacle of the press conference. As Luke talked, Mark moved through the sliding-glass door, setting the unfinished beer on the kitchen counter and moving into his shag-carpeted living room.

Despite having rented this house for two years, the living room, as with most of the house, was largely undecorated. Two pictures hung on the wall over Mark's desk, dangling slightly askew on nails he had driven into the fake-wood paneling – one of Mark and his mother Claire; and one of Mark's immediate family: Mark, along with his father, mother, and younger brother, all smiling, chests adorned with "Claire Ellis for Senate '08" buttons.

On the phone, Luke paused before he reached the key part. "Mark, they identified me as a person of interest."

Mark had been digging through the laundry spilled across his couch, searching for his laptop. He stopped. "They what?"

Certainly he had heard him wrong. Mark had known Luke Lyford for years. They had graduated law school at the same time. Mark had joined a large law firm in Atlanta and Luke had signed on as a legal counsel with the Sierra Club. Three years ago, when Claire Ellis decided to close her private flight school and jump into politics, Luke had taken a leave of absence from the Sierra Club, returned to North Carolina, and joined the campaign. He and Mark had travelled the state together, planting campaign signs and organizing local campaign groups.

They had been together when Claire Ellis died.

"They called me a person of interest," Luke repeated. "The Chief of the United States Capitol Police. On a national broadcast. Called me a person of interest!"

Mark didn't know how to respond. "Luke," he started, but Lyford interrupted him.

"They called me this afternoon and I met them at my office. We talked for over an hour. They said I was not a suspect; they were just trying to piece together a timeline. But, to tell you the truth, I'm not sure I believe that."

Lyford had moved back to DC after Claire Ellis died. With only a month until the election, the Democratic Party had time to replace Ellis's name on the ballot, but no chance at a serious campaign. The party nominated a former Congressman to replace Mark's mother, but support collapsed and the campaign lost in a landslide.

Ellis had steadily gained on the incumbent Senator, Republican David Baker, through the summer and fall, narrowing Baker's lead to four points, according to the last poll taken by the Ellis campaign. The more people heard about her background, and heard about her career as one of the original female pilots in the Air Force, the more they supported her campaign.

But Ellis's death ended the challenge. Any hope of knocking off David Baker died alongside Claire Ellis, her husband, and their younger son.

And so Lyford had moved back to DC and taken a position as the majority counsel for the Senate Judiciary Committee, a position in which he acted as the attorney for the Democratic chairman of the committee. He had asked Mark if he wanted to come with him to DC, but Mark had declined.

Mark Ellis was still trying to piece together the story he was hearing over the phone. "Why did they want to talk to you?"

"He called me this morning, Mark. Iredell called me. Apparently, my office number was the last one dialed from his phone. He said he wanted to meet with me, but that it had to be somewhere other than in my office."

"William Iredell called you?" This might have been the strangest fact that Mark had heard so far. The opposition to Iredell's Supreme Court nomination had been nearly futile; he had steamrolled through the Senate confirmation process. To the extent that there was an attempt at an organized opposition, Luke Lyford was the heart of it.

In fact, most of the time it seemed like Luke Lyford simply was the opposition. From his position as the majority counsel for the Judiciary Committee, he was tasked with "opposition research", the effort to dig into Judge Iredell's background; to read every word of his writing, every opinion; to review every speech. During the confirmation hearings, Lyford had composed many of the questions for the Democratic Senators and had, on occasion, actually questioned Judge Iredell on behalf of a Senator.

However, the only product of the work had been Luke Lyford's growing distaste for Judge Iredell's judicial philosophy. Lyford leaned left; Iredell right – and the more Luke had read the more he had grown concerned about Iredell's impact as a Supreme Court Justice.

"Yeah – it's strange. I read every word that man wrote. Over the last couple of months I've gone through every piece of his life that I could get my hands on. I issued a million memos, talking points, and press releases all aimed at stopping his nomination. I have no idea why he would want to talk to me." Luke's voice sounded both tired and strained. "I can't imagine he was calling to gloat. It doesn't seem like his style.

"I took this morning off," he continued, "to recover from the hearings this week. Apparently, he called while I was at home. I had no idea he had even called my office until the cops called my apartment."

Ellis had found his laptop, but the power cord remained elusively lost in the pile of laundry. He gave up the search and cleared a seat on his faded leather couch, leaning his head back until his brown hair nearly scraped the wood paneling. Mark tried to put the pieces together, pulling what he could from Luke's quick synopsis: a future Supreme Court Justice turns up dead in a DC parking garage and his last phone call was to the one man in America that had fought the hardest to stop his appointment to the Court?

Ellis was trying to puzzle out a reason for the call, while Lyford continued. "The message also said, 'I have something I need to show you.'"

"What the hell does that mean?"

For the first time, there was a pause on the other end of the line. Instinct, premonition, or something like it caused Ellis to sit forward on the couch. He bowed his head while one hand held the phone to his ear. He could see strands of the shag-carpeting pushing up through the space between his first two toes.

"Mark, I . . . ." Luke started, but his voice faded away. His discomfort was apparent. "After the cops left, I sat down and started flipping through some paperwork on my desk. Eventually, I started to make my way through the mail that had been delivered that day.

"I think – and I say 'think' because I'm not at all sure – but I think that Judge Iredell had a letter delivered to me through the Capitol's internal mail system. I have no idea when it arrived, but I didn't see it until well after the cops left."

"You mean through one of those internal mail packets? The reusable brown envelopes with all the lines for delivery information on the front?"

"Exactly," Luke answered. "It was marked to be delivered to me and dated with today's date. The 'From' line only read 'Iredell.'"

"What did the letter say, Luke?" Ellis hadn't moved. "You think that is what Iredell wanted to show you?"

"I'm emailing you a copy. I'm not sure I can really describe . . . ." He trailed off again. "It's on its way to you. This will be obvious when you read it, but I think you should keep this to yourself. I haven't shown it to anyone yet."

Ellis had renewed the search for his power cord. He had worked his way through the pile of laundry and was heading toward his bedroom. Luke's last comment stopped him half-way down the hall. "You haven't shown it to the police, Luke?"

"No. I'm not sure that is the right move. In fact, I have no idea what the right move is. I don't know why Judge Iredell called me. I don't know why he sent me this letter. I don't know why he wanted to meet in secret. I don't know why the police are calling me a 'person of interest' on national television!"

Ellis could hear the panic escalating in his friend's voice. He sounded trapped, boxed in – like he had nowhere to turn. Like he had reached a dead end, but wasn't sure how he got there. *Sometimes you're the mosquito*, Mark thought for the second time that night.

"The only thing I do know is that I'm not going to sit back down with them without an attorney. Which is why I need you."

Ellis had been leaning with one hand on the wall. He pivoted and lowered himself to the aged hardwood floor. He couldn't come close to extending his legs in the cramped hall-way. He hadn't made it to the light switch when he had stopped and the only light that reached him was from the living room. In the near-darkness, Mark tried to think of a way out.

"Luke, I'm happy to help, but you need a real criminal defense attorney. You can't mess around with this."

Luke was ready for this objection and quickly parried with an explanation about how he was not even an official suspect; he needed a smart attorney who could help him fig-ure out what was happening to him, not an experienced one that was just going to play by-the-book.

Ellis threw his last card on the table: "Luke, I've been representing small-town plaintiffs and doing real estate work since my mother's death. Whispering Pines is a long way from Washington." Luke was ready for this one too. *This is like law school all over again*, Ellis thought. *I make one argument and he's got a response before I can even finish my last sentence.*

"Mark, as of tonight I'm virtually untouchable in DC. Any DC attorney that would take me on as a client would be only doing it to benefit his or her career. Most would not even return my call. I need you. I need someone without his own agenda. I need someone I can trust."

Mark Ellis closed his eyes.

Luke let the silence sit. "Listen, Mark, you don't have to decide right now. Take a look at the copy of the letter I emailed you. Then give me a call." Mark Ellis heard the line go dead.

His laptop power cord was on the floor next to his unmade bed. He downloaded the letter to his desktop. Five minutes later he called Luke Lyford back. Three minutes after that Mark Ellis started to plan for an extended stay in Washington, DC.

Chapter Five

Edenton, North Carolina
June 11, 2010

Nineteen days before the execution of Parker Brown

"You had better call your father." Hannah Baker pulled the remote control from her husband's motionless hand and turned off the television. The image of United States Attorney General Edwin Carter walking away from the Capitol Police podium disappeared from the flat-screen imbedded in their living room wall, giving way to a reflected view of the book shelves lining the opposite wall. Four American flags, each folded into a perfect triangle and encased in wood-and-glass displays, lined the top shelf. From his seat next to her on their dark leather couch, her husband did not respond. He seemed stunned by the news of Iredell's death, like a boxer trying to recover his wits after an unexpected uppercut.

"John," she said, gently nudging him on the shoulder. "I'm going to get dinner on the table. Call your dad and then get the kids." Hannah Baker crossed out of their living room and into the kitchen of her family's expansive colonial home. She pulled a pot roast from the oven and left it steaming on the stovetop as she began clearing the remaining portion of her son's birthday cake from their kitchen table.

As she set the antique table for dinner, she watched her two children through the window that looked out onto their backyard. The early-June days were getting pretty long. She could see her son, ten, digging his foot into the earth near "home plate", a patch of worn-out ground that hadn't seen a blade of grass grow in the last three years. On his right shoulder, he was bouncing the wiffle-ball bat his grandfather had given him that morning.

Their sprawling backyard, flat and dotted with pine trees like most yards in this part of Edenton, and manicured like most in their neighborhood, sloped in the back toward the Chowan Golf and Country Club. It was a feature she had always loved about this house. She had come to learn over the last few years that it was also a feature precisely laid-out to serve as a baseball diamond.

His Atlanta Braves hat – another gift from his grandfather – turned backwards, her son faced down the pitcher: the kid from next door. Somewhere in his head, she knew, an imaginary crowd was roaring. Her five-year-old daughter had one hand on a Frisbee. Reagan, their golden retriever, had the other side of the disc. With her free hand she was pointing her index finger toward the dog, repeating, "Drop, Reagan, drop" in her most authoritative voice. Hannah smiled and laughed to herself. *Good luck, sweetie.*

"He's landed, but they're still taxiing," John Baker said, walking through the kitchen on his way toward the backyard. A few inches over six feet tall, he could cover the kitchen's length in a few steps. "He's going to call when he gets back to his office." Through the window, Hannah could see him scoop up their daughter in his arms. The dog trailed them back into the kitchen.

"I feel bad he couldn't spend more time with the kids. I know he wants to." Hannah had pulled some baked potatoes from the oven and was cutting her daughter's into smaller pieces. "He got here, when? Ten last night? After the kids were already in bed." Her daughter scurried past her, climbing onto a step-stool to wash her hands in the kitchen sink. "Then he had to run out again this morning. He barely had time to eat cake with us. And now he's headed back to his office on a Friday night."

John knocked on the kitchen window, signaling to his son that it was time to end the wiffle-ball game. John's father, David Baker, had always kept a busy schedule, one that had seemingly doubled in activity over the last few years. John had grown up with it, but Hannah was still getting used to it. For nearly as long as John could remember, his father had been running or serving in public office: first, a legislative seat; then two terms as North Carolina's attorney general. He had been elected to his first term in the United States Senate almost eight years ago, winning a tough re-election campaign just two years past.

"I know he's sorry he had to miss part of the birthday party," John responded, thinking of the family's celebration earlier that morning.

Grant, John's son, had just unwrapped the wiffle-ball bat when his grandfather had needed to step outside to take a phone call. "The office," he had explained. "I need to run out and meet with a constituent real quick. I'll be back soon." He had tussled Grant's blond hair on the way out.

The blond hair Grant had inherited from his mother, but his build was all Baker men. Long and lean, even at ten he seemed to exhibit the effortless smoothness of an athlete, just like his father and grandfather. Replace the shaggy, blond hair with his father's dark chestnut and there would be no mistaking Grant Baker as being anything other than his father's son, and his grandfather's grandson.

"When I get back, we'll see if you can handle my curveball," his grandfather had told him as he strode toward the door. True to his word, Senator David Baker had made it back with just enough time to throw a few curveballs, eat a piece of cake, kiss his granddaughter on the head, and catch the day's single flight back to DC.

༄

Tonight was John's daughter's turn to bless their food. Head bowed, Grant waited patiently for her to finish the prayer before opening his lecture on the unpredictable nature of wiffle-ball flight. His mother was his chosen audience.

Absentmindedly, John poked at the skin of his baked potato, his brain still processing the death of William Iredell.

John's father, as the senior Republican on the Senate Judiciary Committee, had served as Iredell's unofficial advocate during the confirmation process. He controlled the hearing from the Republican side, not only organizing the issues that each Republican Senator would raise during his turn to question Judge Iredell, but also signing off on the subject matter before they stepped in front of the camera. David Baker had been, as much as anyone else in the Congress, the key supporter of William Iredell.

With Grant momentarily distracted by their dog, Hannah made her break from the wiffle-ball speech and turned toward her husband. "Your father is going to take this pretty hard. He put a lot into Iredell's nomination. I remember him at those hearings."

"Yeah," John agreed, his fork still gently nudging the remnants of his food around his plate. "In front of and behind the camera. He pushed for Judge Iredell as soon as the vacancy on the Court opened."

John rocked back in his chair and rubbed his eyes, his hand reaching for his wine glass. As he watched his daughter drop green beans to their dog, he could hear himself explaining some of his father's efforts to Hannah.

There were, of course, the standard machinations of a political office: the press releases supporting the Judge, the contacts with fundraisers and conservative interest groups used to press Iredell up the President's "short list" of candidates. But John knew it was his father's connections at the Lexington League that provided the driving force. Securing the organization's support and endorsement had propelled Iredell toward the Supreme Court.

And it was those same connections that were now pushing John's own career.

Earlier that year, John and Hannah had learned that John was going to become the United States Attorney for the Eastern District of North Carolina, the federal prosecutor with jurisdiction over every federal crime committed between Raleigh and the Atlantic coast.

His father had been the first to approach him with the idea after the prior U.S. Attorney announced his long-expected retirement. At first, John resisted. With only ten years experience as a local prosecutor, and only three of those as the chief assistant prosecutor, it was the image that concerned him: a well-connected son of a Senator moving into a powerful federal position. That image never played well in the press.

But his father was persistent and had recruited others to his cause. A call from the Governor. Multiple calls from Republican congressmen. *Consider the good you could do from that office*, they said. *Patriotism*, the voices repeated. That one struck a particularly strong chord with John Baker; they knew what motivated him. Eventually, they wore John down. The last voice was Hannah's, and with her support he took the leash off his father.

"Tell your friends I'll accept if the President offers the position," he had told his father nearly six months ago. The Senator had erupted into immediate action, delivering a Lexington League endorsement within a matter of days. The call from the White House followed shortly behind the endorsement.

But his acceptance had a condition attached: any investigation into Parker Brown, and any trial, must be handled by someone else.

"No problem," his father told him. "We'll find someone in DC to take it over."

The Brown investigation had become an open secret. Grand Jury testimony was being leaked. Witnesses were talking with the press. The clerks and the local lawyers that gathered daily around the Chowan County courthouse gossiped about indictments. With the media camping out around the federal courthouse every day the Grand Jury was in session, and with reporters contacting the FBI agents and prosecutors, John Baker knew he wanted no part of the public circus certain to unfold if Parker Brown was indicted.

Two years ago, the death of Claire Ellis had filled the pages of the local papers, and for a few days even held the attention of the national media. As the lead trial attorney in his office, John had been the face of the local investigation into the plane crash that had killed her moments after she took off from Edenton's one-runway airport. Although John brought no charges in the case, and the public lost interest after a few weeks, he had quickly grown tired of conducting an investigation under the glaring light of media attention.

Under no circumstances did he want to walk back onto the front pages by taking responsibility for the investigation into Parker Brown and his defense-contractor company, Echo Industrial.

And so he set his terms: he'd take the U.S. Attorney position, but only if someone else would take the Brown case.

Carol Cushing, the federal prosecutor from DC, was immediately sent to handle the case, and Baker started planning for the transition to a new office. Within a week, he knew he had made the right decision. Cushing set up a temporary staff, comprised mostly of younger attorneys she brought with her from DC. Occupying a previously unused corner of the federal building in Raleigh, her staff hit the ground running. The indictment was handed down within days, and Cushing went for the throat: treason.

What had started as only a local reporter or two following the investigation, grew overnight into roughly twenty media organizations. Camera crews covered every entrance and exit of the federal building, swarming Cushing and her assistants every time they moved. Baker stayed away. Ryan Wentworth, the outgoing prosecutor, simply stopped working from his office.

Cushing, in contrast, met with the media on an almost daily basis, her close-cropped brown hair a fixture on the local news. It became a one-woman show: watch her interviews at night, read about the investigation in the following day's newspaper.

If the investigation was a one-woman show, the trial was a multi-part drama. Cushing was cast perfectly as the crusading prosecutor building her case. She was every bit as confident and courageous as she appeared. And with her nearly around-the-clock media availability, there was no shortage of public appearances.

Parker Brown was the opposite: secretive, secluded, quiet. Cold. Echo Industrial – or as it was commonly called, Echo – described itself as a company focused on logistics and security in the defense sector. As Carol Cushing and the federal indictment described it, the company was a treasonous organization that provided aid and comfort to an enemy of the United States.

Everyone knew her target was Parker Brown, not Echo itself. However, her indictment took a swing at both company and CEO. She would have an easier time painting the portrait she wanted if she started with a broad brush.

It had seemed impossible, but Carol Cushing managed to increase her public exposure as the trial started. She was everywhere. Continuing the stark contrast between the two sides, Parker Brown offered no public response to the indictment other than to enter a "not guilty" plea. He released no statements to the press. Echo Industrial's headquarters, tucked away in the northeastern corner of North Carolina, remained, like always, closed to the media and the public.

The trial lasted seven days, and Cushing's opening statement took up nearly the entire first day. Like her, it was smooth and polished. It was professional. She held the complete attention of not only the jury, but also the spectators packed shoulder-to-shoulder in the creaking, wooden pews of the courtroom. She even made some of the spectators forget about the empty chair sitting next to Parker Brown; that is, until she finished and Brown announced that he would not be making an opening statement.

As Parker Brown took his seat at the otherwise vacant defense table, the only thing left standing in the courtroom was the final enlarged document from Cushing's presentation, an expanded image of Article Three, Section Three of the Constitution: "Treason against the United States, shall consist only in levying War against them, or in adhering to their Enemies, giving them Aid and Comfort."

Cushing called her first witness on the second day and started to construct her case, walking the jury through the structure of Echo's finances and explaining the payments from the Department of Defense. At times she would pace between the prosecution's table and the witness stand, the clicking of her heels intertwining with the typing of the court reporter and rebounding off the old paneled walls. One of her younger attorneys would pass her documents and spreadsheets. She worked through Echo's finances as though the trial had turned into some sort of public audit.

Witnesses described what Echo Industrial actually did, what "logistics and security in the defense sector" actually meant. "In short," Cushing summarized while examining one witness, "Echo Industrial provides private military services in foreign countries. It guards ambassadors, delivers munitions, even conducts offensive military actions alongside, and in coordination with, the American military. Isn't that right?"

"Yes," the witness responded. "It makes money – quite a lot of money – off of conflict and war."

Over three days she pulled back the curtain, unveiling how Echo worked, what it did, and how it got paid. But she had not touched on anything illegal, much less, treasonous.

In fact, the only truly surprising aspect of the first three days of the hearing came from the defense: the chair next to Parker Brown remained empty. Parker Brown had chosen to represent himself and had made no comment other than to graciously decline to cross-examine all of Cushing's witnesses. He would rise each time, his voice clear and stable. "Your honor, I have no questions for this witness. Thank you." And then return to his seat and pull his chair to its original position closer to the table. The same scraping noise: wood on wood. The same ramrod posture, a remnant from his days in uniform.

His forest-green eyes would move between the judge, the witness, and Cushing. Until the end of each day, at which time he would turn to quickly hug his wife and son before the U.S. Marshals escorted him from the room.

On the fourth day, Cushing began to deliver on her allegations and the trial started to draw John Baker's full attention. First, it was former employees taking the stand, one of whom relayed the informal mission statement of Echo Industrial: "war is cash." Then current employees were put on the stand.

Through their sometimes reluctant testimony, Cushing demonstrated the truth of the informal mission statement.

As the press explained throughout its coverage of the trial, the election of President Anderson had been bad for Echo's bottom line. The President had run on a campaign promise of reducing America's role in the world. And now he was beginning to draw down the number of troops deployed abroad. He promised to limit American involvement in foreign crises. President Anderson had even promised to slash defense spending, and pouring public money into private companies like Echo Industrial was first on his chopping block. No war, no cash.

Cushing called her final witness on the morning of day six: Gloria Augusteel, Echo's Vice President for Human Assets. Augusteel had one purpose as a witness: to distinguish and separate Parker Brown from Echo Industrial as a whole. Her testimony delivered a clear message to the jury: *You may not like what Echo does, but it stays within the bounds of the Constitution and federal laws. Parker Brown crossed that line, alone, when he sold those weapons.*

Gloria Augusteel was the last bullet in Cushing's gun and the last nail in Brown's coffin.

John Baker had watched the final prosecution witness from the back bench and left with the same feeling as every other person in the courtroom: this trial is over.

On the seventh day, the prosecution rested its case. And the eyes of the jury turned toward Parker Brown. He rose with the deliberate effort of a man who knows he's the center of attention, the contrast between his light-blue tie and his black suit enhanced by the old fluorescent lighting of the federal courtroom. Nearing seventy, he wore his suit like he had worn his uniform prior to his retirement from the Marine Corps.

"Your honor," he addressed the judge, "I will not offer a defense."

John Baker could barely believe what he had heard. Treason carried the potential for a death sentence; yet, here stood a man with massive personal and financial resources, not only choosing to stand trial without counsel, but apparently choosing to offer no defense. This military man wasn't even putting up a fight.

∾

His kids had just gone to bed and John Baker was reaching for his remote control, hoping to get an update on the William Iredell story. He was two bites into a large slice of his son's birthday cake when his cell phone rang. He looked down at the face of his phone, a dull glow in the Bakers' dark living room:

Dad (Cell)
202-281-2657

Chapter Six

Washington, DC
June 11, 2010

Nineteen days before the execution of Parker Brown

oah Augusteel slid onto the rear seat of the waiting town car. He edged along the cushioned leather toward the far side of the vehicle, dragging his duffel bag behind him as he slid across. He left the bag in the open seat to his right, as he took the seat behind the driver. His right arm rested on the gray canvas of the duffel. The car door clicked shut behind him.

Augusteel's eyes tracked the driver as the younger man rounded the hood of the car and circled toward the driver's side door. Backed by the setting Washington sun, the driver's dark suit faded into deep black. *Gloria would call this reckless,* he thought. *She would never step into a car driven by someone she didn't know.* Of course, his twin sister had that option. Echo assets were at her beck-and-call, each one more than willing to chauffeur the Vice President for Human Assets anywhere her majesty wanted to go.

In the seconds it took the driver to pass across the front of the car, Noah considered unzipping his duffel bag. *Easier access*, he thought. *In case I need it.* His mind automatically weighed the younger man's movements as he settled into the driver's seat. Augusteel's eyes absorbed the driver's actions. Where did he look? What did he touch? How often did he glance in the rearview mirror? The pieces of information fell like raindrops on a slanted roof. They ran together, collecting and coalescing in his mind, forming a stream and flowing into his thought process. Augusteel worked through the situation instantly, instinctively. Just like he had been trained.

No, he concluded. *There is no threat here.* His handgun remained zipped within his duffel bag. They exited the Hertz rental car lot and turned toward Washington, DC.

He relaxed as the engine smoothly accelerated and the town car merged into the highway traffic. His body seemed to sink into the leather seat. Like his twin sister, Noah Augusteel stood five-foot-nine. He was strong, but not necessarily muscular – the type of body that could blend into multiple settings without standing out. Normally tucked behind his ears, his stark, blond hair would frequently break free and swing in front of his ice-blue eyes.

As he sank deeper into the leather, Augusteel rubbed those ice-blue eyes, massaging his temples and forehead as though he could somehow will the exhaustion out of his body. *I had a town car pick me up from a rental car lot. A driver I don't know is taking me to an apartment too sparse to be called a home. I'm returning from a job I never asked for and being tasked with another I don't want.*

The driver was speaking to him. Noah's mind focused on the words faster than his eyes could open. "Still going to Hobart Street?" the driver asked, his dark-brown eyes bouncing between the rush-hour traffic and Augusteel's reflection in the rearview mirror.

Farsi. A trace of it in his English.

Augusteel locked on the accent.

"Yeah," he answered, calling between the two front seats, toward the driver. Augusteel paused, his mind processing the new information, adding it to his earlier assessment. The handgun remained in the duffel bag, but its owner sat forward in the rear seat.

"Persian?" Noah asked, amplifying his voice over the passing cars. "Sounds like a there's a little Farsi in your background." He could sense as much as see the driver's surprised reaction.

"My father came over right before the Shah fell. Middle of '78. After things got bad, but before they got dangerous. Farsi was his native tongue, and he and my mother would speak it around the house. I'm impressed you could pick that up. Did you spend time over there, or something?"

Augusteel continued to lean forward on the rich leather, angling his body to better hear the driver. "A little. Probably right around the time you left."

"I've actually never been to Iran, or anywhere near it," the driver responded, shifting the town car into the neighboring lane as the traffic slowed around them. "First-generation American. I was born a few years after they reached the US."

Noah reclined again. That was one of those facts he wished he had missed — but he never missed any facts. He was built to monitor his environment; his mental calculus was automatic. And that calculus had just handed him a rather depressing result: *This kid's in his late twenties. I'm fifteen years older than him.* It made Noah feel old, and feeling old made the exhaustion come back.

As the town car ground to a halt in the rush-hour traffic, he slipped his phone from his pocket. The screen brought up the list of his missed calls. Three of them in the last twenty-four hours, and all from the same number: his sister. He read her name on the top three lines. "Gloria Augusteel. 8:05 p.m. June 10, 2010. Gloria Augusteel. 8:08 p.m. June 10, 2010. Gloria Augusteel. 8:17 p.m. June 10, 2010." Three calls, all the night before, none of which Noah had answered.

The third time she had finally left a message. As was Gloria's style, especially with her brother, it was short, direct, and authoritative. It was, as she meant it to be, an order from a commanding officer. Noah had listened to the message earlier in the day. He had been assigned another job, and they would be working together on this one. Noah had been instructed to contact her as soon as he reached DC and was directed to be prepared to leave immediately. Sharing details with a subordinate was not Gloria Augusteel's style, but she had left him a couple. The first: they would be travelling to Edenton, North Carolina. The second: this assignment came from on high. *One of the five. One of the people at the top,* Noah had imagined as he memorized her voicemail. *Someone way up the food chain is calling the shots on this one.*

The highway around him had become a parking lot. Augusteel checked the thick, impact-resistant watch around his wrist and called into the front seat of the town car. "You mind turning on the radio? Looks like we're in this for a while." *It is already five forty-five,* he thought. *I've got to be back on the road with Gloria in a few hours.* No rest. There was never any rest. Not for Noah. Not for an Augusteel. Not when the Lexington League had something that needed his unique set of talents – and there was always something. Year after year. Assignment after assignment.

Ahead of him, the driver pressed the power button on the radio and selected a pre-set station. Yet, the voice that came humming through the top-of-the-line speaker system did not have the melodic, Midwestern quality of the usual newscaster. If was rough. *Nervous,* Noah's mind told him. *Different.*

It was the tail end of some sort of press conference, or at least that was how it sounded. A police officer was speaking. Augusteel could pick out voices in the background of the live broadcast, but couldn't quite make out what they were shouting. Suddenly, a deeper voice. *Edwin Carter? The Attorney General?*

A minute or two later it was over, and the voices coming through the speakers reverted back to the standard, flat tone of the professional media. Augusteel brushed his blond hair behind his ears, as his mind worked in parallel, two sets of wheels pulling his train of thought along its track. On the first rail of the track, he was consuming the information from the radio station's political commentators. *William Iredell is dead. The initial toxicological results are consistent with poisoning. He was found this afternoon. Time of death estimate is around 11 a.m.* He absorbed the cold facts as he had the actions of the driver moments before. The data poured into him.

But the cold facts weren't the entire story, there was analysis, there was context surrounding the death. On the second rail of the track, his mind accessed everything he knew about William Iredell and his nomination, and wove the facts together with the data coming over the radio. *Iredell's nomination had been President Anderson's first to the high court. It had been a significant victory for the Republican President. Only a few on the liberal left challenged Iredell's nomination, and their efforts proved largely futile. The president was popular. Iredell was a popular nominee. The final Senate vote was yesterday, and Iredell was overwhelmingly confirmed to a seat on the Supreme Court.*

The town car was beginning to move. Augusteel could see the brake lights extinguishing around him as the vehicles crawled toward the end of the traffic bottleneck and started to release into the open section of the highway. The town car broke free from the congestion and moments later they were passing over the Potomac. The sight of the water clicked something in his memory. His blue eyes closed as he searched for the final fact he knew about William Iredell. Like a man methodically searching an office for a single piece of paper, Noah Augusteel mentally hunted the fact. He could feel it in his mind, something he had noted about William Iredell, some sort of connection between the judge and himself. A coincidental connection, he seemed to recall. Something he had seen? Somewhere he had been?

He found it. *Edenton. The hometown of William Iredell's family.*

The realization landed on him like an anvil. *Edenton.*

Noah Augusteel jerked his phone from his pocket and accessed the list of missed calls on his phone. It was an entirely unnecessary action; his memory had already locked in the information concerning his three missed calls.

Gloria and I are being sent to Edenton. William Iredell's family is from Edenton.

She left me the message on Thursday night, which means she was given the order on Thursday night. Yet, William Iredell didn't die until late Friday morning.

The league knew he was going to die before it happened. How?

There was only one possible answer, and Augusteel had no doubt about its truth: the Lexington League was somehow involved in the death of William Iredell.

And now I'm involved.

The voices of the political commentators droned on, filling the rear seat of the town car. His right hand, as if acting on its own volition, crept over the upper portion of his duffel bag, dragging the zipper as it crossed the canvas. The steel of his Luger was in his hands. It was cold, solid. But it was also familiar. *This is who I am, who I was born and trained to be*, he acknowledged.

Yet, in the dying sunlight of the Washington evening, Noah Augusteel closed his eyes and, not for the first time, wished he was someone else.

Part Two

Chapter Seven

Edenton, North Carolina
August 21, 1798

Supreme Court Justice James Wilson looked up into an unfamiliar face. "Mr. Justice, can you hear me?" the stranger asked and then turned away from Wilson, calling into what appeared to Wilson to be a blurry haze of colors. "Justice Iredell, I believe he's waking up."

Wilson could feel that his face was wet. He could tell that he was lying down. Slowly raising his hand, he felt a cold, damp cloth covering his forehead. He pulled it away, balling the cloth in his hand and dripping a string of water across his bare chest. The joints of his fingers ached. His skin burned.

"Justice Wilson." A deep, familiar voice. Coming from somewhere. Wilson could see the stranger's face move to the side; his eyes were beginning to focus and he could see the outline of broad shapes developing. "Justice Wilson." This time he recognized it.

Focusing his eyes on the approaching figure, he responded, "Justice Iredell." His voice sounded dry, and weaker than he expected.

"Dr. Robinson," Wilson heard Iredell address the stranger, "I'll call for you if we need assistance."

Wilson could feel Iredell's hand reach for his own and remove the cold cloth. The background behind Iredell's face was beginning to take shape. Wilson could see the outline of what looked like a wooden writing desk along the wall opposite the bed he was in. He could see the white coat of the stranger passing through the door to the left of the desk; the wooden boards of the door creaked as they closed behind the doctor. The sound echoed in James Wilson's ears, surrounding him like the groaning bowels of a ship.

Iredell moved through the fog of Wilson's vision. As he rotated the wooden bar used to lock the room's door, Wilson could hear the bar softly landing on the corresponding wood attached to the frame. He tried to sit up. Iredell was back by his side, his hand gently resting on Wilson's left shoulder. It felt like an immovable weight, pressing Wilson into the bed. "Don't strain yourself, James."

Wilson could now see the room's only window, positioned over Iredell's shoulder, on the wall near the head of the bed. The midday sunlight was pouring into the room. He could make out his traveling chest, sitting on the writing desk behind Justice Iredell. Wilson felt cold, which seemed nearly impossible in the sweltering humidity of the North Carolina summer.

He looked toward the wall opposite the window. His clothes hung from hooks attached to the wall, alongside his dark traveling coat. Water dripped from his clothes and fell on the wood floor, pooling next to his boots. His larger travelling chest, the one holding his clothes, had been pushed into a corner of the room.

Iredell was reapplying the cold cloth to his forehead. "The doctor is concerned about your fever, Justice Wilson."

At the sound of his voice, Wilson focused on Iredell's face. "How long have I been here?" He could feel the fresh streams of water running down his forehead and onto the pillow.

"Your coach arrived near daybreak. One of my men found your driver and clerk holding you in the driving rain, standing on my doorstep. I had you and your luggage brought to this spare bedroom." Iredell had drawn the desk chair next to the bed. A bowl of water and clean cloths sat on a small table nearby. As he leaned to soak the cloth, the small chair strained under his weight. "You've been asleep since we brought you to this bed. I summoned the doctor shortly after you arrived. It is near midday. I can have some food brought in if you would like."

Wilson coughed and tried to bring his hand toward his mouth. The sheer act of raising his head slightly off the pillow exhausted him. He waved off Iredell's offer: "Thank you, but I believe I'm not quite prepared for food."

Again, he tried to raise himself onto an elbow. He could instantly feel pain. The area behind Iredell's head faded into a deep red as the pain pushed up from Wilson's abdomen, through his throat, and seemed to settle behind his eyes. The brown of Iredell's vest blurred with the tan wood of the writing desk until the border between the two was indistinguishable. He could see Iredell's white sleeves, the thick cuffs doubled-back and rolled to the elbows. The sleeves reached for Wilson's shoulders and lowered him back down.

Wilson coughed again. The taste of metal in his mouth. "Have you ever heard of the Lexington League?" Wilson turned his head to the side, to face Iredell. This time the liquid running down his face was blood, small drops escaping his mouth as he talked.

"Lexington League? No," Iredell responded, leaning in closer to the bed.

Wilson could clearly distinguish strands of Iredell's white hair. "I met with them yesterday. They've formed a kind of group, a faction of some sort, and wanted me to join." Wilson's voice was fading. "They want to . . ." He trailed off. It was getting more difficult to find each word.

Iredell could read the concern in Wilson's eyes and watched him struggle to speak. "There is no need to rush, sir. Take your time. Catch your breath." He waited a few seconds as he watched Wilson breathe. The visitor's eyes were closed. "Now, what is it that you need to tell me?" Iredell asked.

The room seemed to be moving around James Wilson. He opened his eyes. He could see the yellowing blanket covering his legs and torso. Dust particles moving in the streaks of sunlight across the room. The light played off the pool of water collecting under his drenched clothes.

The memory swept over James Wilson: The coach. The water, pooled around his ankles. Crashing toward it and unable to lift his arms.

Wilson raised his left hand and grabbed Iredell's wrist, holding it across his chest. His pale fingers, turned whiter with the force of his grip and bleak against the tanned skin of Iredell's arm. With his right he pointed away from his bed, toward where he recalled seeing his boots. His voice scratched out the word: "boots."

They must be destroyed. They can't go back. The intensity with which the thought erupted into his mind seemed to increase his pain.

Iredell disappeared into the red mist and instantly returned. He held the brown leather boots over Wilson's chest. Wilson grabbed the left boot with both hands; the leather had dried, but the sole and heel remained slick. Each joint was like a rusted hinge, fighting against his aching muscles to remain still. Holding the sole of the boot with his left, he used his right hand to press against the side of the black heel.

Iredell watched as the heel rotated, slowly at first, but then spun freely on its axis to reveal a small opening embedded in the shoe. A key fell from the opening, landing on Wilson's chest.

Wilson could feel the cool metal, and the small, rounded handle of the key. "Chest." He nodded toward the area where he had seen the writing desk. The room was filling with darkness. Even the sunlight was fading. "Key." Wilson raised his left hand toward his throat, in an instinctual effort to stretch what felt like a collar that had been buttoned too tight. His hand found only skin.

Iredell began to rise from his chair. He reached over Wilson and grabbed the key. As he turned to move toward the desk, Wilson reached for his sleeve. He missed, but felt his hand close again around Iredell's wrist. He could see the white of his rolled cuff, but no longer his face.

"Find. Franklin."

Iredell moved closer, barely able to hear. *Find Franklin? Franklin has been dead for years.*

"Franklin. Notes. Destroy notes." His strength was failing. "You must," he coughed, more blood escaping his lips, "destroy the notes." Wilson's eyes closed and his hand slipped from Iredell's wrist, his arm falling limply and spilling over the side of the bed.

Justice Iredell reached for his Supreme Court colleague. He rested his hand on Wilson's chest. He could see the small drops of blood soaked into the pillow. Labored breathing. It was faint, and uneven, but there without a doubt.

Iredell pulled his chair to the writing desk and examined the traveling chest. It was a small wooden box, worn around the edges and circled by rough leather straps. He unfastened the straps and turned the key in the lock. Pushing aside some wrapped quills and a closed bottle of ink with one hand, he reached the papers stored beneath. Iredell could recognize Benjamin Franklin's distinctive handwriting on the top document. Nevertheless, he removed the entire stack of documents from the chest. The top seven pages were loosely bound together and were doubtless the writing of the late Franklin. He quickly scanned the other documents and confirmed his initial assessment.

Iredell replaced the other documents and locked the chest. The writing on Franklin's pages was virtually indecipherable. Iredell searched the barely legible chemical formulas scratched onto the brown, torn documents for any word he recognized. *Ethanol?* He had at least heard that word before. *Amylon malonate?* The last page was in German and was signed by someone named Albert Ladenburg. It looked like it had been pulled from a letter from Ladenburg. None of these notes meant anything to James Iredell.

None, except the date. He returned to the first page and re-examined it: January 23, 1783. Paris, France. Franklin had been Ambassador to France at the time. Throughout the year he had been locked in negotiations concerning the Treaty of Paris, the treaty that had ended the Revolutionary War.

It did not surprise Iredell that Franklin's mind could travel onto a scientific sidetrack while at the same time negotiating a multi-party treaty that would change the course of global history. It wasn't the contents – to the extent that he could hazard a guess at their meaning – of the notes that interested Iredell. It was the path they had taken over the last fourteen years to reach this old wooden writing desk in the extra bedroom of his eastern North Carolina home.

And it was James Wilson's insistence that the notes be destroyed.

He looked back at his fellow Justice, lying nearly motionless on the bed. Drops of sweat and lukewarm water drained slowly across his ghost-white forehead and mixed with the drops of blood that had dried into the pillow. Why had Wilson appeared on his door step, unannounced and unconscious, in the middle of a downpour? Who was this group – this Lexington League – he had mentioned? *Why did he fight to direct my attention to these notes? Why must they be destroyed?*

Iredell tucked Franklin's notes into the interior pocket of his vest. He rose from his chair and crossed the rough floor, rotating the wooden bar as he reached the door. He could hear Wilson's uneven breathing; its broken rhythm was the only sound in the room.

Supreme Court Justice James Iredell called for the doctor to return and went to look for the clerk that had shown up with James Wilson.

Chapter Eight

Edenton, North Carolina
June 12, 2010

Eighteen days before the execution of Parker Brown

denton's Colonial Park runs along the Atlantic
waterfront and is the last stop on the town's "History
in the Humidity Tour." Houses surround the small harbor.
The view from their porches and lawns sweeps across the blue
water. Waves and wakes lap against the hulls of the docked
boats and the stout retaining wall separating Colonial Park
from the saltwater.

It is peaceful, reserved, and for the most part, quiet.

The Tour, an annual event, had opened in its traditional manner: a fundraising breakfast on the grounds of the
Chowan County courthouse, a nearly 250-year-old structure
and one of the oldest courthouses in the country. The day

had then moved down Broad Street toward the water's edge. Saint Paul's Episcopal Church was the second of the procession's three stops. It had opened its doors to the mid-morning crowd and hosted a series of presentations, stretching from a panel on southern literature to a reenactment of Sir Walter Raleigh's final address.

As the Tour moved down Broad and crossed Water Street, a few participants stopped at Waterman's Grill, cutting their Saturday morning short to escape the summer heat. The majority, however, continued to the final event of the day: Everett Johansson's speech from the front porch of Edenton's historical Barker House.

The crowd slowly shuffled across Water Street and onto the paved parking lot of the Barker House. Knowing the well-established routine, the attendees filed into a line parallel to the folding tables stationed on the border of the lot. Steam rose from the trays of barbeque and baked beans. Cylindrical coolers of sweet tea and lemonade stood atop the last table, next to tilting columns of clear plastic cups. Members of the Edenton Historical Commission scurried among the crowd like the crabs in the nearby sand, energetically greeting their neighbors and friends as the June sun climbed toward its peak.

Everett Johansson had been the first to arrive that morning, having skipped the earlier events to help prepare the grounds surrounding the Barker House. The two-story Barker House, established in 1782, had been built directly along the waterfront and stood as the centerpiece of Colonial Park. The historical home rose three stories above the paved lot. Its white siding rested on a brick foundation, all of which had been power-washed in anticipation of the event. Along the front of the house ran a long, white porch. It bordered the parking area. Black shutters highlighted the two rows of windows along the front of the white house. The Atlantic lapped like a lullaby in the background.

Johansson seemed to almost float among the crowd, shaking hands with his fellow Commission members and the volunteers he knew from the Iredell Family House. His broad smile never left his seventy-one year-old face.

He lived for this day. As chair of the Edenton Historical Commission and caretaker of the Iredell Family House, he was widely regarded as the small town's most authoritative source on all things historical. And, with twenty-one years under his belt at the Iredell House, he was slowly becoming part of the town's history.

Johansson had held the honor of being the final speaker on the historical tour since he first organized it sixteen years ago. And his speech was always the most popular event. "Mr. Everett," as he was known around Edenton, would don his trademark red bowtie, his crisp, white shirt, and his best dark-blue suit. At the stroke of noon, he would climb onto the white, wooden porch of the Barker House. He would pause and look out over the parking lot – the empty trays of barbeque and banana pudding to his right, the folded chairs he had set out that morning now full of his fellow Edentonians and a few honored guests.

At five-foot-three and barely one hundred and thirty pounds, he was nearly swallowed by the gleaming sunlight pounding off the white siding of the Barker House. Bracketed by the American flag waving to his right and the North Carolina flag to his left; and beyond those flags, by the brick double-chimneys running up both sides of the house, Johansson's eyes would narrow in the sun. His hand would reach for the handkerchief in his breast pocket. He would wipe the small drops of sweat from his forehead, replace the handkerchief, and run his hand over his head.

In the early years of the Tour there had been more hair for his hand to brush over. Now, nearly bald, he could feel the sun on his uncovered head.

It was always at this moment that members of the crowd would wonder whether this was the last time they'd get to see Mr. Everett climb those old, wooden steps.

Then a smile. That smile. The one they knew. The one that always came before this speech. The one that he always had ready for the elementary school groups that toured the Iredell Family House. The smile that pushed back the waving flags and the chimneys, that drew the attention of the crowd away from the lapping saltwater in the background. The smile that made them forget about the heat.

And then he would start. It was always a different speech – sometimes Revolutionary history, sometimes North Carolina history, sometimes Edenton history. Sometimes all three woven together. Yet, no matter the subject, the old man always crafted a story that captured the attention of the Tour crowd for the entire hour and left them looking forward to the next year.

༄

Noah Augusteel squinted into the reflected glare of the late-morning sun, then peeled open the heavy, glass door of The Pack House Inn. The scent of bacon, then the enticing smell of vegetables frying on a flat grill, washed over him like a lazy mushroom cloud. He eyed the handful of locals scattered throughout the diner as his sister passed ahead of him, through the open door. He was, he thought as her blonde hair flicked past his chest, a long way from DC.

Lean and long-legged, Gloria Augusteel carried herself like the natural athlete she was. The strong strands of her pale hair ran nearly past her shoulder blades. Dressed to blend with the semi-casual crowd she had expected to find in Edenton, she wore narrow-fitting dark jeans that stretched to her open-toed tan sandals. The sleeves of her crimson blouse ran halfway down her gym-toned arms.

They were on her timetable now, as they had been since they had left Washington the night before. After a midnight ride south, Gloria had at least allowed him a few hours of extra sleep.

During the brief conversation that had periodically raised its head during their drive from DC, and during the even more brief exchange this morning, Gloria had addressed her twin brother with the same "when you need to know" style of which he had long ago grown tired. The concise plan — concise in the sense that she had only provided him a limited number of details: Thirty minutes to eat. One hour to plot and explore the route to and from the Iredell Family House. Thirty minutes for routine reconnaissance work before engaging the target.

Two hours. Two hours until this is over.

His mind automatically pulled in details from the dining area, a magnet drawing in the relevant aspects of the room. This wasn't a meal. This was just another job. One more on a long and growing list.

Noah had lost count of the number of times he had been deployed — domestically and abroad. He had served the

Lexington League his entire adult life, and had forgotten more assignments than the average asset had performed. In the beginning, it was challenging and – if he was being honest about it – entertaining. Yet, the work had grown old and he had grown older. It wasn't about his skills deteriorating over time; he could still move with the speed and dexterity of a field asset half his age. It was simply that most of the other field assets *were* half his age now.

To say that he had "forgotten" the work he had performed over the years wasn't entirely accurate. His mind had been trained as well as his body. He could, if he wanted to, summon the memories, recalling exact times, positions, and people at will. But this morning – like most mornings – he didn't want to. He would rather forget.

His past actions weighed heavily on him, immovable stones on the gilded scale of his soul. Early in his life the stones had been black, each operation a smooth, small rock tilting the scale toward fulfillment. Then, a few years ago, the first white stone had appeared on the opposite side of the scale. The feeling had surprised him. Was it dissatisfaction? Unrest? Regardless, the scale had remained severely tilted. Against the mound of black stones, the one white rock caused no movement.

Yet, other white stones began to appear. Slowly, the scale began to shift. Fulfillment was leaving him. Noah began to internally question his assignments.

Then, a couple of years ago, two large white stones had landed on the scale. He had been commanded to take – and had taken – two innocent lives, the collateral cost of eliminating his target. The weight of the new white stones finally brought an unsteady balance: the importance of loyalty and expectation of his family had been equaled by his growing sense of distrust and distaste. Between the two emotions, Noah Augusteel teetered – and trailed the arrow-straight blonde hair of his sister as she cut through the late-breakfast crowd at The Pack House Inn.

⌒○

His sister had ordered black coffee and toast. The toast sat untouched as she quietly accessed the Echo Industrial internal network, her laptop's universal wireless card providing a connection from their corner table. As she pushed the Echo servers to locate all available information on Everett Johansson, Noah flagged down the waitress.

"You happen to know a Mr. Everett Johansson? He's a historian at the Iredell Family House." He passed her his empty plate, the former home of a western omelet and a pool of buttery grits.

His sister's gaze moved from her laptop to her brother. She didn't need to speak. He knew exactly what his twin sister was thinking: *unnecessary communication creates risk.*

"Mr. Everett? Of course. He's been at the Iredell House for years," the waitress replied. Noah was working to keep up with her heavy accent.

"Do you know what time the Iredell House opens today? Is it likely to be busy?"

The waitress reached for his coffee cup to refill it.

She cleared the table with her right hand, but she poured with her left hand. She has three sets of extra silverware, wrapped, and stuffed in the front pocket of her apron. Each set has a knife. The knife in the set on the right extends past the top of the napkin wrapped around the silverware.

"Well, I suspect it'll be closed today, since the tour's goin' on."

His sister looked up after that answer. She entered the conversation for the first time. "What tour?"

"The history tour. Down by the water. I think Mr. Everett always gives the last talk. I'm sure it's in today's paper, if y'all want to see him talk."

His sister quickly closed her laptop and pushed her plate of untouched toast toward the waitress. "Let's go," she announced, dropping a twenty-dollar bill onto the toast.

As they exited, a local police officer approached the door from the outside. He held the door as they passed though.

Noah Augusteel's training shifted his mind into a higher gear. *His service revolver is strapped to the right side of his belt. It is a nine-millimeter Glock. I can get to mine before he can get to his. He is holding the door with his right hand. I can likely get to his before he can get to his. I can move on him while my sister covers the people in the restaurant. We are twenty-three feet from the rental car. The rental car cannot outrun the police. Worst-case scenario, next three moves: police officer draws his weapon; I shoot him; we drive a short distance, abandon the car, and use her laptop to signal for extraction at night.*

Augusteel could feel the gaze of the officer. But it was not a look of investigation; it was a look of interest. Noah assumed there were not many sets of fraternal twins living in Edenton, certainly not many which looked as similar as he and his sister. Their pale-blond hair – his sister's, now pulled into a single, thick braid, and Noah's curled behind his ears – had always drawn looks from people outside their family.

As he drove, his sister accessed the online version of the local newspaper and acquired the details of the historical tour.

She reassessed and reset their mission schedule, speaking only enough to bark directions at Noah with crisp efficiency.

∽

Noah Augusteel had never eaten banana pudding before. The last time he had been in this part of the South he had tried the sweet tea. He didn't like it. Yet, as the temperature inched past ninety, he was thankful he had refilled the small plastic cup in his hand before he took a seat in one of the unfolded chairs.

He checked his watch. 12:45. He could not believe the old man was still going.

Augusteel was enjoying the speech – in part, because he knew the subject matter nearly as well as the old man. It was also the first time in roughly the last day that he had been able to relax.

He watched the man moving back-and-forth across the porch. A handful of other old men and one heavy-set, middle-aged woman were sitting on the porch behind the old man in the red tie, their eyes tracking him as he moved across the white planks. On the left side of the porch, a younger man was recording a video of the speech. He was struggling to keep the short, bowtied man in the frame as the speaker paced between the two flags flanking the presentation area. Augusteel noticed that, every so often, the cameraman would stop following the presentation and would scan the crowd, an amateur effort to give the recording a sense of setting.

Noah closed his eyes. His mind automatically catalogued the scene before him. *The old man has a red bowtie. Two other men also have red ties, but they are wearing neckties. The videographer is wearing khaki shorts. His right shoe is untied. I am four rows back from the front. Three seats in from the left edge of the crowd. It is 12:47. My gun is loaded and holstered along my flank, hidden by my sport coat. There are three ice cubes left in my cup.*

༄

The old man was now reaching his conclusion. Johansson's voice, unexpectedly powerful given his slight frame, rose as he reached the end. He had been talking about "breaking points" in American history: points where historical figures were forced to choose between one side or the other in an era of conflict. His last example was Samuel Adams.

"The British occupation of Boston," he called over the crowd, "broke Samuel Adams. It forced him to make a choice; it forced his hand. His long hope for reconciliation came to an end that day. The overbearing British, the occupation – they cracked his dedication to reconciliation and pushed him into the arms of the Revolution." He smiled. "And the rest, as y'all have heard me say before, is history!"

The old man paused, eyed the crowd once again, and closed the presentation. "Thank you. And thank you for another great Tour!"

Noah Augusteel rose with the rest of the crowd to applaud the speech. Sitting beside him, his sister did not. As he stood, he could feel the vial of white powder move inside his jacket pocket.

∽

Noah and Gloria Augusteel watched as Johansson made his way off the porch, and received handshakes and hugs from some of the spectators. As the crowd dispersed, brother and sister moved in opposite directions.

She followed the crowd, on foot, as it reversed its earlier course and made its way up Broad Street. She stopped at Waterman's Grill, taking an outside table on the sidewalk. From her vantage point, she could observe both Water Street and back down Broad, toward the Barker House.

Noah moved down Broad in the other direction – to the position his sister had selected for him during their earlier review of the area. He purchased a Diet Coke from a vender working the small boardwalk running along the dock and found a shady, wooden bench. If Johansson left the Barker House in his direction, Noah would see him either make his way down the street or turn into one of the smaller gravel parking areas.

Everett Johansson waited until the chairs had been packaged and were on their way back to the Episcopal Church. He helped the caterers move the empty trays back into their van. And, when every small plastic cup had been removed from the parking lot, he stepped back onto Broad Street and turned right.

Noah watched him leave. He raised the inside of his wrist to his mouth and notified his sister that the target was heading toward her.

I am departing Beta position and am half a block behind target. Target has removed his coat. No evidence of a weapon. Target is approaching Alpha position. Alpha asset is moving.

As Noah trailed Johansson, he could see Gloria crossing Water Street. Johansson was between them now. The old man was not moving fast, but was walking toward his sister. She was closing toward Johansson. Noah quickened his pace to close the gap.

Suddenly he lost sight of Johansson. His earpiece crackled: "He's turned into the bank parking lot. I'm moving to reach him before he makes it to his car. Close and provide back-up."

Ahead he could see the white-and-green Albemarle Bank & Trust sign. Augusteel checked the area around him and saw a family strolling along the boardwalk far behind him. Otherwise, the block was empty. He broke into a jog.

As he rounded the corner into the parking lot, he could see his sister. She had gotten Johansson's attention and was approaching him. As her slender legs covered the space between them, her platinum-blonde braid bounced in rhythm with her step and the small purse strapped over her shoulder.

Noah could hear her expressing how much she enjoyed Johansson's speech as he neared. Johansson was smiling. Noah was about ten feet away when Johansson caught sight of him. The smile flickered; the old man's eyes darting between the two nearly identical twins. Although they were only five-foot-nine, both towered over Everett Johansson.

Johansson's Buick was parked behind the bank and the building shielded all three of them from Broad Street. They were alone in the deserted parking lot. "Mr. Johansson," his sister asked, "my brother and I were wondering if you might be able to give us a tour of the Iredell House."

Johansson had already removed his coat. As it hung over one arm, he started to roll up the sleeves of his white dress shirt. "I, um, would be," his speech was halting, not nearly as smooth as his earlier presentation. "I would be happy to, if you would be so kind as to stop by on Monday. We open at nine." He tried a smile.

He is nervous. He rolled up one sleeve, but then reached into his pocket. He is searching for his keys. They are already in the door of his car.

Johansson reached toward the car door, unlocked it, and started to open it. He slid his coat into his hand and moved as though he was going to toss it in the passenger seat. Noah saw his sister's hands move. With her left she reached for the top frame of the opening door. Grabbing it, she held it in place. Her right disappeared into the open mouth of her purse.

Johansson turned toward her and opened his mouth to speak.

Gloria's gun pressed against his ribs. The old man tottered back against the Buick. "Mr. Johansson, I must insist on that tour. Please back away from your car."

Johansson didn't move a part of his body other than his eyes. He didn't seem to register what was happening.

Noah interjected. "Mr. Johansson, please just back away from the car."

His sister's eyes never left Johansson. "Noah. Get the car. Follow us to the museum." She raised the barrel of the gun until it rested on the soft skin under Everett Johansson's chin. This time the old man moved.

∾

Everett Johansson opened the screen door and unlocked the front door of the Iredell Family House. The house was a white, two-story colonial-era home. It had been renovated and remodeled to serve as the official museum of the Iredell family's documents, pictures, and other historical artifacts. It sat along Church Street, only a few minutes from Edenton's downtown area.

A red-and-white "Closed" sign hung on the door of the house and fluttered as they passed into the foyer. His sister circled around Johansson, keeping the barrel of her gun trained on his sweat-soaked chest as she instructed the old man to stop.

Noah found a light switch, and the dim light of an old crystal-paned lamp came to life over their heads.

There are two cars in the parking lot. Our rental car and target's Buick. It is 15:37 on a Saturday afternoon. Some traffic will pass the house while we are inside. Likely visiting the downtown shopping area near here. It is possible that a visitor will arrive while we are here as this location is normally open on Saturday.

His twin sister, equally trained, had the same thought, and got straight to the point. "Mr. Johansson, I want a letter that is part of the Iredell collection. It was drafted in 1798."

There was no weakness in her voice. She calmly, efficiently restated the information she had received the previous night. "The letter is addressed to James Wilson and is from James Madison."

She was standing directly in front of Johansson, purposely separating Johansson and the visitor information desk in the foyer. Noah presumed she had also noticed the telephone on the desk and had angled herself to cut off any desperate attempt Johansson might make.

Contrasting sharply with Gloria's quick assertiveness, the old man's voice was weak, wavering, like a candle flame nearing the end of its wick. "I don't know what letter you're talking about."

Noah Augusteel hand instinctively moved toward the vial in the side pocket of his sport coat. He knew Gloria had one too.

In the curt manner that she always used, especially with Noah, she had explained that she had been given two vials of the substance – the only two that remained. She had been authorized to use it, but only if it was absolutely necessary.

After learning of the historical tour, and Everett Johansson's scheduled appearance, she had been forced to adjust her plan. Her original plan called for them to approach Mr. Johansson together while he worked at the Iredell House. Accordingly, she had seen no reason to *trust* – that was the word she chose to use – Noah with one of the Lexington League's remaining two vials. However, when it became apparent they would need to split up to cover both potential exit routes from the Barker House, she had been forced to divide the remaining two vials between them.

Noah watched his sister calmly raise her gun. Johansson took a step back, his heel clicking on the hardwood floor as he stepped beyond the edge of the thick Oriental rug.

Photographs lined the wall behind the historian: Aged images of James Iredell, one of the first Justices on the United States Supreme Court. Other pictures of his son, James Iredell, Jr., a former governor and senator from North

Carolina. A photograph of a younger Johansson, posing at what looked to be a family reunion. Johansson, kneeling next to a group of school children.

"Mr. Johansson." His sister stepped toward the old man. Her hand was steady, as always. The weapon was leveled at his forehead. "I am not a person who responds well to lies." She inched closer. "Either you will show me the letter or I'll tear this place apart until I find it."

"Why . . . why," he stammered. "Why do you want it?"

"I want it because I want it. That is all you need to know. Where is it?"

The old man's knees buckled. He caught himself on the chair rail of the wall.

Noah suppressed the urge to reach for him.

"That letter is part of history. It is not yours and you have no right to take it, especially by force. What are you going to do with it?" Johansson balanced himself with one hand on the wall behind him.

Destroy it, most likely, thought Noah. In fact, what would happen was what always happened: his sister would follow instructions. Gloria had given him the barest of descriptions of the letter's contents as they drove to Edenton. He felt quite certain that this document – a letter between two of the authors of the Constitution – was going to be destroyed, either by his sister later this evening or by someone above her in the league once they delivered it to Washington.

He was drawing conclusions, fitting pieces of the puzzle together as he watched the scene unfold in front of him. *The league killed William Iredell and now they've sent us down here to destroy this letter in his family's collection. They are trying to cover something up. Something that's in the letter. Something that William Iredell knew.*

It pained Noah to watch the old man struggle to keep his balance along the wall. These moments seemed to be growing in frequency, and in strength. More often than not, his heart was pulling against the reins of the Lexington League. The league jerked the bit in his mouth one way; he longed to go in the opposite direction.

"It doesn't matter what I'm going to do with it," he heard his sister respond to Johansson. "What matters is that you take me to it."

Resistance costs time. Unknown: is target wasting time on purpose? She will use the substance if he does not comply within one minute.

The old man pushed himself off the wall and began to unsteadily walk toward the converted former dining room of the house. Noah fell in line behind his sister. She pushed her gun into the small of Johansson's slightly bent back. They passed through the dining room and into a confined storage area.

"We keep it in this environmentally sealed box." The old man climbed onto a small stepstool and pulled down a box marked 7A. Noah could see the label on the top: "Wilson-Madison Letter."

"We've only known about it for three or four months," the breaking voice quietly mumbled. "It was stored with a great many other documents. It was buried until Judge Iredell found it himself."

Johansson reached for a large set of keys hanging next to the rack of boxes. He fumbled with the keys; his hands shaking as he tried to find 7A.

Noah stepped past his sister and gently lifted the ring from Johansson's hand. He quickly singled out 7A and handed the set back to the old man.

As Johansson inserted and turned the key, Noah stepped back.

"You are lying to me, Mr. Johansson. And your time is up." His sister moved the barrel of her gun to the old man's temple. He fell to his knees and her weapon followed him down.

"Please. I swear I'm not lying. It should be in there."

Noah looked over his sister's shoulder. Box 7A was sitting on the top step of the stool. The metal lid was open, folded partially back at the hinge. It was empty.

He could feel his sister's calculation. The signs they had been trained to look for in an interrogation indicated that the old man was not lying. She could give him a vial of the substance and make sure he was telling the truth, but it would not be worth the cost if it didn't produce the letter.

"This is your last chance. If the document is not here, someone took it. Who is that someone, Mr. Johansson?"

Johansson was sobbing. "I don't know." His head was in his hands. The single bulb of the overhead light created the image of the old man seemingly kneeling into his shadow. "I've been gone since Wednesday night. Been helping set up the Tour. Volunteers . . . volunteers have been watching the collection for me."

"Wait." Noah turned and ran back toward the foyer. He had seen a sign-in log on the visitor information desk. He grabbed it and sprinted back into the room. He knew where this was heading. His heart pushed him to prevent it; his obligation pulled him back.

"Mr. Johansson, if one of the volunteers had shown the document to someone or given it to someone would their name be in this book?" He kneeled beside the old man and handed him the bound visitor log.

Johansson choked out a response that sounded like "maybe." He took the book from Noah as Noah looked up toward his sister. His training told him exactly what his sister was thinking.

Either way target dies. Option one: target provides a name and is then killed. Option two: target does not provide a name and is then killed.

Noah and his sister locked eyes as Johansson flipped through the thick book to locate the last few days of visitor names. As they had done since they were children, they argued without speaking. Noah's mind moved through every tactical possibility that did not require Johansson's death: *They take target with them. They leave target behind and take the visitor log, working through each name in order. They wait for target to provide name and then move quickly against secondary target. They wait for target to provide name and then delay their approach until police give up search . . .*

He combined the approaches. He worked in new factors. He systematically played through each possible outcome of each tactical option.

But he could hear her voice, the second voice in his head. There were two unavoidable conclusions. If Everett Johansson was allowed to live he could identify both of them. He and the police could also notify every person that had signed the visitor log.

She knew it and he knew it.

His train of thought was interrupted by the sound of Johansson dropping the visitor log. "There are too many names. There must be a hundred in there. I have no idea where to even start. We've had huge crowds come through because of the Tour."

Noah watched his sister's reaction and knew the clock had expired. In frustration, she kicked the visitor log away from the old man. It skidded across the storage room floor and disappeared under the wall-sized rack of document boxes. "I'm sorry to hear that, Mr. Johansson."

Noah's heart screamed through the dense, increasing pressure in the small room. A new white stone appeared on the gilded scale – a thick one, heavy. The unsteady balance inside him began to gently shift. For the first time, his regret, his disgust, his dissatisfaction with his life – they were outweighing his loyalty.

There has to be something, he felt. *Some way to prevent this.*

Noah Augusteel glanced to his side, measuring his sister's determination. As usual, she was fully committed. He studied her weapon. He felt the weight of his own.

The conclusion he reached was simple: he could not kill his sister, not even to save the old man. As he stood here, pressed to the edge, caught between his duty to the league and the pain that duty caused, he knew he could not turn on her. Noah looked down at her gun resting on the side of Johansson's head. He thought about the pictures on the wall of the foyer, the smiles on the faces of the people sitting next to him in the Barker House parking lot.

Noah thought about all the years he had served the league. All the jobs. Everything he had done in the name of the Lexington League. They swelled inside of him. The details he longed to forget involuntarily scrolled through his mind.

He thought about the document: a letter between two Founding Fathers that he was being asked to locate and destroy. He could see Everett Johansson, moving between the two flags, leading the tour crowd through Revolutionary history, to Boston, to the breaking point of Samuel Adams.

Nothing justified what his sister was about to do. Yet, he felt powerless to prevent it. Something had to be done;

something had to change if Everett Johansson was going to survive. He had to alter the environment, alter the course of her calculation. It was his only move — and it was a desperate one.

Throw a variable into the equation.

He turned and ran.

He could sense Gloria turning her head, her braid swinging over her shoulder, looking back as he bounded through the dining room and toward the front door.

He could feel her weighing the options. She could not chase him and stay with Johansson. She had to choose: one or the other. Noah Augusteel prayed she chose him.

Every second built his lead. He slammed through the front door, hurling himself toward their rental car.

He never heard the shot that killed Everett Johansson.

Chapter Nine

Washington, DC

June 14, 2010

Sixteen days before the execution of Parker Brown

Dr. Samuel Ortiz pushed through the revolving glass door of the Office of the Medical Examiner at exactly 8:15 on the morning of Tuesday, June 14. At the suggestion of his boss, DC's Chief Medical Examiner, he had taken Monday off. Sam had raised no objection to his boss's idea; after being unexpectedly thrown into the middle of a national press conference on the previous Friday evening, he needed a three-day weekend.

Ortiz crossed the sterile, marble floor of the lobby and drew his ID card from the pocket of his gray dress pants. His white, long-sleeve dress shirt was unbuttoned at the collar, his sleeves rolled to the elbows. His white shirt accentuated his light-brown skin. Out of a sense of protocol, he flashed his ID card at the security guard. The guard missed the movement entirely as he noisily flipped to an interior page of the newspaper on his raised, circular desk. Ortiz pulled his card through the reader next to the door handle, heard the familiar beep, and stepped into the executive suite of offices.

He nodded at a few of his co-workers as he passed and accepted a handful of good-natured comments about his prime-time performance. The trailing comment caught his attention. "You looked good up there, Sheriff. I hear you're organizing a posse."

Without breaking stride, Ortiz called back over his shoulder at the other physician. "Be careful, Tom. I might just deputize you and send you up on that podium for the next one."

"Sheriff" was short for "Sheriff Sam". In a moment of pure stupidity, Ortiz had once mentioned to some of his co-workers that he had graduated at the top of his medical school class. "Then what the heck are you doing grinding out a nine-to-five in the DC medical examiner's office?" one of the staff physicians had asked. "Shouldn't you be doing research somewhere? Or running some medical center?"

Sam had then compounded his mistake, making it much worse. "I wanted to fight crime," he answered, before realizing how ridiculous it sounded to actually say that sentence out loud. "You know – be part of the process. Catch some bad guys."

The laughter had been so loud it commanded the attention of the entire lunch-hour crowd crammed into the downtown sushi restaurant. "Sheriff Sam" was instantly born. He didn't mind it. Plus, it was easier to just go along with the joke.

❧

Ortiz turned down a small side hallway toward his office and could see his assistant was already stationed at her desk. She saw him approaching and lifted a small pile of documents toward him. "We missed you yesterday. It was busy."

"I heard Paul on NPR as I was driving in," Ortiz replied, reaching with both hands for the stack of documents. "Phenobarbital, huh? You got a copy of the report in here?" He gestured with the pile of documents then leaned down to press the lever on his office door with an elbow.

"No. I haven't seen it. I'll let you know when it gets up here."

Ortiz entered his office and dropped the stack of documents on his desk. It spilled to one side and fanned out toward his laptop docking station. It looked like the standard mix of toxicology reports, requests from various local law enforcement agencies, and office mail.

He pulled his shoulder-bag strap over his nearly-black hair and balanced the bag on the seat of his desk chair. After removing his laptop from the bag, Ortiz set the computer on the docking station and hit the power button. The monitor on his desk flashed to life as he stored his shoulder bag in the narrow opening between his desk and the nearby wall.

Sam crossed back toward his office door. Closing it halfway to reach the hook on the back of the door, he returned his white physician's coat to its usual spot. In his line of medicine, the traditional attire was largely unnecessary. In fact, when Paul Sorenson, his boss, had notified him that he wanted Ortiz to handle the William Iredell press conference, it had taken Ortiz a minute to recall where he had hung his white coat.

Ortiz stepped back around his desk, pulling up his chair and nestling into the cramped office. Between his dated, wooden desk and the electronic equipment – some of which he was forced to position on the floor behind him – there was little remaining space in the tight office. He slipped into the confined area like he was easing a car into a tight DC parking space and immediately started to sort through the pile of documents from his assistant. Flipping past the first few reports on the top of the stack, he reached a pile of pink phone-message slips from Monday. The pile was even larger than he had expected. He looked up and noticed that his voicemail light was blinking.

"Joshua Michaels" read the first message slip. "Monday. 8:27. Please call re: Iredell." The second slip: "Richard Austin. New York Weekly. Monday. 8:34. Call re: Iredell." He flipped through a few more, all from journalists. "Kelly Addison. NBC15. Iredell." *The local television station. Is she the cute one? I'll call her first.* "Joshua Michaels (again!!!). Monday. 3:45. Call re ~~phenaba~~ poison."

Sam Ortiz was beginning to get the picture, and it was starting to look like it may be a long morning. Part of him had enjoyed the press conference, and was enjoying the residual attention. Yet, as he looked ahead over a morning full of identical conversations with hungry reporters, he could feel the enjoyment fading. He rotated toward his keyboard and logged onto the office's internal network. It took only a second to locate the file from the Iredell exam.

A couple of years ago, the office had moved toward what was supposed to be a completely paperless filing system. While he still received more than a few reports on paper – as evidenced by the pile in the center of his desk – most of the office's physicians had embraced the computerized approach. The electronic Iredell file on the network would contain copies of the findings from the autopsy and any toxicology reports that had been generated. The original versions of the reports would be stored in the office's main file room, a couple of floors below. Ortiz knew enough about DC reporters to know that he needed to have the facts down cold before he started returning the phone calls.

Kelly Addison. The name floated back into his mind as a grin floated across his youthful face.

The Iredell folder opened on his screen. It contained four files. The first was a Word document, titled "Toxicology Report." The other three, titled "ToxRep1", "AutRep1", and "DNARep1", were .esi documents. The .esi filename extension designated the files as being generated by the office's internal network. Ortiz had expected to find these three .esi documents, but not the Word document.

He double-clicked ToxRep1.esi. As usual, a prompt appeared and asked for his clearance password. He entered his password, watching as seven black circles filled the password entry space.

A message immediately popped onto his monitor screen: "Access to this document has been denied by the system administrator."

What? As a deputy medical examiner, he had global access to every file on the system. He clicked "OK" and tried his password again. This time he typed it slowly, confirming each letter and number.

The same response.

Ortiz moved the cursor to AutRep1.esi. He carefully entered his password.

"Access to this document as been denied by the system administrator."

He tried DNARep1.esi. Access to that document was also denied.

He backed out of the Iredell file and tried the one next to it: Ivanson, Carlton. He double-clicked on the ToxRep1 file in the Ivanson folder, entered his password, and the file opened on his screen. *I guess that rules out a problem with my password.*

He moved back into the Iredell file and tried AutRep1 again. The same message.

His curser moved to the Word document, "Toxicology Report." It opened without prompting him for his password and Ortiz quickly scanned the contents. The document looked very similar to an .esi ToxRep1 report. The seal of the Office of the Medical Examiner was included at the top.

Ortiz clicked on the print button in the upper left corner of his screen and sat back in his chair while the paper worked its way through the printer behind him. *This must be the version they released to the press. Maybe it is just converted into Word from the internal version.* He spun toward the printer on the floor behind him and grabbed the one-page report. As he read through it, he put his feet up on the ancient radiator under his window. Another small flake of its white paint chipped off and fell to the wood floor next to the printer, revealing the rusty metal beneath.

The report listed a series of toxins that comprised the traditional toxicological scan. The "no" box had been marked for each toxin other than Phenobarbital. Next to Phenobarbital the "yes" box had been marked, indicating that the toxicology scan had detected a significant amount of the chemical.

To the right of the yes/no column the report detailed the exact amount of each chemical detected in the blood sample taken from William Iredell.

At the end of the report, additional notes had been automatically included on the findings: "Phenobarbital Chemistry: 5-ethyl-5-phenylbarbituric acid or 5-ethyl-5-phenylhexahydropyrimindin-2,4,6-trione. Phenobarbital oral bioavailability: approximately 90%. Peak plasma concentrations are reached 8 to 12 hours after oral administration." Ortiz automatically considered the medical examiner perspective that had gone unstated in the single-page toxicology report: *Phenobarbital is an old, but widely available barbiturate. It has sedative and potentially hypnotic effects, even when given in a prescribed dose. An overdose slows the central nervous system, potentially leading to death.*

Below the automatically generated notes the report included a section for the physician's notes. This was blank. In the bottom right corner of the document was the signature: "Paul Sorenson, Chief Medical Examiner."

Ortiz scanned the remainder of the document for any additional information. He returned to the far right column, where the amount of the detected barbiturate had been recorded. That was the key conclusion. If the reporters asked, he felt very confident giving a conclusive medical opinion: this was, without a doubt, a significant overdose of Phenobarbital.

He grabbed the message slip with Kelly Addison's name and number, and spun back within reach of the phone on the corner of his desk. *If I can squeeze a date out of this, that press conference will be worth it.* Pulling the phone to his left ear, he started to dial with his right hand, reaching over the spilled pile of documents. 2-0-2-8-9-. He paused.

Abruptly, Ortiz rose from his black chair and slipped from behind his desk. The chair rolled back a few inches on the wood floor and stopped as it came to rest against the printer. He pulled his office door completely open, passed into the hallway, and spoke absentmindedly in his assistant's general direction as he passed. "Be right back."

He was moving back down the hallway as the thoughts formed in his mind. Ortiz quickly backtracked through the main section of the office suite and passed back into the lobby. He hit the down button on the elevator and listened as the tired chains dragged the elevator up from the floors below. The sound crept slowly upwards. Ortiz could feel the nervousness climbing in his stomach. The thoughts were still forming in his mind, each tracing a separate line of concern like multiple streams flowing toward the same dry riverbed. He wasn't quite sure why, but something felt wrong. He couldn't put his finger on it.

It wasn't that there was a discernable problem. It was that — in a culture and an office that functioned on predictable, repeatable, consistent bureaucracy — the number of unusual aspects about the Iredell autopsy was growing at a startling rate. It was his lack of access to the reports. Plus, the fact that the Chief Medical Examiner had signed the toxicology report as the responsible physician. Plus, the fact that he had chosen to make no additional notes on the apparent poisoning, or overdose, of a future Supreme Court Justice.

Why was the youngest deputy medical examiner asked to address the press instead of the chief or one of the more senior deputies?

As the elevator doors opened, two people walked out. He stepped into the elevator and hit the "B" button as the doors sealed in front of him. Sam Ortiz began his decent.

The basement level held the facility's autopsy rooms, forensic laboratory, and the entrance to the attached underground parking garage. Like most federal buildings the structure was dated. However, the office's laboratory had been updated only a year earlier. The office could now perform onsite, thin-layer chromatography, enabling the physicians and chemists employed by the Office of the Medical Examiner to complete an entire autopsy and toxicology examination simply by examining the body in one room and walking the blood sample into the adjoining laboratory.

Ortiz took a deep breath and tried to shake off his nervousness. *Everything can be explained. Iredell was a high-profile autopsy. I shouldn't be surprised that Paul wanted to be involved. I also can understand why he didn't want to add any notes to a document that was going to be released to the press. He sent me to the press because I was in the office on a Friday afternoon and he needed to stay behind to oversee this high-profile case.*

On the other hand, something was making Ortiz uncomfortable. It was more of a general feeling than anything else. Once he took a look at the hard-copy reports, he knew he would feel better. He could confirm the results and start calling the journalists back.

Ortiz pulled his ID card from the pocket of his dress pants and passed it through the reader on the white hallway wall. Seven feet ahead of him, he heard the automatic lock of the double doors retract. Simultaneously, the doors swung toward him, opening in the center and moving until they reached the end of their arc against the walls. The sound of the contact echoed off the hard, empty hallway floor. The doorway gaped wide before him, like a pair of open horizontal jaws. It was wide enough to pass a stretcher through and led into the examination room. He could feel the burst of cold air expanding into the hall.

Ahead of him, three bodies were lying on the examination tables. He could tell from the exposed faces of the first two that they were female. The body on table three was covered completely in a white sheet, indicating that the autopsy had been completed.

He entered the examination room and pivoted to his right, crossing into the neighboring file room. He quickly located William Iredell's file in the metal cabinet. The notes on the exterior of the manila folder indicated that the autopsy had been performed two days prior, on Saturday. Sam recalled the timeline from the press conference. *Subject discovered on early Friday afternoon. Subject identified and brought to our office for preliminary examination shortly thereafter. Time of death determined to be Friday morning, around 11 a.m. Press conference late Friday afternoon. Comprehensive autopsy Saturday morning. Cause of death: Phenobarbital poisoning.*

On the exterior of the Iredell file, the space next to "Removal Date:" remained blank, which confirmed for Ortiz that Iredell's body had not been moved and was very likely still on Examination Table Three.

Paul Sorenson's signature was the only one next to "Physician Performing Autopsy:".

When was the last time Paul performed an autopsy? Much less, performed one alone? The office had three deputy medical examiners — Ortiz and two others — and five staff physicians. The deputies did not even perform many autopsies; it was almost exclusively a staff physician function. *If he does anything down here it is simply observation or some kind of administrative review. Does he even remember how to do an autopsy?*

This didn't help. His feeling of unease was continuing to grow. He flipped open the folder. The only document inside was a copy of the Word document Ortiz had reviewed in his office. *Where are the hard-copy reports? Where is the DNA test?* Two years earlier, his office had started performing routine DNA examinations along with each autopsy, and he had expected to find it along with the official toxicology and autopsy documents.

His mind spun as his hands returned the file and pressed the drawer back into the cabinet. Sam could hear the drawer rolling along its tracks. He could hear the metallic sound of its green face locking back into place. His hand remained on the small, silver handle of the drawer as he looked back into the examination room.

The third body was easily visible from the file room. The flexible overhead lights had been extinguished and faced away from the body. At the head of the third examination table he could see the table's storage locker, a small cabinet that rose to waist-level and held the instruments used during a routine autopsy. On its flat, stainless steel top was an attached rack used to hold the blood samples.

Iredell's samples are still in the rack.

The first step was the hardest for Sam Ortiz to take.

He wove his way across the examination room, the floor slightly angling under his feet, sloping toward the drains under the tables. As he reached for the blood samples, his hand hovered above the rack.

The new chromatography set-up only takes a drop. He knew he could offer any of a thousand reasons why his ID card had passed through the reader in the hall. He knew the odds were overwhelming that one drop of blood out of the ten test tubes that had been filled would never be missed, especially since the autopsy had already been performed. *I can run the scan myself and set the results protocol to email the report directly to me instead of printing a hard copy. I can cover my tracks.*

Ortiz grabbed the last sample of blood in the rack, leaving behind nine red-topped glass containers and one empty position. Two steps later he pushed through the swinging door into the small laboratory. The three work tables were empty and Ortiz quickly moved toward the closest, taking a seat on an old, round stool, and wheeling himself toward the work space.

As Ortiz removed a single drop of blood and mixed it with the solvent, he could hear the sound of the swinging door behind him: a dull *thwack-thwack-thwack*, increasing as it settled back in line with the door frame.

Setting the test tube of Iredell's blood to the side, he started to carefully spread the solvent on a small plate. He placed the plate in the analytical chamber and closed the lid. The sound of the door was softer, but faster. A rapid *thwack-thwack-thwack-thwack*. It finally settled back into its original position and the room became quiet. He reached for the green circular button to start the toxicological scan.

A new sound.

He held his thumb on the green circle. He could feel the hard plastic against his skin. *Voices. In the examination room.* Ortiz looked around the laboratory. The swinging door he had just passed through was the only way in and the only way out. He could see the shadows moving through the Plexiglas window in the door. The line of light between the door and the frame disappeared for a moment as the voices moved closer.

He searched the room for a place to hide the sample. If he was caught with William Iredell's blood he would have a very difficult time explaining why he was running an unauthorized, unnecessary toxicological scan. He may be the press contact on this case, but he was not the physician responsible for the autopsy. Interfering with another physician's autopsy without any sort of authorization could get Ortiz demoted back to staff physician, if not fired outright.

His best option seemed to be to move to the far end of the room and hide the test tube behind the centrifuge used for the DNA testing. No-one would have a reason to be in that area and he could return later in the day to retrieve the blood. He knew the blood smeared on the plate in the scanner was not attached to any label indicating its source. It could not be traced back to Iredell's body without running a new series of tests. *There's a way out*, he thought. *Hide the blood and I won't have anything to explain.*

Ortiz started to lift off the small stool. The squeal of the aging metal sounded like a gunshot in the silent room. He stopped, holding himself midway off the torn, black cushion. The voices in the other room had reached the third examination table. He could make out two – no, three – distinct voices. As they approached he heard a female voice. The only words he could clearly make out were "quick funeral." Ortiz was sure the voice did not belong to anyone that worked in his office.

He could now hear another sound. *They're pushing one of the stretchers with them.*

He glanced toward the test tube, weighing the distance between himself, the blood, and the centrifuge across the room. If he startled the people in the other room, they could be in the laboratory in a matter of seconds. He did not have time to reach, and then hide, the test tube.

A male voice he did not know: "No. He's not going to lie in state at the Capital. I spoke to Senator Baker this morning. The first step is to get the body in the ground; then we'll work on nominating a replacement for him on the bench."

Then a second male voice. This one Ortiz recognized.

Paul?

The voices were directly outside the door. He was bracing himself on the stool, praying that it would not make another sound and semi-hovering over the cracked cushion. Paul Sorenson's voice again: "Give me a hand with this. There are some latches near the feet."

"You need a third set of hands?" The female voice again.

"No, we got him," his boss responded. "There's a box on the counter over there. Put those blood samples in it; then drop the box on the shelf under the stretcher bed."

Ortiz could feel his heart pounding. His eyes were locked on the Plexiglas window. *The rack of blood samples. Paul will notice the empty slot in the rack.*

"Lift on three." He heard his boss count to three and gathered that he and the other man were moving Iredell's body.

Then the sound of the stretcher rolling out of the room and the voices fading away. The metallic lock of the automatic double-doors. The parallel thuds of the stretcher wheels crossing the raised threshold into the hall. The double doors closing.

Ortiz lowered himself onto the stool. His dark hair was damp with sweat. He took four deep breaths and waited until enough time had passed for Paul and the other two people to leave the basement area. He punched the button to start the toxicological scan and walked back in the examination room.

Table three was empty. The rack on the stainless steel locker was empty. *Paul was at the head of the body. His back was to the rack of samples. Maybe he didn't see that one was missing. Maybe the woman didn't know how many should have been there.*

Or maybe he noticed and is going to check the electronic entry log after they move the body.

Sam Ortiz resealed the blood sample and carefully lowered it into the right pocket of his pants. The muffled, whirling sound of the chromatography machine followed him out of the room.

Chapter Ten

Washington, DC
June 14, 2010

Sixteen days before the execution of Parker Brown

Mark Ellis confirmed that he had reached the right apartment before he knocked on the door. The building at 425 Massachusetts Avenue had eleven floors. The apartment was on the seventh.

Ellis tapped his knuckles on the apartment door and stepped back, looking both ways down the empty hall. The exposed HVAC piping running along the ceiling and the hard, concrete floor gave the building an especially modern feeling. He could see two elevator doors at one end of the hall. At the opposite, a stairwell, separated from the hall by a door. Sunlight trickled into the hallway through the window in the door. Mark had his laptop and a small document folder tucked under his right arm. His suitcase remained in his truck, parked a few blocks away. In front of him, the light of the peephole darkened and a second later he heard the deadbolt withdraw.

Luke Lyford ushered him into the apartment, quickly closing the door behind Mark. They stood in silence for a moment. Mark smiled, shifted his laptop and folder to his left arm, and extended his right hand to Lyford.

Luke glanced down at the offered hand, then swatted it away and hugged Mark, patting him twice across the shoulder blades before releasing his guest. "Thank you for coming, Mark. I really appreciate your help. I know it couldn't have been easy to shut down your practice on such short notice and make the drive up here." He was pivoting, angling his body to invite Mark into the apartment. "It's great to see you – despite all of this."

"Great to see you too, Lyford. It's been too long."

Mark's eyes looked past Luke and examined the apartment behind his old friend, and his new client. It had the sleek, spartan feel of an executive apartment. The room opened to Mark's left, its far wall providing a view of the Washington Monument and the Capitol Building. To his right was a small kitchen area and directly in front of him was an opening into a short hall. "I see you have a short walk to work. And one heck of a view." He nodded in the direction of the Capitol.

His friend looked thinner than he remembered. Luke had always been thin, even during the days of pizza and barbeque while they campaigned for Mark's mother. As Lyford led Ellis into the living area to the left, toward the window, Luke removed his glasses and rubbed his eyes. Mark couldn't help but notice the dark circles.

"The short walk is great – when you can leave the apartment. I haven't been outside that door since Saturday. I tried to run to the office to pick up some paperwork on Monday morning and was swarmed by the press." He walked to the edge of the room, looked out the widow, and pointed to a few of the camera trucks parked on the street below. "They're out there again today," he said, eyeing the street below like a gargoyle.

Luke turned his back to the window and extended his arm toward the rest of the small apartment. "So, um, the living area is obviously here. Kitchen over there. Down the hall is the bedroom and a small office. I hope we can work out of here since I'm kind of trapped." He gestured back toward the media. "Unfortunately, I've only got the one bedroom. You don't mind a hotel, do you?"

Ellis settled into the couch and laid his laptop on the coffee table near his knees. "Sounds like a plan to me," he responded, running his hand along the smooth, dark teak wood of the table, admiring the lack of dust almost as much as the table itself.

It had been nearly four days since Ellis and Lyford had spoken on the phone. Over the weekend Ellis had caught up on some outstanding legal work and found a neighbor that would feed his dog while he was away. He had spent Monday tying up some loose ends in his law office and had driven to DC the following morning. "I'll try to find a place near here later this afternoon."

The time Mark Ellis spent between the first phone call and his arrival in DC had largely been filled by preparation for an open-ended stay in DC. He had not had time to consider what it would be like to be working around Luke again.

They had not seen each other since Mark's family's funeral, two years ago.

Luke was pacing, crossing back and forth in front of Ellis. Lyford moved like a metronome and Mark couldn't tell if he was simply nervous or was lost in thought. He stopped directly in front of Ellis and ran his fingers through his shaggy brown hair, twice; the ends of the brown strands tucked behind his ears, curling away from his head like a pair of small wings.

"You gonna keep wearing out that carpet, or we gonna get down to work?" Mark asked.

"Don't know if you saw it or not – I guess not; you were probably driving – but Edwin Carter, our show-horse of an Attorney General, was kind enough to note during his tour of the morning news shows that I was not a suspect." Luke sat down, balancing on the arm of a chair next to the television. His speech had a rapid cadence. Even sitting, he had that look of restlessness. "He didn't even need to say 'yet'. It was more or less implied in his statement."

"Better than being a called a suspect," Ellis offered.

"I recorded all his appearances." Luke tilted his head toward the television to his left. The flat-screen television sat on top of a low set of glass and metal cabinets, filled with a cable box, receiver, and the other components of his entertainment system. "I also managed to track down a copy of the entire press conference from Friday. It's saved on my laptop, in the office, if you'd like to see it."

"I'll take a look later on."

Luke Lyford pushed himself to his feet and walked toward his kitchen, crossing from the pristine, white rug covering the center of the living room back onto the light-colored bamboo floor. Mark rotated on the couch. For the first time, he noticed the "Claire Ellis for Senate '08" sign hanging near the opening into the kitchen area. Matted and framed, it was perfectly straight on the cream-colored wall.

Watching Luke pass the campaign sign brought that familiar memory back to Mark Ellis. The memory was actually more of a feeling. He felt the cell phone in his pocket. He felt the ring. He felt the voice on the other end, his mother's campaign manager. He felt Luke talking in the passenger seat of the truck, growing silent as his attention shifted to the one side of the phone call he could hear. He felt himself pulling his truck onto the shoulder of the road. He felt the gravel under the wheels. He felt the sand and grass as he kneeled on the side of the highway. He felt the end of nearly everything he had known.

Luke was back, this time sitting fully in the chair across from the couch. "As I see it, here is what we need to do. First we talk to the police. We make them understand that I'm innocent. We find a way to make them believe me. Second, we need to issue a statement to the press indicating that you are representing me."

"You're the political one, so tell me if I'm wrong," Mark interjected. "We might want to avoid the term 'representing.' I can hear the question already: 'Why does Luke Lyford need a lawyer to represent him if he's innocent?' Maybe we just go with 'assisting' or something like that."

Luke was nodding his head in agreement.

Mark continued. "As for the police, I'm inclined to hold off on contacting them right now. You're technically just a person of interest. As the Attorney General noted, you're not a suspect. You certainly aren't under arrest. I say we hold off on getting in touch with them until they want to talk with you again, or there is a big change in the circumstances."

Luke was up and pacing again. Mark noticed that, even when he was not going to leave his apartment, Luke was wearing what the folks in Whispering Pines would consider "business attire": a pressed, light-blue dress shirt tucked into black dress pants. Mark's wrinkled khakis seemed out of place in this apartment. His red, short-sleeve polo shirt, untucked in places, seemed even more foreign.

"Good. Good point." Luke smiled, affirming Mark's opinion to refrain from immediately contacting the police. "I told you I needed you."

Mark had placed his leather document folder on the couch next to him. It was an inch-thick binder with room on one side to hold a handful of documents and a legal pad embedded in the other side. He reached over, picked it up, and unfolded it across his knees like a magazine. "Luke, I think we need to talk about this letter." Mark had printed a copy of the letter from Luke's email and he pulled the copy from the folder, reclining back into the couch as he did.

Luke retrieved his copy of the letter from the small kitchen table on the other side of the room. Returning to the living area, where Mark was still sitting, Luke dropped the Capitol Mail envelope it had arrived in on the coffee table.

"I guess we need to start with the biggest question: is this real?" Mark asked, after watching his friend settle back into the seat across from the couch.

Luke shrugged his bony shoulders. "I have no idea, Mark. The version I received is obviously a copy. I believe that we can safely assume that this copy was actually mailed by Iredell. The police linked his cell phone to my office number. I listened to the voicemail. It sounded like Iredell – and, believe me, I grew familiar with his voice during the confirmation process."

Luke continued his assessment. "So, if we assume it was actually Iredell who called, and we know that the message indicated that he had something to show me, I think we can assume he was talking about this letter. And, therefore, we can assume that the copy I have was mailed by Iredell."

"OK. I'll buy that," Mark responded. "But it doesn't get us any closer to an answer on whether there is – or was – an original version of this letter."

"I'm not sure we can get to a definite answer on that, Mark. I ran every search I could think of, and even called a few history professors at Georgetown, but haven't found any evidence of this letter." As he spoke, he flipped through the three-page document, his eyes coming to rest on Madison's signature at the end. "I was, however, able to locate a good amount of information on the relationship between James Wilson and James Madison."

Mark was also flipping through the pages of the letter, reading back over the text that he had reviewed – it seemed – at least twenty times over the weekend. "I hate to admit this, buddy, but I don't really know who James Wilson was. I haven't had a chance to dig into the history books." If Luke was surprised by the comment, Mark thought he hid it well – as he always had in law school when Mark showed up unprepared for their study sessions.

Luke rose from his chair, again starting to pace along the edge of the carpet. His nervous energy appeared to subside as he presented James Wilson's abbreviated biography to Mark. "James Wilson was one of the country's Founding Fathers," he announced, unraveling the words like he was beginning a sermon. As he progressed, Luke explained how Wilson, when compared to some of his better known contemporaries, has gone largely unnoticed in the tales of Revolutionary history.

"Many scholars of American history consider him to have been one of the principal minds behind the Constitution," he offered.

"There are not many biographies on Wilson that I've been able to locate, but he is mentioned in numerous other works. I downloaded a handful of books that mention Wilson, but I've only been able to make it through a few. Yet, one story keeps reappearing. It seems he defended a group of alleged traitors during the movement toward independence. Some of his fellow revolutionaries hated him for it, but – in the end – he proved the innocence of most of the group.

"Apparently this led to the insertion of the Treason Clause into the Constitution – you know, the one about 'giving our enemies aid and comfort?' History seems to give Wilson credit for coming up with that part of the Constitution.

"He was also one of the first Justices appointed to the Supreme Court by Washington," Luke concluded, still pacing in the small apartment. "And many historians have argued that, when you consider the impact of his whole career, Wilson's contribution to the creation of the Constitution was second only to James Madison's."

Mark had started to take notes on the legal pad in his folder. "James Wilson was important – got it. And there is no doubt that there could be a connection between Madison and Wilson. So it's possible that Madison actually wrote this letter," Mark said, tapping the cap of his pen on James Madison's signature at the bottom of his copy.

"I'd say more like 'probable' than 'possible.'" Luke picked up his copy of the letter again. "Look at the date on this letter. May 15, 1794. We're a year after Chisholm versus Georgia." Luke paused and looked down at Ellis.

Ellis sheepishly smiled.

"Come on, Mark. Chisholm versus Georgia? The first big Supreme Court case? There were only five Supreme Court Justices back then, including some Revolutionary giants. Wilson was on the Court; John Jay was the Chief Justice. James Iredell was also on the Court at this point."

Mark looked up from his note-taking. Luke continued, stepping toward the window and gesturing toward the buildings in the background. "For the first time the brand-new Supreme Court is actually handling a significant case. It is actually *interpreting* the Constitution.

"I'm guessing that it is pretty reasonable that Madison and Wilson – two great intellects of the time and former partners at the Constitutional Convention – might write some letters back and forth discussing how the Supreme Court will actually work." Luke stopped and turned back toward Mark. The mid-afternoon sun was glaring off the windows across the street from his apartment, creating a backdrop of brilliant light directly behind Luke Lyford. "Looking at the history and the substance of the letter, I think we have to assume this is real. I think James Madison wrote this letter to James Wilson."

Mark flipped to the last page of the letter. He dropped it on the coffee table in front of him and laid a finger next to the middle paragraph, his finger covering some handwritten notes in the margin. He read the paragraph aloud as Luke listened. When he reached the final sentence, he looked up toward Luke and finished from memory: "To each generation, its own interpretation."

Their eyes met. "If you're right, Luke. If this is actually a copy of a letter from James Madison. Then this tells us *how* Madison thought we should interpret the Constitution."

"And that means . . ."

"I think I can take it from here, Professor Lyford."

Mark turned his head back toward his notepad. Neither attorney needed an explanation concerning the significance of James Madison's words.

A central battleground in American legal thought – if not *the* central battleground – is the question of *how* to interpret the Constitution. On one side of the argument is the concept of "originalism", the idea that the appropriate way to interpret the language of the Constitution is to look for its original intent: in essence, what did the authors of the Constitution intend by their words? On the opposing side stands the idea of an evolving interpretation of the Constitution, one that embraces the idea that the interpretation changes – evolves – over time and takes into account the values of the contemporary society. Most often, it has been conservative judges taking up the cause of the "originalism" theory, while liberal judges have carried the flag of an evolving interpretation.

This high-minded theoretical dispute has very real effects in the lives of Americans. Civil liberties, civil rights, and a host of other constitutional ideas could be expanded, contracted, or even cease to exist, depending on the outcome of the theoretical battle.

If Luke Lyford was right, Mark knew, it meant two things.

One: Somewhere out there, there might be an original version of this letter – a letter from James Madison that may go a long way toward resolving the theoretical dispute. From the letter it appeared that James Madison, the author of the Constitution, supported the "evolving" method of interpretation. *To each generation, its own interpretation.* If the original version of the letter – real proof of Madison's views – came to light, it would substantially undercut a massive portion of conservative constitutional philosophy.

Two: Mark Ellis also knew that Judge William Iredell had held the copy that now rested on Luke Lyford's coffee table. And he held that copy right before he died.

Luke was off his perch and moving toward the hall leading to the back rooms of the apartment. Mark reached across to the end table next to where his friend had been sitting and lifted Luke's copy of the letter. He was examining the copy, holding it near the large, sunlit windows when Luke returned to the living area.

"Mark," Luke called, tossing him a set of keys. "Just in case I'm not around and you need to get in. One gets you in the front door. The second is for the office door. I also made the change from 'representing' to 'assisting' in the statement to the press, and emailed you that press conference video file." Luke dropped a copy of the updated press statement on the coffee table.

Mark continued to examine Luke's copy of the letter. "What do you make of this writing in the margin?" He turned to the third page of the letter and pointed to the notes next to the paragraph he had read earlier:

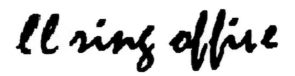

"I'm not sure what to make of them. I've been trying to figure that out since I got the letter on Friday," Luke answered.

Mark was still examining the page in the sunlight. "The coloring looks a little darker than the text of the letter."

Luke rose, walking to the window to look over Mark's shoulder. "I assumed the 'll' is my initials: Luke Lyford. Probably a note that Iredell wrote before he mailed the document."

"I'm with you on the 'll', especially since it is next to the important paragraph. But what is this second part? Sing office?"

For a few more seconds, Luke lingered over the document as Mark held it in the sunlight. "My best guess is 'ring office'. You know, like 'call office,'" Luke responded. Returning to the edge of the chair he had been sitting in, he continued. "My assumption is that he was reading this copy of letter, got to that part, and made a note to call my office – and he called my office on the morning he died. Then he dropped the document in the Capitol Mail when he couldn't get in touch with me. They found him in the Senate office parking lot so we know he was near the Capitol."

"Ring office?" Mark asked, looking over his shoulder back at Luke. "What is he, British?"

Mark moved across the room and grabbed his copy from the table. Returning to the window he held them both to the light. "Luke, have you taken a look at this stain in the top right corner?"

"What stain?"

"Compare the copy you scanned and emailed to me, and the original copy you had. There is a very light stain that covers the top right corner of each page of your copy. It is not there on my copy."

Luke was moving back toward the window and was watching as Mark pointed to the differences in the pages.

"When you hold it up to the light, you also see a difference among the pages in your copy. The back page seems to be slightly darker, in this corner, than the middle page." He turned back to the first page. "And the middle page is slightly darker than this first page." Mark was pressing the individual pages against the glass of the window. The stain started in the corner of the page, yet was uneven where it ended, a waving line with rounded peaks and valleys angled toward the middle of the document.

Luke looked over Mark's shoulder and could see that it matched the description Mark was giving: the back page was the darkest; the first page was the lightest. "It sort of looks like it got damp in that corner and then dried before it was delivered to me."

Mark handed both copies to his friend and picked up the press statement from the coffee table.

Luke was now holding both copies in the sunlight, comparing the light, off-colored stain on his copy with clean copy that had been scanned, emailed, and printed. Mark collected his laptop and document folder, and started to make his way toward the door. "I think it's time I made this statement to the press. I'm going to flag down some of those vans outside and get this over with."

Luke crossed to where Mark was standing, picking up the Capitol Mail envelope on his way. He dropped both copies of the letter in the brown envelope and handed it to Mark. "Take these with you. I've been staring at this letter for days. I need a break from it."

"I'll call you when I find a hotel room and we can try to determine our next move." Mark put the envelope in his document folder and stepped into the hall.

Luke laughed for the first time since Mark had arrived. "I'll have the mystery of William Iredell's death solved before you figure out how to find a hotel in DC."

Mark responded as he turned to walk toward the elevators. "You just worry about figuring out how a copy of a two-hundred year-old letter that James Madison wrote to James Wilson ended up in William Iredell's hands before he died."

Luke called to his old friend, and newly retained attorney, as Mark walked away, his raised voice slightly echoing in the empty hall. "I must not have told you the end of the James Wilson story: Wilson died on August 21, 1798. At James Iredell's house."

෴

Cumberland, Maryland
June 14, 2010

Sixteen days before the execution of Parker Brown

The television was mounted to the ceiling of the dining room at the Federal Correctional Institution in Cumberland, Maryland. As he did for most meals, Parker Brown sat alone, occupying the far-left circular seat of a six-person, institutional dining table. The screen flickered above him, a window into the outside world. On most evenings, the prisoners were allowed to watch the national evening news while they ate. Brown would customarily collect his dinner from the serving line and take up his solitary position. Not to his surprise, he was one of only a few prisoners at this high-security facility who watched the evening news.

Toward the end of the program, the broadcast displayed footage of a middle-aged man, his faded, red polo shirt tucked into his wrinkled khaki pants. He was standing outside what looked to be a modern apartment building. The man squinted in the sunlight as he read a prepared statement for the camera.

As required by federal correctional policy, the television was available for the prisoners, but was without sound. Parker Brown read the closed captioning to keep up with the broadcast. He watched the footage of the younger man, while he read the comments from the news anchor: "Luke Lyford, previously identified as a person of interest in the death of William Iredell, is now being assisted by an attorney. Mark Ellis, an attorney from North Carolina, made a statement today on behalf of Luke Lyford . . . ."

Parker Brown laid his plastic fork on his Styrofoam plate. He quietly watched the silent video of Mark Ellis, as the noises of the other inmates filled the prison dining room.

Chapter Eleven

Edenton, North Carolina
June 14, 2010

Sixteen days before the execution of Parker Brown

Six hours earlier, three hundred and fifty miles south of Parker Brown, and on the opposite side of the line that separates prosecutor from prosecuted, United States Attorney John Baker held his Styrofoam container of salad over the center of his desk as he cleared a space for his lunch. As he opened the container, his assistant leaned her head through the door of his office. "I'm sorry to interrupt you, sir. There's an FBI agent here to see you."

Baker glanced at the calendar open on his computer screen. It was nearing 1:30 in the afternoon. Most of his morning had been taken up with a conference call and a meeting with local prosecutors. "Did I forget to schedule something?"

"No, sir," she replied. "He doesn't have an appointment, but says he would like to talk with you if you have a few minutes."

John Baker had hoped to keep this Tuesday afternoon open. The corner of his desk held a pile of case reports on federal investigations, most of which had been opened before he accepted the position as United States Attorney. He was still trying to catch up. Reluctantly, he pushed his lunch to the side. "Please send the agent in. Thanks."

The primary offices of the United States Attorney for Eastern North Carolina were in downtown Raleigh. Most of the attorneys on his staff worked from those offices. After accepting the position, one of Baker's first decisions had been to open a small satellite office in Edenton. This allowed him to put in a full day of work and still make it home in time for dinner with his children.

The satellite office was smaller, but still had the feel of a federal prosecutor's office. There were three attorney offices and a smaller office for a paralegal. Baker's assistant worked from the desk in the entryway, a hardwood-covered space that connected the office's main door with two of the attorney offices. Plush red carpet covered the remainder of the space and blanketed the hallway leading from the reception area to John Baker's office.

Counting the one in his office and the one in the reception area, there were four American flags displayed in various corners. Behind the reception desk hung the two standard pictures: President Anderson and Attorney General Edwin Carter. The flags and the pictures, along with the recently delivered dark-brown leather furniture, made clear to anyone that entered from the lazy Edenton sidewalk that they had walked into a federal office.

The assistant had retreated to her front desk, the sound of her footsteps absorbed by the thick, new carpet. She was the first person Baker hired to work in the small office. A paralegal from Raleigh had also accepted his offer to move to Edenton, jumping at the opportunity to live closer to the ocean. He knew he needed to fill the attorney offices, but his tight budget and mountain of yet-to-be-reviewed case files were limiting his efforts. All things considered, John Baker was pleased with his decision to become the U.S. Attorney for this section of the state. Yet, there had been more than a couple of days on which he couldn't help but miss his old position as a local prosecutor. As he rechecked the calendar on his computer screen, and overlooked the surrounding stacks of work to be done, he knew this was going to be one of those days.

"Mr. Baker, I'm Agent Carl Kittleson." Kittleson passed through the office door and extended his hand to John. "I appreciate you working me in, sir. This shouldn't take much of your time."

"No problem, Agent Kittleson. Please have a seat." Baker pointed in the general direction of the chair sitting opposite his desk, its stuffed, dark-green seat accented by brass tacks running along its edge. The matching chair had been pushed back against the far wall and rested next to the flag in the right corner of the office. The tassels of the flag draped across the back of the chair and rested on another pile of unreviewed investigation reports that Baker had asked his paralegal to collect.

As Kittleson crossed the red carpet of the office, the unattached ear piece of his communication equipment dangled on the shoulder of his black suit. He was nearly as tall as John Baker, but much thicker across the chest. His graying hair had been allowed to grow only a half-inch from his scalp. His eyes were serious and a notch or two away from intimidating.

The agent took his seat and admired some of the photographs arranged along the credenza behind Baker's desk: in one, a younger John Baker was shaking hands with George Bush, the first one. In another, John Baker had his left hand on a Bible, his right in the air, and was facing President Anderson. The FBI agent recognized a couple of the people in the background of that picture: Senator David Baker and the agent's boss, Edwin Carter, the Attorney General.

"Sir, our office was just notified about what looks like a murder and potential robbery," Agent Kittleson began. "Everett Johansson was found dead this morning. He was the historian at the Iredell Family House."

John Baker had been looking for a legal pad. His hand froze on the half-open drawer to his right. "Everett Johansson? That's terrible. I just saw him speak over the weekend."

"Yes, sir. One of the volunteers at the Iredell House found him this morning. She called 911 and word eventually reached our office. Our working theory is that he may have been killed as early as Saturday evening. The medical examiner is trying to confirm a time of death for us now."

Baker pushed out of his chair. He circled behind it and sat on the edge of the credenza. He slid a picture of his family and a decorative, carved quote from Samuel Adams a few inches to the side to clear enough space for him to sit along the edge.

Agent Kittleson's voice matched his eyes. He ticked through a matter-of-fact summary of the investigation. "The victim was absent from church on Sunday, which was unusual according to people in his Sunday morning Bible-study class. Since the volunteer found the Iredell House locked, we believe the door was likely locked throughout Monday."

DREW NELSON

"Agent, I'm sorry to interrupt you." Baker crossed his arms, the buttoned cuffs of his white dress shirt pinning his striped tie to his chest. "Why are you bringing this to me? Isn't this an investigation for the state prosecutor?"

"The Iredell Family House is federal property," Kittleson answered. "Apparently, it was established, and has been managed, by the federal government since it was opened twenty-odd years ago. So it is kind of like a national park."

Baker finished the explanation: "So any crime committed on that land falls under federal jurisdiction, and therefore right into my lap."

"Yes, sir."

There was a note of resignation in John Baker's voice. He glanced at the pile of unread case reports on the chair behind the FBI agent. "OK. I guess you better fill me in on what we know so far."

"Well, we don't know much, yet, sir." Agent Kittleson pulled a hand-sized notebook from the interior pocket of his suit and flipped a couple of pages into it, his voice settling back into its mechanical pace. "As I mentioned, our working theory is that he was killed on Saturday. We have some agents checking with his neighbors, but there are no reports of Mr. Johansson being seen after he left the Barker House. There are countless sets of fingerprints in the House; we're not optimistic we'll pull any leads from the prints we've taken so far."

The agent turned another page in the small notebook, flipping the paper over the spiral binding at the top. "Single gunshot to the head. Close range. We found his body in an interior room of the house. There was no blood trail in the house so our assumption is that is that he was killed in that interior room."

"You mentioned a potential robbery," Baker interjected. "Tell me about that. Could that have been the motive behind the murder?"

"Yes — right now, robbery is looking like the most likely motive. However, there are no signs of forced entry. The door had an old-fashioned kind of lock that required it be locked from the outside. Our theory is that either Mr. Johansson or the suspect unlocked the door upon arrival, and then the suspect locked the door, from the outside, when he left."

Kittleson continued to work through his notes, offering a more-detailed explanation of the potential motive. "The robbery issue really has two components. The first is that the victim's car is missing. No keys were found on his person.

"As a side note, when we combine the fact that his keys and his car are missing, along with the fact that the front door had to have been locked from the outside, we start to see the outline of a suspect that was not necessarily in a hurry to leave. He found the victim's keys, took the time to lock the door, and then — we assume — left in the victim's car."

Baker was taking his own set of notes, jotting down questions as they came to him. "You said the potential robbery has two components?" he asked without looking up from the legal pad he was balancing against his legs.

"Yes, sir. We've been working through the file index for the house with one of the volunteers. We started with the boxes in the storage room in which we found the victim. Each box was locked and each document was accounted for. Except one. The index and the label on the top of the box describe the contents as 'Wilson-Madison Letter'. The volunteer said she had never seen the document that was stored in this box."

Agent Kittleson looked up, checked to make sure he wasn't moving too fast for the attorney's note-taking, and then continued. "We found the box in its proper place on the shelf, and it was locked. Our technicians tried to lift some prints, but the outside had been wiped clean. They tried the inside but could not pull any usable sets. However, there appear to be multiple spots of dried blood on the interior of the lid. Our crime scene techs have sampled it, and I'll keep you updated on their results."

Baker responded, his head bent over his legal pad. "I'm guessing that your assumption is the box was open at the time of the murder. That is how the blood was splattered inside the box."

"Yes, sir."

"And then it was closed and returned to the shelf?"

"Yes, sir."

"And I'm guessing that you believe the suspect may have taken this 'Wilson-Madison' document with him?"

"Yes, sir. That is the second component of the potential robbery."

"Anything else, agent?"

"No, sir." Kittleson closed his notepad and returned it the interior pocket of his suit coat.

Baker rested the yellow legal pad on the credenza and laid the pen across the top page. He rubbed his eyes and ran his fingers through his hair. The office was silent, like it was waiting on Baker to speak. "So let me see if I can summarize this. We've got an elderly historian, last seen on Saturday morning in a public place. No sign of him since then. He shows up dead on Tuesday morning. A single gunshot to the head from close range. A potentially missing historical document, but no evidence of a break-in. No witnesses and no suspects."

"Yes, sir."

"And we've got a killer with what we are assuming is a three-day head start on us."

"Yes, sir. On the suspect front: The volunteer told one of our agents that there was a visitor's log, but we haven't been able to find it. If it turns up, we'll start working through the list of people that were on the premises in the days leading up to the weekend."

"So we don't know much, do we?" Baker offered, the note of resignation growing in his voice.

"No, sir."

Baker tore the pages off his legal pad, stapled them, and slipped them into a manila folder. "I guess we know one thing, at least."

Agent Kittleson was standing, preparing to leave. He buttoned the top button on his coat as he responded. "What's that, sir?"

"A descendant of the Iredell family and the historian who keeps the Iredell family documents were both killed within a couple of days of each other. What is that saying about random crimes? One is random, two is a trend?"

"And three is a pattern, sir."

∽

Washington, DC
June 14, 2010

Sixteen days before the execution of Parker Brown

I am in Cabin John, Maryland. I am thirteen-point-six miles away from Washington. I am travelling three miles-per-hour over the speed limit in the right lane of MacArthur Boulevard. No evidence indicates that am being followed.

Noah Augusteel turned the rental car into the parking lot of the roadside motel. It was late evening and the sun had just disappeared below the horizon. In the dusk, he could see the few neon letters still in working condition: the small sign on the front office read "Vac n y".

The small sedan jerked slightly as its right wheels passed over a large hole in the broken concrete. Instinctively, he scanned the other cars in the parking lot and drove past the motel's office, guiding the rental car around the edge of the two-story motel. The building was on the course to dilapidation. Two broken windows in the back had been boarded-up instead of being replaced. As he circled, the owner's decision to invest only in the façade along the front was becoming apparent to Noah. *This will work,* he thought. *For tonight.*

The rear parking area held two vehicles other than his rental car. Noah backed his foot off the accelerator as he approached. Neither gave any indication of a threat. He parked the car between two nearly invisible yellow lines and stepped onto the rough pavement, again scanning the windows of the other two cars. Confident he was alone, he stretched and attempted to work some life into his dulled, numb lower back. He had discarded the blazer, but had returned to the casual khaki pants he had been wearing in Edenton.

Now on foot, Augusteel circled one of the cinder-block corners of the building, working his way back toward the entrance. He consumed the details of the building like a fire marshal. The white paint on the side wall was fading.

No more than a handful of shingles clung to the edge of the second-story roof. Gravel and the shattered remains of a Budweiser bottle crunched under his shoe. For the second time, he examined the four cars in the front lot. Seeing no movement and feeling no hesitation from his instinct, he pulled the glass door leading to the motel's small office. It was loose and rattled on its hinge as he swung the dirty glass outward. Noah stepped onto the threadbare, light-red carpet. He was alone in the room.

Noah Augusteel was northwest of Washington. Since his sprint from the Iredell Family House on the previous Saturday night, he had been almost constantly on the move. He had made two initial decisions. First, he had removed the battery from his sister's laptop computer. His training had been in operational and field work, not in technology. He was unsure whether Echo could track his movement through the laptop, and accordingly had removed the battery as a precautionary step.

Augusteel's second move had been to withdraw as much cash as possible, as quickly as possible. He had used the rental car's GPS to locate the nearest Bank of America. Accessing his personal account he had withdrawn his maximum daily limit of $5000. Electronic purchases would be instantly flagged so his credit and debit cards were now out of play. In the sprawling grocery-store parking lot next to the bank, he had exchanged the license plate on their rental car with a plate from a blue Ford Escape.

The dashboard GPS had skipped twice on the North Carolina highway before he saw it fracture into pieces in his rear-view mirror. He had bought a replacement handheld GPS – with cash – in southern Virginia. Then he had turned west and spent the remainder of Saturday night driving away from Washington. He had travelled north on Sunday, reaching middle Pennsylvania before he stopped for the night. He had spent both of the first two nights in his car. On Monday, he had turned back south and slowly worked his way toward DC. The rental car's license plate had been traded out twice more since leaving North Carolina. He spent Monday night in a small hotel in northern Maryland. It was now Tuesday night.

Noah Augusteel knew his sister would immediately initiate a search. She would deploy as many Lexington League resources as she needed. His decision in Edenton would not be misinterpreted. He had not simply abandoned a mission and disobeyed the commanding asset. He had moved to intervene, to prevent the mission objective. He had crossed the bridge between asset and threat — and each running step he had taken out of the Iredell House had burned a plank of that bridge, until none remained. There was no going back.

As if Noah Augusteel would ever entertain the concept.

She knows who my target is, he thought. *She knows I will avoid a direct route from Edenton to Washington. She knows that it will be impossible to locate me as I approach DC. She will, therefore, concentrate her energy on finding me in DC.*

It had been rejuvenating to be free of her. For the first time in his life, Noah was not being directed, hounded by his twin sister.

While his mind retraced his path over the last few days and nights, his senses registered the hotel clerk, as the twenty-something man entered the small office. Augusteel paid cash for one night. His room key was attached to a worn-down wooden oval by what appeared to be one-half of a leather shoelace. Like an ornament, the leather circle hung on the outstretched index finger of the clerk's right hand. The clerk spun his wrist, catching the key and the oval in his palm. As he used his left hand to reach for the cash Noah had laid on the particle-board counter, the younger man dropped the key and oval in his right hand to his waist, imitating a gunfighter holstering his weapon.

The clerk's slight physical movement was enough to restart Augusteel's operational mind, his training so engrained that the information came to him without any consideration.

Inventory: $4687.95, laptop, and battery. Echo Industrial Standard Field Kit: binoculars, 9mm Luger handgun, two ammunition clips, detachable silencer, first aid kit, hammer, wrench, three screwdrivers. Personal 9mm Luger with full ammunition clip. One change of clothes. My sister's change of clothes. One vial of the substance.

After moving the small inventory into his hotel room, Noah Augusteel searched his surroundings. He removed the pastel-colored bedspread and examined the yellowed mattress and box spring. He examined the rear-projection television. It was bolted to the small chest of drawers. After removing each of the drawers, he examined their bottom panels. He disconnected the phone and then worked his way through each light fixture. The small table in the corner of the room was not secured to the floor, so Augusteel repositioned it to block the locked door. He had performed the same routine the night before. It still felt overly cautious. Yet, until it was finished, he knew this was how he had to live.

Sitting on the edge of the aging mattress, he passed his Luger back and forth between his hands. He ejected the clip and ran his thumb across the top. His sister was out there. So was Echo. So was the Lexington League. He could sense them waiting on him, crawling like insects in the streets of the city, watching for any sign of his approach, preparing – knowing all the while, that they could afford to wait, that time was on their side. Knowing that he would eventually have to go to them.

Noah Augusteel's target was also out there. He only knew one of the five. But that was enough.

He passed the Luger into his right hand and slowly pressed the clip into the handle of the handgun. The satisfying click of it locking into place was the only noise in the tired motel room.

Chapter Twelve

Fifteen days before the execution of Parker Brown

ark Ellis swore as his red pick-up truck rolled past Massachusetts Avenue. He slammed his palm into his turn signal and swerved into the right lane, weaving among the other cars with all the grace of a boulder. The angry horns of the surrounding midday traffic echoed off the rusty tailgate of his truck bed. Ellis had been in Washington for nearly twenty-four hours; he was already tired of the city. His red truck made the next right on I Street and circled around the city block, eventually making its way back to Massachusetts. He waited for a break in the traffic and then made what was now a left turn onto the street where Luke Lyford's apartment was located.

Two police cars were parked perpendicular to the street, blocking traffic in both directions. Their spinning lights blazed over the hood of Mark's truck. He pumped his bare foot into the brake, and brought his truck to a stop just a few feet short of the painted shield covering the door of one of the cars.

Confusion. Then a sense of panic swept over Mark Ellis.

He could see the activity escalating as it progressed down Massachusetts. Even in the harsh sun, the blue and red lights reflected off the glass windows of the buildings. The cab of his truck suddenly felt like a bubble, the windshield and windows separating him from the noise and activity outside.

Ellis rammed the silver transmission shifter up the column of his steering wheel, jerking his truck into Park and leaving it in the middle of the blocked street. *Luke.* He sprinted the half-block between the barricade and Luke's apartment, the rotating lights burning red and blue and red again as he passed through the parked police vehicles. The intensity of the cars and the lights grew with his accelerating heartbeat, and concentrated around the front door of 425 Massachusetts.

Press vans. He recognized some from his impromptu press conference on the curb of Luke's apartment. *Are these still here from yesterday? Or did someone allow them inside the police perimeter?*

He reached the front door of the apartment building. The one-word thought pulsed in his mind. *Luke.* To his left, standing exactly where he had stood one day earlier, and surrounded by media cameramen and reporters, was a woman. Her short brown hair and pinstriped suit looked familiar to Mark, but he couldn't place where he had seen her before. She looked like she was handing out a single-page document to the reporters in the crowd. Mark slowed as he approached the melee.

Other cameramen were moving toward the woman, filing in from the side opposite Mark. His gaze ran back down the line of the approaching cameramen as he pressed into the crowd. Farther down the street, and on the other side of the crowd of reporters, he could see Luke Lyford's stringy brown hair. A police officer had one hand on the top of his head, another on the handcuffs binding Luke's wrists behind his back. A few cameramen were still filming Lyford.

Ellis started to push through the crowd, elbowing reporters, trying to create a path. "Luke!" He tripped over one leg of a tripod and sent the camera spilling back into the hands of the man behind it. Like the horns before, the angry shouts went ignored. "Luke! Stop!" He tried to pick his way through the equipment, but couldn't move fast enough.

Ellis broke through the other side, his stride extending as he pushed to reach the car. Heads were turning at the sound of his flip-flops popping against the asphalt. It was too late.

He could see the red brake lights of the police car as it slowed at the other side of the perimeter. He could see one of the barricading cars pull forward, creating enough space for the departing car to pass through. Mark's pace slowed to a choppy jog. Hands on his knees, he watched as the police car disappeared down Massachusetts. The lights and sound rained down around him. Yet, for a brief second, he felt like he was back in the cab of his truck, like a sheer divider had closed around him, muffling the world and the cacophony of Massachusetts Avenue. Or was it that he wished he was back in the cab of his truck?

The authoritative voice of the woman behind him pierced the bubble, yanking him back into the action surrounding him. As he walked back toward her he realized she was already halfway through her announcement. "What I've distributed today is a copy of the toxicology report from the Office of the Medical Examiner. This is the same version that was released by that office this past weekend. As you will note, the report points directly toward a significant overdose of Phenobarbital.

"Accordingly, I have great confidence," she continued, as Mark worked his way around the circle of cameras and toward the front, "that my office will prosecute and convict Luke Lyford for the murder of William Iredell. Thank you for your time today."

Mark was weaving through cameramen and piles of cords. Duct tape held some of the cords to the ground, making it easier to pass over them. He also noted that many of the vans had been able to back up directly in front of the apartment. *Not only did someone notify the press and let them through the police barricade*, he thought, *they also had enough of a head start to get properly set up.*

Stepping over the final set of taped power cords running between the press vans and the cameras, Mark Ellis cut the woman off as she turned back toward the front door of the gleaming apartment building. "I'm Mr. Lyford's attorney," he said, as he approached.

The woman turned toward him, her indifferent eyes engaging his. He felt like he was being strip-searched. Mark had dressed casually for a day of working in Luke's apartment. He could feel the woman's eyes as they silently judged his less-than-professional attire of tan cargo-shorts and a faded Durham Bulls t-shirt.

The recollection finally settled in. *Carol Cushing.*

Her hand was extended. "Mr. Ellis, right? I saw your name in the *Post* this morning. I'm Carol Cushing, the federal prosecutor for DC."

"What is going on? Why was Luke loaded into that squad car?"

"Luke," she paused, letting the mocking tone she used as she said his first name linger in the air. "Has been arrested for the murder of William Iredell."

Ellis recalled liking Carol Cushing when she was prosecuting Parker Brown. That feeling was fading fast. Before her death, Claire Ellis, Mark's mother, had campaigned against Brown's company, Echo Industrial, and other defense-contractors like it. It had been a key part of her campaign for the United States Senate. Carol Cushing had arrived in North Carolina with the same goal, only she had the backing of the federal courts.

Images of her dropped into his mind. Cushing in court, examining witnesses. Cushing on the day of Parker Brown's treason conviction, shaking hands with John Baker — then the incoming federal prosecutor. *I remember thinking that I had hoped you would stay, and save us from political hacks like John Baker.* He could see Cushing in front of the cameras on the steps of the federal courthouse in Raleigh.

Mark no longer wondered who had called the press.

Before him on the steps to the apartment building, Carol Cushing was returning the remaining copies of the toxicology report to her briefcase, resting it on the handrail leading toward the building's door.

"Arrested? That's a joke, right? Based on what evidence?" Mark asked. To Mark's right, a man with a gray, knit, short-sleeve shirt walked out of the apartment door, eyeing the underdressed attorney as he stepped past. In stark, black letters "FBI" was printed across the upper left portion of the man's shirt. Two other agents followed him out. Each carried a large box. Mark could see a laptop computer resting on the top of the items in the second box that passed. *Please tell me you erased that copy of the letter after you emailed me*, Mark thought as his mind shot back to his truck, to the brown envelope resting on his passenger seat and the two hard copies of the letter inside.

"Mr. Ellis, why don't you step upstairs with me?" Carol Cushing asked, responding to Mark, and gesturing toward the door.

As they crossed the threshold into Luke Lyford's apartment, Mark could see other FBI agents pulling apart nearly everything in the living area. The entertainment center had been dismantled. Another agent, "FBI" emblazoned across the back of her blue windbreaker, was working her way through the contents of the teak coffee table.

Cushing had remained silent on their ride up the elevator and their walk down the concrete hallway toward Lyford's door. However, as soon as they had moved into the apartment, she pivoted on a heel toward Mark Ellis. "It is straightforward criminal law, Mr. Ellis." She was overlooking the scene around them, a queen bee commanding her drones. "Means, motive, and opportunity."

She raised a closed fist, the back of her hand extended, facing Ellis. "One." Her index finger uncurled in front of Mark's face. Cushing's voice was crisp, efficient. The same voice Mark remembered from the Parker Brown trial in North Carolina. "Motive. It is no secret that your client went to great lengths to try to subvert Judge Iredell's nomination to the Supreme Court. I'm certain that he was – shall we say – less than enthusiastic that Iredell was confirmed by the

Senate last week and was going to take his seat on the Court this week." Her harsh voice seemed to reverberate off the hardwood floors.

"This is ridiculous. I've known Luke for years." Mark was trying to focus on Carol Cushing, but was being distracted by the FBI agents moving around the apartment. *There must be seven or eight of them in here.* "Of course, Mark opposed Iredell. So did I. So did millions of other people. That doesn't mean any of us killed him."

Cushing took a step toward the entrance of the short hall leading to the back of the apartment. "That is true, Mr. Ellis. It does not, *by itself*, mean that your client killed Judge Iredell." She entered the hallway; Mark trailed her, turning his shoulders parallel to the wall to let an FBI agent pass with another box of material.

Cushing held her hand back up in the air, speaking over her shoulder as she walked toward the bedroom of the apartment. Mark could see the door to the office to his right. It was open. An agent was rifling through Lyford's desk. Ahead of him, Carol Cushing uncurled her middle finger, extending it next to her index finger.

"Two. Opportunity. Judge Iredell called your client on the morning of his death. We know that from his cell phone records. He asked to meet your client that morning. We know that from the message he left on your client's voicemail. And we know that Judge Iredell died shortly thereafter."

She paused before she finished the thought. "In the basement parking garage under your client's office. Therefore, your client clearly had the opportunity to murder William Iredell."

Mark's voice was a mix of frustration and disbelief. "I know Iredell called Luke. It was not the other way around: Luke *did not* call Iredell. And they never met." Frustration had overtaken disbelief. He could feel the shift from Luke's friend to Luke's advocate as he approached the open bedroom door.

Cushing stepped into the door frame and turned to face Mark. They were a foot apart from each other in the small hallway. Mark stood only a few inches taller than Cushing. A smile cracked across her stern lips. "According to your client," she responded. The smile broadened, growing like a pool of water slowly spreading across a hardwood floor. "He could not provide an alibi for the morning of Iredell's murder. Can you provide one for him?"

Ellis hesitated. *Luke said he had taken the morning off. How can I prove that he was here the whole morning?*

Cushing leaped into the void created by Mark's hesitation. "Your client told the Capitol Police that he was in this apartment, alone, for the entire morning of Iredell's death. Did he speak to anyone? Did anyone see him? Do you have any evidence to corroborate his story?"

No. Mark could not bring himself to admit that out loud.

Carol Cushing uncurled the ring finger of her right hand. "Three. Means." She stepped into the bedroom and held the door open for Mark to enter.

Means? The means to kill Iredell? Mark's mind was moving. *Iredell was poisoned. Motive is easy to imagine. Opportunity is hard to disprove without an alibi. But the means to kill? That requires some hard evidence.*

Carol stood to the side, allowing Mark to view the bedroom. It was a compact space and matched the other rooms of the apartment. Despite the FBI's search, the room still had that executive, sleek feel. The mattresses had obviously been lifted, cut open, and returned to the frame; the furniture had been moved.

One agent was still in the room and Mark could see him kneeling next to one of the bedside tables. Cushing approached the back of the kneeling man and reached over his shoulder. She picked up two large, clear plastic bags off the surface of the bedside table. Both bags had "EVIDENCE" stenciled across the front. Mark Ellis circled the corner of the bed and followed Cushing. She held one bag in each hand, gently shaking the one in her right as she lifted it. Mark could see four or five light brown prescription bottles rattling in the bag.

"Phenobarbital." Cushing's smile had been replaced by the same stern look Mark remembered. "Multiple prescriptions. None of which are in your client's name. My guess is that I'll charge him with possession too."

She lowered her right hand and raised her left. A handful of loose, white pills rattled in the bag. "These will be taken immediately to the lab. My expectation is that we'll soon confirm that they are also Phenobarbital. We found all of these in the space under your client's bedside table."

The FBI agent rose to his feet, removing his latex gloves as he stood. Cushing handed both bags to him. The agent slid past Mark and left the room.

"Mr. Ellis, there is more than enough of the drug in those bags to kill *several* men."

Mark was overwhelmed. *Phenobarbital? In here?*

Cushing stepped past him as Mark stared at the small opening at the base of the bedside table. She was leaving; Mark followed her back into the living area of the apartment. The FBI agents had completed their search and the last one was stepping into the external hallway.

How do I stop this?

The authoritative click of Cushing's briefcase clasps broke through his thoughts. She had opened the case and was handing him a copy of the document she had distributed to the press. "This is the toxicology report, Mr. Ellis. Phenobarbital killed Judge Iredell. And we found the same poison in your client's apartment."

She raised her hand, three fingers extended. "Means, motive, and opportunity. That is why your client is under arrest, and that is how I intend to convict him."

Mark could see Carol Cushing closing her briefcase and opening the apartment door. *I told Luke he needed a real criminal lawyer.* He was reaching back to law school, trying to recall something, anything about search and seizure law.

"Hang on one second." He stepped toward Cushing. "If you just found this pheno-whatever this morning, how did you have enough evidence to get a search warrant? You can't just tear this place apart based on the fact that my client took the morning off from work and didn't agree with Iredell's thoughts on constitutional law."

"That's true, counselor." She stepped into the hall. "We had more, enough to get a search warrant."

More?

"A copy of the warrant is on the table, if you would like to read it." She pointed to the kitchen table to her right. "We had a source, a tip. Someone sold your client one of those bottles of Phenobarbital last week."

Mark felt like he had been punched. "Who? What kind of source?"

"The very helpful, anonymous kind." She smiled and closed the apartment door leaving Mark Ellis alone, standing among the remnants of the FBI's search.

⌒)

Washington, DC
June 16, 2010

Fourteen days before the execution of Parker Brown

The funeral of Judge William Iredell took place on a Thursday, exactly one week after he had been confirmed by the United States Senate and six days after his body had been found in a Senate parking garage. The President spoke. Iredell's wife and son sat in the front row. Every other row of the Capitol Hill Baptist Church was filled with the black suits of Washington dignitaries, fellow judges, members of Congress, and the crowd of Iredell family and friends that had travelled from North Carolina.

In downtown DC, A Street had been blocked off, as had the two blocks of Sixth Street that stretch from A Street toward Stanton Park. Dark town cars lined the street, double-parked in some cases. The President's motorcade had parked a block away on Constitution during the service, but now had been pulled up in front of the church steps as President Anderson left the sanctuary. The crowd slowly followed him out, the dark clothing a stream of ink spilling from the old church.

It had rained most of the previous night and the mid-morning sun was raising the remaining puddles into the humid Washington air. The President navigated the gray, stone steps of the church as he left, carefully avoiding the few spots of standing water and slick rock. He lifted a hand to shield his eyes from the sun.

President Anderson stalled as he approached his armored limousine. For a moment he scanned the crowd exiting the church, his head swiveling like the heads of the Secret Service agents to his right and left. He quickly spotted the man he was looking for, the Attorney General. Attorney General Edwin Carter had been a few steps behind the President, and as he reached the final stone step, had moved to the side and found an open area of sidewalk.

The President waited outside his limousine until Edwin Carter turned in his direction. As soon as he made eye contact with the Attorney General, Anderson lowered his hand and nodded his head toward Carter. It was nearly imperceptible, but both men understood what had been conveyed by the quick sign. Anderson's face, now drenched in the unblocked morning sunlight, looked older, and paler than it had in his campaign commercials. He turned his back and entered the waiting car.

Edwin Carter received the silent message – or rather the silent order – and looked back into the crowd exiting the church. He could see Senator David Baker working his way down the steps, talking with people the Attorney General did not recognize. As Carter knew everyone there was to know in the capitol, he assumed they must be some of the people that had made the trip from North Carolina. He caught Senator Baker's eye as the Senator passed. Baker offered a few final hugs and handshakes and worked his way toward Carter. "Beautiful service."

"Yes it was, Senator. I thought your comments were especially moving."

"Thank you. It's been one hell of a week around here."

Carter watched the crowd moving behind Baker. Some were making their way toward their cars. The Secret Service was removing the barricade it had erected for the President's exit. "David, I'm hoping that I might be able to ride with you to the cemetery. There is something I'd like to discuss."

"I believe my driver parked around the corner. Give me a minute or two and I'll be ready to leave," Baker responded.

The two men said a few more parting words to members of the crowd and worked their way toward Baker's dark sedan. They walked in silence – two black suits, side-by-side – until they reached the car.

"The President wants to move quickly on this, Senator." The car had pulled into the procession on its way to Arlington National Cemetery. "Very quickly."

"I agree," David Baker said. "We need to keep the momentum we have."

The Attorney General turned toward Baker, shifting on the cushioned leather of the town car's rear seat. His eyes watched the Senator. "The President thinks you're the answer."

David Baker stared straight toward the headrest in front of him. He could see cars pulling to the shoulder of the road as the funeral procession passed through downtown Washington.

Carter continued. "You would certainly get support from the Lexington League. And he thinks that your fellow Senators would quickly fall into line behind you. You'd sail through the confirmation process. Plus, the base of our party loves you and the country knows you from your work during the Iredell hearings. You'd be perfect."

Baker turned away from Edwin Carter. He now knew where this was going, and like the parked cars rushing past the window to his right, images from his career sped through his mind. He could see his early legislative races – a young man with talent, and ambition to match. His first statewide run: a competitive battle, but he had pulled it out in the closing days. An image of his wife joined the procession. She was on stage with him after his election to the Senate, her eyes sweeter and prouder than the victory. *Christ, I miss her*, he thought as the caravan of dark sedans picked up speed. *She would know what to do, what to say.* The Lincoln Memorial passed outside his window. Baker watched water splash onto the sidewalk as the cars ahead found the leftover puddles.

"If he calls you . . . If the President calls you, will you accept the nomination to fill Iredell's seat on the Court?"

Senator David Baker did not respond.

"David, if the President offers you the seat on the Supreme Court, will you accept?"

Chapter Thirteen

Washington, DC
June 17, 2010

Thirteen days before the execution of Parker Brown

It took most of Friday afternoon to straighten up Luke Lyford's apartment. After confirming with Carol Cushing's office that the apartment had no "crime scene" designation that required him to leave the rooms untouched, Mark had tried to reset the apartment as best he could.

He had returned from visiting Luke in the Capitol Police holding facility around two o'clock that afternoon. He spent the next couple of hours moving furniture back to its original location – or as close to it as he could recall – and reconnecting most of the electronic equipment in the apartment. Mark had reached his third beer by the time he figured out how to get the television and all of its associated technology back up and running.

Now around five o'clock, he had finally settled into the couch in the reconstituted living area of the apartment. His black-socked feet on the coffee table, Mark was looking forward to returning to his hotel, ordering some Chinese food, and trying to find a movie to take his mind off this case. The sleeves of his dress shirt were rolled past the elbows; he had long ago shed his tie and coat.

The clock on the wall above the television seemed to be moving so slowly that Mark wondered whether he had forgotten to plug it back in. The FBI had contacted him earlier that day; an agent had some paperwork or something that needed to be delivered in person, and Mark was waiting on the agent to arrive. Knowing it would take some time to rearrange Luke's apartment, Mark had told the agent he could find him here. *Plus, it probably gives us more privacy than the hotel and it can keep us away from the press*, he had considered as he spoke with the agent. Once he met with the agent and officially received the documents, he could lock up the apartment and make his way back to his hotel.

The apartment building across the street was partially blocking the sunlight, causing a half-shadow to fall over part of Luke's large window. Looking past the opposite apartment building, Mark could see downtown Washington. The apartment was quiet and the quiet only amplified Luke Lyford's absence.

Mark had not found the remote control during his cleanup effort. So he sat his beer on the coffee table and circled toward the television. Sitting on the other edge of the table, he found the power button and started to manually scroll through the channels.

MSNBC. Some press conference. The television blinked through a few channels. *CNN. Press conference.* Another click, another channel.

Mark paused, then hit the Channel Down button and returned to CNN.

As if the connection between his mind and his eyes had faltered, it took a split-second before he realized what he was watching. His first organized thought was about the man in the background. Then he read the network caption across the bottom of the screen: "Anderson Nominates Baker to Supreme Court."

Son of a . . .

He found the Volume Up button on the side of the flat-screen television and returned to the couch. Tipping the beer up, he finished the last half of the can in three swallows.

President Anderson was in the Rose Garden of the White House. Backed by the recognizable glass-paneled doors and two American flags, he was standing at the wooden podium with Senator David Baker to his right, patriotism personified.

Could this week get any worse? Mark thought.

The announcement seemed to be nearing its end. The President was conveying his hope for a swift confirmation process. The President seemed to emphasize that phrase, *"swift confirmation process."* Mark heard something else about "carrying on the work" of William Iredell, but his focus had turned to the face in the background, standing to the President's left on the small steps leading to the glass-paneled doors.

John Baker.

Maybe the pain and anger were still close to the surface. Maybe seeing Luke Lyford again had stirred up the emotion. Maybe it was some sense of injustice that he felt. *Here I am, alone, trying to dig my friend out of trouble; and there John Baker is, watching his father being nominated to the Supreme Court.*

The dislike was tangible, and almost overwhelming. He felt like crushing the empty beer can. He could recall his last conversation with Baker. *It must have been about two years ago,* he thought. Mark had returned to his parents' home in Pinehurst after the plane crash. His mother's campaign was still going through the motions with the substitute candidate, but everyone knew it was over. Senator David Baker was extending his lead and was going to cruise to reelection.

Two months had passed since his mother's death when John Baker called and suggested they meet to discuss the investigation. Baker had crossed southeastern North Carolina, making the drive from Edenton, on the Atlantic coast, to Pinehurst, a small town closer to the middle of the state. *I'll give him credit for at least delivering the news in person.* The two attorneys had sat on Mark's parents' back porch. John had accepted a glass of lemonade; Mark was at least a beer or two deep.

Baker had laid out the basic components of the investigation into Claire Ellis's plane crash, highlighting the involvement of multiple investigative agencies and the thorough, professional work of the Edenton police. The prosecutor – the son of David Baker, the son of his mother's opponent – had then placed the empty lemonade glass on Claire Ellis's own porch table and sat forward in Claire Ellis's own deck chair. "Mark, we're going to bring this investigation to an end," he had said with earnestness that Mark couldn't bring himself to believe was genuine.

Baker had tried to explain. There was no evidence of a crime. Claire Ellis simply died in a plane crash.

His words echoed in Mark's head: "The most we have been able to determine is what you already know. Her plane left

Edenton that afternoon. Your mother was piloting the plane. Your father and brother were on board. It crashed about ten minutes after take-off . . . ."

Friends had tried to discuss the closing of the case with Mark – some even to the point of saying that John Baker had made a courageous decision. Intellectually, Mark understood the awkward position Baker was in. As the senior assistant prosecutor for the jurisdiction from which the plane departed, and in which it crashed, he was charged with running the investigation.

But, he was also his father's son – and Senator David Baker had politically benefited from Claire Ellis's death.

Baker's final explanation of the case was the least satisfying part for Mark: "We have gone through every video we could find of the speech your mother gave before her plane took off. We have attempted to locate and interview every person we saw in the tapes. Your mother's campaign office helped us identify people." Then he had paused. Mark could still recall that pause. It had felt like the world had paused.

"Mark, we talked to everyone we could find," Baker had said, trying to defend his decision.

It was a nice effort at a justification, but Mark had also been in touch with his mother's campaign. He had also watched the video footage of the speech. "Everyone we could find" had a very literal meaning in this investigation. It meant everyone, except for one man.

That one man. The one man that approached Claire Ellis as she made her final walk from shaking hands at the rope line to the small concrete runway. He had trailed her, easily slipping behind the loose security of a campaign event, and handed her a bottle of water.

Mark could still see the image. The man casually approaching his mother, walking within feet of other campaign aides. *She must have thought he was just another volunteer when she took the bottle.* The man walking away, exiting the frame of the video. His mother climbing the movable stairs to the cockpit door and turning to wave to the crowd. The water bottle was clearly visible in her hand. Closing the cockpit door. Through the window he could see his mother slipping the communication gear onto her head. The plane turning and taxiing down the runway toward a fundraiser in Charlotte.

The man had never been identified. Mark had questioned every campaign volunteer he could find. So had John Baker and his state-level investigators. So had the FBI.

Eventually, the investigation had focused on that one man. The plane crash and subsequent fire had destroyed every other potential piece of evidence. Every other person at the event had been questioned. Yet the man was never identified, and when John Baker travelled across southeastern North Carolina, sat in Claire Ellis's backyard, and closed the investigation, the search for that man ended.

∾

On the television in front of Mark Ellis, Senator – and now Supreme Court-nominee – David Baker had been joined by his grandchildren, John Baker's son and daughter. The press conference was ending and the President was bending down to greet the children as they shyly hovered around John Baker's legs.

Mark turned the television off and checked the clock above the screen. 5:27. He expected the FBI agent to arrive around 5:45. Time crawled forward.

He picked up his document folder, looking for something to kill the last few minutes. The brown Capitol Mail envelope was inside. The two copies in the brown envelope – Luke's original copy from Iredell, and the scanned version Mark had printed – remained, as far as he knew, the only two that existed. Thankfully, Luke had removed the scanned version of the letter from his laptop and email account after he had emailed it to Mark. That had been Mark's first question after the guard had closed them into the attorney-visitation room during his visit earlier that day.

After discussing the confiscated computer, Mark and Luke had started to piece together what they could about the prosecution's case against Luke. The anonymous source was a dead-end. If the source was truly anonymous – as the copy of the search warrant Carol Cushing had left in the apartment indicated – then there was no witness for Mark to locate.

Real or fake: it didn't matter at this point. The Phenobarbital had been discovered in Luke's apartment. Cushing would not need a witness to link the drug to Luke – no matter how strongly Luke denied knowing anything about the drug.

The alibi was also a problem. A significant problem. Luke had spent most of the morning of the murder sleeping, recovering from the long week of William Iredell's confirmation hearing. The remainder of the time had been spent watching the morning news shows.

"I may have checked my email once or twice," Luke had told Mark, leaning back in his visitation-room chair as he tried to recall the morning before Iredell's body was found.

Mark had made a note to look into whether they could establish that he was in his apartment by showing that his computer had been connected to the apartment building's wireless network. They both considered this unlikely to help. Luke had explained that his computer was always connected to the network. And, even if they could prove it had been disconnected and reconnected sometime that morning, Cushing would just argue that he signed on to the network and then left to poison Iredell. It was another dead-end.

After covering the old – and problematic – evidence, Mark had updated Luke on the single piece of new information that had developed since his arrest. The FBI had been able to make an addition to the timeline of Iredell's death. A fellow appellate court judge had been with Iredell after his confirmation, on the night before his body was discovered. The judge had apparently called the FBI shortly after the press conference and explained that he had left the Capitol with Iredell. The two judges had walked together until they separated near the corner of K Street and 14th.

Visitation time was nearly exhausted when Luke had asked Mark to check one other potential piece of evidence. As Mark gathered his documents together and prepared to leave the visitation room, he listened as Luke briefly outlined a way they might be able to use Madison's letter. Ellis had promised his client that he would look into the idea later in the day.

ᏮᎧ

And with a few minutes to spare before the expected arrival of the FBI agent, Mark decided it was as good a time as any to keep his promise. He reached for the lamp on the end table to his left and pulled it closer to his seat on the couch. He had already removed Luke's copy of Madison's letter and held it aloft in the lamplight. The stained corners were in the same condition as when he had first examined this copy of the document.

Mark closely studied the stain on each of the three pages and compared it to his scanned version. He turned Luke's copy over, then over again. The stain appeared to be identical on both sides of each page. The darkness – as it had appeared when he first noticed it – decreased from the third page of the letter to the first page.

Mark reset the pages in their correct order and straightened the letter on the coffee table. The pages of Luke's copy naturally folded along a rounded crease in the middle. He ran his finger along the crease then flipped through the stained edges one more time. *Maybe Luke is onto something*, he thought.

As he examined the third page, his eyes ran to the writing in the margin.

ll ring office

He and Luke had not had time to discuss the writing since Mark's first day in Washington. As part of that original discussion, Mark had offered the idea that it might read "sing office." But that seemed to make little sense. Luke's reading seemed much more likely: "ring office" – as in a note

Iredell left for himself, reminding him to call Luke Lyford. This made sense to Mark, when he read it in conjunction with Luke's initials, which were positioned next to it in the margin.

He rotated the third page, trying to read the scrawled letters from every possible angle. He flipped it over and read the words backwards in the lamplight. *Nothing.*

Mark closed his eyes and leaned his head back against the pillow of the couch. *Ring office. Sing office.* He moved the words around his mind. *Nothing.*

He landed on something. *Could "ring" maybe be a physical description of the office?*

He opened his eyes and looked at the paper in his lap. *An office shaped like a ring?* He rolled his head back onto the couch pillow and stared at the ceiling. *An office that is shaped like a ring? Maybe a circle? An office that is shaped a circle?*

An office that is shaped like an oval?

The knock on the door came suddenly, interrupting his meandering reflection. Swiftly, but carefully, Mark slid the letter back into the envelope and put the envelope in his leather folder.

The FBI agent knocked again as Mark walked toward the door. He retracted the deadbolt and turned the door's silver handle to let the agent enter.

"Mr. Ellis?" The agent raised his badge and identification card as Mark pulled the door open.

"Guilty as charged. Y'all ready to let my client out of jail yet?"

Without answering, the agent crossed into the apartment, taking a step to the side to allow Mark to close the door behind him. He handed Mark a few pages of paper that had been stapled together.

Mark glanced down as he reached for the documents. They looked like a spreadsheet with some introductory text above it. Behind the documents was a small handbook. The agent handed this to Mark at the same time.

"Did I forget to sign something when I left today?" Mark looked at the cover of the stapled documents as he spoke. He paused, then examined the face of the booklet. The materials looked to be a visitation schedule and a booklet on attorney-visitation regulations.

"Agent, um . . ." If the man had offered his name, Mark had forgotten it. "I think y'all have made a mistake here. My client is in the Capitol Police lock-up downtown." He rotated the booklet to show the agent the cover. "Luke Lyford is not being held at the . . ." Mark turned the booklet back over and read from the cover. "Federal Correctional Institution at Cumberland, Maryland."

"This is not about Luke Lyford, Mr. Ellis."

Confused, Mark looked up at the FBI agent. "Then why are you . . ."

"Mr. Ellis," the agent interrupted. "Parker Brown is looking for an attorney. He would like to talk to you."

Part Three

Chapter Fourteen

Washington, DC
June 17, 2010

Thirteen days before the execution of Parker Brown

The crowd of tourists on a Friday afternoon, alone, would not have been enough. However, the media presence outside the White House, and the extra spectators it had drawn, gave Noah Augusteel cover to operate.

In a light breeze, a few dead leaves swirled around the feet of the crowd. He could hear their brittleness as they scraped along the concrete and were trampled under rubber soles. A double-decker tour bus on the street twenty yards to his left pulled forward as the light changed to green. He could feel the rumble of the groaning acceleration. The guide barked something about the White House's Rose Garden to the passengers baking on the upper deck.

His blond hair had been severely cut back by the electric clippers he had purchased the night before. It was temporarily dyed a deep brown. Sunglasses, baseball hat, t-shirt, and shorts gave him the look of a traditional DC tourist. He could feel the weight of the Luger in the small backpack hanging from his shoulder. It lightly bounced with each step as he walked along the wrought-iron fence enclosing the White House grounds.

Visibility of target is obstructed. Target is roughly fifty yards to the northeast.

He fell in behind a family as they worked their way through the crowd on the western side of the White House. As they slowed to angle for a glimpse into the press conference, Augusteel moved past them and stole a look to his right. Senator David Baker's nomination to the Supreme Court was underway. Noah's view was largely obstructed by the collection of news cameras set up between his position and the Rose Garden's podium.

Something moved along the iron fence. A woman in running clothes. Augusteel sidestepped as she moved toward him, then past him, and broke into a jog. He briefly caught sight of President Anderson and Senator Baker through the space her departure had created. As though it had been pulled into the vacuum, another body filled the space along the White House fence, and Augusteel's view was gone.

Target is thirty-five yards to the northeast. It is 17:18. I am approximately two miles from my vehicle. I am in a crowd of moderate density. There is a group of fifteen tourists twelve feet to my left. Their tour guide is wearing a straw hat and walking backward as he speaks. There are two smaller groups ahead of me. Each group is comprised of two adults and one child. One of the women is taking a picture with her phone. The man with her is approximately 235 pounds. He is tired and looks bored. He is wearing an imitation New York Yankees jersey.

Assault window undetermined.

His Echo training was taking over, structuring his thinking as he approached.

Level one assessment: White House uniformed guards. Four threats in area. All inside fence. Two on fence ahead. One behind. One stationed in guardhouse ahead. All armed.

The faces moved past him in the crowd. He could catch brief portions of conversations as they flowed around him. He searched each face. Nothing registered.

There. Two watching the crowd, facing away from the fence.

Level two assessment: plain-clothed Secret Service. Two threats ahead. Fifteen feet. Armed.

He adjusted the backpack on his shoulder.

Ten feet. Three feet.

He was past them. Augusteel shuffled to his right, closer to the fence and behind a man pushing a baby stroller.

His senses were alert, his eyes and ears absorbing the environment as he flowed through the spectators. Ahead he could hear the muffled sound of the press conference. Someone – Anderson or Baker – speaking through the amplified sound system. The stroller ahead rolled over an empty McDonald's bag. He could hear the paper under the wheel. Two conversations to his left. One behind.

Target is twenty yards east-northeast. No line of sight. Assault assessment: Direct approach unavailable. Potential assault window while target in vehicle.

Augusteel was approaching the western exit of the White House grounds. Traditional White House planning would schedule the press conference participants to pass through this exit. *Security is increasing*, he thought, as he approached the driveway. He could see Secret Service agents moving into position. The uniformed agents were forming parallel lines along the route away from the building, preparing to guard the course through which the cars would pass.

He could see two plain-clothed agents in the crowd, each with his right hand pressed against his ear as he received instructions. They also moved toward the exit route.

Then Noah Augusteel saw something else.

Level three assessment: Echo Industrial assets.

Two across the exit route, on the opposite side of the pathway the guards were creating. Then a third farther down, across the driveway and to his left.

The ceremony was over in the Rose Garden and the Secret Service detail was opening the exit. The tourists were moving away from the fence; some watched as the first cars left the White House.

It was the head movement that had given away the Echo assets. It was subtle, but Augusteel could easily read and recognize the tactics. The two across from him had stopped looking skyward and were moving toward the exit route. He looked left. The third asset was still searching the nearby rooftops. *He's looking for a sniper. Does she really think I'd take up a vertical position this close to the Secret Service?*

Noah reached the blockaded alley that had opened before him. He turned to his right. The crowd was dispersing, the tide of people now flowing toward him and away from the fence.

Cover reduced, he registered automatically, calculating the new factor into his environment.

Augusteel moved against the crowd flow, toward the White House fence, toward the Rose Garden. He could feel himself becoming more apparent – easier to spot – as he moved against the direction of the tourists.

I am alone. Fifteen identified threats. It is 17:28. One weapon, in shoulder bag. One extra ammunition clip.

Target visibility zero.

He slipped past a pair of college students and earned a clear view through the fence.

Target acquired.

He could see the few remaining guests at the nomination announcement moving into their cars. The Vice President and the Attorney General stepping into a black sedan. The United States Attorney for the district was speaking to two people Augusteel did not recognize. She stopped shaking the hand of one of the people and entered another dark sedan. He could see David Baker and his family ducking into the final car in the long line.

Recognition. The middle-aged man behind Senator Baker.

I know that face, Noah thought. He paused. His mind spinning, working to recall where he had seen the man before.

Cover reduced. Like a red beacon appearing in the fog, the repeated thought interrupted his memory. The crowd had all but left this area.

He glanced across the driveway. Only one of the Echo assets remained across from him. The asset was watching as the final cars moved past the White House guard post.

Target approaching.

Noah Augusteel slung the small backpack over his shoulder, catching it in his right arm. He started to raise his left hand to unzip the bag. His eyes scanned the exit. There were three cars lined up at the guard post. The last three in line.

Echo Industrial threats. Two. Left. Twenty yards. Closing.

Two of the men he had seen across the street had crossed and were moving toward his position.

The wrought-iron fence was beside him. White House uniformed agents behind it. Directly in front of him was the guarded exit route. Two sides of a square. *I am in the corner.* The Echo agents were the third side of the square. His only opening was behind him, back along the fence.

Ten yards.

In his peripheral vision, he could see the White House guard waving through the last set of three cars. They were pulling into the route outlined by Secret Service personnel and the portable hard-plastic barricades.

Target window: now.

Noah Augusteel's left hand hovered. *If I open this bag there is no going back. The federal agents will see the move and swarm toward me. I can get only a few shots off.*

Assault assessment: Likelihood of success limited. Likelihood of success and survival approaching zero.

But if I don't open this bag . . .

He could see his target in front of him. He could feel the threat closing from his left.

Choose.

Augusteel could hear the German-accented English of one of his earliest Echo instructors: "It always comes down to a choice." He pivoted toward the approaching men and grabbed the zipper of his bag.

Wait. The thought came like a hammer. It was all instinct now.

Threats looking up. Slowing. The Echo assets were mirroring their counterpart on the opposite side of the exit route. They scanned the surrounding rooftops as they backed toward the passing cars.

Fifteen yards. Moving away.

The final set of three cars passed. The Secret Service was closing the barricades behind them. Each Echo asset simultaneously touched his left ear.

Noah could see two black sport-utility vehicles pull behind the final set of cars as they turned right onto Executive Avenue.

Target out of range.

∽

Her assets had focused on the long-range threat. His sister had left the defense against the short-range tactical options to the federal agents. That close to the White House, with that much security – anything in the short-range was a suicide mission.

She knew it and he knew it.

It was a standard Echo Industrial approach. Basic, but thorough and effective. So long as his target stayed within Gloria's protective bubble, Noah Augusteel knew he may never get a clean shot.

He knew it and she knew it.

Chapter Fifteen

Edenton, North Carolina
August 21, 1798

Thomas Augusteel had been watching his clothes dry. His traveling coat, and the shirt, vest and pants he had been wearing in the stagecoach, dangled like dead men on a line that stretched between two of the pine trees behind Justice James Iredell's house. Augusteel watched the clothes as they clung to the line, motionless in the summer heat. Some pine needles had fallen onto his coat. He could see darker areas in the sandy soil, where the water dripped from his clothes.

He had managed to pull a few semi-dry clothes from the bottom of his travelling case. As he rose from the wooden steps of Iredell's back porch, he tried to straighten his mis-matched vest and pants. His wrinkled – and now dusty – formal dress coat hung over the porch railing. He retrieved it as he stepped toward the rear door of Iredell's house. One of the women who worked in Iredell's house was holding the door open for him, and she inspected Augusteel as he passed: an unusual combination of formality, sweat, and dirt.

He moved down the white-walled hall and through the Southern home, following the woman who had been sent to find him. As he passed, Augusteel could see two other women working in the kitchen. Steam was rising from a boiling pot and drifting out the open window into the side yard. To his left, he could see the door to the bedroom where they had taken James Wilson. It was closed, separating Wilson and Thomas Augusteel. Of equal importance, it also separated Franklin's notes and Thomas Augusteel. He took a second glance at the bedroom door. *They've had someone in there since we arrived – the doctor, Iredell, or his clerk.*

He could still hear the conversation in the common room of the Hillsborough inn: *If he has the notes, he can end us.*

It seemed like an age ago, but it had only been a day and a half. Yet in that day and a half, Augusteel had moved from confidence to near desperation. The league had trusted him to handle the recruitment of James Wilson. *I played my part*, he thought. *I got him to Hillsborough. I delivered him to the five. They failed. They and the other senior members. Not me.* He knew, however, that was most certainly not how it would be perceived by the Lexington League. They wouldn't care if he had done what they originally asked. No, the five would only care about his new assignment, the second assignment they had given him: *Find out whether he has the notes. Take them back if he does. Allow Wilson to discuss this with no-one.*

He had accomplished the first part, though only after giving Wilson the powder. *He has the notes.*

The second part was growing more complicated. Franklin's notes were with Wilson's other documents, in his small travelling trunk. The trunk had been taken into the room with Wilson. Augusteel desperately needed to get into the room, and he had to get in alone. But he was being hurried down the hall, a feeble boat in a strong current, helplessly passing its dock and being carried farther down-river.

The third part – making sure Wilson told no other person about Franklin's notes – was out of Augusteel's hands. He knew that time was on his side. If the abbreviated description he had received was correct, Wilson would be dead soon. *But, has he already told someone about the notes? How can I find out without implicating myself?*

He was working through his options as the woman opened a door ahead of him. He entered what looked like a small library, or a large study. *Would a second dose accelerate the effect?* His thoughts trailed a few steps behind his body and were still pondering what to do about James Wilson. Augusteel instinctively moved his left hand into the pocket of his pants. He could feel the second vial he had been given.

He extended his right hand to James Iredell as he entered the warm room. "Mr. Justice. Please, sir, provide me with good news about Justice Wilson's condition."

Two stuffed chairs faced an empty fireplace. Iredell rose from the one farthest from his guest. His desk stood to the side, behind the chair he had been sitting in. Bookshelves lined the opposite wall, to Augusteel's left as he crossed into the room. "Young man, I've been told you were with Justice Wilson last night." James Iredell was living up to his well-earned reputation of getting to the point. He was half a foot shorter than Thomas Augusteel and much older. "What is your name?"

"Thomas Augusteel, sir. I apologize for being introduced in this manner . . . ." He cast an overly dramatic look down at his dusty coat. ". . . and under these circumstances. I've been Justice Wilson's clerk for nearly a full year, sir."

"And you were with him in the coach last night?" Iredell was settling back into the chair and he motioned for Augusteel to take the other, directly across from Iredell. Augusteel was not familiar enough with Justice Iredell's speech to recognize the slight note of interrogation coloring the question.

The Justice was shorter than Augusteel expected. *But just as substantial around the waist as they say*, he thought. Augusteel noticed small red specks on the rolled up sleeves of Iredell's shirt. *Is that blood? Wilson's blood?*

"I was, sir. We had a long ride from Hillsborough."

"What were you doing in Hillsborough?"

This time Augusteel caught the hard edge of the question. He shifted in the stuffed seat. "Justice Wilson attended a meeting with some gentlemen there, sir."

"What sort of meeting?"

If Wilson told him, he's not going to reveal it to me. He wants to know how much I already know. "I'm not sure, Mr. Justice. I was not in attendance."

"Certainly he told you the nature of the meeting, Mr. Augusteel. You were . . . are . . . his clerk."

Were? Is Wilson already dead? Iredell's eyes were locked on his. Augusteel looked away, his gaze searching along the back of Iredell's chair and over the wooden desk behind the older man. A few open books had been stacked on top of the desk. A lamp, lit despite the sunlight entering through a small window farther down the wall, glowed from the back of the desk.

"No, sir. He did not." That much was at least technically true. *Wilson* had not told him what the meeting was about. That wasn't to say that he had not been told by *someone*.

"Justice Wilson wasn't – I mean, isn't – the kind of gentle-men who reveals the details of his affairs to a clerk."

Iredell's eyes were locked on him.

Damn this. He knows Wilson. He knows Wilson would tell the world about his affairs, if it would listen.

Iredell was quietly watching Augusteel.

"Sir, how is Justice Wilson? He was so sick that we feared he would not make it through the night." Augusteel crossed, then uncrossed, his legs. He could see a streak of dirt running along the back of the right leg of his pants, a remainder from his time sitting on the back steps. He started to bend to wipe it off – paused – and then abruptly sat back in his chair.

James Iredell's eyes never left Augusteel as he reached into the interior pocket of his vest. He pulled out the seven pages of Benjamin Franklin's notes and ran his finger down the crease in the paper, straightening the pages against his crossed leg.

Augusteel could not read the documents from his chair, but he could suddenly feel the quiet settle over the room.

Iredell had stopped straightening the pages. He pulled a small set of reading glasses from his shirt pocket, unfolded them, retracted some strands of white hair, and hooked the frame of the glasses around his ears. He slowly read through the top page, while he let the clerk stew in the silence. As he finished, Iredell lowered the pages and looked at Augusteel, his eyes peering over the top edge of his glasses and boring into the clerk like two small drills. "Mr. Augusteel, Justice Wilson directed me to these pages. They appear to be notes from Ambassador Franklin."

The second line of the directive ran through Thomas Augusteel's mind. *Take them back if he does.* He thought about feigning surprise. Instead he froze, staring at the documents in Justice Iredell's hands. It was slipping away. *Wilson told Iredell about the documents. Iredell has the documents.* It was all slipping away.

The vial in his pocket called for his attention; it weighed on him. Suddenly, an image he hadn't recalled in years appeared in his mind's eye. Thomas Augusteel could see his father standing next to him, listening as Thomas repeated the words of the league's initiation ritual: " . . . to be a man of action . . ." Was this his moment of action?

Before him in the study, James Iredell was reading from the documents, slowly turning their pages. Augusteel could see that the Justice was watching for his reaction. "Amylon malonate? You know what that means, Mr. Augusteel?"

His reaction was slow. "Um, no. No, sir. I've never heard that term. Is it, um, French?"

Iredell again glanced over the top of his half-moon glasses. "No. You've never heard that term? What about anti-spasmodic tincture?"

"No, sir."

Iredell ran his finger down the page, reading off six more terms. Augusteel's response was the same to each question. His left hand had moved into his pocket; his fingers grasped the vial. Quickly, he removed his hand and firmly gripped the arm of the chair.

Iredell studied the clerk's nervous movement, observing the restless action in the chair across the warm room. The Justice lowered the notes back onto his lap, and the commanding, collected tone of his voice sliced through the humid air between the two chairs. "Mr. Augusteel, who is Albert Ladenburg?"

"I do not know, sir." Augusteel was sweating profusely now. He could feel it on his palms. He rubbed his hands on the arms of the chair and looked toward the fireplace in front of him. "Do you think I might be able to visit Justice Wilson, sir? I would like to help if possible."

Iredell slowly rose from his chair and walked toward the desk behind him. He reached over the open books and lifted the small reading lamp. Deliberately, and slowly, as though it were some cherished relic, he carried it between the chairs and to the brick hearth in front of the fireplace. He lowered himself onto a small footstool next to the fireplace and removed the glass covering of the lamp.

The small flame seemed to hover over the dull brass of the lamp.

Augusteel could suddenly see the floor of the stagecoach. The water shifting around the lamp at his feet as he lurched to catch Wilson.

"Young man." Iredell was holding the notes over the flame. "I am a Justice on the United States Supreme Court. I practiced criminal law for years before my appointment." He looked up from the documents.

Take them back if he does. It was pounding in Augusteel's head.

"I've been in more courtrooms and seen more liars than you can count, son," Iredell continued. "And I believe I'm looking at another one right now."

"Sir, I . . ." *I cannot be linked to those documents.* His thoughts were panic.

Iredell did not stop to let him reply. He lowered the corner of the notes into the flame.

Take them back if he does.

Augusteel flexed his fingers. Wilson was dying in the other room. Augusteel's life may be following the notes into that flame. *If he knows about the notes, what else does he know? Does he know what happened to Wilson?*

But in that moment of reflection, the decision was made. The flame licked at the corner of the first document and then tore into the dry, fifteen-year-old pages. Iredell tossed them into the empty fireplace, the seven pages briefly fluttering as they landed on the steel grate.

As he moved to replace the covering of the lamp, a quick knock on the wooden door drew the attention of both men. The doctor's white coat shifted around his legs as he breathlessly stopped before the two chairs. "Justice Wilson is awake, sir."

With some effort, Iredell lifted himself from the footstool and rushed back through the open door.

Augusteel, hands still gripping the arms of the chair, looked at the lamp before him. Roughly twelve hours ago a serviceable lamp was all he needed to find Franklin's notes. But, he had lost them. The Lexington League had lost them. He forced himself to relax his hands on the chair and reached into his pocket. It was time to remove some of the evidence. He couldn't allow himself to lose the notes *and* be linked to Wilson's death.

After checking to make sure he was alone, he crossed to the fireplace and dumped the contents of the vial onto the burning pages. The white powder sparked as it hit the flame. The light-gray smoke lifted from the fire, pushed against the closed flume, and rolled into the study. It briefly engulfed Thomas Augusteel, causing him to close his eyes.

For the second time that day, he was in darkness.

Chapter Sixteen

Cumberland, Maryland
June 23, 2010

Seven days before the execution of Parker Brown

The door closed behind him. The first click was expected: the sound of a lock springing into place. Its sound was distinct in the small visitation room. The second sound came from the iron bar sealing the door in place. The sound was much heavier, and it reminded Mark Ellis of the difference between the small Capitol Police holding cell where he had visited Luke Lyford and the maximum-security facility in which he now stood.

There were only three attorney-client visitation rooms at the federal correctional facility in Cumberland. The limited number of rooms prevented Mark Ellis from scheduling a visitation earlier in the week, despite the profile of the inmate who had requested the visitation. He had been contacted on Friday evening. It was now Wednesday.

Parker Brown rose as Ellis turned toward the thick, glass divider that split the room. Brown was nearly thirty years older than Mark Ellis, yet appeared to be in much better shape. His broad shoulders filled the mandated prison attire. Over six-feet tall, his bearing remained militaristic, intense. His hair was the metal-gray of a darkening sky and remained buzz-cut short despite his time in captivity. His eyes seemed to catalogue everything about Mark Ellis with a single glance.

A tabletop ran along both sides of the glass divider. The chair on Mark's side sat empty, facing the glass. In the center of the tabletop, and at the edge where it met the glass, was a small slit through which documents could be passed between attorney and client.

The parties could speak through a small hole in the glass. A grate covered the hole and prevented materials from being passed through. As it had been explained to Ellis, a guard would watch their entire interaction through closed-circuit video and would interrupt if anything other than paper was handed under the glass. The senior guard who had escorted Mark to the room had explained that, if he were to become Mr. Brown's attorney, the sound would be removed from the closed-circuit broadcast. However, so long as he was simply a prospective attorney, the guard monitoring the room would also listen to their discussion. There would be no privacy so long as Mark Ellis remained only a routine visitor.

As he pulled the chair away from the tabletop, Mark noticed that Brown still had the same ramrod posture Mark remembered. *But the orange jumpsuit doesn't hang quite as well as that black suit from the trial*, Mark thought, recalling the footage he had seen of Brown's treason trial and taking his seat on his side of the divider.

"Thank you for coming, Mr. Ellis." Brown returned to the seat on the opposite side of the glass, parallel to Mark's. Behind Brown, a guard exited through the rear door of the room, leaving the two men alone.

Mark examined the glass domes, affixed upside-down on the ceiling. He assumed they broadcast the video to the guard. There was one on each side of the room, black pupils tracking the two men. He nodded, but did not respond to Parker Brown's comments.

"Since you are not officially my attorney . . ."

"Let's get this straight right now, Mr. Brown. I am not your attorney in any capacity, and I don't plan to be." Mark was staring through the glass divider. Vague memories of his mother's campaign speeches came flooding back. The memories had been all he could think about during the hundred-mile drive from DC to this cramped visitation chamber. She was gone, but Brown was still here. *But not for long*, Ellis thought.

"Since you are . . . ." Brown's pause was theatrical. "*Not* my attorney, they will only give us fifteen minutes to talk." Brown had crossed his left leg over his right knee. He slightly reclined in the hard-plastic chair and tapped the watch on his left wrist.

"I'm surprised they'll let you wear a watch in here. But, I guess you got a countdown to keep an eye on."

The look of annoyance sweeping over Parker Brown's face was obvious through the thick glass. He uncrossed his legs and leaned forward onto the tabletop on his side of the divider. "Personal effects are allowed in supervised visits." Brown pointed to the domed camera above his seat.

"Mr. Ellis, we have limited time. And – as you have so delicately pointed out – my country has determined that I should be put to death in sixty-three days. So, let's cut through the crap.

"I have an offer for you," Brown continued. "I want to retain you as my attorney."

Ellis pushed his chair back from the table and bent to rise from it. "Again, I'll pass. Best of luck with your sixty-three days."

"Hear me out, Mr. Ellis. I do not need you to represent me in court. In fact, I doubt that I will need much legal assistance at all."

Now steps away, Mark Ellis turned to face the glass.

Parker Brown continued to speak, his eyes locked on the younger attorney standing on the opposite side of the room. "But, before I can discuss my legal difficulties with you, I need to retain you as counsel."

Through the glass, Mark Ellis and Parker Brown scrutinized each other. Brown's eyes quickly rotated up, taking a short glance at the watchful dome above his head. Mark recalled the explanation: once he officially represented the prisoner, the guard would be required to stop monitoring the audio component of their conversation.

Ellis remained standing a few feet from the glass divider as he assessed Parker Brown.

"If you accept, Mr. Ellis, I'll knock on the door and confirm for them that you are now my attorney. It won't buy us any additional time today, but it will allow us to speak in private."

"Why? Why the hell would I represent you? You sat in your compound, getting rich off American tax dollars and playing war games in the marshes of my home state. And when the country started turning off the spigot, you put guns in the hands of people shooting Americans just to keep your little game alive." Mark was edging back toward the glass. "As far as I'm concerned you're about to get what you deserve."

"Technically, the United States Attorney called it facilitating the acquisition of . . ."

Mark interrupted him. "And why the hell would you want *me* to represent you? My mother tore you and your friends to pieces in her campaign."

Parker Brown breathed deeply, bringing a moment of near-silence into the small room. "Mr. Ellis, consider your situation," he said with slight exasperation. "If you say 'yes' it creates an attorney-client relationship between us. It protects our conversation, makes it private and privileged. That is all it does.

"If you hear me out and are no longer interested in representing me, you can walk directly out that door and never come back. You have nothing to lose."

"Fine." Ellis was pacing in the confined space behind the chair on his side of the room. "Consider me your attorney, for now." He emphasized the last part.

Parker Brown rose from his chair and crossed to the back of the room. He knocked on the door, briefly spoke to the guard, and returned to his seat. "Thank you," he said quietly as he sat down.

"If you don't need me to represent you in court, what do you need an attorney for?"

"As I said, Mr. Ellis, I doubt I need an attorney. But I do need *you*." Parker Brown tapped the face of his watch. "Nine minutes until we're done for today." He looked up, through the glass at the younger man. "Here is my offer: I want you to fill me in on every detail of the Iredell investigation." He paused. Mark started to interrupt him, but Brown raised his right hand, signaling for the attorney to hold his objection. "And . . . ," he spoke over Mark. "And, *in exchange*, I will provide you with details about your mother's murder."

The words hung in the room, their weight heavy in the sudden silence, their implication filling the confined space like an expanding gas. Mark had been walking toward the door, preparing to end the discussion after Brown's request for details on the Iredell case. He stopped.

Mark Ellis glared at the unflinching eyes of the older man. The prisoner's face seemed to grow colder. The room seemed to grow smaller. He could see Brown checking his watch again.

"Eight minutes, Mr. Ellis. While you're thinking, I'll give you a free one: I did not kill your mother, have her killed, or agree that she ought to be killed."

Mark Ellis advanced toward the glass pane that separated him from Parker Brown. "Who did?"

"That is not how this is going to work, Mr. Ellis." Parker Brown had re-crossed his left leg over his right. His slightly reclined posture did not change as Ellis pressed closer to the glass divider. "Quid pro quo, Mr. Ellis. I give you one; you give me one. And I just gave you your first. Do we have a deal, young man?"

If Mark had been paying attention to anything other than the fact that the man in front of him knew, and was now withholding, details concerning his mother's death – *no, her murder* – he would have detected the hint of condescension in Brown's voice.

"Seven minutes left."

The table pressed against Mark's thighs as he leaned toward the glass. *This man knows who killed my mother.*

"Deal." Mark pulled the chair back out. *I can't give up any confidential information without Luke's permission, but I can hand him this.* "Here's a detail: Luke Lyford did not kill William Iredell, have him killed, or agree that he ought to be killed."

The faint movement of a smile passed through Parker Brown's lips.

"Mr. Brown, twelve of your peers found you guilty of treason for selling guns to Hezbollah – or *facilitating the acquisition* – or whatever – in an effort to justify your private army of mercenaries. You've got a well-deserved date with the gas chamber in a couple of months. Why do you care about a dead judge?"

Parker Brown shifted in his chair, paused, and then tilted his upper-body toward the glass. He intertwined his fingers in front of him, his elbows resting on the hard, white surface of the table. He said nothing.

Mark continued. "Listen, it's your time, Mr. Brown – but, I'm guessing we only have about four or five minutes left, so I'm hoping you've got something to say."

The older man answered, his words adding to the tension in the room. "I believe that the people that killed Judge Iredell are the same people that put me in here. And the same people that killed your mother."

"Mr. Brown, *as your attorney,*" Mark started, this time adding a thick tone of sarcasm to his reply. "You put yourself in here when you gave the green light on that arms deal. You put yourself in here when you went to trial without an attorney." His voice was rising. Mark could feel the time expiring and he needed to hear more about his mother. "You put yourself in here when you didn't question a single witness at your trial."

"You are exactly right, young man." The condescension was back, answering Mark's sarcasm. "I made the deal and am beyond a reasonable doubt guilty as charged. I don't challenge that. But let me make this clear for you: I was not the person that put me in here. Making a deal and exposing a deal are two very different things."

This time it was Parker Brown who rose from his chair. Mark could hear the chair's metallic legs scraping along the hard floor of the visitation room. Parker Brown seemed to lose his composure for the first time in their conversation. "You think all that evidence just fell into Carol Cushing's lap?" Brown pointed through the glass at Ellis. The veins in Brown's neck pressed against his skin as his anger increased. "Your mother called me many things in her campaign, but she never called me negligent, lazy, or sloppy. You think Gloria Augusteel ever takes the stand against me – the man that built her career – if someone does not have her back?

"I am guilty," Brown concluded. "That doesn't mean they didn't set me up."

Mark Ellis was not quite sure how to respond. He tried to trace back through the steps of their conversation. He tried to work through what Parker Brown was telling him. *He admits that he was guilty, but believes that the conviction was only possible because he was "set up." He thinks the people that set him up were the same people that killed my mother?*

Mark's next question was the obvious one. "Who is 'they'? Who set you up?"

A pounding on the door behind Parker Brown. Mark could see Brown quickly glance at his watch, then back at Mark. Brown strode back toward the glass divider. "Remember the rules, Mr. Ellis: one for me, *then* one for you."

The door opened behind Brown, and Mark could see the dark boot of a guard stepping into the visitation room. *There is nothing wrong with me giving away information that is already public*, he thought. "They found Phenobarbital in my client's apartment. The toxicology report on Iredell names Phenobarbital as the poison that killed him." Mark rushed through the sentence as the guard closed toward Parker Brown.

Brown had moved as far from the door as possible. His face was now inches from the glass divider. His hands pressed flat against the tabletop directly in front of Mark. Mark could see the skin on Brown's hands turning white as he put his weight on the table.

In that moment, he noticed the ring on Parker Brown's right hand, thick and silver and wider than a normal ring. The upper side of the ring was slightly elevated off the fourth finger of Brown's hand as he pressed against the table. That side of the ring was flat, or at least appeared that way through the glass. It looked like a star had been etched onto the surface.

The first guard had reached Parker Brown and had pulled away the prisoner's chair. A second guard entered the room. Brown's eyes remained on Mark Ellis. He seemed to be ignoring the instructions to leave. "Phenobarbital? You're sure?"

"Time's up." The guard was pulling Parker Brown away from the glass.

A look of confusion covered the prisoner's face. "It was Phenobarbital? Not Amobarbital?" he called toward the glass as the guards ushered him toward the door.

Mark Ellis watched the heavy door close behind Parker Brown. "You owe me one, Mr. Brown," he said to the empty half of the room.

Chapter Seventeen

Washington, DC
June 24, 2010

Six days before the execution of Parker Brown

*A*mobarbital?

      Sam Ortiz stared at the paper. The same paper he had been staring at for a week. His interest had become a habit; his habit had become a routine. He would examine the paper, and then lock it away in a file drawer in his desk, buried under other documents. But he always felt it. It pulled at him. He would withdraw it again.

      He had come in early that morning and been alone for a while. But he could now see the glare from the rising summer sun starting to appear on his laptop screen. The Office of the Medical Examiner was slowly coming to life as other members of the staff drifted in. Their voices echoed down the hall, through his slightly ajar door, and off the weary, wooden floor of his office.

For a week he had tried to put it out of his mind. He would bury it in his desk drawer and turn to another project. But his mind would wander back to Judge William Iredell's toxicological report. It was Thursday morning. Nine days since he had tried to access the official version of Iredell's toxicology and autopsy reports. Nine days since he had ventured into the basement autopsy room, located the blood samples taken from William Iredell, and run an unauthorized toxicological scan.

Nine days since he had listened as Paul Sorenson, his boss, and two other people removed Iredell's body from the examination room.

Eight days since the FBI had arrested Luke Lyford for the murder of William Iredell.

Seven days since they had buried the body.

It might be more accurate, he had thought as he read through the press account of the ceremony, to say that it had been seven days since they had buried the evidence.

Ortiz had received the results of the unauthorized test on the morning of Iredell's funeral. And every day since then he had stared at the one-page report that, again this morning, rested in his hand.

The official toxicology report had been released to the press. In clear and unambiguous terms, it offered conclusive medical evidence of an overdose of Phenobarbital. But the report in his hand indicated that there was no trace of Phenobarbital in Iredell's blood. Instead, a series of different chemicals had been detected.

Although he knew it by memory, his eyes worked through the list. Ethanol. *The report found a significant amount.*

Mebeverine. *An antispasmodic drug? A significant amount in the blood of a man with no reported problems with spasms?* Scopolamine. *Isn't that a derivative of nightshade or some other poisonous plant?* He read through the others, until he landed on the final chemical identified by the test.

Amobarbital. *A significant amount. Certainly enough to kill a man.*

Amobarbital was a close cousin of Phenobarbital, Ortiz knew – and had confirmed with some research as soon as the toxicology report has been electronically delivered. Both were of the barbiturate family. Both could cause substantial damage to the nervous system. In high quantities, both could cause death. Oritz turned the one-page report over and placed it face-down on the copy of the *Washington Post* resting on his desk. He rotated in his black office chair, spinning toward the window behind him.

The white, wooden dividers separated the lower pane of the old window into six smaller rectangles. Ortiz could see the sun climbing higher through the old glass. It was eight thirty in the morning. He had been in his office for nearly an hour and a half. His co-workers were arriving. *I've had this report for a week*, he thought. *Time to fish or cut bait.*

The sample of Iredell's blood that Oritz had removed minutes before the body had been taken had been smuggled to his apartment. Ortiz had never been questioned. Its absence had apparently gone unnoticed. The report had been delivered directly to his email account. After realizing the discrepancies between it and the official report, he had printed it and removed all traces of the report from the office's network. As far as he knew, the document resting on his desk was the only piece of evidence of . . . *what?* A mistake? A conspiracy? A cover-up?

He could still feel the heat of the press conference even though it had been nearly two weeks ago. The recollection of the cameras felt like a firing squad encircling him. He could still see Chief Evanston, sweating off to the side. *Did he know about this?* Paul Sorenson, his boss and the Chief Medical Examiner, had pushed Ortiz onto the stage. He had also been there when Iredell's body had been removed. And he had performed the autopsy and signed the official toxicology report. Ortiz did not like where this was heading.

Carol Cushing had stood opposite Evanston, her gray suit and Evanston's dark-blue uniform enunciating the clean white of Ortiz's medical coat. *White like lamb's wool*, he thought, as he, for the first time, contemplated the actors around him. *She made the decision to reveal the cause of death, but sent me to deliver the message – sent me to the slaughter. What other decisions had she made?*

The morning's *Post* had summarized the case against Luke Lyford. Phenobarbital had been found in his apartment. There were loose pills and prescriptions bottles filled for other people, and the heavy implication that Luke Lyford had purchased or stolen the barbiturate. The article noted that the drug was the cause of death, according to the Office of the Medical Examiner.

Ortiz turned back toward his desk. His palms rested on the pock-marked wooden surface. He slid them outward. His fingers traced the well-worn dents and chips as he weighed his next move. The edge of his right hand bumped against the side of his laptop and stopped his arms. The report remained face-down. Eight-and-a-half by eleven square inches of information that could open a box some people clearly wanted to remain closed.

To the side of the report he could see Senator David Baker's picture in the newspaper. *Was he part of this?* Ortiz could recall his name being mentioned as Iredell's body was removed, but the doors of the laboratory had separated him from the conversation, and he had not been able to entirely understand the context.

Baker was pictured with President Anderson. *How high does this go?*

According to the article, the two men had walked the halls of Congress yesterday in an entirely unnecessary, symbolic introduction of David Baker as Anderson's pick to replace William Iredell on the Supreme Court. The caption below the picture read: "The President and Senator Baker prepare for next week's Senate confirmation hearings."

Ortiz reached toward the paper and slid the toxicological report to the side. He could now see the cover story, and the same two pictures of Luke Lyford that had saturated the Washington media market over the last week. Lyford had an attorney, but neither had spoken to the media since his arrest.

In the first picture, Lyford was in the Senate Judiciary Committee's ornamental hearing room, questioning William Iredell as part of Iredell's confirmation process. In the second, Lyford walked outside his apartment, head forced down by the hand of an unnamed FBI agent, as he was being escorted into the rear seat of a police car.

Ortiz made his decision. Yet, he hesitated before he acted. *One more time*, he thought. *I'll look one more time.*

༄

It was cool in the office's basement and the feel of the file cabinet was familiar. The green, metal face rolled toward him. The plastic tabs of the thin folders flowed past his fingers as his hand scampered toward the file.

He glanced over his shoulder as he withdrew William Iredell's thin file. Ortiz examined the outside of the manila folder. Someone had entered "June 14" as the Removal Date. He counted backwards to the previous Tuesday. June 14 had been the date on which he had heard Paul and two others roll Iredell's body out of the autopsy room. Other than the addition of the Removal Date, nothing had changed. The outside of the folder still listed Paul Sorenson as the physician that had performed the autopsy.

He opened the thin file. Nothing new inside. It was only the Word version of the toxicology report, the one that had been provided to the press. The autopsy results and the DNA information remained missing.

Part of him had hoped he would open the file and find an explanation. Maybe the missing documents, maybe a memorandum from Paul. But there was nothing. No new documents, no explanation. And now no reason not to . . .

The authoritative voice came from the doorway behind him. "What brings you down to the file room today, Sheriff Sam? I thought you were a loyal disciple of technology."

His head jerked, spinning to look over his shoulder, while his hands fumbled with the Iredell file. Sam recognized the voice – and recognized how guilty his uncoordinated response must look.

Paul Sorenson stood in the doorway. He leaned against the door frame, his body angled to the side and covering the exit.

"I was just checking on something, Paul. When in doubt, check the records, right?" he said, hoping to appeal to the older man's distrust of the office's new electronic-filing system.

Paul crossed the small space between them and stepped to the side of Sam. Sam had been holding the Iredell file aloft when Sorenson had entered, and now he was unsure whether he should attempt to hastily re-file it or ease it out of Paul's sight. He felt like prey, frozen by the unexpected arrival of a predator.

The internal debate became irrelevant a split-second later. Paul was next to him and from his vantage point could easily read the name on the elevated plastic tab. "Checking on something in the Iredell file?"

Sam could hear his voice slightly crack as the nervousness overpowered the calm he was trying to portray. "Um, yes," he started. "I've gotten a few more calls from some reporters and I wanted to double-check the results before I called them back." Ortiz tilted the folder toward his boss as he spoke. "Phenobarbital it is." He tried to laugh. "Same as it was last week, I guess." The prey was shuffling toward the edge of the clearing – no sudden moves, nothing to attract the predator.

He could tell Paul was watching him carefully. The man's eyes searched Ortiz's face and then eyed the folder as Sam slowly lowered it back into the file drawer. He pressed the drawer back into place. The holding pin clicked as Paul continued to silently watch, stalking Sam Ortiz, following the younger physician's nervous movement.

"Well, I . . . um . . . guess I should get back to returning those calls." He was sliding past Paul now, edging toward the door and trying to force a smile. As he cleared the Chief Medical Examiner's shoulders, Sam turned and quickly strode from the room.

Paul studied him until he turned toward the elevators. Ortiz never looked back.

◌

He was still sweating as he planted himself in front of his desk. Ortiz double-checked the attorney's name in the newspaper article and then spent the next few minutes tracking down an email address for Mark Ellis, through Ellis's law firm in North Carolina.

Ortiz made a few notes with a thick Sharpie on the toxicological report and ran it through the small scanner on the floor next to his desk. As the document uploaded onto his computer, he created an anonymous email address through Gmail. He attached the scanned version of the document, typed a few words into the body of the email, and, before his courage ran out, clicked the Send button.

Then for the second time in the last two weeks, he went about covering his tracks.

◌

Washington, DC
June 24, 2010

Six days before the execution of Parker Brown

There are two cameras on the front. One on each corner, attached to the underside of the second level. The second level extends over the front door. Both cameras face the front door. Neither rotate. I am on the sidewalk. I am fourteen feet from the door.

There are no side entrances. I am twelve feet from the door.

Noah Augusteel wove through the morning foot traffic on the G Street sidewalk. Nearing eight thirty on a Thursday morning, the sidewalks of downtown DC were thick with people. Dressed in a light-gray suit, he blended with the traffic and was compressed in the crowd. His sky-blue shirt was open at the collar. Today's copy of the *Washington Post* was folded under his arm. He had left his Luger in the car as he anticipated that the Martin Luther King public library would have a metal detector.

Augusteel had circled the block twice, checking and double-checking that he was not being followed. This had become a standard practice since his close-call outside the White House. At 7:39 he had taken an outside table at the Starbucks across Ninth Street. From his view he could see the library's front door. He read through the two articles above-the-fold on the *Post*'s front page: an update on the case against Luke Lyford and a preview of Senator David Baker's upcoming confirmation hearings in the Senate.

Through the glass doors of the library he could see someone approach and then unlock the doors. It was exactly 8:00 a.m.

It is 08:10. I am travelling north on Ninth Street.

Seizing a break in the traffic, he darted across Ninth and onto G Place, a small cut-through street running between the back of the library and the steak house opposite the building.

Eighteen. Nineteen. Twenty.

After twenty steps he knelt to tie his shoe. Sliding to the side of the walk, he watched the mouth of the small street through which he had just come. Two women entered. One man. Then another. Images spun in his memory, like the wheel of a slot machine: people he knew, faces he had seen in the foot traffic. None of the people in the alley registered. He was clean, so far as he could tell.

Noah continued down G Place, turned left on Tenth, turned left on G Street to complete the square, and entered the front door of the public library. With a calm, deliberate pace he strode through the metal detector and opened the heavy interior door. Beyond him, he could see two librarians behind the circulation desk. It was quiet, empty – as he had expected. This was the trade-off he had accepted: he could move along the sidewalks under the cover of the morning crowd, but he would stand out in the empty library.

He quickly found the public computers and created a new email address. After activating the email program's encryption feature, he typed the message he had mentally drafted the night before and sent the email. His next move was to open an online map of downtown DC. After three minutes Augusteel found a suitable location and then clicked back to his new email account. *A response already*. He replied immediately, then deleted the email account.

Noah Augusteel squinted as he stepped into the sunlight outside the library's front door. The sound of the commuting cars moving past was more apparent after the quiet of the library.

I am on G Street in Washington. It is 08:37. I am unarmed. I need . . .

The realization pushed away his other thoughts.

I have just made a mistake.

Chapter Eighteen

Washington, DC
June 24, 2010

Six days before the execution of Parker Brown

*L*uke Lyford's apartment had the disheveled look of being in a confused changeover. The majority of the material that had been collected by the FBI had been returned, and Mark Ellis had made an effort to unpack it. He quickly realized, however, that he had no clue as to where most of it had been originally stored.

Mark had moved one of the cardboard boxes into the office, and dragged one of the larger ones down the hall and into the bedroom. The others had been pushed to the side and stacked against the wall in the small dining area of the apartment. The combination of packed boxes, a couple of unpacked boxes, Mark's half-way reorganization of the apartment, and

Mark's conversion of the living area of the apartment into a workspace, gave the formerly clean, coordinated apartment the appearance of one in transition: either someone moving in or someone moving out.

In a way, both had occurred. Luke Lyford remained in federal custody and had been transferred from the small Capitol Police holding facility to a larger, more-secure FBI facility. It had been over a week since his arrest.

Mark Ellis, meanwhile, had found that the apartment created the best private workspace available to him. He had used Luke's television to review the press coverage of Iredell's murder and had used his digital recording equipment to record additional news reports and interviews. He had even figured out how to connect his laptop to Luke's television in order to get a larger view of the initial press conference. Luke had downloaded a video of the press conference and emailed it to Mark on his first day in Washington. Mark had reviewed it a few times over the past week.

His half-empty coffee cup was on the end table to his left. The empty bag and greasy containers of the bacon, egg, and cheese biscuits he had brought for breakfast lay on Lyford's coffee table, along with the corresponding used napkins. They looked out-of-place on the polished, teak table. But sitting next to Mark's outstretched bare feet, they seemed somehow in their element.

Mark was on Luke's couch, his laptop open on his legs. He was hoping to spend some time triaging the emails that had accumulated in his work email account, addressing those that needed immediate attention and shelving those that could wait for him to return home.

He and Luke had met yesterday, in the late afternoon, after his visit with Parker Brown. Mark had quickly recounted his conversation with Brown and asked Luke for permission to reveal confidential information about his case with the prisoner. They both agreed that an exchange with the former Echo Industrial executive would, at least, provide a new angle in their defense.

"It may be a deal with the devil," Luke had observed. "But we don't have any better options, right now."

They had spent the rest of their limited time re-plowing the ground around Luke's lack of an alibi. Their best guess was that Carol Cushing would argue that Luke checked his voicemail during the morning of Iredell's death, received the message from the judge, scheduled a meeting with him, and poisoned him.

The first line of defense they would offer would be that there was no record of a phone call from Luke's cell phone to his office voicemail. "Perhaps it is more accurate to say that we don't believe there will be a record," Luke had argued. "Someone planted that Phenobarbital in my apartment. We can't rule out that they will also change the call log on my phone."

Mark had promised to contact the cell-service provider and request a copy of his call log as soon as possible. "I've looked into this from the other end, too," Mark explained. "I was hoping that the voicemail from Iredell had not been accessed until *after* the police contacted you. That wasn't the case. An intern in your office was covering the phones while you were out and checked the message shortly after it was recorded. I don't know why the little moron didn't call you.

"The voicemail system only makes a record the first time the message is listened to. That means Cushing can argue that you called in, from a number other than your cell phone, *after* the intern checked the message. Once you realized the judge wanted to meet, you jumped on your opportunity."

"It's convoluted," Luke assessed. "But given the hard evidence of the Phenobarbital, the location of the body, and the supposed motive, it is probably enough to convict me." The end of their discussion brought them right back to the beginning: Luke could not disprove Cushing's theory that he had the opportunity to kill Judge Iredell. There was no solid evidence proving that he was at home on the morning of the murder.

Mark had pondered their alibi problem while he consumed the biscuits. His eyes drifted around the apartment, hoping that something would leap out at him – something that could prove that Luke spent the morning of the murder exactly where Mark now sat.

But nothing did. They were stuck.

And so he turned toward his law firm email account with the intention of taking up the alibi problem again in the afternoon. He had clicked though four or five emails before he realized that he had not actually thought about the contents. His conversation with Parker Brown – as much as he tried to prevent it from distracting him – was demanding his attention.

Why was Brown surprised at the results of the toxicological test? Why did he think it was Amobarbital and not Phenobarbital?

Mark opened a new Internet Explorer window and searched for both drugs. While he didn't understand the chemistry, he could appreciate the similarity between the two. They were both barbiturates and both could easily be used as a toxin if a substantial amount was ingested. *The similarity doesn't explain Brown's reaction though.*

Was he confused? That didn't seem like Parker Brown.

Nor did it explain the fundamental question about their conversation. Mark worked through the loose pieces of information that he received from Brown. *He said my mother was murdered, but not by him. And he said that he did not "agree" that she should be killed?*

Agree with whom?

Parker Brown had seemed convinced – or had at least acted convinced – that the same person, or people, responsible for the plane crash that killed Claire Ellis were also the people responsible for his conviction. He believed that he had been "set up."

Should I even trust that he is telling me the truth? Am I the one being set up?

Mark reached for his coffee. Outside, the morning was opening over Washington. He could hear the traffic coming to life seven floors below and see the reflection of movement in the windows across Massachusetts Avenue.

He felt frustrated, and weak. After a week of working, he and Luke had gotten no closer to a plan for Luke's defense. His trial date would soon be set and, if they didn't have a better plan by then, Luke was going to be convicted.

And now Parker Brown had emerged into the equation and had adamantly stated that Claire Ellis had been murdered. Her death was not accidental. Mark knew he couldn't trust Brown, but if Brown had evidence of his mother's murder, he couldn't walk away either – at least not until he had learned all he could.

The three crimes circled each other, approaching, but never quite touching.

William Iredell had been killed, and an innocent man, who knew nothing about the crime, had been charged with the murder.

Claire Ellis had been killed, and a guilty man, who professed to know everything about her murder, withheld the information behind his prison bars.

Parker Brown had been convicted and admitted his guilt, but maintained that his trial had been the result of a conspiracy against him.

At least according to Parker Brown, the three crimes were connected at their core: the same group of people had killed William Iredell and Claire Ellis, and arranged the conviction of Brown.

Mark tried to concentrate on the emails in front of him. He closed the window of Amobarbital search results and turned back to his email account. He had received four new messages in the last few minutes. Two were internal emails from one of the other attorneys in his firm, but the other two seemed to be from email addresses composed of a random set of numbers. Out of habit, he moved to erase them from his mailbox. Both appeared likely to be some sort of spam email or maybe an email containing a virus.

He glimpsed the subject line of the first email a split-second before he moved it into his trash folder. The portion he could see read "Toxicol." He expanded the subject line until he could read the entire note: "Toxicology Report Iredell."

Mark could feel his pulse quicken as he read the body of the email: "From a friend. The actual toxicological findings for William Iredell." He double-clicked the attachment. The PDF document downloaded onto his laptop and opened. The seal of the Office of the Medical Examiner hovered over the lines of text on the document. A few hand-drawn black stars appeared along the right side, tracing down a list of chemicals. Beside each, Mark noticed, the report indicated a "significant" amount of the chemical. *Ethanol. Mebeverine.*

Near the end of the report someone had drawn two dark ovals around an entire line of data. *Amobarbital.* Below the ovals, the words "lethal dose" had been written.

Mark doubled-back to the email. He hadn't missed anything in the text or the subject line. He checked the address: a line of numbers.

Mark set the laptop on the coffee table and crossed the room, looking for his document folder. He retrieved the folder and removed the copy of the toxicological results that Carol Cushing had been passing out during her press conference. A sense of her still lingered in this apartment, her arm extended and a copy of the report in her hand – the report that linked the cause of death to the Phenobarbital that had been found in Luke's apartment.

The report from Cushing and the report from his email account looked like they came from the same source. The templates matched, or at least seemed to. The seal was identical and the list of standard chemicals was identical. *But it wouldn't be too hard to fake this document*, Mark thought.

He stared at the computer screen. *Amobarbital.* It seemed impossible that Parker Brown would have sent this email. *Could he be coordinating with someone else outside the prison?* If not, Mark considered, then he had run into two references to Amobarbital – two independent references – within less than twenty-four hours.

If I can prove these results are real, I can undercut the whole case against Luke, he thought. *But how can I determine if these results are real without knowing where they came from?*

He moved to the second email, hopeful that he could find more information. The email address from which it was sent was a different, but equally long list of numbers. There was no subject line.

YOU WILL NEVER PROVE YOUR CLIENT'S INNOCENCE. THE EVIDENCE AGAINST HIM WILL BE FLAWLESS. THE LEXINGTON LEAGUE WILL ENSURE A CONVICTION.

MY FAMILY AND I HAVE SERVED THE LEAGUE SINCE THE REVOLUTION, SO PLEASE TRUST ME. YOU EITHER BEAT THEM AT THEIR OWN GAME OR YOU LOSE.

FOR THE REPUBLIC.

Mark rushed to reply. "Who are you? Can we meet? Where did you get the tox report?"

The puzzle pieces swirled in his head, but none seemed to fit together. Parker Brown expected Amobarbital to appear in the toxicology report, but the official one listed only Phenobarbital. Then an alternate report arrives from an anonymous email account, this one listing Amobarbital, but not Phenobarbital.

The author of the anonymous emails called the evidence against Luke "flawless." *Didn't he just provide me with information that directly challenged the evidence? How can it be "flawless" if it is false?*

Mark could not make the pieces fit together. And now there was a new puzzle piece on the board. *What the hell is this person talking about the Lexington League for?* He re-read the email. It made no sense.

He glanced back at his email account to make sure he had not missed a response from the anonymous email source and then opened a new search window. Google: The Lexington League.

The group's website confirmed what Mark already knew. "The Lexington League is an association of conservative and libertarian activists deeply committed the ideas of a limited federal government and a constitutional republic," he read. It was founded in the 1990s.

How can this guy claim he worked for them – no, served them – since the Revolution, if this was started in the 90s?

Mark continued to read, further confirming what he already knew. The main purpose of the Lexington League was to press forward conservative causes and candidates. It was a national network of students, scholars, political activists, and lawyers. Ellis closed the website and closed his eyes. He was more confused than he had been at any point since that first phone call from Luke Lyford.

Opening his eyes, he could see the tattered brown cardboard of the FBI evidence boxes, so jarringly out-of-place in the modern apartment. He was also out-of-place. *Luke should be here.* His document folder was open on the couch next to him. He could see the brown Capitol Mail folder. It held both copies of the letter from James Madison to James Wilson.

He checked his email. No response.

The biscuit containers from his breakfast sat open on the table in front of him, alone on the sleek surface. In the growing sunlight, the grease stains on the white paper bag seemed more pronounced than they had earlier.

In his mind, two of the puzzle pieces bumped into each other. Mark held his breath, trying to focus on the new thought, but the pieces would not quite interlock. He opened the PDF of the toxicology report on his laptop. *If I can't find the source, I can't use it in court.* He looked back at the Capitol Mail envelope.

But maybe I can use it in a different way, without having to find the source.

It was time he looked into Luke's idea about the stains on the letter. It was a long-shot, but that was the only kind of shot they had left.

He closed the PDF document. His finger moved the cursor and prepared to open a new window. He needed to find a phone number. The top line of his email inbox stopped his hand. In bold, an unopened email from the second set of random numbers. *A response.*

TOX REPORT? PORTICO CAFÉ. OUTSIDE. 8TH AND F. WEDNESDAY, NEXT WEEK. 11 AM. I'LL FIND YOU.

Chapter Nineteen

Edenton, NC
June 25, 2010

Five days before the execution of Parker Brown

John Baker stretched his arms, and hooked his left behind his head to pull his right farther back. He was tired. It was nearing nine o'clock. His dark-blue tie remained knotted around his collar. The sleeves of his white dress shirt had been rolled past his elbows.

Night had finally closed out the long summer day. The window along the right wall of his office was open. The humidity seeped in from the outside street, but it was worth the fresh air. The American flag in the corner briefly moved in the slight breeze. The corner of the flag resting on the pile of untouched case reports slipped, and fell toward the office's red carpet. Like the pile of reports on the chair, the paperwork on his desk had been largely neglected over the past few days. Baker had been with his father and family in Washington and had barely touched the briefcase he had carried to the capitol.

The light on his phone blinked an annoying red. *More reporters*, he thought, cursing their unwillingness to take "no comment" for an answer. Pink message slips threatened to overflow the black, plastic inbox on the corner of his desk, each one clamoring for a quote about his father's nomination to the Supreme Court. He had even been followed as he left his office earlier that evening, the aggressive reporter asking repeatedly whether he would run for his father's vacant Senate seat.

U.S. Attorney John Baker had actually answered that question: "No, I will not. Write that down. It is not going to change, so you can stop asking the question – and by the way, my father is still in that Senate seat. He has not been confirmed yet. Until he is confirmed, he will not be part of the Supreme Court."

The confirmation hearing was scheduled to start the following week. If everything went as expected, there would be a day or two of testimony from some liberal groups that opposed his father's nomination. The few liberal Senators who were against him would likely make their stand during these days. The days dedicated to his opposition would be followed by a day or two of testimony from conservative attorneys and fellow Senators that supported his nomination. The final days would consist of testimony from high-level legal representatives from the Anderson administration and the testimony of the nominee himself, Senator David Baker.

At the end of it, David Baker would take the open seat on the Supreme Court of the United States; on that much, the pundits agreed.

John Baker planned to return toward the end of the confirmation process. He knew a second trip to Washington would cost him at least another couple of days of work. It would be another delay in getting up to speed in his new position, but he couldn't skip the ceremonial final vote in the Judiciary Committee. And he couldn't let his kids miss it.

"Will the President be there?" his daughter had asked over dinner that evening. Ever since she had met President Anderson last Friday at David Baker's nomination announcement that was all she wanted to talk about. Her follow up: "Did you know President Annersin is the president of the United States?" It was about the fifth time she had asked the question since they had returned from DC and it finally drew an irritated response from her older brother.

John Baker smiled at the memory and then tried to force himself to focus on the work on his desk. Three more federal investigations had been opened over the last few days.

He reached toward the corner of his desk and scraped the accumulated message slips from the top of his mail pile. Baker thumbed through a few letters; opened one, then discarded it; and then quickly read through a letter from a prosecutor in North Carolina's Middle District. As he re-folded the letter and placed it back in the envelope, he noticed a larger envelope on the bottom of the pile.

He lifted the brown envelope from his in-box and tore it open, ripping the perforated seal across the top. A small hand-written note fell out as he turned the envelope sideways over his desk. Inside was a plastic DVD case. The note read: "We are still working on putting together the timeline regarding Mr. Johansson. Interviews: He saw many people at the festival and we are talking to them as we locate them. Will be in touch with an update soon. Enclosed copy of video from his speech." It was signed by agent Carl Kittleson, the FBI agent who had visited him a week and a half ago.

Baker removed the DVD from the case and inserted it into his computer. He opened the video file. The view was from the side of the Barker House's white porch. Baker instantly recalled the scene; he had been seated in the second row of the folding chairs that morning. His memory matched the video. He recalled seeing the videographer, standing to the left of Everett Johansson, and turning back-and-forth like a sprinkler as he filmed the crowd and the speaker.

On the computer screen he could see Johansson. The old man was slowly pacing on the white, wooden slats of the porch. The video seemed to have picked up the speech midway through. As the camera moved to follow Johansson, it caught glimpses of the other members of the historical society that sat behind him, nearly lifeless statues baking in the midday heat. Baker could see the North Carolina flag, still and quiet in the sunlight, hanging to Johansson's left. From the videographer's angle, on the opposite side of the porch, it was behind the speaker. The image on the video began to vibrate as the videographer's shaky hand turned the camera toward the crowd. It was a rapid movement, but slowed as it reached the faces of the crowd.

John Baker let the video play as he turned back toward the documents on his desk. He listened as he worked his way through the remainder of the unopened mail and then opened one of the new investigation files.

He could hear Johansson's voice filling his quiet office. The historian was reaching the final portion of his speech: the story of Samuel Adams reaching his "breaking point" during the British occupation of Boston – the moment that Adams had shrugged off his hope of a peaceful conclusion and fully embraced the need for a powerful, and likely violent, revolution.

His mind wandered from the investigation report in his hands. He rotated in his desk chair, turning in a half-circle to face the credenza behind his desk. Pictures from his career and of his children were neatly arranged along the polished top of the oak credenza. Standing among those pictures was what Johansson's speech had brought to his mind. Baker's favorite quote, soldered into a rough square of wood — a piece salvaged from a revolutionary-era stagecoach — and given to him by his father:

THE LIBERTIES OF OUR COUNTRY, THE FREEDOM OF OUR CIVIL CONSTITUTION, ARE WORTH DEFENDING AT ALL HAZARDS; AND IT IS OUR DUTY TO DEFEND THEM AGAINST ALL ATTACKS. IT WILL BRING AN EVERLASTING MARK OF INFAMY ON THE PRESENT GENERATION, ENLIGHTENED AS IT IS, IF WE SHOULD SUFFER THEM TO BE WRESTED FROM US BY VIOLENCE WITHOUT A STRUGGLE, OR TO BE CHEATED OUT OF THEM BY THE ARTIFICES OF FALSE AND DESIGNING MEN.

SAMUEL ADAMS

A nearly identical piece hung in his father's office – the same quote burned into a second piece of the same stagecoach.

He could hear the crowd on the video. They were applauding Everett Johansson. *For the last time*, thought John.

He turned back toward his computer in time to catch the rattled motion of the video as the camera operator swung from the crowd back to Everett Johansson. He watched as Johansson smiled – broad, satisfied, happy – wiped the sweat from his bald head, and turned toward the camera as he left the porch.

The video ended and it was silent again. Baker could hear a car pass outside the open window of his office.

The video had stopped on its last frame. Johansson had turned to his right. As he approached the video camera he had looked directly into the lens at the same instant the videographer had stopped recording. Johansson's eyes were open, frozen in time, and staring out of John Baker's computer screen. *I will find him. Wherever the killer is, I will find him*, Baker thought, silently speaking to the motionless image of the old man.

He reached down and removed the DVD from his computer. The screen reverted to his desktop and Baker turned the monitor off. He closed the investigative report he had been reviewing and started to collect a few files to take home. John Baker picked up his briefcase and pulled the golden cord on his desk lamp. The office darkened slightly as the desk lamp was extinguished. He could hear the phone ringing in the reception area down the hall. *Another reporter or another case?*

The few files he had collected barely made a dent in the mountain of unfinished work on his desk. Open cases. Investigations and pending prosecutions. Everett Johansson was in that mountain. It was a small file now, thin by comparison.

But it would grow, he knew. Transcripts from the interviews with people in the crowd. Evidence from the museum.

Unfortunately, he also knew what the relative lack of communication from the FBI meant: Agent Kittleson had made little progress so far. By now, the murder was approximately two weeks old. They had no suspects and no notable leads.

The familiarity was uncomfortable for John Baker. It was Claire Ellis, all over again. A speech, then a death. No witnesses. In the Ellis case she had died with her husband and one of her sons. Johansson had died alone.

He could still recall watching the videos of Claire Ellis's last campaign speech. The most informative video had actually come from his father's campaign. David Baker had assigned one of the younger members of his campaign staff to trail Ellis at all of her public appearances and to record as much video footage of her as possible. The staff member had been at the speech at the airport, and the prosecutor's office had used that recording to identify the potential witnesses and suspects. They had tracked down every person they had seen on the video, except one.

As Baker flipped off the overhead light in his office and walked into the dark hall, he could visualize that video footage. *I must have watched that video a hundred times*. He could see Claire Ellis walking off the stage, waving to the crowd. With her family at her side, as well as some campaign workers, she had turned toward the small plane on the runway behind her.

A man had approached her as she neared the plane. He had been youngish – maybe middle-aged. It had been hard to tell in the fading light of the video. The edge of his blond hair had been barely visible under his baseball hat. Wearing jeans and an "Ellis for Senate" t-shirt, the man had handed

Claire Ellis a bottle of water and walked away. Just as he had reached the edge of the video frame he had turned toward the campaign worker's camera.

John Baker could still feel the old chairs in the media room at the state prosecutor's office. They had watched it over and over again as the search narrowed toward that man. The side of his head, turning. His face. Pause. Rewind.

Again. The side of his head. His face turned toward the camera.

Pause.

Play. The man had exited the frame. The campaign worker had filmed for another few minutes as Ellis entered the plane's cockpit and started the take-off procedures. The video had ended as the plane turned and accelerated down the runway.

ᘯ

Washington, DC
June 25, 2010

Five days before the execution of Parker Brown

"We may have a problem."

Paul Sorenson's assistant had just handed him the report and he had it open on his desk. The telephone was balanced between the shoulder of his striped dress shirt and his ear. His hands turned the pages before him as he checked that he was reading the technical document correctly.

Nearly a quarter of an inch thick, the document provided details correlating to every action of the office's security-management system. Every time an employee passed his or her security card across a wall-mounted reading device the central computer recorded the date, time, location, and identification of the employee. In essence, the data allowed him to track the movement of his medical staff. He could look into the past and watch each employee travel through the building. He could follow them minute-by-minute, door-by-door.

"Fill me in. Quickly," Gloria Augusteel replied, from the other end of the phone call.

"I found one of our deputy medical examiners – Sam Ortiz, the one I sent to the press conference – looking through the Iredell file yesterday. He fed me some line about needing to return some calls to reporters."

"You're his boss. If he asks questions, make something up and move on, Paul."

"The file is not the whole problem. I asked our IT guy to give me a list of how our employees have been passing through our security system. With the dates and times, we can . . . ."

Augusteel cut him off. "Get to the point. If the file is not the whole problem, what is?"

"The same physician accessed the autopsy room – the one in the basement. I'm looking at the report for Tuesday of last week. Apparently, he swiped his card just a few minutes before mine." He paused and let the implication pass through the phone line. "Unless he swiped his card and left seconds later – and we missed him on our way down there –

Ortiz was either in the laboratory attached to the examination room or in the file room on the other side."

Gloria Augusteel replied with silence.

"He could have heard us," the Chief Medical Examiner concluded.

"Is there any way to confirm he was in the room?"

"Not that I can think of."

He could tell her tone had changed. Annoyance had become focus. Her questions were rapid-fire, one after another. "Has he done anything yet? Confronted you?"

"No."

"Any reason to believe he has contacted the police? Or told anyone else about this?"

"If he has, I haven't been informed. Or questioned."

"Are you sure he heard us? Are you certain he was there?"

"Like I said, he could have left shortly before we moved the judge, but it seems more reasonable to believe he was in one of the adjoining rooms."

Silence returned. Paul held the phone to his ear, waiting for direction. His eyes left the report on his desk and landed on his office door. *He's just down the hall*, he thought. *If he heard something, why hasn't he said anything?*

"Paul," the voice of the higher-ranking Lexington League member began. "Don't do anything. We don't need to overreact. I'm going to put something in place. A card we can play if we need it, if he talks to someone. For now, act normal."

"Tell me his name again," Augusteel said.

"Sam Ortiz."

Paul Sorenson started to object to her instructions, but realized halfway into his first sentence that he was the only person left on the line.

Chapter Twenty

Cumberland, Maryland
June 28, 2010

Two days before the execution of Parker Brown

This time Mark Ellis was the first to arrive. Through the thick, glass divider halving the attorney-visitation room he could see the closed door on the opposite side. He impatiently drummed his fingers on the blank legal pad on the table in front of him as he waited for Parker Brown.

Ellis was more prepared this time, if only slightly. Over the weekend, he had attempted to determine a couple of non-public facts about the Iredell investigation. He hoped that the facts he had gathered, combined with whatever he could come up with on his feet that day, would be enough to pry the identity of his mother's killer from the prisoner.

It won't be an easy conversation, Mark thought, as he reminded himself — for the fifth or sixth time that morning — to stay as calm as possible. *The killer's identity is his ace-in-the-hole, and he's not going to just give it up.* Mark checked the date on his watch. *He's got fifty-some days until he's put to death. I have to get that name before he dies. If not today, then tomorrow, or the next day — but it has to happen.*

The institutional-gray door opposite his chair creaked open like a coffin as Parker Brown was led into the room. There was no smile on his chiseled face. Mark could tell Brown was sizing him up as the older man moved toward the single chair opposite Mark.

The guard backed through the door. The sound of it landing against the metal frame reverberated through Mark's side of the room. Again, they were alone. Mark could feel his blood-pressure rising. He breathed deeply, willing his head to remain level.

Parker Brown pulled his chair away from the table. The metal legs grated on the floor.

"You owe me one from last time, Mr. Brown," Mark said, referring to the end of their prior conversation. Directly before Parker Brown had been removed from the visitation room, Mark had informed him that the toxicology report had revealed an overdose of Phenobarbital. The deal between them called for Brown to then offer Mark a piece of information about his mother's death. However, their time had expired and Brown had been removed from the discussion before he had provided any information.

"Yes, counselor, I do. I intend to honor my part of the agreement. What would you like to know?"

"There's a lot I'd like to know, but we actually need to talk about your case before I cash in my chip. I've notified

Carol Cushing about my new role as your attorney. We've got a court appearance set for Wednesday morning. Because of the profile of your case and your death sentence, the judge is requiring me to be officially entered into the record as your attorney, in open court. Then we can continue to have these meetings as attorney and client."

Mark continued. "I've spoken to the warden's office, and they'll get you to the hearing."

The message did not seem to reach Parker Brown. He seemed stagnant. His eyes remained on Mark.

Mark momentarily matched his silence. For a few seconds he could hear the quiet hum of the electronic monitoring equipment surrounding the small room. "Is there some kind of problem?" he asked. "You got somewhere better to be on Wednesday?"

The prisoner remained silent. He had, again, crossed his left leg over his right, and reclined in the small chair. His hands rested on his elevated left thigh. Brown seemed to be studying the silver ring on his right hand. With his left he slowly rotated it. "I would prefer to stay incarcerated rather than appear in court."

"With only a couple of months to live, I figured you'd want to take in as much free air as possible."

Brown was silent again, his eyes downcast.

"Listen," Mark jumped in. "You've got to be there. I can't just show up and say I'm your attorney. You've got to authorize it before the judge."

Parker Brown raised his gaze toward Mark. In the florescent light of the room, his concern was evident on his face. "Can it be a closed proceeding?"

"No. It'll only take five minutes. You're in; then you're right back out, and they'll rush you straight back to your

comfortable cell. OK?" The quiet set back in. Mark was surprised by Brown's hesitation. The man never seemed to hesitate. "What is the problem, Mr. Brown?"

This time it was Parker Brown who took a deep breath.
He rose from his chair. Mark watched as the older man
stepped behind the chair and then leaned forward, his arms
braced against the hard-plastic seat, his weight leaning on
the back of the chair. He remained quiet. Brown seemed to
be studying Mark Ellis, balancing something in his mind.

"Do you ever wonder why I did not defend myself during
my trial, Mr. Ellis?"

"Do I wonder?" There was a tone of incredulity in his
response. "Half the country probably wonders."

"Their objective was to remove me. To get me out of the
top spot." Brown completed his suspended orbit of the chair
and sat back down. He bent forward, placing his elbows on
the long table. "You have to think about this from a strategic
perspective," he continued. His forearms rested on the table;
his fingers were interlaced and close to the glass.

"They kill me, and people look into it and maybe look
back at them. So what do they do instead? They set me up.
They turn me in. They take me to trial.

"Now, where do people look? Right at me. Now, I'm not
being *murdered*; I'm being *punished*. That makes people feel
better. It feels right. The story has an end; the press moves on
to the next spectacle."

"OK." Mark had pulled a pen from his pocket and started
to take notes on the legal pad in front of him.

"Put the pen down, son. You don't need notes. You need
to understand. You need to *think*. You need to *learn* if you
want to handle this Lyford trial in the right way."

Mark let the "son" comment pass. He laid the pen down.

Brown continued. "So I'm going to trial. What is my move? I fight them in court, right? I call witnesses. I take the stand. I hire an attorney. Maybe I get desperate and reveal some secrets. But that is no good, from their perspective." Parker Brown looked like his thoughts were somewhere other than this confined visitation room in Maryland. "So how do you keep someone quiet without killing that person?"

Mark could not tell if that was a rhetorical question or if he was actually supposed to answer.

Brown's hands were near the glass divider. Again, Mark noticed, Brown was rotating his thick ring. It was the same ring he had seen during the last visit. It was silver and broad, and Mark could see angles in the metal as the ring slowly spun. The angles looked like intersections between two flat sides. As he watched, Brown separated his hands and sat back in his chair.

Mark offered a response to the question Brown had asked, piercing the silence. "You keep a person quiet by threatening that person or threatening something that person wants to keep safe?"

A slight smile cracked Brown's lips for the first time that morning. Devious. Mark had seen it before – in videos taken by reporters when Brown had responded to his mother's campaign. He liked the smile even less in person.

"Exactly." Brown had now connected with his one-man audience and was looking through the glass at Mark. "It is one of the first things we teach our assets. For instance, you threaten that person's family. I got a son, a wife. Right now, they're ashamed. But they are *safe*." He emphasized the last word. "When I die, my secrets – the league's secrets – die with me.

"You see how this works, of course," Brown continued. "I don't threaten them; they don't threaten my family. I don't harm them; they don't harm my family."

With his right hand, he pointed toward Mark. "I got an attorney. I'm willing to take the risk, because I need *you*. I want information about William Iredell's death and I want to know about Luke Lyford's trial.

"However, there is a significant difference between our little private conversations in this room and a public court appearance. Once I set foot in open court, their reaction will depend on their interpretation. If they think I'm going to appeal my sentence, then . . . well, let's say that is an unacceptable outcome in their eyes."

Mark had absorbed the message from Parker Brown. His thoughts told him to disregard it as the paranoia of a man whose life had been lived in the gray area between personal glory and patriotic sacrifice, between hunter and hunted. But his instinct heard something else. Above all, he felt himself being painted into a corner. If Parker Brown did not appear in court, the judge was unlikely to recognize him as Brown's attorney. If he was no longer his attorney, these "little private conversations" would end, along with his only pipeline for information about his mother's death.

"Listen, Mr. Brown," he started. "It is not that I don't appreciate your situation. However, it can't be done without you. Here's the best I can offer: I'll talk to the prosecutor. As you say, she will most likely be expecting an appeal. You know she's going to hold a press conference at some point, but I think she will wait until we actually file the appeal documents. I think I can convince her to stay quiet about this short hearing."

Parker Brown looked skeptical.

Mark made his last point. "I'll be there on Wednesday morning. Federal marshals will be prepared to transport you. If you're there, we move forward. If not, I'll assume our conversations have reached an end." *That is the best I can do.* He could see that he had not convinced Parker Brown, but he had nothing left to say.

Mark took advantage of the opportunity to change the subject. "Here's your question: You said my mother was killed. Who killed her?"

"The same people that set up my prosecution and put me in here."

"Not good enough, Mr. Brown. I want a name."

Parker Brown coughed a short laugh in reply. "Do you think I'll let you jump right to the end and then walk out of here? Not a chance, son."

Mark did not bother to take another deep breath. No effort to remain calm was going to help. It had taken only one question. His thoughts shot back to Luke's apartment. *Am I being set up?* He rose from his chair and collected the legal pad from the table.

"Where are you going?"

"We're through here, Mr. Brown. I asked my question. You dodged it. Game's over."

Mark was halfway to the door and closing fast.

"How about a different question instead: *why* was your mother killed?"

Brown's words stopped him. Mark's fingers had formed a fist. He held it airborne, poised to knock and call the guard. Mark did not turn back to face Parker Brown.

In the still visitation room, the prisoner offered an answer to his own question: "Your mother was killed because she posed a substantial threat to Echo."

Mark spun toward the glass, furiously measuring whether he could somehow break through it before the guard could reach Parker Brown. "You said you did not have her killed!" He formed the sentence, but his anger blurred the pronunciation as the words violently erupted toward the glass.

Brown remained seated. The indecisiveness and hesitation were gone. The coldness was back. He noticed Mark Ellis's fist, absorbed the attorney's growled shouting, and smiled. "If you will take a seat, counselor, there is more.

"As I said, your mother was a threat to Echo. She was gaining on Senator Baker in the polls. She was making some key people very nervous.

"We had no concerns about criminal prosecution. What concerned us was a congressional hearing, a congressional subpoena. We did not need some idealistic liberal taking control of a North Carolina Senate seat and turning the power of that office on our company."

Brown continued to speak. "Trust me when I say that we were not worried about David Baker launching an investigation." The devious smile returned. "What worried us . . . what worried me – I was in charge of the league then – was what would happen if Baker lost that election to your mother. Some people understand that this world is a complicated and dangerous place. Your mother was *not* one of those people.

"I thought we should wait it out. We should give the Baker campaign time to win the race. Others thought differently. They acted without my consent and against my authority. They killed your mother. Then they went to work to get rid of me."

Mark remained standing. He was as close to the glass partition as he could get. He was paying near-absolute attention to Parker Brown, but his mind was also working on a parallel circuit. The anonymous email registered in his memory. *The Lexington League will ensure a conviction.*

"You keep saying 'the league.' Do you mean the Lexington League?"

"Of course. Certainly you know that by now." Not only was the confidence back, but the condescension Mark recognized from their last meeting had returned. "And certainly you've figured out that our little legal institution is just our public face."

This can't be true, Mark thought. "Mr. Brown, let me make sure I have this correct: you're telling me that there is a connection between Echo Industrial and the Lexington League? That is hard to believe."

Parker Brown let the question linger in the room. "That is a new question, Mr. Ellis. Accordingly, it will cost you new information. I paid you back from last time. Now, it is my turn. What have you got for me?"

Mark had one solid piece of non-public information on the Iredell murder. He reached into the interior pocket of his suit coat and retrieved a one-page document. It had been folded along the longer axis. Recalling that the guard was monitoring the action in the room and was especially concerned with any material passed through the small opening in the glass, Mark raised the document, unfolded it, and briefly displayed it to the glass dome in the ceiling. "This was sent to me last week. It appears to be an alternate toxicology report on Judge Iredell," he explained as he passed the document through.

Parker Brown opened the single page of paper. His eyes moved side-to-side, then scanned down the paper's right side as he examined the chemicals that had been identified in significant quantities.

As he read, Mark spoke. "The last time you seemed to think that Phenobarbital was *not* the poison that killed Iredell. You seemed to believe that it was Amobarbital, instead. As you can read, this report found Amobarbital in Iredell's blood." Mark gestured toward the document. "How did you know that?"

Parker Brown had finished reading the document. He passed it back through the divider.

"Mr. Ellis, you seem to be having trouble with the rules today. You've now asked me two questions: one about the connection between the league and Echo, and one about Amobarbital. Yet, you have only given me one piece of information. Which question would you like me to answer?"

"Amobarbital." Mark was quick to reply. His first priority had to be Luke Lyford's defense. If he could somehow prove that the official toxicology report was false, he might be able to get the charges dropped. "How did you know to ask about it?"

Parker Brown shifted in the hard chair. He collected his thoughts before he answered. "First, some background: Years ago . . . many years . . . Revolutionary times," he started, then hesitated and looked across the dividing table. "Do you know where the first battle of the Revolutionary War was fought?"

Mark Ellis answered immediately. "Lexington. Massachusetts. 'The shot heard 'round the world.' The shot that kick-started the American Revolution. Everyone's heard of that."

"Lexington. That first battle. That's where the name of the league comes from, in case you haven't put that together." There was a glint in Parker Brown's eyes that wasn't there moments before. A smile crept over his iron features like a snake easing from its den. "And you're right about the first shot of the War. It all started with Lexington. Do you happen to know who fired that first shot, son?"

This time Ellis hesitated. The answer did not immediately come to mind. Instead, confused by the look in the older man's eyes, he fired back with a question. "Do *you* know who fired that shot?"

The smile broadened and Parker Brown seemed to leave the confined room, his thoughts escaping his prison cell and fleeing the execution date that was gaining on him by the second. "The same hand that has fired more than a few shots over the course of American history: the unseen hand, the one that moves in the background, that hides in plain sight. The one that topples the first domino and has the last word."

"What does that mean?"

Suddenly, Brown's focus shifted back the conversation. "Another question, Mr. Ellis. I would imagine you would rather me answer your original question, the one about Amobarbital," he said. "How about we leave the history lessons to the side, for now? Call it another story for another time."

Parker Brown didn't wait for a response from Mark. He picked back up where he had left off moments before. "Some of the original members of the Lexington League . . . um, let's say 'came into possession of' a set of notes that were once Benjamin Franklin's. These notes *partially* explained the chemical composition of a particular sort of mixture. The person that had developed the mixture – Franklin, we assume – had originally expected it to serve as a sort of truth serum, a powder that could be dissolved in a liquid.

"Maybe he planned to use it as part of the war against the British. Maybe not. We really have no idea. While it worked – *the recipient will tell the truth* – it had one rather unfortunate side effect: it was lethal. So he never actually put the mixture to use."

Parker Brown had Mark's attention. He held back the next sentence with a dramatic pause. "The league did not share the inventor's reservation.

"After we relieved Franklin of his notes, we realized they were incomplete. Some of our science-minded friends worked for years to comprehend the notes, to recreate the mixture. They were not successful. After a few years, my predecessors shelved the project.

"Years pass. Then the German gets involved." Another pause as Brown's eyes rolled toward the ceiling in thought. "Lautenberg? Ladenburg, maybe? Something like that. Anyway, he was a German chemist. He starts publishing some research that sounds familiar to our scientists. Eventually, his work leads to the creation of a drug that we now call scopolamine." Brown stopped and pointed to the toxicology report sitting on the table in front of Mark. "You'll recognize that from the report."

He continued his explanation. "So the people on our side of the Atlantic are gradually seeing the work as it is published and makes its way to the States. They decide to pull the notes back out. They take some of the German's work and combine it with the instructions in the notes. And start to produce a rough approximation of the mixture.

"Now, the people at the top of the league start to get interested, and worried. They don't want the chemists passing this around. They demand that the original version of the notes be held by one of the Lexington League leaders and that all copies be destroyed. The mixture is only to be produced under the supervision of one of the five."

Brown glanced at his watch and continued. "This proves to be a grave mistake. It is unclear exactly how it happened, but the original copy of the notes was stolen shortly thereafter. They were not able to retrieve them and were left with only the limited quantity that the chemists had been able to produce prior to the theft.

"Now let me answer your question. One of the active chemicals in the mixture was called Amylon Malonate – or, to use its modern name: Amobarbital."

Mark added the conclusion. "So, if one assumes that the Lexington League was involved in Iredell's death – as you assume – and one knows Iredell was poisoned, then one might expect to find Amobarbital in his blood sample."

Brown turned in his chair and leaned toward Mark. "That is correct, counselor. I've now given you something. What do you have for me?"

Mark knew this moment was coming. He had two firm, private pieces of information. The alternative toxicology report had been the first and he had given that up. The second was the letter from James Madison to James Wilson. *I can't show that to him. Not yet.* Everything else that he had been able to think of was already public information. By now, Brown had certainly consumed everything that had been in the media coverage.

He had one card left to play. But it wasn't truly a fact. Or at least he didn't know if it was a fact. Yet, it was the only thing he knew that Parker Brown did not.

He had to try.

"There are families that have served the Lexington League for generations, some stretching as far back as the Revolution." He stopped. "And one of them, at least, is tied up in the Iredell murder." The last part was a calculated risk; it was not in the anonymous email he had received. *But he couldn't know that.*

The light changed in Parker Brown's eyes. They narrowed as he seemed to grow more alert. "How do you know that, Mr. Ellis? Who is your source?"

This time it was Mark's turn. He tried to stifle it, but a grin crept onto his face as he replied. "That sounded an awful lot like a question to me, Parker. I gave you a piece of information. What you owe is an answer to my earlier question: what is the connection between the Lexington League and Echo Industrial?"

"Echo is effectively the operational arm of the league. Now, tell me your source."

"That is ridiculous." Mark couldn't suppress his incredulity. "The Lexington League is a group of lawyers and law students. That's all. They push conservative causes and ideas. I really doubt they have an *operational arm.*

"You asked me to reveal my source," Mark said. "Maybe you should be revealing yours, too."

Brown remained concentrated on Mark. He inched closer to the glass divider.

"You've got to stop limiting yourself to what you believe you know. Did you ever stop to ask yourself how that legal organization was able to grow so fast? It is within one appointment of a majority on the Supreme Court – after being officially non-existent twenty years ago. That would be an extraordinary *unassisted* climb to power."

He returned to the original discussion, his voice slightly declining in intensity. "Mr. Ellis, most of the lawyers that work in that office building, or are members of our organization around the country, have no idea what happens in that top-floor conference room. Most of the judges we endorse and the politicians we support think we're just a regular, conservative interest group. We're not. We never have been.

The league is multi-layered. And has a lot of moving parts. However, there are always five at the top."

"Like some kind of board of directors?" The mocking tone made its way through the glass. "Y'all got stockholders, too? I bet you have corporate retreats every summer."

Brown was quiet. And the quiet unsettled the attorney across the room from him. "You laugh, son. But your mother is dead and the case is unsolved. A judge is dead and your friend is about to be wrongly convicted." He stopped. "If I didn't believe this to be true, then why didn't I put up a defense at my trial? Why would I just roll over and accept my sentence?"

Mark moved to interrupt him, but Brown stopped him with the same palm he had raised in their first meeting. "You called it a 'board of directors.' That is not far off. There are five members at the top. One of the five is the ultimate decision-maker. The other four offer advice.

"No-one other than the five knows who the one at the top is. I used to be the one, the ultimate authority. Until the other four turned against me after your mother's death."

This was the second mention of his mother's death in the last couple of minutes and it brought Mark's thoughts back into focus. He was struggling to believe Parker Brown, but he needed to at least hear what he had to say about his mother. The better he kept his emotions in check, and the more he kept the conversation on target, the more likely he was to pull the information he needed from the man on the opposite side of the room. "Get to Echo. You said she was killed because she was a threat. How is it connected?"

"I am getting to it, counselor.

"As I said, the one makes the significant decisions. The five, including the one, direct the action of the other members.

As far as the other members know, any of the five could be the one. So they treat each of the five in the same manner.

"Some of these other members – and, in some cases, one of the five – are installed within key positions in Echo. Like I was. Others hold positions in government. Some in business. And, of course, as you have noted, we have our public face: some control our group working within the legal realm, the organization that most people believe to be the true Lexington League."

The explanation continued. "When it is called upon, Echo works in the field, so to speak. Sometimes it protects the five. Sometimes it has a more offensive mission."

"On American soil? It would have to be deployed here if the organization is based here."

Parker Brown did not blink at the suggestion that Echo Industrial was secretly violating an armful of American laws. "Not just have been," he responded. "They *are* deployed. Listen to me carefully, Mr. Ellis. Any effort to move against a high-level member of the league – especially one of the five – will run headlong into an Echo-created defense. You will not see them, but they will be there. Believe me, they will be there. In an unsettled time like this – with my execution date approaching and Iredell's murder being investigated – the league will be especially vigilant."

Brown tapped his finger on the glass divider. "You'll have to either go through it or around it. You beat them at their own game or you will lose."

His words resonated in Mark's head. Certainly the similarity between Brown's last sentence and the anonymous email he had received was not a coincidence. It had to be something more. Mark Ellis rocked on the back two legs of his chair as he examined Parker Brown. He was trying to process the story, the information Brown had given him. One piece of information – *the* piece – remained missing. "Mr. Brown. You keep dancing around the most important part." Mark settled his chair and leaned toward the table. "I want a name. Who killed my mother? Who took your place at the top of the Lexington League? Are they the same person?"

"If you want a name, Mr. Ellis, you need to give me one first. Who provided you with the information about the Lexington League's involvement in William Iredell's murder?"

"It was in an anonymous email," Mark answered. "I don't know the name." He could tell by the look on Parker Brown's face that he believed Mark was lying.

"No name for me, son, means no name for you."

Mark paused momentarily. "I'm meeting with the person next week."

Brown's response was expected and immediate. "Then come back next week and we'll trade."

Mark collected his pen from the table in front of him and slid it into the right pocket of his pants as he rose from his chair. Picking up the legal pad with his left hand, he looked through the glass divider as he rose from his chair.

"I'll be in court on Wednesday, Mr. Brown. I hope to see you there."

Chapter Twenty-One

Washington, DC
June 29, 2010

One day until the execution of Parker Brown

"Yes." Gloria Augusteel's voice was direct. "I understand."
She closed the office door behind her as she entered. As the Vice President for Human Assets she occupied one of the corner offices in Echo Industrial's Washington branch. Her black heels, silenced as she crossed from the marble floor of the suite's hallway onto the tan carpet of her office, traced a line toward the communication console embedded in one of her bookshelves. The voice on her cell phone continued its explanation as she rushed to enter her password. Impatiently, she watched the small silver cover of the console retract. With a few more keystrokes her cell phone frequency was

masked. Anyone attempting to monitor her call would hear only static.

Receiving mission objective. It is Tuesday, June 29, 2010. It is 19:54.

I have less than twenty-four hours, she thought.

She could hear the voice on the other end through the touch of cell phone static caused by Echo's frequency-masking technology. "He will be available and alone. The rest is up to you.

"I'm sorry to put you in this position," the voice continued, "but this has to be handled with precision. And it has to be handled now. The league simply will not risk a retrial or any sort of public spectacle. It is time to finish what we started a couple of years ago."

"I understand," Augusteel repeated. "Mark Ellis actually called my office earlier today. He asked for a meeting with me. He wanted to talk about Parker Brown."

There was a moment of contemplation before the voice responded. "Have your assistant call him tonight or tomorrow morning. We don't need to give him a reason to be suspicious. Tell him the only available time you have is around ten thirty in the morning. That should be directly after the hearing. He'll be too busy afterwards and will certainly miss the meeting."

Like a gear engaging a chain, like clockwork, her mind began to plot the operation. The timing. The approach.

Short-range. Potential hand-to-hand. Target unarmed. Assault window likely limited.

The voice on the phone was providing her with the final details. She listened, as she planned. The potential outcomes and the likelihood of each. The consequences. The exit strategy. The weapon.

Inventory: Echo Industrial cache available. Concealable hand-guns available.

She moved toward her glass-topped desk as the voice continued to speak. The silver drawers along the right side were locked. Shifting her cell phone to her left ear, she held her right palm to the electronic reader on the side of the desk. The lock on her desk softly clicked as it released; the drawers, now loose, extended slightly from the desk frame. She opened the bottom drawer. Her right hand reached toward the back and her fingers closed around the vial.

Inventory: Echo Industrial cache available. Concealable hand-guns available. One vial of the substance.

She waited until the voice had completed the final notes on the operation. Only the vague outline of a plan had been assembled. The details were being left to her. "I still have one of the vials I took to North Carolina. Is information extraction required?"

"No. This should be a clean, quick hit. Get in; get out."

The conversation fell silent. Gloria Augusteel knew her role: to plot and often accomplish the objectives of her superiors. It was in her blood. Her father had worked for the Lexington League. Her grandfather had even been one of the five. Her family had done this for generations. She pushed the thought of her brother from her mind. *Noah made his choice.* Gloria could hear the German-accented English of one of their earliest Echo instructors: "It always comes down to a choice."

She ventured into the stalled conversation. "May I make a suggestion?"

"Of course."

"Once the press discovers that Mark Ellis was hired to represent Parker Brown — and especially after tomorrow

– Mark Ellis is going to attract a significant amount of media attention. I believe we can use that to our advantage."

"How so?"

"We need to control the story. If we spoon-feed the media an easy-to-grasp plot, they'll run with it." As she talked, she absentmindedly balanced the vial of substance on the flat glass of her desk. She could see the white powder in the glass case, sliding into a flat line parallel to the desktop as she settled the bottom of the cylinder. Her white-blonde hair fell evenly across her shoulder blades as she leaned forward in her chair.

"Step one: we release Luke Lyford from custody. We do so this evening. He can remain technically under arrest, but we need him out of federal control." She paused as the suggestion hung between the two sides of the conversation. It was a bold and potentially reckless idea. Augusteel knew that, and she momentarily hesitated to see if it would garner a response. There was no reply from the voice and she took the silence as a sign to continue. "After tomorrow there are going to be two high-profile murders and no convictions. Step two: we turn to our media contacts – first the online sources, then some in the more traditional media. They push the connection between Parker Brown and William Iredell."

The voice on the other end of the line remained silent. She was not sure whether to interpret that as a note of support or outright rejection of her idea. Gloria decided to press on. "The connection between the two is Mark Ellis and Luke Lyford. We've already linked Lyford to Iredell through the murder investigation. Ellis represents Lyford, so he's also connected."

The wall-length window behind her, and its partner along the left side of her office, were dark with the DC night.

Lights from the low-slung skyline shone through the windows and reflected off her glass-topped desk as she transitioned to explain the second connection she believed could be used to manipulate the media coverage. "Mark Ellis also represents Parker Brown. So they're connected, too. More importantly, Mark Ellis is responsible for Brown's public appearance tomorrow. Iredell, Lyford, Brown, Ellis – they are all interconnected.

"If we play this right, the focus of the public will be on Ellis and Lyford. Two liberal activists and two dead conservatives. We let the media draw its own conclusions."

Finally, a word from the other side of the conversation: "I'm not sure we can simply dump a man that has been accused of murdering a future Supreme Court Justice back on the streets, without so much as an explanation. The press will go wild."

Cautiously, Augusteel responded. "It doesn't have to be a long-term release. We simply need him out of federal control tomorrow – and tomorrow only. You can have him picked back up the day after tomorrow, if you decide to. Call it an administrative mistake by some low-level employee, or a computer error. Call it anything that implies it was not intentional. Someone down the chain of command will take some heat for making the 'mistake', but our purpose will be achieved, so long as he's out of federal control by tomorrow morning."

More silence from the other end of the phone call.

"All we need it to do is distract the press and create a credible reason to turn the investigation toward Ellis and Lyford . . . ." Gloria Augusteel was completing her explanation.

The voice finished her sentence. ". . . and away from anything that might bring the focus back to Echo. We buy enough time to make sure we've erased any connection to us. I'll give it some thought."

The line went dead.

In less than a minute, Augusteel was rotating a three-dimensional diagram of the federal courthouse on her computer screen. She located the courtroom where Brown was expected to be and examined the surrounding hallways and stairwells.

Limited approach vectors.

Her mind organized the details that she had been provided. This was what she did best. Brown moved within the three-dimensional diagram. She held his imaginary position in her mind and mentally inserted the U.S. Marshals that would be escorting him. Mark Ellis appeared in her calculations. As she had been taught, she moved each player through its expected positions. She considered the likelihood of a variety of options.

She tried to imagine variables that could enter the equation.

He taught me that. She violently shoved the memory of her brother, trying to remove it from her planning session. *He was always better than me at the variables. But I could plot the fixed pieces, set the plan. Organize. Build.*

She could hear their first supervising case officer. This part of her training always returned to Gloria in the supervisor's dense Russian. Her mind instinctively translated it into English. She and Noah had been stationed in Europe in the early Nineties. The Berlin Wall had come down a few years before, but the world was still changing. The league had sent them there to train, to learn, together. They had been educated in a series of different forums, by a series of different European instructors.

I could always see the whole board. Time the arrival of the cars, even in traffic. Determine which assets had the right set of skills. Move them into the right position. Give them the right tools. Prepare the extraction protocol.

It was this set of talents – expectation, patience, thoroughness – that had fueled her upward acceleration through the Echo Industrial ranks. She was not only meeting, but was exceeding, the passionate guarantees her father and grandfather had made as they argued for her expanded role in field operations.

Think. Plan. Execute. Like clockwork.

Noah was the sand that slowed the gears and stopped the clock. He would take her well-crafted mission plans and pick at them, sometimes after the assets had already been put in play. He would work around the edges, probing, testing each element. Looking for a faulty assumption, a weak link in her chain of actions and reactions. Looking for a variable.

He would not always find one, but when he did, Gloria could barely contain her frustration.

In the early years of their training, senior members of the Lexington League would pit them against each other. They called it war games for field operatives. Parker Brown – then a newly inducted member of the five – loved to do that. Gloria would be required to trap an imaginary threat within different computerized environments. Noah would control the threat and try to avoid capture, while still accomplishing his theoretical mission.

She would capture him as often as he would escape, but that was never enough. She demanded perfection from herself. He prevented it.

The similarity between now and then wasn't lost on Gloria Augusteel. But this time, Noah had made a mistake.

The final round would be hers. As she reached to return the vial to the back of her secure desk drawer, she wondered whether Noah knew of his mistake. *Probably*, she assumed. *But he doesn't know the significance of it.*

Noah had used a public computer to send an email to Mark Ellis. It was the kind of careless mistake that had stalled his advancement at Echo, the kind of mistake she would never make. It took very little effort to monitor the email messages entering Mark Ellis's work account. Once they traced one of the emails back to the computer at the public library, it was equally simple to gain access to the security footage and identify Noah Augusteel, despite the changes he had made to his physical appearance.

At least he was smart enough to encrypt the message.

His serious problem, she knew, was not that they had identified him in disguise. It was that he was not aware of the recent advances Echo had made in decryption programming. His clearance within the company was far too low for that sort of information. *He'll assume that it will take months before we can break the encryption. He'll be wrong. Again.*

Instead of months, her analysts estimated that the text of the email would be decrypted and delivered to her by tomorrow morning.

Then we'll see how many variables you have left up your sleeve, Noah.

৩৩

"Mr. Ellis?" The annoyingly assertive female voice was unfamiliar.

He glanced over his shoulder as he used his left hand to merge his truck onto the elevated bypass. His right held the cell phone to his ear. "Yeah. This is Mark Ellis." Two cars sped past him. He swerved to miss a third, changing lanes as he entered the highway.

"I am returning your call. This is Ms. Gloria Augusteel's office."

A green sports car shot past, pulling ahead of him as his truck growled toward the speed limit. He glanced into his rear-view mirror, but failed to notice that a blue SUV had changed lanes with him and was a few car-lengths back, matching his pace.

"Ms. Augusteel is available to meet at ten-thirty tomorrow morning."

"Is there any other time? Could she do eleven?"

"I'm sorry, sir, but that is the only time she is available this week. Should I schedule the appointment?"

"Um . . . yes." Ellis was distracted by a Honda that had moved in front of him and was traveling far too slow in the left lane. *The hearing is at ten. I can be out of court by ten-fifteen. Or we can split the work between us . . .*

"Thank you. Ms. Augusteel will see you at ten-thirty tomorrow."

Mark Ellis tossed his phone onto the passenger seat. It skidded across some loose documents that were shifting with the momentum of his truck and slid over the far edge of the upholstered seat. Ellis steered his truck to the right and passed the Honda. Behind him, the blue SUV made the same maneuver.

His dashboard clock read 9:04. Frustrated, he reached for the dial of his radio. Mark had hoped to catch a news update at 9:00, but the phone call had come moments before the top of the hour. The David Baker confirmation hearings had started yesterday. It was mostly the usual pomp and circumstance of a Senate hearing. The Senators were listening to each other "question" the witnesses, which mostly involved only the Senators reading their prepared remarks. There would be between "no" and "absolutely no" surprises. *Especially since the conclusion is already determined*, he thought.

Even some of the moderate Democratic Senators were starting to endorse Baker, including the Senator who would be chairing his confirmation hearings. *I'm not sure how they managed to create a hearing with less drama than William Iredell's, but they sure did.* It was going to be a week of air-filled speeches and token opposition, culminating in the confirmation – *more like coronation*, Mark seethed – of David Baker as the next Supreme Court Justice.

He had been watching replays of the prepared remarks when he had gotten the call from Luke Lyford.

"Released?"

"Yeah," he had heard Luke respond. "Tonight. Right now. What did you do?"

"Nothing . . . that I know of." Mark had not spoken to Carol Cushing since he had been asked to represent Parker Brown. As far as Mark knew, he had not done anything that would have caused Luke's immediate release.

"I'll be right there," he had said, already looking for the keys to his truck.

Ellis dropped his speed as he eased into the expanding exit lane on the right. The SUV passed on his left, remaining on the elevated bypass. As he pulled into the parking lot, he could see Luke standing on the edge of the concrete curb outside the FBI holding facility. The powerful flood-light directly behind his head stretched his shadow into the empty parking lot as he waved down his powerhouse defense team of Mark Ellis and his red truck.

Mark's cell phone fell onto the pavement as Luke pulled open the side door of the truck. He tossed it back to Mark. "Never look a gift horse in the mouth, I guess."

"This is kind of hard to believe, Luke. What happened in there?"

Luke gathered the loose pages off the passenger seat as he stepped into the truck. Out of habit, he started to straighten the pages and look for a more secure storage spot. He kicked a couple of fast food containers to the side to make room for his feet on the floorboard.

Luke Lyford was wearing the same tan dress slacks and white golf shirt he had on when he was arrested, but the shirt was now untucked. His eyes were darker, more tired. His face, somehow more thin. He looked like he hadn't had a good night's sleep in three weeks – which was almost literally the case. "One minute I'm sitting in my cell. Then the guard opens the door and leads me down the hall. Next thing I know they've processed me, released me 'on my own recognizance', and I'm out the door. They didn't even have time to collect my stuff from the holding facility. My wallet, keys, phone – maybe a few other small things that were on me – are still in storage. I'm supposed to just give them a call when I can come pick them up."

Mark's truck was turning out of the parking lot. He glanced at Luke. Their eyes met.

"I know," Luke said, "but at least I'm out. We'll work on determining the 'why' part later."

The NPR commentator was reporting on the Baker hearings and Mark turned the volume up. He sat in silence as Luke listened, trying to catch up on what was happening outside the walls of his cell. After the report finished, Mark spun the silver knob of the radio until it clicked. As the old truck plowed over the highway, the creaking of its frame filled the quiet cab. Both men were thinking about David Baker's nomination. And thinking about David Baker made both of them think about the death of Claire Ellis.

Mark broke the silence. As they merged back onto the surface streets of DC he gave Luke a blow-by-blow account of his time with Parker Brown. "I also dropped off a sample of the stained part of the James Wilson letter for a chemical analysis. I found a professor at Georgetown that thinks he might be able to get a read on what caused the stain. We should have some results soon."

"Thanks."

"One more thing: Parker Brown's selling this story that Echo Industrial is kind of like the operational arm, right? He also said that Gloria Augusteel never would have testified against him if someone didn't have her back. So, I figure, let's go to the source."

Mark looked across the dark cab of the truck. "I've got an appointment set up for ten-thirty tomorrow morning. She's expecting me. I say we send you, the deadly assassin of a Supreme Court Justice. Shake her up. See if we can rattle her, and get her off her game. It is high-time we played some offense."

Luke Lyford leaned his head back against the dirty headrest and smiled.

Mark could see the bright lights of the street lamps lining Massachusetts Avenue. Against the dark backdrop, they were blurred flashes, rushing past beyond Luke's smile.

Part Four

Chapter Twenty-Two

Washington, DC
June 30, 2010

It was Wednesday morning and the single courtroom on the fourth floor of the E. Barrett Prettyman Federal Courthouse in Washington, DC was virtually empty. The tight-spun carpet sloped under the twelve rows of seats as it led from the double-doored entrance toward the judge's bench. Mark Ellis checked his watch. 9:47. He checked the door along the wall to his left.

Carol Cushing sat at the counsel table opposite him, to his right. She had traded in her gray suit for a black one, and was turned away from Ellis. Hunched toward the other seat at her table, she was quietly addressing a U.S. Marshal sitting in the wooden chair next to her. The much taller Marshal was forced to nearly double-over in his chair to bring his ear to the same plane as her mouth. Ellis could see the Marshal nodding as she spoke inches from his ear.

Beyond her sat the silent twelve seats of the empty jury box. In front of their counsel tables, and across the open well of the courtroom, rose the seal of the United States District Court for the District of Columbia. It rested like a coat of arms, separating the high-backed, black chair behind the bench from the rest of the courtroom. The judge's clerk, seated to the left of the bench, whispered into her desk telephone.

Mark Ellis nervously rolled his shoulders and adjusted the sleeves of his coat. 9:49.

He rotated his chair and scanned the curved backs of the wooden benches behind him. Cushing had apparently kept her word: there was no sign of the press. A younger couple sat a few rows behind the prosecutor's table. Behind them, a man in a suit was turning the pages of a stapled document. One woman sat, alone, on Mark's side of the courtroom. Her blonde hair caught the sunlight as it passed through the tall windows of the old courtroom.

The door to his left opened at 9:51. The dark suit of a U.S. Marshal passed through first. Parker Brown followed, and was trailed by a second Marshal. The handcuffs around Brown's wrists were the first – and only obvious – aspect of his appearance that distinguished him from the two federal agents. He was older, but his build was similar, and his perfectly-tailored dark suit mirrored the two worn by his guards.

They moved along the wood-paneled wall, passing down a short corridor created by the wall and a waist-level railing. Mark watched as his soon-to-be official client was escorted into the well of the courtroom and toward the seat next to him at the defense counsel's table. *This is his first time back in a courtroom since his sentencing a few weeks ago*, Mark considered. The handcuffs did nothing to diminish Brown's outward appearance of confidence. His stride was sure, smooth. He nodded as Mark rose to meet him.

He could see Brown's eyes, evaluating the room and searching the faces. The clerk. Then toward the prosecutor's table. He lingered on Cushing and then moved toward the few people in the rows behind her. It was the searching review of a veteran field operative. It was reconnaissance.

Mark had settled back into his seat and checked his watch. 9:56. The hearing was scheduled to begin at ten o'clock. With his future client in the courtroom, he felt slightly more relaxed. He had spent all morning wavering, undecided about whether he wanted Parker Brown to appear this morning. On the one hand, if he failed to appear, Mark knew he would find a sense of relief. He would no longer have to be concerned about being publicly associated with a convicted traitor. On the other hand, he desperately needed confidential access to Brown – both to enhance Luke Lyford's defense and to learn all he could about his mother's death. If Brown had not walked into the courtroom, his access would most likely have come to an abrupt stop.

Ultimately, he had decided, he needed the information more than he feared the association. Their exchange – while frustrating and, at times, painful – had provided the only spark of hope he had felt since John Baker had closed the investigation.

As his feet reached the seat next to Mark, Parker Brown completed his review of the courtroom, his eyes sweeping toward the rows of seats behind the defense table. His head gradually turned, then snapped back toward Mark. Ellis could see the change in his eyes. They had grown wide. The calm, steady review of his environment had been interrupted.

"What is she doing here?" His whispered voice was insistent.

"Who?" Mark angled his head toward Brown in response.

"Augusteel. The woman behind us."

He immediately had Mark's full attention. Instinctively the attorney began to turn toward the blonde woman, but stopped himself, and instead leaned closer to Brown. "Gloria Augusteel?"

"Yes." It wasn't quite panic, but his voice was failing to mirror the confidence of his appearance. "How did she find out about this?"

Mark glanced at Brown. He could see the older man examining the handcuffs around his hands. The examination then turned to a slow study of the water pitcher set out along the top of the defense table. Finally, Brown turned slightly, rotating until he had confirmed that the U.S. Marshals were seated directly behind his chair.

"I don't know," Mark replied, answering Brown's question, "but I'll find out." He rose and moved across the opening between the two tables. The Marshal that had been talking to Carol Cushing was gone and she sat alone at the prosecution table.

"Excuse me, Carol?" Mark got her attention as he stepped toward her seat. "It appears to me that one of the main witnesses from your prosecution of Mr. Brown just happens to be sitting in the courtroom today. Seems like a rather large coincidence. What's she doing here?"

A look of measured annoyance on her face, Cushing closed the folder of documents she had been reviewing. "I don't know. I suppose she has an interest in your client's case."

"I thought I had your word that you would not publicize this."

"She didn't hear about it from me," Cushing answered, her attention travelling back to the documents on the table in front of her.

Mark paused as he stood between the tables and watched Cushing dismissively turn away from him. He allowed himself a quick look to the side. The blonde woman's hair had been worked into a single, thick braid, and it fell to the side along her shoulder. By the angle of her arms, it appeared her hands were resting in her lap. Her eyes hadn't left the back of Parker Brown's head.

Brown leaned toward Mark as Ellis returned to his seat. "When this is over, follow her." It wasn't a request.

A rush of anger. Mark began to reply, then stopped himself. Whatever the agreement he had with Parker Brown, it certainly did not allow for Brown to direct him like he was some Echo underling. Yet, there were multiple concerns playing through his mind, and it forced Mark Ellis to pause. He was stalled by the number of different roles Gloria Augusteel had taken on over the last few weeks of his life.

A chief Echo officer who may provide some insight into the death of William Iredell and potentially the death of Mark's mother.

The woman who testified against Parker Brown and then, without explanation, appeared at a routine procedural hearing.

The woman that he was scheduled to meet in roughly half an hour . . . and had hoped to rattle into making a mistake by sending Luke Lyford, the man publicly accused of poisoning William Iredell, to her office instead of himself.

Instead, Mark felt rattled. And unsure.

Along the right side of the wall behind the judge's bench, a door opened. "All rise!" The bailiff was calling the traditional judicial introduction. As he rose from his chair he stole one more look behind him. He was struck by a new thought as he watched the judge take her seat. *Carol Cushing never looked back when I spoke to her. She knew Gloria Augusteel was there. Had she already seen her or did she expect her to be in the courtroom?*

∾

As Mark had promised, the hearing took no time at all. He introduced Parker Brown. Brown acknowledged him as his attorney. The clerk entered his name into the record of the case. The judge signaled for the U.S. Marshals to remove Parker Brown. Less than five minutes.

Brown had been sitting with the same rock-backed posture he displayed during his trial. He rose with the same precision and control. The man was hardwood timber in a three-piece suit. As one of the Marshals gently steered him back toward the side door of the courtroom, the other moved toward Cushing.

Mark watched Brown's shoulders pass through the door. Directive or not, he had decided to follow Gloria Augusteel. He gathered his legal pad and other materials under his arm and turned to look for the blonde woman.

Her seat along the bench was empty.

Ellis pressed through the swinging gate of the bar and hastily stepped toward, then through, the rear doors. There was no movement in the tiled hallway of the old building. He could see the stairwell doors at the far end of the hall. Two other doors stood closed between Mark and the stairwell. The elevator door, to his left, was also closed. He could see by the illuminated number above the elevator that the lift was stationed on the ground floor, four floors below. *Did she leave during the hearing? Or did I simply take too long?*

Mark reached for the courtroom door behind him. The prosecutor would still be in there. Would she admit that she had notified Gloria Augusteel now that the hearing was over? *Maybe she'll at least explain to me why Luke got released last night.* As he pulled open the gilded oaken door he could see Cushing. She remained at the prosecutor's table and was talking with one of the U.S. Marshals who had escorted Brown into the courtroom.

Mark observed them as he made his way back down the aisle between the two sets of benches. Cushing was looking up at the taller man. Suddenly, the man reached for his ear. His left hand rose, fingers extended, signaling Cushing to stop talking. Mark enjoyed the brief look on her face. *I doubt anyone ever interrupts Carol Cushing with the palm of a hand.* Then he noticed the look on the Marshal's face.

In the fleeting moment before Brown's guard ran for the side door, Mark saw the look move from alert, to concern, to all-out panic.

Cushing seemed momentarily suspended. She called something toward the clerk as she crossed the courtroom. Mark could hear other movement in the main hallway behind him. Voices and footfalls, their volume increasing as they approached. It was loud enough to penetrate the thick door and enter the solemn courtroom. Cushing heard it too. Her steps quickened as she reached the side door – the same door through which Brown had arrived and departed.

Mark was only a few steps behind her. He barreled through the side door.

He had entered a narrow hallway. It was darker than the sunlit courtroom, and it took a split-second for his eyes to adjust. There was movement to his right. He caught sight of Cushing as she turned out of the end of the corridor.

Mark followed. The smaller hallway he had just exited ran from the courtroom door to a second hallway, the one Cushing had entered. The second hallway was slightly larger. Old fluorescent lights ran across the ceiling. Ellis could see two doorways along the right side of the hall in the dusty light. Cracks crossed sections of the checked, tiled floor. Cushing was a few steps ahead of him. Over her shoulder he could see the last door at the end of the hall closing.

Mark slowed his pace to parallel Cushing's. So far, she had either not noticed he was there or was not concerned about his presence. The faded wood sign, attached to the wall over first door on the right, read "Judge's Chambers." They passed the second: "Office of the Clerk."

He could hear other footsteps behind him. The solid pounding of dress shoes on the old tiles. He looked back. One man in a suit, presumably another U.S. Marshal. Two uniformed officers, static-covered voices coming through their handheld radios. The voices echoed down the empty hall, pushing ahead of the oncoming officers like foam in front of a wave of water.

Cushing reached the third door a couple of steps before him. As she opened the door, she noticed him over her shoulder. She ignored Mark and kept moving. Mark read the sign above as he passed through: "Prisoner Holding."

There were two small cells built into the holding room. Their barred doors had been constructed to open into the area where Cushing and Ellis now stood. The one nearest the two attorneys stood open; the cell, empty.

A uniformed guard stood with a U.S. Marshal near the second door. It was the Marshal they had been following. The courthouse guard was fumbling with a set of keys as the Marshal watched in unrestrained agitation. Cushing moved forward. Mark continued to follow in her footsteps. From his vantage point he could see over the shorter woman's shoulder, and between the courthouse guard and the U.S. Marshal.

Parker Brown's right hand hung limply between the vertical bars of the holding cell. The midpoint of his forearm rested on a flat, horizontal bar. His hand extended into the open space of the room, reaching out of the cell and through the bars.

Mark could hear the other guards entering behind him. He could feel one of their hands on his shoulder. *They don't know who I am.* The U.S. Marshal in front of him briefly glanced back and then returned his attention to the guard attempting to unlock the cell door.

They were pulling him back, away from the holding cell. Mark struggled against the grip on his shoulder, bending his knees to weaken the hold on him. He took a step forward, pivoting around Carol Cushing until he could see his client. Blood was slowly flowing from a small entry wound above Parker Brown's right eye. Brown's body was leaning against the holding-cell door. Slumped, he had come to rest on his knees. Mark looked down, and for the first time, noticed the pool of blood spreading around his own feet. It was then that he noticed the three other dark stains on Brown's upper chest.

He knew this would happen. I should have found a way to keep him out of the courtroom.

Gloria Augusteel. He thought about telling Carol Cushing, telling the Marshals. That could wait. He needed to talk to Luke.

Luke. Mark looked at his watch. 10:26. Luke would be at her office by now.

Hands firmly grasped Mark and pulled him backwards, dragging the heels of his shoes along the hard floor as he scrambled to keep his footing. His soles, slick with blood, slipped every time he tried to stand. As they wrenched him away from the cell, he could see Brown's right arm and hand. They stretched through the bars. The flat-sided ring Mark had studied during their conversations was gone.

Chapter Twenty-Three

Edenton, North Carolina
August 20, 1798

For the third time, the physician gently held two fingers to Justice James Wilson's wrist. The pulse was thready and uneven, faint. It matched his breathing. His face was taut, like the pale skin had stretched against the bone as the color ran from it. His eyes were closed, but there was movement beneath. *Whatever this is, he's fighting it*, the physician thought. *But he's losing.*

He had been alone with Justice Wilson for nearly half an hour. Once, he had heard Iredell moving outside the room's wooden door. Then footsteps passing. In the quiet, he could make out another voice. Iredell and the other voice sounded as though they were talking in a room down the hall.

The physician dipped the damp cloth into the bowl of water to his left and leaned forward in his chair. Droplets splashed across the white sheets as he reached toward Justice Wilson's head. The pale face did not move. Water ran down

Wilson's cheek, toward the doctor. He could see it adding to the dampness where Wilson's face met his pillow. Other droplets ran down the skin of his forehead and into his eyes. The bedridden man remained frozen in place.

Gently, the physician wiped the drops away as he watched the body of the Supreme Court Justice. There was little he could do, but watch. The feet twitched every so often. An arm would move periodically. *James Wilson is going to die in this room*, he thought. The physician adjusted the white sheets after each movement. It was about comfort now. With as much care as possible, he rolled Wilson's right arm away from his torso, exposing the interior of the lower arm. He could see the dark blue of his veins. He thought about a sedative, but given the unusual nature of his condition, it was difficult to gauge the impact.

The physician was settling the arm back into its original position when it jerked from his grasp. He recoiled, shocked by the abrupt movement. His left foot clipped one leg of the wooden stool next to the bed, sending the pile of clean cloths and the bowl of water tumbling onto the floor of the spare bedroom.

As the physician kneeled to recover the bowl, he glanced at Wilson's face. His eyes were open. The green pupils searched the room with jerky movement, flashing to one point, holding the spot, and then flashing to another.

Ignoring he bowl, the physician ran from the room, toward the sound of James Iredell's voice.

Seconds later, James Iredell was following the physician back down the hall, leaving Wilson's clerk – leaving Thomas Augusteel – sitting alone in the study.

∽

There was a hazy light. Red, then a light blue. Steaks of yellow from one side. He was in a room. In a bed. A numbness ached through him. It was getting worse as his sight improved.

The wooden door was opening. He could see that now. The yellow streaks arrowed from the window along the side wall. People were moving toward him. *Iredell.* Recollection dripped a useable collection of facts. He was at Iredell's house. He had been travelling. He had been running – running from something.

He could see Iredell's mouth moving. There was no sound. He tried to focus on the lips of his fellow Justice, but it brought nothing but pain. The haziness was overwhelming Iredell's face.

Wilson closed his eyes. *Breathe?* he asked himself. *Can I breathe?*

It brought some relief. He could faintly hear Iredell now: "Justice Wilson, can you hear us?"

He tried to answer, but the words failed him. It was heavy sandpaper, scratching gravel. He opened his eyes. More recollection: his documents, the notes.

Iredell again. "I found Franklin's notes. I destroyed them, as you asked."

Wilson could now clearly hear the other man. There was aggressiveness in his voice. "I think your clerk is hiding something. He may be responsible for your condition. Is there anything you can tell me?" He could tell Iredell was pressing. His speech was hurried.

Wilson tried to answer. *Nothing.*

Iredell had bent toward him. He could feel Iredell's hand, heavy on his arm. "What would you like me to do, Justice Wilson?"

His mind seemed to pulse against his skull. He grasped a thought and then lost it. More recollection: He could hear himself telling Iredell about the Lexington League. It was flowing backwards. The coach. The documents. The meeting. The faces.

The images fell from his mind. James Wilson closed his eyes and tried to collect them.

Breathe. It was a command now.

He opened one eye toward Iredell. He jerked his right arm away from the bed. The burning increased exponentially, tracing its way from his wrist into his shoulder. He pointed toward his traveling chest sitting on the desk in the corner. A white flutter. The physician had understood and brought the wooden chest. He was holding documents up. *No. Not that one. Next.*

Iredell could help, but there was another man who needed to know.

Slowly, the doctor was turning through the documents, holding them above Wilson in the bed. The extra quills and ink had fallen onto the white sheet covering his legs. The background behind the physician was darkening. He could no longer see the slats of the door, nor his clothes hanging on the far wall.

No. Hurry. He could feel it coming now. *Not that one.* He directed the physician with his eyes, pleading, begging him to move faster.

Finally. Wilson jerked his head.

Iredell grabbed the letter from the physician.

Wilson rotated his head toward the letter, toward Iredell. Iredell seemed at a loss.

Wilson lifted his right arm again. Pulling away from the hard wooden frame of the bed, he held his arm aloft, one finger extended. The darkness behind the physician deepened. The sunlight was a deep red. It flowed behind James Iredell, like water over barely submerged rocks, spilling into the room.

Iredell looked like he understood. He held the letter toward Wilson's extended arm. Wilson's finger shook. He tried to manipulate the pages. Iredell understood this movement; he turned to the second page. Then to the last page of the letter.

The index finger landed on the signature at the bottom: James Madison.

"Madison? Madison is part of this? Part of the Lexington League?"

Wilson tried to move his head. The muscles did not respond. He moved his eyes side-to-side.

Iredell paused. His eyes met the dying green light of Wilson's pupils. "Tell Madison about this? About the notes? The Lexington League?"

He willed his eyes to move. *Look down. Look up. Look down.*

"What do I tell him?" Iredell seemed to realize the question was too complex. He leaned back in the small wooden chair. The letter from Madison rested on Wilson's chest.

The coach. The documents. The meeting. The faces. The thoughts were untamed, roaming in Wilson's mind.

The water. The lamp. The notes. The wine. The meeting. The faces.

He could barely hear Iredell.

He drew on everything he had left. The blood-red light was spilling over Iredell's shoulders. He could see it swaying, sloshing around the floor. Filling the room. Rising toward the edge of the bed frame.

The coach. The documents. The water. The lamp. The notes. The wine. The meeting. The faces. The rings.

With his left hand he reached for the extra ink bottle at his waist.

Iredell followed his movement and grabbed it for him. Iredell opened the bottle. He was helping now: fitting one of the extra quills into Wilson's weak right hand.

The red light had overtaken the side of the bed. Wilson could hear the light, a river roaring as it crested slightly below his ears. The quill was in his hand now. Iredell was holding his right arm and reaching to steady the letter beneath the quill. James Wilson's hand was moving, writing on the third page of the letter.

ll ring office

The red light washed over his ears. His arms dropped to his side: his left hitting feathers, his right landing half-way over the edge of the wooden frame. He tried to raise his head. Iredell was gone, but he could hear his voice in the distance. The light sloshed higher on his cheeks. He could smell it now. He closed his eyes and released his head. It did not move, but he could feel it sink into the pillow. The blood-red light washed over his eyes.

And James Wilson died.

James Iredell gently rested his hand on his friend and fellow Justice's eyes. He could feel the fire of his skin. He collected the ink well from where it had spilled through the sheet. He lifted the letter from Wilson's lap, sorted the pages to their original order, and locked it back into the traveling chest.

He spoke a few quiet words to the physician and walked through the open door leading into the hall.

The study was empty. The ashes had cooled in the fireplace.

Thomas Augusteel was gone.

Chapter Twenty-Four

Washington, DC
June 30, 2010

"Ms. Augusteel is running slightly behind schedule, Mr. Ellis. She asked that I apologize on her behalf and show you into our conference room." The receptionist had crossed the white marble of the reception area and was approaching the light-gray leather chair in which Luke Lyford sat.

Luke could hear the contact between her tall heels and the marble floor echo in the empty room. He returned a brochure broadcasting the patriotic work of Echo Industrial's employees to the coffee table in front of him, piling it on top of this morning's copy of the *Washington Post*.

"I'm actually not Mark Ellis," he said as he rose to follow the receptionist. "I'm Luke Lyford. Mr. Ellis was not available." He noticed a slight hesitation in her step as she recognized his name. She paused, but continued to stare straight ahead.

They crossed the reception area of Echo's seventh-floor office suite, moving through the white-on-gray color scheme of the conservatively decorated area. Behind him, the elevator doors faced directly into the reception area. Before him were three smoked-glass doors. Two occupied corners of the rectangular room; the third was off to his right, near the receptionist's desk. Luke guessed that each door opened into a hallway leading to a different wing of the office suite. The woman extended a security card from her hip and swiped it across a reader along the wall. Luke could hear the lock release on the nearest of the three glass doors.

Luke Lyford could feel the confrontation ahead, looming, waiting for him. In the hallway, he felt gladiatorial, a combatant being ushered below the thirsty crowds and toward the sandy pit, toward the confrontation. *The lion?* he asked himself, his confidence surging. *Or the Christian?*

Pictures lined the interior wall of the hallway. Some, Luke assumed, were from Echo Industrial's primary training facility in North Carolina. He could see a firing range, taken as it would be seen through the scope of a rifle. The crosshairs marked thin black lines across the picture. Another picture showed what looked like an advanced ropes-course. The external wall, to his right as they walked toward the conference room, was comprised of large windows, through which one could look out over the Washington morning. The thick glass was split by two horizontal metal dividers. Every ten feet or so they intersected with a matching vertical piece: a black grate, laid over the spotless glass. For a few steps, he traced his fingers along the cool, metal edge.

The receptionist followed the window until it ended at the first and only door on the right side of the hall. Only a few feet down the hall, and directly ahead of him, Luke could see another door, one leading to the corner office. Like a shroud, the smoked-glass entrance matched the one they had passed through as they left the reception area. He read the name and title affixed to the door: Gloria Augusteel, Vice President for Human Assets.

"May I bring you something to drink?" the receptionist asked as she showed Luke into the conference room.

"No, thanks."

"Ms. Augusteel will be here momentarily." She closed the door behind her as she left.

Luke tossed the legal pad he had brought with him on the conference table and reclined in one of the cushioned chairs. He spun toward the outer wall and leaned forward. The chair rocked with his movement, allowing him to look down the seven stories onto the street below. He could hear neither the traffic nor the people walking on the sidewalk. *That was me three weeks ago*, he thought, considering the course of his life since William Iredell's confirmation hearing. He now felt separated from the people below, as if the allegations against him had walled him off, trapping him behind the thick glass.

Work hard. Try to make a difference. It had been the Sierra Club first. His first job as an attorney. Then the campaign. He could still recall the idealistic days of the Claire Ellis race. Day in, day out – they had gained on Senator David Baker. *We could have won that campaign*, Luke daydreamed.

Then it had been Washington and the counsel position on the Senate Judiciary Committee. The Iredell nomination. In some ways, it had felt to Luke like a continuation of the campaign. David Baker had returned to his Senate seat and was leading the charge for Iredell, lining up a phalanx of conservative activists in support of his confirmation. Luke had been on the other side – and sometimes it felt like he had been the only person on the other side, the only person standing between William Iredell and the Supreme Court.

All around him, moderate Democrats had folded their hands. Liberal interests groups had offered tepid, half-hearted support, but they knew the cause was lost. David Baker and the Lexington League had been poised for a huge victory: William Iredell had been a lock for a seat on the Supreme Court. Through it all, Luke kept fighting, following the path his natural instinct laid before him. *Work hard*, he told himself. *Try to make a difference.* Yet, they had lost. Luke had lost. Iredell had been confirmed with overwhelming, bipartisan support.

And the phone call from the police the following morning had sent his life spiraling off its predictable path. The unexpected phone message from William Iredell followed by the unexplained copy of the James Madison letter. The announcement at the press conference followed by the arrest. The detention in the holding facility followed by the unanticipated release.

He looked down at the few notes he had made on his yellow legal pad. It was like a whirlwind had gathered him from his high-rise apartment and deposited him, nearly full-circle, right back in this high-rise office. *I went from asking questions about the Lexington League's nominee for the Court to asking questions about the Lexington League itself.*

The door opened behind him and intruded on his recollection. He angled his chair back toward the table and saw Gloria Augusteel enter through the same doorway through which he had just walked. As she approached the conference table, Luke noticed a second door, beyond her, at the narrow end of the rectangular room.

"Mr. Lyford." Her hand was extended as she approached. "I was expecting Mr. Ellis."

"He couldn't make it, so he asked me to meet with you instead. I hope that will not be a problem."

"Of course not," she answered. "I apologize for running late."

She sat opposite Luke Lyford. "What can I do for you?"

❧

Is there blood on my clothes?

Gloria Augusteel had changed into a new suit coat while her assistant sped from the federal courthouse to her office. She had also changed her blouse. She had examined the pants of her suit and failed to find any traces of Parker Brown's blood. The discarded clothes were with her assistant along with strict instructions on disposal. Once this meeting ended, she could change the remainder of her outfit, destroying the few clothes she still wore from the courthouse.

I am sitting across from Luke Lyford. We are in the conference room next to my office. We are alone. It is 10:39. His back is to the window. We are on the seventh floor. He is likely unarmed. I have a small handgun located in the briefcase near the foot of my chair.

She was aware of her accelerated pulse. Her training had engrained the necessity of – and the ability to create – a controlled physical condition. However, the feeling of the weapon, the resistance of the trigger, the look on Parker Brown's face, remained. They lingered.

And she remained affected by them.

I have received no communication concerning target.

Gloria always felt uncomfortable in this period: the unte-thered window of time between conclusion and confirmation. *He's dead*, she reassured herself.

A single-asset assault within a confined and guarded area. How much the U.S. Marshals knew remained an unknown in her planning. It really didn't matter. They had been moved – either with their knowledge or without – and the window had opened. He had approached her as she entered, walking to the front of the cell. Like he was expecting her.

Four close-range shots.

Her mind demanded that she move into the present. Luke Lyford was saying something, his voice slicing through her memory.

". . . and my attorney has had an opportunity to visit with Parker Brown."

He was looking at her for a response, a reaction. She gave him none. Slowly, she was engaging in the conversation, leaving the courthouse behind.

Lyford continued. "Mr. Brown believes your testimony at his trial may not have been entirely truthful. He's consider-ing that as a potential ground for an appeal."

Gloria Augusteel offered the most dismissive look she could summon. "Mr. Lyford, if Mr. Brown wants to appeal the verdict against him that, of course, is his right. However, my testimony was absolutely accurate." Her hair remained in a single braid. She smoothed some loose strands behind her ears as she spoke.

"It is interesting though, isn't it?" asked Luke from his seat across the table. He was looking past her now, study-ing the pictures of Echo Industrial employees hanging on the white wall behind her. "Interesting to think through what a new trial might look like. Or maybe not even a new trial?

Maybe just a press conference where Parker Brown tells the story he failed to tell in his trial." As he finished the sentence, his eyes landed on Gloria's.

The veiled threat in his speech was obvious. The tactical portion of her mind engaged as her crystal-blue eyes studied Luke Lyford. His right hand rested on his legal pad. The sunlight from the window behind him glared off the watch on his left wrist.

It is 10:43 on Wednesday morning. I am alone with Luke Lyford.

She watched his eyes, the movement of his face. There was no nervous twitch in his hands.

It was not the threat itself that bothered Gloria Augusteel. It was that he knew enough to deliver it. *If he thinks I might be threatened by Parker Brown talking, then he knows I have something to fear. If he knows that I have something to fear, then Brown – or someone – has told him something about the league.* She worked through the possibilities. The most direct seemed the most likely: *Parker Brown has been talking to Mark Ellis, who in turn has been talking to Luke Lyford.*

The situation in the Echo conference room instantly changed.

It is 10:44 on Wednesday morning. I am alone with target.

"Mr. Lyford, I testified truthfully at his trial and, as far as I'm concerned, Mr. Brown can say whatever he wants, whenever he wants, in public." Gloria leaned forward in her chair. She heard the slow squeak as it tilted toward the conference table. Placing her hands on the polished-wood table between them, she mirrored the position of Luke's hands.

The younger man began to speak. She quickly moved to interrupt him. "Sir, I appreciate the fact that Mr. Brown has the right to an attorney and that he has hired Mark Ellis.

I also appreciate the fact that you have some rather significant legal difficulties of your own at this time. What I do not understand is why you are here. Has Mr. Brown also retained you as his counsel?"

"I'm here," he answered, "because your name came up in the conversation between Parker Brown and Mark Ellis, and . . ."

Her tone moved up a notch in emphasis as she interrupted him for a second time. "I understand that, Mr. Lyford. And that would explain why Mark Ellis might want to meet with me. What I want to know – and what I asked – is: why are *you* here?

The question hung, as it was supposed to, like a challenge. Would he claim to be Brown's attorney? A claim they both knew she could easily refute, and then potentially expose to the press – thereby labeling him a liar and calling into question any answers he might give at his own trial. Or would he offer some version of the real motivation behind his visit?

Truth or lie?

She watched his face again. It was steady. His eyes remained fixed on her.

Fight or flight?

She could see his left hand, tightening into a fist. His watch rotated, the new angle moved the circle of reflected light on the wall. "I am here . . ." Luke Lyford started, the words crawled from his mouth, but the determination was thick in his voice. "I am here because I believe there might be a connection between Parker Brown's case and the death of William Iredell."

Fight.

It was the answer she needed to hear, even if it was not the one she had hoped for.

It is 10:49 on Wednesday morning. I am alone with target.

❦

I got her, Luke Lyford thought, as he watched her response. It seemed forced. She had leaned back, away from the table. She had tried to laugh it off. "Maybe so, Mr. Lyford. But if there is a connection, I have no idea what it is."

Gloria continued, rising from the rich, tan leather of the conference-table chair. "Mr. Lyford, everything I know about Parker Brown's conviction is in the transcript of my testimony." She looked at the clock above the conference room door. "But, I have about ten more minutes before my next meeting and I'd be willing to answer some questions if you have them. Just let me get some notes from my office."

Luke watched as Gloria Augusteel stepped away from the table, moved past the door to the hall, and approached the door at the end of the room. He could see her right hand pass a white security card over the reader attached to the wall. As the door clicked open, she stepped through, closing it behind her.

Ten minutes. *Rattle her*, he thought. *Mark's idea. Connect the Lexington League to Echo Industrial and see what she says.*

Augusteel was moving back through the conference room. She had a manila folder under her arm and two glasses of water in her hand. "Would you mind grabbing a couple of the coasters?"

Luke reached into the center of the table and removed two coasters from the stack, passing one across the table to her. He reached for the extended glass of water as he returned to his seat.

On the other side of the table, Gloria Augusteel held the folder in the air, tipping its corner toward him. "My notes from the trial," she offered. She took a sip of her water. "I feel I must warn you, Mr. Lyford. I'm willing to answer some questions, but if we touch on confidential Echo Industrial maters or classified information, I'm going to have to bring our lawyers into this."

Luke nodded in response. He reached for his glass and pulled it closer to him.

"Have you ever heard of the Lexington League, Ms. Augusteel?"

"Yes. I believe it is a legal organization. Sometimes when I'm in DC I work with our lobbyists on the Hill. I've heard them mention it."

"Is that all you know about it?"

"I think so. Is this somehow connected to Parker Brown?"

Luke looked up from his legal pad. He had been making notes as she spoke. He watched her response, trying to gauge her reaction. Sidestepping her question, he dove deeper into the informal interrogation. "Parker Brown seems to think Echo Industrial is connected to the Lexington League. Do you know anything about that?"

"No. As I mentioned, I've heard our lobbyists refer to the Lexington League, so maybe we work toward some common legislative goals . . . ," she answered, trailing off.

Luke examined her as he reached for the glass to his right. She was still answering. "How is this connected to my testimony? What does this have to do with Brown's trial?"

Luke brought the glass to his lips and tilted it, sipping the water before he started to respond. He looked at Gloria

Augusteel. Her eyes seemed to track the glass as he moved it back to the table.

"Parker Brown claims that the Lexington Leag . . . ." The words stopped. Slowly, he lowered his right hand. He gripped the edge of the table, his fingers curling around the bottom of the beveled edge and clawing the back of the wood.

An electric current. From the base of his neck, running along his spine.

She was moving on the opposite side of the table, circling the end and approached his chair. Her questions came at him fast, one after another. Like single pellets lodging in his chest.

"Did Parker Brown provide the name of anyone associated with the Lexington League?"

She fired again, not waiting as he struggled to suppress the answer.

"Did Parker Brown tell Mark Ellis that the league killed Claire Ellis?

His grip slipped from the table as his fingers involuntarily extended. Luke Lyford tried to stand. His legs were weak. He rose unsteadily, grasping for the table. His chair tumbled to his side, its wheels upturned. She was near him now. He could feel the electric current running through his legs, towards his feet.

"Yes."

Another pellet lodged between his ribs. "Did he tell Mark Ellis that the league killed William Iredell?"

Luke tried to move from her. He stumbled over the upturned leg of the chair, sprawling onto the center of the table. His arm connected with the pile of coasters and they spilled away from him.

"Yes," he heard himself answer. Leaning face-down on the polished surface, he could see two of the coasters rolling down the long conference table. Suddenly, he was confused. *Did they fall? Where was the end of the table?*

Darkness seemed to spread from the corners of the room, like clouds rolling in before a storm. He could hear her in the background, her voice echoing into the dark.

She was pulling on his shirt, flipping him over on the conference table. He was on his back now. His face was wet. She was dropping one of the glasses to the floor. "Do you have the letter that James Madison sent to James Wilson?"

Another question. Another pellet. He flinched. He fought against it. He fought against the current. He could feel his eyes closing. Strands of brown hair swung loose from behind his ears. Wet from the water she had poured over him, the hair stuck to his forehead and face.

She was lifting him now. He was leaning against the edge of the table. He was standing, spinning. Trying to catch himself. Falling. His back was against the window. The sun burned through the glass, searing him, holding him. The heat slowly invaded. The current flowed through him. She was holding his eyes open.

"Do you have the letter . . ." Again.

Luke could no longer fight. "Yes, but . . . ."

The heat from the window passed into his chest. It met the current.

Chapter Twenty-Five

Washington, DC
June 30, 2010

*M*ark Ellis pressed the Redial button on his cell phone and held it to his ear. His calls were going straight to voicemail.

Maybe Luke turned his phone off.

The U.S. Marshals had dragged him from the holding room and away from Parker Brown's body. A courthouse guard had escorted him back down the tiled hall. "It's a crime scene now," the rough voice of the guard dictated toward Mark. He held the door open for Ellis to pass through, depositing the attorney back into the public section of the building. "Even if he was your client."

As soon as they had removed him from the holding room, his thoughts had turned to Luke. *I have to warn him.* Desperate, he had found his cell phone in his briefcase. He turned it on as he pounded down the four flights of stairs and exited the front of the federal building. Having left his truck behind this morning, he flagged down a cab.

"Give me one second." He was searching for the Echo Industrial address. He found it and shouted it through the opening in the thick plastic divider. From the rear seat of the cab, he could read the red numbers of the dashboard clock: 10:50. *Luke's been there for twenty minutes. Why would he turn his cell . . .*

Realization finally came: *He doesn't have it. It was still in storage when he was released from the holding facility. He was going to get it after the meeting at Echo.* Mark tapped the screen of his phone, found the phone number he wanted, and dialed the Echo Industrial office.

"Echo Industrial DC." The receptionist's voice gave him a brief moment of hope.

"Gloria Augusteel, please. This is Mark Ellis."

"Ms. Augusteel is unavailable."

Of course she is. The fleeting hope was gone.

"May I take a . . . ."

Mark ended the call and sat back on the torn vinyl. The plastic divider separating him from the driver brought back images of the attorney-visitation room from the federal prison. He could see Parker Brown's face.

The cab was weaving through the early stages of lunchtime traffic in the capitol. It slowed. Changed lanes. Then back again. Beside him on the black vinyl, Mark's briefcase slid against his leg as the driver pumped the accelerator. He reconsidered his plan. *Luke is in a public place. She has no reason to harm him.* The cab stopped for a red light.

10:52 on the dashboard clock. *I'm supposed to be there at 11.*

Parker Brown was dead. They had no other potential sources of information on the Lexington League – no other way to even confirm whether he was telling the truth.

No other way to find out about my mother.

And most likely, no other way to discover who killed William Iredell.

291

He opened his briefcase and shuffled through the papers in one of the internal pockets. His fingers located the anonymous email he had received last week. "Change of plans," he called through the opening. "8th and F. A place called the Portico Café. I think it's inside the National Portrait Gallery."

∾

Gloria Augusteel had accessed the security-control center of the Echo Industrial office suite. With a few adjustments she reassigned the recognition software controlling the security-card readers. The two controlling access to her office – the one stationed at the primary doorway leading from the hall and the one controlling access through the smaller conference-room door – would now only respond to her card. She finalized the changes and exited the security program. Augusteel eyed the conference-room door through which she had just passed. It was closed, like a stone sealing a tomb – and thanks to the changes she had just made in the security program she was the only person who could roll away the stone.

Luke Lyford was face-down on the carpeted floor of her office, a few feet inside the conference-room door. He hadn't moved since she had hauled his body into her office. The thin man in the gray slacks was still breathing. She could see that as she stepped past his body to open the communication console in her bookshelf. His hair and the left shoulder of his shirt were still wet from where she had poured the glass of water over his face.

She initiated the cell phone masking procedure, but this time it was for an outgoing call. Augusteel hesitated before she dialed. Putting Luke Lyford back in play was her idea. Now, not only was his absence going to be noticed by the press, but she had used the league's last remaining vial on him.

In her estimation, it had been worth it. They had misunderstood the threat from Parker Brown. She had assumed he would try to use an appeal, and potentially a second trial if the appellate court ordered one, to expose the league. Instead, he had been feeding information to Mark Ellis. She knew Parker Brown well enough to know what would have come next: he would gradually drip out the information to Mark Ellis until he was confident that Ellis would use the Lyford trial to expose the Lexington League. The trial would have been his vessel, and Brown would have captained the ship from behind the safe walls of his prison cell.

You should have stayed behind those walls, Parker, she thought as she waited.

A voice answered her call. "Yes?"

"The operation this morning was a success . . . as you certainly know. However, there's been a complication," she started. Without taking a breath, she continued, hoping to head off any criticism. "But it has generated new information and a new opportunity."

There was silence on the other end, accented by the light crackle of static from the signal-masking device. Then the voice. "Go on."

Gloria Augusteel immediately began a detailed explanation of what had taken place moments ago at her office. She spoke into what seemed to be an empty phone; there was no response from the other end. "This is where I believe we are," she concluded. "Brown has provided at least some information to Mark Ellis. Ellis has provided that information to Luke Lyford. We do not know if it has gone farther than those two.

"It leaves us with three potential problems. First, Luke Lyford. He is incapacitated, but – as you know – he will likely regain consciousness for a limited time. We don't know what he'll remember.

"Second, Mark Ellis. He has some information from Parker Brown. We don't know what he plans to do with it.

"And third, the Madison letter. Lyford indicated that he had the letter. It is safe to assume he's shared it with Ellis." Augusteel held the phone to her ear as she moved toward her desk. She waited for a response, waited for direction.

"As to the last two issues," the voice began. "Do not do anything. Leave Ellis and the letter alone, for now. We've reached the point where I need to contact the other four. They will likely want to hear directly from you. I'll be in touch about a time and place." There was yet another pause. "As for Mr. Lyford, if you are worried about what he's going to say when he wakes up, then it's pretty simple: don't let him wake up."

She glanced at the crumpled body in the corner of her office.

It is 10:58. I am alone with target.

The static was gone. She glanced at her phone and saw that the other party had ended the call.

Within seconds she had determined at least three ways to remove the body from her office. As she weighed the risks and benefits of each option, her right hand reached for the side of her desk and passed over the identification reader. The locks holding her desk drawers retracted.

The ring Gloria had removed from Parker Brown's hand was in her pocket and she withdrew it as she pondered how to manage the body erratically breathing mere feet from her desk. She examined the ring, sliding her fingers over the five silver sides and touching the five-sided star engraved on each face. The light from her desk lamp reflected off each upturned side as she slowly spun the ring around her index finger. She dropped the dense metal into the center drawer of her desk and gently pressed the compartment back into the frame until she heard the soft click of the bolt sliding into place.

Augusteel watched Luke Lyford as she undid the braid of hair trailing down her neck. For a moment her blonde hair fell over the black plastic and woven mesh of her office chair. She collected the loose strands from her ears and, as much from habit as from anything else, expertly rewove the thick braid. It ran along the top of her chair as she stood. Then it fell between her shoulder blades, swaying as she pivoted past the corner of her desk and crossed the room toward the small couch along the far wall of her office.

She removed one of the pillows from the couch, then returned to her desk and partially removed the bag lining her small trash can. Below the bag – as she had expected – the cleaning service had left a replacement bag. She straightened the clear plastic in her hands, inspected it for holes, and calmly walked toward the incapacitated body of Luke Lyford.

It is 11:01. I am alone with target.

ல

Nestled in the heart of DC's Penn Quarter, the gray face of the National Portrait Gallery stretches two full blocks in downtown Washington. The front of the building runs along F Street, between Ninth and Seventh. Eighth Street intersects the front of the large, stone structure at its central point. The street deposits the approaching foot traffic on the fifteen, cement-colored front steps. The steps climb to five revolving doors, and connect the classical Roman architecture of the Gallery to the pavement below.

Standing at the base of the front steps one can take in the entire scope of the façade. To the left and right, the wings of the Gallery extend from the corners of the building, shrugging shoulders that bulge from the primary body of the exhibition hall toward the intersections of Ninth and Seventh.

The eight massive columns are what dominate the appearance. Ten feet wide and reaching up like stone fingers from the second floor, they carry the granite roof that extends to create the portico: the covered, outdoor space that sits among the stone columns and directly above the revolving entry doors.

Mark Ellis checked his watch one more time. It was a few minutes before eleven. He was slightly early. Exiting the taxi, he had noted the few rectangular banners flying between the stone pillars, advertising the collections within. The expansive banners stretched nearly as high as the columns. Raised and lowered by a pulley system, the Gallery staff alternated and replaced the banners as the exhibits opened and closed. Their bright colors contrasted sharply with the stone of the columns and presented the image of gray stone alternating with large stretches of vivid color.

The wrought-iron tables of the Portico Café occupied half of the open area around the columns. From the tables one could view the traffic moving parallel to the building on F Street or watch the cars making a perpendicular approach on Eighth. Mark Ellis had selected a table near the front ledge of the open space. He opened the white napkin and returned the enclosed silverware to the grated tabletop. The waiter brought water.

He scanned the nearly empty café even though he had no idea what sort of person to expect, or whether he should expect someone at all. There were two couples nearby. Like him, they had selected one of the open tables near the ledge. A group of four tourists sat three tables back, toward the entrance to the Gallery. Beyond the tables he could see the plastic-coated chain that separated the café from public area of the porch. At the opening of the chain he could see the back of the wooden hostess stand, and beyond that the double doors leading back into the Gallery.

Security cameras swiveled above the door. He could see other fixtures near them: hard plastic boxes and two metal domes that were much too modern to have been part of the original construction. They were part of an elaborate security system, guarding the portraits displayed just inside the glass doors, Mark assumed. To his left, he could hear a string quartet warming up, preparing for the lunch crowd. The sound of multiple instruments being simultaneously tuned echoed between the columns and off the hard stone squares making up the portico floor. On the opposite side of the railing: the sound of midday traffic.

Above him he could hear the large banners rolling in the breeze. He was directly under a three-story portrait of James Madison, advertising the collection of Revolutionary-era portraits displayed on the Third Floor. An equally large General Washington was to Madison's right, taking up the space between the next two columns. His eyes followed one of the ropes that ran from the metal crank at the base of a column, up behind the fluttering banner, and to the wheel of the pulley system at the top.

The waiter retuned. Mark checked his watch. 11:02. He ordered an overpriced buffalo chicken wrap and looked back down Eighth Street.

He missed the other man's approach and startled as the metal chair scraped along the stone. The other man was approximately Mark's age and took a seat at the table as he glanced past Mark's shoulder toward the other diners. His blond hair looked almost Nordic in the sunlight. "Mark Ellis?" the blond man asked, now fully seated and focused on Mark.

"Yes."

"I'm Noah. I sent the email."

❧

It was finished, and Gloria Augusteel was mapping out the process by which she would remove Luke Lyford's body from her office.

She opened her database of Echo personnel and narrowed it to active field assets. Then she narrowed the list again to only include those currently deployed in DC. To her benefit, the number of assets in DC was somewhat inflated. Some had been brought in for additional security in the wake of the Iredell murder. Others were detailed to urban field teams focused on locating her brother. Scrolling through the list of names, she searched for two or three that could be trusted with this sort of delicate operation – one with such an obvious connection to their office, and to her personally.

Gloria had identified two potential names when she noticed her email system indicating the arrival of a new email. She clicked on the icon in the lower right corner of her screen, opening her email program in a window that replaced the database of names on her display.

There was one new message, from "Iris Farlington (Technology and Softwa . . .)". The title ran longer than the available space, but she recognized the name. She had tasked Farlington with the decryption of the email chain they had retrieved from Mark Ellis's email account. Assuming the asset had performed as expected, Farlington's email should be the translation of the emails her brother had sent to Ellis.

Using a public computer had been a mistake. She was certain that even Noah had realized that by now. They had accessed the footage from the library's security cameras and had easily identified her brother. Now she would be able to read the message he had sent to Mark Ellis.

The decoded text materialized on her screen as she opened the email.

The first portion was from the first email Noah had sent. She read it in growing frustration.

You will never prove your client's innocence. The evidence against him will be flawless. The Lexington League will ensure a conviction.

My family and I have served the league since the Revolution, so please trust me. You either beat them at their own game or you lose.

For the Republic.

The word came to her, not for the first time: *traitor*.

The second part came from Mark Ellis's reply, which had been included – and encrypted – as part of the second email from Noah's anonymous account. She was already familiar with this email, however, as they had copied the outgoing message directly from Mark Ellis's email account.

\

Who are you? Can we meet? Where did you get the tox report?

She enjoyed that Mark Ellis had confused the two anonymous emails. Echo had easily copied the first anonymous email he had received – the one with the toxicology report attached – so Gloria already understood that someone had provided Ellis with an accurate analysis of the toxins in William Iredell's blood.

After learning of that email, they had worked to locate the sender. However, since it came from a private computer and a good number of people could have removed a sample of Iredell's blood after his autopsy, it had proved impossible – so far – to determine who had emailed Ellis. Nevertheless, she appreciated that the coincidental timing of the anonymous emails had confused Mark Ellis. Ultimately, she knew, it would mean nothing.

The final decrypted section came from the second, and final, email sent from Noah's anonymous account:

Tox report? Portico Café. Outside. 8th and F. Wednesday, next week. 11am. I'll find you.

It is 11:06. I am four blocks from target. Advance immediately. Move supporting assets into position.

She was moving. The Luke Lyford problem would have to wait.

Her phone was back at her ear. She reached for the bag she had brought back from the courthouse. The familiar weight inside was slung over her shoulder as she sprinted toward the door of her office.

She moved down the hallway, her long strides rushing between the wall-length window and the framed images of Echo's North Carolina training facility. She pushed through the glass door and ran across the marble floor, calling to the receptionist to have her car brought to the front of the parking garage.

Alone in the elevator, she reloaded.

◌

Mark Ellis watched the blond man's eyes as they took in their surroundings. They seemed to pause on the security cameras toggling back-and-forth above the Gallery's door. For a moment, the blue eyes and black cameras mimicked each other, as both swept over the open-air café. They moved across the faces of the diners, the few members of the wait staff weaving between the iron tables, and the faces of the musicians in the corner.

The attorney watched the eyes and cameras for another heartbeat, then addressed the anonymous author of the emails he had received a week before. "Your email said you think my client is innocent. What makes you say that?"

Noah Augusteel glanced toward Mark, then back over the stone ledge of the porch, toward the crowd moving beneath. As the clock inched toward noon, the crowd of tourists was blending with men and women in business suits entering the street from nearby office buildings.

Mark's eyes were drawn to the perpendicular, intersecting street. Back down Eighth Street, he could see the International Spy Museum on his right, across F Street from their second-story café. He could see the columns of the National Archives – similar to those next to his table – at the other end of Eighth Street.

"I don't think he killed Iredell. I think he's being set up as the scapegoat," Noah Augusteel answered. The temporary hair dye had been removed days ago and this was the most publicly exposed he had been since his visit to DC's library. He had scouted this café twice before assigning it as the meeting location. The view from the portico allowed him to cover every approach vector. He watched as the density of the crowd slowly increased below their seats, a steadily swelling mass shuffling below them. He scanned the faces walking up F Street toward their position. He turned and looked back down the opposite direction. *Nothing.*

There was, of course, a downside to their position: for every angle he could see, someone approaching from that angle could see him. He had weighed the possibilities. Unless an asset knew his location ahead of time and entered the building through an entrance other than the revolving doors along the front, he would see the asset as it approached.

Mark studied the anxious movement across the table as the waiter refilled his water glass. Noah declined to order. As the waiter walked away, Mark re-initiated the conversation. "I gathered that you thought Luke was set up. I'm asking: why? What makes you so sure?"

Augusteel seemed to turn his complete attention to Mark, the cold glint of his gaze coming to rest on the attorney for the first time. He unwrapped the silverware in front of him. Mark watched as Noah unconsciously twirled his knife between the fingers of his right hand.

"First, the Iredell hit . . . ." Augusteel hesitated. "By that I mean 'killing'."

"I got that much. Thanks."

Noah leaned closer to Mark as he continued, placing the knife on the unwrapped white napkin to his right. "The Iredell hit fits the league's MO – its modus operandi. You know, how we get stuff done. Someone high-profile like Iredell can't just disappear. Although – to be honest – this has the feel of something that was rushed. That is to say, it wasn't carefully planned.

"Your client is perfect evidence of this," he continued. "He's only hooked in to this because of a phone call and message from Iredell himself. Does that sound like a well-planned operation to you?" Noah Augusteel checked the busy sidewalk again as he spoke. "My guess is that your client just stumbled into this. They are taking advantage of the coincidence. I think they decided to set him up after the murder, not before."

Mark lowered his water glass onto the table. He started to interrupt, but Noah's rapid-fire speech blocked his attempt.

"Second, you could say I was part of a hastily put-together second phase of this operation. Somehow the league learned about some letter Iredell's family had been keeping for generations." His serene blue eyes looked back toward the Gallery doors as Augusteel paused.

"You know about the lett . . ." Mark started, then abruptly stopped.

"Are you telling me that you are part of the Lexington League?" Mark glanced at the knife next to Noah's elbow as he asked. Without considering the movement, he slid toward the back of his chair.

"You could say I've recently tendered my resignation." Noah smiled.

Still nothing. Noah was searching the rooftops of the buildings across F Street. There was no movement. He watched the body-language, the action of the people on the sidewalk. *There is no organized pattern.* He looked skyward, studying the banners above their table. He could see the air rolling up the banner as the breeze drifted through the open-air café.

As Noah continued to methodically monitor the street, Mark examined Noah's face. *There is something about him.* It was as much a feeling as a thought. Suspicion was creeping in. "Your email said your family had served the Lexington League for generations," Mark said. "Your resignation must have come has a big disappointment."

"You could say that." Noah was smiling again as his eyes followed the rope holding the massive banner. It ran down from the top of the column behind Mark. His concentration settled back at their table. "My family has served for a long time. All the way back to the Revolution."

"Next, you're gonna tell me one of the Founding Fathers was in the Lexington League." This time it was Mark's turn to

304

look skyward, and he pointed toward the back of the oversized James Madison portrait waving above them. "That is what I think of when I think of James Madison: natural-born killer."

Noah decided not to parry the sarcasm. "Maybe so," he answered. "Wouldn't surprise me if one of them was in it. All I've ever been told is that my family helped recruit one of them – or at least try to recruit one of them. Apparently it didn't work, so in true Lexington League fashion, the threat of potential exposure was quickly extinguished."

Despite what he had seen at the courthouse, despite Parker Brown, despite everything that had taken place since he had driven his truck into the nation's capital, Mark could not contain his disbelief. "Now you're telling me they killed a Founding Father?"

Noah tilted his neck slightly to one side and scanned the sidewalk below. "James Wilson. I doubt you've heard of him. I really don't know if it's true. Probably not. It is probably just some family legend."

"Your family's been at it that long?" Mark responded. His mind was frozen on two words: *James Wilson*.

"Pretty much been serving since the founding of the league. A lot of wasted generations."

Mark watched his eyes as he spoke. *He looks familiar.* Mark couldn't place it. It was like the remnant of a dream that holds on just long enough for the dreamer to know he's forgotten.

Augusteel continued. "One of my family members still takes her orders from them."

Somewhere in the back of Mark Ellis's mind the words sparked recognition. No – not recognition. More of a general familiarity. *Takes her orders . . . .*

"What is your last name?"

"Augusteel."

That's it, Mark thought. He reached for his leather document folder leaning against the ledge of the porch. *He looks just like her.*

But Mark wasn't the only one at the table whose suspicion was accelerating. Noah's grew simultaneously. His, however, had no middle gear.

❦

Noah watched as Mark Ellis quickly pushed away from the table. Ellis's white napkin spilled onto the ground as he rose.

"I just saw your sister's handiwork. She killed Parker Brown about half an hour ago," the attorney said, initiating his retreat from the table.

Noah watched as Mark took a step to the side, then two backwards away from Noah. "Wait. It's not . . . ," Noah began to respond.

It is 11:17. I am on the second-floor of an outdoor café.

His instinct was taking over before he could realize why. His right hand dropped from the table and reached for the backpack resting on the ground next to him.

Ellis had backed farther away. He had put one of the outdoor tables between himself and Noah.

Twelve other people in close vicinity. Two cameras. Security system. Thirty-five feet to the door.

His pulse was rising. He had seen something but . . .

He looked up again. Retracing the review of his surroundings he had performed prior to Mark stepping away from the table. He tried to find what was causing his reaction, what was causing his suspicion to grow. Then he looked straight across the table, through the opening that had been created by Mark's departure.

He could see a wider view of F Street.

Threats. Three. Sidewalk. Forty feet. Closing.

There were two more across the street, moving toward the café. He spun around. The same approach from the opposite side of F Street. Three men were closing at a near-jog. They were only performing a cursory review of the people as they passed. Another two were working in parallel across the street.

Thirty feet. Ten threats.

"Ellis, we don't have much time." Noah was on his feet now, reaching into the backpack. The stone ledge of the porch pressed against his legs. *They won't risk a public shot from the street.* "You have to trust me."

The approach looked like a textbook Echo containment pattern. The two sets of plain-clothed operatives would advance to the corner of F and Eighth, remaining on the far side of the street. They would be positioned to monitor the revolving doors. One from each of the three-man groups would remain on the side of the steps leading into the Gallery. The other four would enter the Gallery to capture their target or flush it into the street.

"Why? Why the hell would I trust you?" Mark had stopped his retreat once Noah rose from the table. He followed Noah's line of sight. He could see the men moving through the crowd below. They were pushing through the tourists, moving faster than the businessmen walking to lunch. From his vantage point above the street he could see them closing toward the front steps of the National Portrait Gallery.

"OK." Noah was looking toward the rooftops on the opposite side of the street now. He called back over his shoulder toward

Mark. The couples at the next two tables had noticed the raised voices and were watching Noah. "Don't trust me. Just listen."

Fifteen feet from entrance. Ten threats.

Noah wheeled toward Mark, looking over his shoulder toward the door leading into the second-floor of the Gallery.

They are disregarding everyone else on the street. They know where I am. He recalled his initial assessment of the location. *And if they know where I am, then others may have already entered through one of the private access points.*

Ten threats. More?

"Listen," he repeated as he looked toward Mark. "Innocent or not, Luke Lyford is going to take the fall if you go to trial. I suspect you know that by now. This is older and deeper and larger than Luke Lyford. And you. And me. We will not be allowed to stand in the way."

The automatic part of his mind calculated the progress: *Groups across the street have reached their position. Others are nearing the front doors. Approximately two minutes until they reach this level.*

"Why are you telling me this?"

Noah's right hand was on his Luger, hovering just below the zipper of the bag – a sword, sheathed, but loose in the scabbard. He had turned back to the street. Two of the men were pointing toward him. Two others had their wrists to their mouths, speaking into the microphones covered by the ends of their sleeves. He looked down at the crowd thickening below. Tourists were moving into the revolving doors. A steady flow of people was spilling onto F Street from the neighboring office buildings. Behind him, others were entering the patio restaurant.

It is 11:19. I am on the second-floor of an outdoor café. My weapon is . . . The thoughts were coming so fast they were becoming action before they were fully formed.

He answered Mark's question. "I'm telling you this because force must be met with force. Blood must be paid with blood. The idea that you'll go to court, file some paperwork, and beat back the concentrated effort of an organization as old as the country is a joke."

He could see the doors opening across the porch. *Too early. The threats on the street could not have made it yet. There must have been more inside.*

Augusteel called to Mark Ellis. "They've been watching you. And Luke Lyford. You have to be careful."

He drew his Luger from his bag.

The diners at the table next to him scrambled past Ellis. Stock-still and surrounded by the wrought-iron tables, he stared at Noah Augusteel. One of the diners was screaming as she ran toward the string quartet in the corner. Two of its members noticed Noah's gun and dropped their instruments, fleeing toward the stone interior walls of the café.

"The league has used me my entire life. Some things are just about revenge." Noah watched the Gallery doors. "I imagine that is something you can appreciate on a personal level."

He saw his sister at the same moment she saw him.

There were three with her, advancing against the flow of people pushing through the doors. The four from the street were directly behind her. The six remaining below had taken up their positions surrounding the steps.

The memory pushed through. It was Europe again. It was training again. *Her planning. His response.*

Gloria had advanced past the hostess stand and through the plastic-coated chain. She was drawing her weapon, nearing the two men and approaching from directly behind Mark Ellis. Two others had moved into the public portion of the open area and were closing from his left.

She just learned I was here, he reasoned. *Otherwise, she would have been in place before I arrived.*

She hasn't had time to completely map this out.

He raised his right hand toward the double doors.

Throw a variable into the equation.

Mark Ellis dropped to the floor as the barrel of the Luger swung toward him.

Two shots. The first hit one of the rotating cameras over the door. The second bullet found the domed security device. The report of the shots was lost in the alarm. It was deafening, crashing and rebounding off the rock columns.

"Stay down." His voice was the only remaining aspect of calm in the cacophony. He saw Mark's head turn in response. "I'll be in touch." Noah Augusteel took two steps toward Mark and pivoted back toward the stone ledge. Gloria had dropped to the ground as the bullets passed over her head, but Noah knew she would instantly recover and take aim. He flipped the nearest table on its side. He felt a series of shots bounce off the iron. The reverberations ran along the metal and through his forearm.

Left. Noah's next shot destroyed the old crank holding one of the ropes. He could hear the confused panic below, on the street.

Madison was falling. The frayed rope swung free of the crank and shot upward. The massive banner rippled and billowed out away from the column. It was dropping on the crowd below.

Right. Another shot. Washington was following Madison.

The table behind him shielded him from three more shots. They deflected off the iron and clanged away from Augusteel.

It is 11:21. I am on the second-floor of an outdoor café.

Noah Augusteel turned and fired two more shots over the table. Bursts of stone exploded from the wall of the gallery. It bought him a split-second. He covered the two steps he had taken away from the ledge and jumped. He could feel the shards of stone fracturing from the ledge as the bullets passed his legs.

With his left hand he grabbed the side of the Madison banner. It was still attached at the base of the column. The border of it ran through his loose grip, slowing his descent to the pavement below.

∽

Mark Ellis saw him jump, but never saw him land. He crawled to the edge of the portico and looked out through the small stone posts that formed the body of the ornate half-wall. The buttons of his dress shirt were grinding against the café floor. He could feel the footsteps behind him, but between the noise rising from the street and the alarm he couldn't hear them.

It was pandemonium below. People were moving in all directions. Some were still trying to crawl out from under the banners. Their heads and hands looked like small, mobile pyramids under the fabric. He could see two police cars advancing along Eighth toward him. Gallery guards were mixing with the crowd. Some ran alongside the building, coming toward the front from the side doors. They were trying to enter the front doors. Mark saw others trying to exit through those same doors onto the sidewalk. Sirens down F

Street to his right. Tourists running down Eighth Street into the oncoming lights of the police cruisers.

He could not see Noah Augusteel anywhere in the roiling crowd.

His heart pounded against the floor. His breathing was spreading dust and dirt along the stone. Mark Ellis rolled onto his back and looked directly up at Gloria Augusteel. Her lips were moving. He couldn't tell if it was the storm of noise and action around him or the rush of adrenaline, but Mark couldn't hear what she said. The edge of her lips curled upward; it was something between a smile and a snarl, a knowing look that delivered its message: she had only begun to focus on the attorney at her feet.

Gloria Augusteel looked out over the edge of the café. The cry of the police sirens had reached the crowd below. She took one last look down at Mark Ellis, turned, and calmly walked back through the upturned tables of the Portico Café.

Chapter Twenty-Six

Washington, DC
July 1, 2010

He could still hear the calm voice of Noah Augusteel: *They've been watching you.*

Not *they are* or *they will*. "They have been," he had said.

At least they won't get lonely out there, Mark Ellis thought, as he surveyed the news vans stationed along Massachusetts Avenue. He had inspected them through the window of Luke Lyford's apartment over the last couple of hours. As evening had drawn in, two had pulled away from the curb. The others, he knew, would spend the night.

Mark looked around the vacant apartment. He had retreated here – the only safe haven he had – after leaving the National Portrait Gallery. He had given a brief, and extremely general, statement to the police after the shooting. Mark had no idea whether anyone would discover that he had left out some key details, like how he had recognized Gloria Augusteel and that Noah Augusteel had been there to meet with him. Yet, he knew it was only a matter of time before some intrepid media intern discovered his name in the police report and added his appearance at the café to the growing list of reasons the press had to follow him.

He reflexively checked the street below again.

A bilateral, unplanned media blackout was underway. And, rising from the quiet, still street below, he could sense the gnawing restlessness in the assembled media. He could read it in the rehashed coverage of the investigation. Its questions were going unanswered. It was going hungry. And, like a living mass, it stirred, searching.

Luke Lyford had been released from the federal holding facility without so much as an announcement. The DC newsrooms clamored for an explanation from the law enforcement agencies.

Parker Brown had hired an attorney – who just so happened to be the same attorney that was representing Luke Lyford. *Why hadn't the prosecutor informed them until after the hearing?* it asked.

Then Parker Brown was killed inside a guarded and secluded section of a federal courthouse. And there was no statement from his recently-hired attorney?

The media had found Mark Ellis. Now it waited on him to move.

He had reached Luke's apartment around one in the afternoon on Wednesday and, roughly a day and a half later, had come to fully appreciate the sentiment Luke had expressed during their first meeting: *trapped.* One by one the trucks had parked in front of the external door of the apartment building.

Mark crossed the white carpet spread across the bamboo floor of the small living area. In the background, he could hear the television: a panel of commentators was reviewing what had transpired during David Baker's confirmation hearings earlier that day. The process was well under way at this point. Days earlier, the few liberal Democratic Senators that opposed Senator Baker had said their piece. They had made their hopeless stand and then shuffled out of the public eye. After taking a break from the hearings on Wednesday, the committee had resumed, with David Baker's supporters entering the arena like the color guard of a conquering general. The first of the supporting witnesses had testified this morning.

Mark stopped, stood next to the coffee table in Luke's apartment, and watched some of the video footage running on the screen. The image served as a backdrop for the commentators' discussion. The wide camera angle showed almost the entire scope of the Senate Judiciary Committee's hearing room. A great wall of wood paneling gleamed along the back. In front of it, and raised from the floor, was the curved bench on which the Senators sat, perched above the remainder of the room.

He could see that each seat along the bench was filled. Except one. The seat directly to the right of the center seat – the center seat was the Chairman's – was empty. The empty seat was Senator David Baker's.

Baker was the senior member of his party on the committee. As the ranking Republican, he sat immediately to the Democratic Chairman's right. In front of the empty seat, Mark could see the gold-bordered nameplate: *Mr. Baker.* Behind it, he could see the seal of the United States Senate adorning the headrest of the empty, navy-blue chair that occupied the space.

Having left his seat along the panel, David Baker sat at the table in the center of the well, the open area in front of the curved bench. Mark could see the back of his chestnut hair, as well has the head of another man – presumably a witness that had been called to support Senator Baker. They sat side-by-side at the polished table.

Mark listened to the talking heads as he watched the images flash over the television. The heads agreed on the outcome: David Baker had already garnered enough commitments to secure his seat on the Supreme Court. They were calling it a "master stroke", a second win for President Anderson – exactly the sort of quick and decisive confirmation he needed after the untimely death of William Iredell.

The conservative train, they said, not only remained on the track, but was gaining steam. If things moved as planned, there would be more testimony in support of Senator Baker on the following day, Friday, and the hearing would conclude on Monday, with the final witnesses from the Anderson administration and the vote of the committee.

Mark continued through the apartment. The framed "Claire Ellis for Senate" campaign sign caught his eye, as it always did when he turned into the small kitchen. The blocked, blue letters stood out against the white background.

It had been over a day since he had heard from Luke. He was beyond fearing the worst; he now suspected it. Even more than that, part of him knew it.

With his right hand, Mark held the refrigerator open and bent at the waist to remove the fourth beer from the six-pack resting on the bottom shelf. He placed it on the stovetop next to the refrigerator and reached back down for the box of pizza. The last couple of slices slid inside the cardboard container as he closed the door and scooped the beer off the stovetop.

He had called the Echo office twice yesterday. Once again this morning. It was a dead-end. The receptionist would not even confirm that Luke Lyford had been there. "The identity of our visitors is confidential," her cheerful voice had explained. "It is Echo Industrial policy to protect their privacy." Mark had not even bothered to ask whether Gloria Augusteel was available to take his call.

He had nowhere to turn. What would he say if he called the police? The FBI? That a man on death row had told him about a secret organization? They would laugh him out of their office. A desperate effort from yet another desperate defense attorney.

That Gloria Augusteel was part of it? That she had unexpectedly been in the courtroom before Parker Brown had been shot? That she had been at the café and tried to kill Noah Augusteel?

"And why isn't this in the statement you gave to the police, Mr. Ellis?" he could hear them asking.

That Luke Lyford – the accused killer of a Supreme Court nominee, and Mark's client – was not only innocent, but had dropped off the radar after visiting Gloria Augusteel?

"And do you have proof that any crime has been committed, counselor?"

There was no reason to pursue this route. It was hopeless.

Was there any physical evidence linking Gloria Augusteel to Parker Brown's death? None that Mark knew of.

Was there any physical evidence that she was involved in the café shooting? Maybe, but Noah Augusteel had fired his first shots into the security system, one directly into the security camera. Chaos had broken out after that. He doubted that there was a credible eyewitness left in the restaurant by the time she had pulled her gun.

And she had managed to leave before the police reached the cafe. *Or had she been allowed to leave?* He thought.

In addition to all of this, there was one last reason why Mark knew he could not go to the police: he simply could not trust them. Parker Brown's killing had established that, beyond a reasonable doubt. Someone had created the opening for Gloria Augusteel. Where were the U.S. Marshals who were supposed to be escorting Brown? Where were the courthouse guards?

Someone had placed that Phenobarbital in Luke's apartment and the only persons he had seen holding the poison had "FBI" emblazed on their windbreakers or "U.S. Attorney" emblazoned on her business card.

He was on his own.

Mark walked back toward the living area, eyeing the dimming lights of the city beyond the glass. He could hear a truck pass on the street below. It reminded him of the vans and the video cameras lurking outside.

He was on his own. *Trapped and alone.*

☙

As he laid the red-and-white cardboard pizza box on the end table, the thought settled on him: *what am I supposed to do now?* Both of his clients were gone – one dead, the other most likely. Moreover, his only source of information about his mother's death had died with Parker Brown.

Mark shoved the end of one of the cold slices of pepperoni pizza in his mouth. He gripped the slice between his teeth as his hands started to flip through the pile of mail that had accumulated on Luke's coffee table over the last two days. A few pieces of junk mail and a community newsletter were tossed aside. He tore the remainder of the slice from his mouth and dropped it back in the open pizza box.

Midway through the stack of mail, he stopped chewing and stared at the envelope in his hands. *The test results.* In all that had happened since the Brown hearing he had completely forgotten about the sample of the Madison letter he had provided to the Georgetown chemistry professor.

At Luke's suggestion, Mark had cut off a small piece of the stained portion of the Madison letter. The piece was cut from the copy of the letter Luke had received from William Iredell. The stain – whatever it was – had appeared to Mark to run through each of the three pages of the document. After providing the small portion of the letter, Mark had simply asked the professor to identify whatever chemicals he could find in the paper, and to mail his results back to Luke's apartment when he had finished.

He discarded the rest of the pile and nudged the unopened PBR can to the side of the table. Inside the package, there was a two-page report along with a cover letter from the professor. The cover letter explained that a great deal of alcohol was present in the sample. However, other chemicals also were found during the testing. The attached report, according to the cover letter, described the results of the analytical tests the professor had run.

His briefcase was sitting in the chair on the opposite side of the small living area – exactly where he had dropped it when he returned from the café. Mark removed the documents he had been carrying in the case and found the toxicology report that he had received over email, the one from the anonymous email account.

Mark laid the anonymous toxicology report on the coffee table in front of him and scanned the test results, his finger tracing the right column of the one-page document. At each of the six chemicals whose presence had been "significant" in William Iredell's blood, he stopped and compared the anonymous report with the testing results that he had just received in the mail. *Ethanol? Yes. Mebeverine? Yes.* He moved through the other chemicals until he reached the final one.

Amobarbital?

Yes. The test had found it in the stained corner of the Madison letter. The results were a near-perfect match with the anonymous toxicology test. He looked down at the words scrawled in black marker on the anonymous toxicology report: "lethal dose."

Next, Mark reached for the official toxicology report, the document Carol Cushing had handed out on the steps of the apartment building. He checked the right column. None of the chemicals that had been found in the Madison letter's stain were listed in the official report.

The documents were back on the table. He was sinking into the couch. The large window to his right was dark. He had silenced the television in front of him, but the muted images flickered into the room. Mark Ellis closed his eyes and turned on the couch, laying his head on one of the pillows and crossing his bare feet on the armrest near the wall-sized window.

Slow down, he told himself. *Slow down and think through what you know.*

He tried to mentally line up the facts. William Iredell had dropped this letter off in the Capitol's mail system before he died. Therefore, Mark concluded, the letter was with Iredell shortly before he died.

The letter was exposed to a specific set of six chemicals. It must have somehow soaked them up because the chemicals were in the stained part of the letter. The six chemicals were also present in Iredell's blood, according to the anonymous toxicology report.

Since they matched, Mark reasoned, it seemed very likely that the anonymous report was the accurate of the two on the table. And therefore, according to the note on the report – as well as the online research Mark had done – it seemed like Amobarbital was the poison that had killed William Iredell.

It was not, as Carol Cushing believed, and had told the press, Phenobarbital.

His next thought was about Luke Lyford. *If I provide the Madison letter to the cops maybe I can get the charges dropp . . . .* He stopped, the thought incomplete. *Luke may be dead. There may not be a trial. There may not be any more charges to disprove.*

Each step he took toward a firm acknowledgement that Luke may be dead was more painful than the one before it. But with each passing minute, the conclusion became more and more likely.

Mark Ellis opened his eyes and stared at the ceiling of Luke's apartment. He let his eyes trace the pipes in the exposed ceiling, following one, then another as they ran into the wall. He could see the thin layer of insulation and the small, black, plastic pipes holding the electrical wires. Mark followed one pipe as it ran from near the kitchen to the light over his head. The dome of the light triggered something in his memory. *The security cameras in the attorney-visitation rooms. Parker Brown glancing at the domed security camera the first time they met, trying to convince Mark to sign on as his attorney.*

Parker Brown's infuriating game of questions and answers. The guard pulling Brown away from the glass divider. The question as he was pulled away from the room.

Amobarbital?

Mark dropped his feet to the floor. *Where are those notes from that conversation?* He flipped through documents and legal pads until he found the hand-written notes buried in one of the interior pockets of his briefcase. It wasn't Brown's question about Amobarbital that he wanted to find. It was something else, something the prisoner had said in their second conversation.

Mark thumbed through his notes until he found Brown's comments about Amobarbital. Parker Brown had explained why he had expected Amobarbital, and not Phenobarbital, to be in William Iredell's blood. In the process, he had walked Ellis through a rather long history lesson, one that stretched back to the late 1700s.

He double-checked his notes. His memory was correct. Brown had mentioned scopolamine. According to Brown that was the modern name of one of the chemicals in the poison the Lexington League had been using. An image of Parker Brown pointing out the word "scopolamine" in the anonymous report flashed through Mark's mind, the word ringing like a bell as he reached for the anonymous toxicology report to confirm his memory.

Scopolamine. A significant amount was present in Iredell's blood.

Mark grabbed the report from the chemist. *Scopolamine.* It was also present in the stained part of letter.

His pulse was rising. Energy, but a restless energy. He walked toward the large window. Mark could see himself, weeks before, in the sunlight. He was holding the two copies of Madison's letter to the window and examining the stain.

The vans were still below. The motionless skulking of a stakeout. He paced back through the living area. He was making connections. *The poison on the letter matches the poison in Iredell's blood. Therefore, the anonymous toxicological results are the accurate results.*

According to Parker Brown, the Lexington League uses a poison with Amobarbital and scopolamine – a poison that has the same chemical composition as one that killed William Iredell. Therefore . . .

He couldn't quite get himself to believe.

He was face-to-face with the campaign sign. He retraced a few steps, turned, and paced down the hall. Then back into the living area. *Could this really be true?*

As Mark Ellis reached the apartment door he rotated on his bare feet. From his vantage point he surveyed the apartment. He could see the living area. The open pizza box was on the end table. Its lid rested against the lamp shade. His briefcase, open on the couch. Images of the Baker hearing replayed on the television screen. Outside the glass window on the far side of the room, the night and the media waited.

The dark-wood coffee table stood silent, an anchor in the center of the room. The two toxicology reports. The test results on the Madison letter had been dropped on top of them. To the side, his document folder, holding the copies of the letter. His PBR can, unopened. He stared at it all.

Sweat streaked down the face of his fourth PBR can of the evening.

Mark Ellis recalled standing in this same spot weeks before, on the day of Luke's arrest. It was the same place he had stood after following Carol Cushing into the apartment. He could see the ghosts of the FBI agents searching, overturning the furniture. He could hear her making the case against Luke Lyford, leading Mark through the apartment. *Means. Motive. Opportunity.*

The translucent ghost of her extended three fingers lingered ahead of Mark. Her confident, insulting tone filled his recollection. *Means, motive, and opportunity. That is why your client is under arrest and that is how I intended to convict him.*

His thoughts were flowing now.

Means.

William Iredell was poisoned. The evidence indicates that he was exposed to a specific set of six chemicals prior to his death. Amobarbital is one of the six. Amobarbital is a particularly deadly poison. The Lexington League has used Amobarbital for generations, according to Parker Brown.

His mind found one other voice. Noah Augusteel. *The Iredell hit fits the league's MO – its modus operandi. You know, how we get stuff done.*

Opportunity.

The hole in the Iredell timeline. The FBI had initially focused on Luke Lyford because he was the last person that Iredell called before he died. This was an understandable approach: Iredell had contacted Luke on the same day as his death.

But what about the last person that had *actually seen* Iredell?

Mark raced for his notes, scrambling through the pages. The FBI had been obligated to disclose the information since he was Luke's attorney, and he knew the information was somewhere in this pile. Seconds later, Mark laid his hands on the exact page he wanted. Again – as with the drug Parker Brown had mentioned – his memory was accurate. An appellate judge had been with Iredell. He had walked with Iredell through downtown DC after the confirmation hearing. Mark checked the date: the night before Iredell's death. The judge and William Iredell had parted, according to the judge's interview with the FBI, near the corner of K Street and 14th.

His laptop came to life and Mark opened a map of downtown DC. *An ice cream store. A park. An embassy. Some law firms?* Could that be it?

There it was. *The Lexington League. 1290 K St., Washington D.C.* Just west of the corner of K Street and 14th.

The opportunity had been there. He moved to the last element.

Motive.

This was the hardest part for Mark Ellis. The point of no return. His Rubicon. To believe the motive was to believe the case.

He reached for the Madison letter. *James Madison writing to James Wilson. Two Founding Fathers. Two giants of the American Revolution; two great minds of the Constitutional Convention.* Mark turned to the third page. As he held the document, he could still recall his conversation with Luke.

Luke had paced. Mark had been stationed on the couch.

Mark re-read the key phrase: "To each generation, its own interpretation." If this was, in fact, James Madison's thinking then the phrase had the potential to upset an entire legal doctrine, to undermine much of the conservative side of the judicial ledger. It could undercut the goals and objectives of a generation of Lexington League scholars and attorneys.

If William Iredell had the original and believed this was actually the work of James Madison . . .

And William Iredell had just been given a lifetime appointment on the Supreme Court, where he would determine the proper manner to interpret the Constitution . . .

Did the Lexington League kill William Iredell because he had this letter?

The thought echoed off the clean walls of the quiet apartment. It fit with what Noah Augusteel had told him in the café. *Somehow the league learned about some letter Iredell's family had been keeping for generations.*

The next thought came directly on the heels of the prior one. *And they killed Parker Brown because they thought he was going to expose them.*

The next conclusion followed after half a heartbeat. *And they killed Luke because he knew what Parker Brown had revealed to me.*

Am I next? The idea struck him and twisted his head toward the window.

They are watching.

He forced himself back to his original train of thought. *If Parker Brown was telling the truth about the Lexington League, was he telling the truth about my mother's death?*

The skepticism was fading.

He could hear Noah Augusteel: *Force must be met with force.*

He could see Parker Brown's arm reaching through the bars of the holding cell. He could hear the gunshots in the café; the crescendo of panic rising over the railing, boiling up from the street. He could hear Noah Augusteel's voice again: *Some things are just about revenge.*

Mark closed his eyes again. In the self-imposed darkness, the question remained. He needed a name. Not Gloria Augusteel. He wanted the person directing her actions.

He wanted *the* name. He wanted the one at the top.

Chapter Twenty-Seven

Edenton, North Carolina
July 2, 2010

John Baker dragged the white, paper napkin over his lips and glanced at the clock in the lower right corner of his computer screen. He had fifteen minutes until his next meeting.

He reached for the drink on the left-hand side of his desk, bridging over a pile of investigative reports to reach the small space he had temporarily cleared to hold the Styrofoam cup of sweet tea. The napkin beneath the cup was wet, and it stuck to the bottom of the cup as he lifted it. Flicking it off, the federal prosecutor watched it drop back into a valley between two of the mountains of paperwork.

He took a healthy sip of the tea as his right hand worked to dig through the piles on his desk. The DVD was somewhere in the mounds of manila and recycled white. It was the one from the Johansson speech, and he needed it. John Baker returned the condensation-covered cup to its corner and dug both hands into the piles of paper. He was standing now, towing his red tie over the mountains as he moved from one side of his wooden desk to the other.

There had been no substantial updates on the Johansson case since the FBI agent had mailed him the video of the victim's final speech. In fact, there had hardly been any communication at all, until this morning. Agent Kittleson had called and asked for – actually, the agent had more or less demanded – a meeting. And he had stressed the need to meet in person. In the privacy of Baker's office.

And so one more appointment had been added to John Baker's calendar, landing dead in the middle of the small break he had carved out for lunch. His dream of a relaxing Friday lunch had been buried. Instead of meeting his family at Bunn's Barbeque, he had been forced to cancel. Again. Instead, his wife and kids had dropped off the sandwich he was now halfway through, along with the fried okra and slaw that remained untouched in the container on his credenza.

Where is that DVD? John Baker had worked his way through the piles of folders on his desk. He turned to the few piles that had migrated to the low bookshelves behind him. Finally, he found what he was looking for. Ignored over the last week, it had worked its way to the bottom of one of the stacks. He took another bite of his sandwich and dropped it back into the white Styrofoam as he loaded the Johansson DVD into his computer.

Between monitoring his father's confirmation hearing and trying to manage a series of new drug investigations that had cropped up, John Baker was losing ground on his caseload.

The new drug investigations had been especially difficult. Two North Carolina State Troopers had made six separate arrests over the past two weeks. Each had followed the same pattern.

The Troopers, riding in the same patrol vehicle, would closely follow a vehicle on Interstate 95, the major north-south highway that bisected John Baker's prosecutorial district. It was a major narcotics pipeline between Florida and New York City. After a mile or so of following the vehicle, the Troopers would engage their siren and lights, and direct the other car to the side of the road. At that point, one of the officers would always explain to the driver that he had crossed into a neighboring lane without signaling. The other officer would circle the car and examine the interior compartment of the vehicle through the windows.

In each of the arrests, the driver had been removed based on what the officers would later describe as "an unwillingness to comply with their directives." The officers then – considering this to be probable cause to conduct a wider search – would search the entire vehicle. On six occasions they had found a substantial amount of narcotics in the trunk of the car.

The repetition and similarity bothered John, as did another question. *Who knows how many times they have pulled this maneuver and found nothing in the car?*

The six arrested drivers, being most likely interstate drug-traffickers, had then been turned over to federal agents for prosecution. And so, earlier that morning, John Baker had found himself asking some pointed questions about the arrest procedure. The Captain, to whom the troopers reported, had called to find out when he would need to make the Troopers available to testify against the arrested drivers. With as much tact as his doubt would allow, Baker had asked a few questions about the nature of the arrests. *Wasn't the Captain at all concerned about the way these people had been arrested? The way the cars had been searched? Did he really believe that these two Troopers — in a span of two weeks — just happened to see six cars cross over a dividing line? And felt the need to pull each of these cars over? And that each of these drivers had failed to comply with the orders they had given at the scene? And then each of these cars just happened to have a load of drugs in the trunk?*

The conversation had quickly deteriorated into a one-sided shouting match, with the Captain all but accusing Baker of working hand-in-hand with an East Coast drug cartel.

"I don't care if I sound like a defense attorney, Captain." Baker voice remained steady, but had taken on a more authoritative tone. "I look at these reports and I start to get the distinct impression that your boys are out there randomly stopping cars and then coming up with a pretext for a search."

The Captain had violently tried to defend the arrests. In response, John Baker's eyes had rolled, and then landed on the undeveloped lot next to his office. Through the window behind his desk he could see a magnolia tree. Its wide leaves were catching the summer wind and swaying the branches. It stood next to three quiet pines in the untouched lot.

The Captain continued to yell into his ear, but the words were simply fading into the background as Baker's mind wandered from his desk chair. The Captain was shouting something — something about how Baker had better "get serious about his new job or he wouldn't last too long."

Part of him admired the Captain. There weren't many mid-level employees in the law-enforcement community that would sandblast a U.S. Attorney like the Captain was giving it to Baker. Much less, one whose father was a U.S. Senator and was days away from being appointed to the Supreme Court. However, John Baker had never flexed his family's political muscle to settle a dispute. He was certainly not going to do so simply because he was tired of hearing the Captain's empty threat. *Just let him burn himself out*, he thought.

He scanned the pictures of his family along the top of the credenza, his chair shifting to the right as he moved through the pictures. He re-read, for the thousandth time, the Samuel Adams quote from his father: *The liberties of our country, the freedom of our civil Constitution, are worth defending at all hazards; and it is our duty to defend them against all attacks . . . .*

Eventually the Captain, red-faced in John's mental image, took a breath, and John Baker calmly spoke into the phone. "Sir, I appreciate your position," he started. "However, let me make this very clear: I am going to take a thorough, and complete, look at each of those arrests. If I believe I can convict the defendants, we'll move forward.

"If I don't, I'm dropping the charges."

The Captain tried to interject, but John cut him off. "In the meantime – and from here on out – I expect everyone in your command to 'get serious' about the Fourth Amendment. I've got far too many cases on my docket to waste time with illegal searches and seizures. I took an oath to protect and defend the Constitution. I'm going to do that – whether I'm protecting it from two overzealous Troopers, drug mules running up I-95, or anyone else.

"Thank you for your call, Captain. I will let you know if we need the Troopers to testify."

The Captain did not immediately respond. John waited a second or two and then lowered the receiver back onto its cradle.

∽

The DVD had loaded on his computer and was replaying the scene from the front porch of the Barker house. John cleared a space and settled his lunch tray onto his desk. He unfurled the napkin, letting the plastic fork fall into his hand. Alternating between mouthfuls of fried okra and coleslaw, he watched Everett Johansson pacing along the porch. He recalled the beginning of the video from the last time he had watched it. It also matched his memory from being in the crowd that day. He again watched as Johansson entertained the crowd. The North Carolina flag was motionless, standing guard on the far side of the porch.

Toward the middle portion of the speech, the image began to shake as the videographer turned toward the crowd. The camera caught the glare of the sun as it hit the lens. Johansson disappeared from view as the camera panned the attentive faces of the crowd. Briefly Baker saw himself, sitting in the second row, next to his wife. In the direct sunlight, her winding, blonde curls radiated through the computer screen.

He realized that this was where he had stopped watching the video the first time. During that initial viewing, he had let it play in the background, listening to Johansson's final march through history. But he had not actually watched this part; he hadn't been interested in the amateurish recording of the crowd.

Baker reached for his sandwich and took another bite, catching a small piece of barbeque as it fell from the opposite side of the bun. He tilted his head back and dropped it in his mouth.

The slow-motion roll of the camera had nearly covered the entire crowd. It closed toward the edge of the faces, the last row of chairs. Baker could see the tables of empty metal food containers and large cylindrical coolers enter the shot. The high-noon sun that had crested the sky during Johansson's speech glared of the greasy metal of the semi-empty pans. He could tell every eye in the crowd was on Everett Johansson. The videographer started to shift the view back the way it had come, overlooking the crowd once again as the camera presumably started its arc back to the porch.

My God.

Baker had been reaching for the Styrofoam cup. His arm froze in midair.

My God.

Could that be him?

The image had, at one time, been etched in his mind. After all the hours he had logged in front of his old office's DVD player, he thought he would never forget the face. *It's been two years.*

He wasn't quite sure. Baker reached for his mouse and backed the DVD up a few minutes. He clicked the Play arrow on the video program and watched as the image rolled back into the crowd.

The videographer was on the left side of the porch, from the perspective of the audience. As the young man had turned to record the crowd, he had revolved on the same spot. The image John Baker was seeing, accordingly, was a direct shot of the faces in front of the videographer, a direct image of the left side of the crowd. Baker could again see the line of tables on the right side of the screen.

Pause. The same bleach-blond hair? Just as it had with his wife's, the noon sunlight was emphasizing the near-white color. He could see the man. His eyes were fixed on Everett Johansson.

To the man's right, John Baker could see another head of glowing blonde. *A woman?* He asked himself. It was difficult to tell from the angle of the camera. Her head was turned away from the stage, like she was watching something in the crowd. Her hair was either short or had been pulled tight behind her head. The more John Baker studied her the more he realized that she was clearly not paying attention to Everett Johansson's speech. The blond woman looked bored, like she was simply waiting for the speech to end.

Baker quickly shifted his concentration back to the male. The camera was exactly in line with his face, and less than twenty feet away. *It really does look like the same man.*

He reached for his phone. From memory, he dialed his old office.

The female voice on the other line was familiar, as well as welcoming. "District Attorney's Office."

"Suzanne. It's John Baker. How are you?"

"Well," her southern drawl drew out the word for a few syllables. "I guess United States Attorney John Baker does remember his old friends," she joked. "How can I help you, John?"

"I need someone to dig out that old video from the Claire Ellis investigation, the one from her last campaign event. Should be in a 2008 file. And – I hate to say it – but I really need someone to run it over here right away."

৩৯

John Baker was still staring at the blond-haired man, the face paused and frozen on his monitor, when his secretary's

DREW NELSON

voice brought him back to the present. "Mr. Baker. Agent Kittleson is here, sir."

"Thank you. Please send him back."

Baker rose from his chair as his partially open office door was gently pushed the rest of the way by his secretary. She held it open as the solid face of the FBI agent entered. Kittleson crossed the short distance to Baker's desk in two lengthy, no-nonsense strides.

"Mr. Baker, I appreciate you seeing me in person, sir." He glanced back over his shoulder. The unattached ear piece dangling on his shoulder swung with his head, bouncing over the front of his shoulder then back into its original position.

"No problem, Agent. Have a seat." Baker waved his hand toward the open seat across from his desk as he returned to the large chair behind it.

Kittleson hesitated before he accepted the seat, retraced his two steps to the office door, and quietly closed it.

Baker's assistant had opened the window along the side wall of his office earlier that morning. The summer breeze that had been moving the magnolia leaves eased its way in. Behind Agent Kittleson, Baker could see the heavy folds of the American flag giving way to the breeze. Slowly, they turned, touching the file cabinet in the corner of his office and then yielding back to gravity as the breeze weakened.

As he did the last time – as he probably had a hundred times before – Agent Carl Kittleson reached into the interior pocket of his dark-blue coat and removed his hand-sized, spiral notepad. Moving with what looked to John Baker like sheer muscle memory, Kittleson flipped deep into the small notepad, rotating the white pages over the metal rings along the top. He found what he was looking for about halfway through.

Baker's eyes flicked to the right as Kittleson searched his notes. The image from Johansson's speech was still on the screen. The blond hair. The cobalt eyes, stilled in the shot, but obviously trained on the old man to the left of the camera.

Although he was certain, Baker double-checked the angle: Kittleson could not see the computer screen from his seat across the desk. Baker weighed whether to discuss his theory with the agent. On the one hand, it could be an incredibly important connection in an otherwise stalled investigation. On the other hand, he simply was not sure that it was the same man.

As John Baker debated, Kittleson spoke up. "There have not been many new developments in the Everett Johansson investigation," he started. His eyes lifted from his notes to meet John Baker's. "Have you had a chance to review the video?"

"I have."

"We've been trying to use it to identify all of the people that might have been in contact with Mr. Johansson on the day of the history tour. We're working our way through the crowd. The victim gave the speech on a Saturday." His voice was methodical. Unemotional. He was simply detailing a list of facts.

"The medical examiner has examined the body." He continued, now reading from his notes as he briefed the attorney. "Her opinion is that he was likely killed that same Saturday. However, she doesn't believe that she'll be able to give us a concrete time of death. A few days passed between when the victim was killed and when she had a chance to examine the body. That being said, our working theory is that he was likely killed that Saturday or that Saturday night, in the museum."

Baker had reclined in his leather chair and was taking notes on the yellow legal pad stretched over his crossed leg.

"Unfortunately," the FBI agent explained, closing his notepad, "we've made little progress on suspects." There was something in his voice, a hesitancy that wasn't there moments before.

John Baker noted that the agent had used the word "little" instead of the word "no" when describing their search for a suspect. FBI agents typically prided themselves on the exactness of their speech – and Kittleson, Baker could immediately tell, was no exception. As he looked up from his legal pad, he wondered whether there had been *some* progress. Why else would he use the word "little"? *Do they know about the blond man in the crowd?*

Kittleson had returned his small notebook to his coat pocket and was looking to his right. He was reaching downward toward the base of his chair. The far side of Baker's desk rose too high to allow him to see Kittleson's hand from the reclined position of his desk chair.

"It took our crime scene agents a while to find it, but they located it yesterday." Kittleson had bent to his side and looked like he was searching for something in his briefcase. He sat back up. "They found it wedged far underneath the locked storage boxes – the set of boxes that were in the room with the body." Agent Kittleson looked up from the bended position he was holding in the chair. He saw the quizzical look in Baker's eyes.

"I'm sorry," the FBI agent said in response to the confused look from the prosecutor. "I'm talking about the visitor log from the museum. The book that visitors sign as they come in the front door. I believe I mentioned, in our first meeting, that it was missing from its usual location. One of the volunteers from the museum – the one helping our investigator – told us that it was kept at the desk in the foyer. It wasn't there when we searched the crime scene."

Kittleson's iron spine straightened in his chair and he raised the visitor's log from the Iredell Family House onto his lap. It was an oversized book, heavy and bound with a thick cover. Even closed, it spread over the both legs of the FBI agent. "As I mentioned, our investigator spotted it under the set of storage boxes that the museum used to protect some of the more important documents. We're not sure how it ended up there." He was flipping through the wide pages of the ornate book. Baker could see the double rows of signatures as the pages spun through Kittleson's hands.

The hands slowed, then stopped. John Baker could see the agent's auburn eyes quickly scanning the page of signatures. Kittleson seemed to find the one he was looking for. For a few seconds, the agent was unexpectedly quiet. The break felt strange. It was a departure from the agent's checklist, matter-of-fact briefing style – and it got Baker's attention.

Kittleson looked up from the columns of signatures and met Baker's line of sight. "There is a name in here you need to see, sir." He lifted the thick book and rotated it in the air, setting its spine on top of a stack of papers on Baker's desk. The weighty cover of the book and the rounded piles of its long pages opened over the mounds of folders. The agent pointed to the date at the top of the column as he stood facing the desk. "This is from the last Friday before Johansson's speech. Presumably, the day before he was killed." His finger followed the page down, directing Baker to a name toward the end of the left column.

Baker rocked forward in his seat, the legal pad folded under his arm. He rose to his feet, leaning over his lunch, toward the front portion of the desk. His eyes followed the signature column to Kittleson's index finger.

The "D" was clear, as it always was. The "B" was semi-legible. Everything else – the loops and angles of the signature – took much more liberty with traditional cursive style.

But John Baker knew the signature at first sight: David Baker. It was his father's signature.

Agent Kittleson left the book open on the desk and sat back down in the chair opposite John Baker.

What was my father doing in the Iredell Family museum on the day before Everett Johansson was murdered?

A second thought came to John Baker as he silently returned to his seat. *What was he doing in the Iredell House hours before they found William Iredell's body?*

"Thanks, Agent Kittleson. I appreciate you handling this discretely." John Baker gave nonchalance his best effort. "I'll get in touch with him and find out what his name is doing in this book."

꩜

It was later that afternoon before John Baker could get in touch with his father. Senator David Baker's hearings had concluded around two and he had immediately retreated to his Senate office to meet with a small team of attorneys from the White House and a handful of Republican strategists. Numerous supporters – and some opponents – had been scheduled to appear on the Sunday morning news shows. Everyone needed to be on the same political page over the critical final weekend. The committee was scheduled to vote on his nomination on Monday. Their team was not going to fumble on the goal line.

"Dad. It's me. Hearings go OK today?" John Baker was walking through the front door, entering the office's reception area from the street. The small waiting room had the conservative decoration of most U.S. Attorney offices. A picture of the President. A picture of the Attorney General. The North Carolina flag in the corner stood immobile behind his assistant's desk, opposite the American flag near the door.

His assistant caught his eye as he entered the room. "For you." She mouthed the words as he passed. She held a DVD in her hand, reaching over her desk to hold it in Baker's path.

He lifted it from her hand as he walked toward the hallway. "Claire Ellis Video" had been hand-written across the folded paper underneath the plastic case.

"I'm glad to hear that," he responded into the phone, after listening to his father's summary of the day's hearings and the game-plan for the weekend's news shows. "Yeah. We're coming up there tomorrow."

Another break in his side of the conversation. Baker moved down the carpeted hallway toward his door, the sound of his footsteps dissolving into the plush material. He entered as his father finished speaking.

"Listen, Dad, the FBI just came by here with the visitor's log from the Iredell Family House."

There was silence on the other end. John Baker considered, for a split-second, whether he had lost the connection between the cell phones.

"Hello? You there?"

He closed the office door behind him and stood in the center of the red carpet. In a half-sitting position, he leaned his weight against the arm of the chair Agent Kittleson had sat in earlier that day. His chestnut-colored head tilted slightly to the left as he held the phone to his ear. Baker could imagine a mirror image taking place in his father's Senate office.

He heard his father answer in the affirmative. He was still on the line. It was a short answer. Then another pause.

"You know Everett Johansson's murder falls under federal jurisdiction, right? They are probably going to be getting in touch with you about the log book. It may happen as early as this weekend."

John Baker closed his eyes as his father spoke. This time the response was much longer.

Through the open window behind him he could hear the first drops of rain hitting the pavement.

∽

After he hung up with his father, John Baker slumped into the dark-green, leather chair facing the front of his desk. An afternoon thunderstorm had blown in from the Atlantic. The sky had darkened outside and waves of rain were drenching the pine-straw covered lot next to his office. He could hear them rhythmically pounding the window behind his desk.

He watched the magnolia leaves moving outside his window. They were bouncing haphazardly, battered by the falling rain. In the foreground, his eyes traced the faces of his family in the pictures on the credenza. The Samuel Adams quote, carved into the piece of the old stagecoach.

A gift from my father, he thought.

To his left, the other office window remained open. Cars were passing in the street. John Baker could hear their wheels spraying puddled water along the sidewalk. He thought about the consequences of what his father had just told him. *It feels strange to sit on this side*, he thought. The storm had dropped the temperature by a few degrees and a cool breeze was blowing into his office. He noticed how the air seemed to flow much better on this side of his desk.

He mindlessly turned his cell phone in his hands, spinning it and passing it from one hand to the other as he studied the piles of folders on his desk. After a few more contemplative minutes he walked around the side of his desk, trailing his hand along the curved edge of the cherry.

Baker inserted the DVD from his old office in his computer. It was the same familiar video from the Claire Ellis investigation. He fast-forwarded through her speech, quickly reaching the first image of the man he had never identified.

There he was. Approaching Ellis as she walked toward her plane. It felt like déjà vu.

It surprised him how easily the timing came back. He reacted to the movements of the man, his steps. He had watched him a hundred times. Probably more. He knew the exact moment when he would give the camera a slight glimpse of his face. The only view of his face the man had ever offered to John Baker.

Until now.

Pause. His face. His blond hair.

The same face. The same blond hair.

John Baker opened his internet browser and looked up a phone number he never thought he would need. He spoke four sentences into his cell phone before hanging up.

"Can I leave an important message for Mark Ellis?"

"Can you get in touch with him today?"

"Please tell him John Baker needs to meet with him. It's about his mother and it's urgent."

Part Five

Chapter Twenty-Eight

Washington, DC
July 2, 2010

In one sense, the trouble had started roughly two years ago, in the summer of 2008.

What began as whispers in hallways and at quiet restaurant tables had grown with Claire Ellis's standing in the polls. She was surging in the North Carolina Senate race, drawing closer to David Baker by the week. The whispers had grown into questions – sometimes vocalized, sometimes unstated. The questions had grown into open insurrection, and the insurrection into an unofficial meeting in the formal drawing room of Four's country house.

The servants dismissed for the evening, Four had served the other three himself. The room smelled of leather and antiques, of wood-polish and scotch, of wealth and legacy. Tucked away in the Tidewater region, near the Virginia coast, the four people could feel the seclusion. It had taken weeks to organize, but they had found a safe place away from Washington, somewhere they could openly talk.

So this is where it happens, Five had thought. *This is how it starts*. She was the group's most recent inductee and had paced, circling the Oriental rug, time and again. Two had led the discussion. Four had mostly listened as the dissatisfaction with their leader swelled to a boiling point.

"He is unwilling to do what must be done. It is just that simple," Three had said. "Or – if not unwilling – he is simply unable." Three's sentiment had been the group's sentiment; his thoughts, their thoughts. Most importantly, his conclusion had been their conclusion: Parker Brown had to be removed. He no longer had their support, and without it, he could no longer lead the Lexington League.

None of the four in the room misunderstood the consequences of their vote. If they were going to remove Parker Brown, the vote needed to be unanimous, and it had been.

It had also been, they believed, unprecedented. Never before had four of the five turned against *the one*, as far as the remaining four knew. Of course, there had been examples in their history of members leaving the five. Some departures had been due to death; others had essentially retired as they crept toward old age. There had also been some examples of more forceful exits, even violent ones – but never against *the one*, the person at the top.

So far as they knew. It was a point they all had recognized. There were always five at the table, but only those five knew which one was actually *the one*. Therefore, they pondered, there was really no way of knowing what sort of internal shuffling had transpired before their time.

Maybe this isn't so unprecedented after all, Five had considered, her nervous steps crossing behind Four, her nervous eyes taking in the spacious room for the hundredth time and noting the distinguished gray hair of their host. *Maybe there had been others before Parker Brown, other leaders that had failed to act when action was required. Maybe there had been other* Ones *that had been removed prior to the ascension of Four, the longest serving member of the current five – and thus the person with the longest memory.*

While it momentarily intrigued Five to consider their decision in this historical context, touching on the potential uniqueness of the moment had no impact on her decision. The time had come. Claire Ellis was rising, gaining strength in her Senate campaign. Something had to be done. Five knew that. They all knew that. Yet, Parker Brown was unwilling.

෴

It was late summer 2008. Quietly they put the pieces of their plan in place. Only the most discreet, the most trusted assets – and only a very limited number of those – had been brought into the operation. The first step had been the easiest: eliminate the threat of Claire Ellis.

Parker Brown grew suspicious after Ellis's plane crash. He already regarded his fellow members warily, and he certainly could recognize the hand of the league in the death of Claire Ellis – even if the hand was acting without the head.

The plane crash changed the top level of the Lexington League, changed the relationship between Parker Brown and the other four. It wasn't an open dispute; it was an undercurrent.

~~

It was early 2009. The four secretly met again and hashed out the details of the final stage. Over the next few months the pieces were lined up on the board, the evidence gathered, and the witnesses identified. By the summer, the plot was set and the four went about determining how to influence each witness. They each understood that a trial against Parker Brown would damage Echo Industrial. But the secretive paramilitary organization would survive, even if its chief executive did not. The process began, and once it started, it moved forward rapidly, and of its own volition.

December brought the first winds of winter and the arrest. Parker Brown and his driver passed through the iron gates marking the exit of Echo Industrial's administrative complex and drove directly into the waiting arms of the FBI.

As Two had guaranteed, the trial came quickly after the arrest. A charge of treason against a figure such as Parker Brown easily landed the case at the front of the docket. It moved swiftly toward conviction, just as Two had promised.

Seven days after Carol Cushing gave her opening statement, Parker Brown was convicted, and effectively removed as the leader of the Lexington League. The implied threat against his family, unspoken but still potent, found its mark: he was going to quietly spend the last weeks of his life in a prison cell in Maryland.

As the jury read its verdict, Two became One.

And Three took his place as the new Two. The distinguished, gray-haired Four became Three. And Five took her first relaxed breath in nearly two years and became Four.

❦

It was July 2, 2010.

The fifth side of the five-sided table was empty, as it had been since the other four had moved against Parker Brown. It was Friday night and the remaining four had gathered for the first time since Brown's arrest. It was also the first time since the ascension of their new leader that they had gathered in this room: their conference room atop the Lexington League offices in Washington.

One gently tapped the side of his drink against the hard edge of the table. The hollow thump of the heavy glass gathered the attention of the other three. Two and Four had been quietly speaking to each other, already in their seats at the conference table. The backs of their chairs tilted toward the bank of windows behind them, and the lights of the city that dotted the late DC night. Three had filled his glass at the small wet bar to One's right and had made his way toward Madison's portrait. He had been examining the picture when One's glass had shifted their gathering toward the business of the evening. He took his seat to One's right. To Three's right was the open chair. A vacancy they would soon have to fill – although that problem was of less immediacy than the others at hand.

"Thank you all for making yourselves available tonight," One started. The view from One's chair extended across the open table and ran parallel along the long axis of the room. The elevators doors were directly ahead and their presence was momentarily distracting.

An image of William Iredell. Stumbling backwards into the doors. Holding himself as the elevator climbed, as the doors opened. Falling back, across the threshold.

Above him. Pouring their two drinks onto his unconscious chest, dousing the hands that instinctively protected the folded copy of Madison's letter secured in the chest pocket of his coat.

Shortly after One had poisoned William Iredell, the other three had been notified. Whether they agreed or disagreed with One's actions was irrelevant. Whether they considered it rushed or foolishly hasty was immaterial. The decision – like all decisions – had been One's to make.

"I've asked you to gather this evening to discuss a few aspects of our current . . . ." There was a pause as One searched for the word. ". . . situation." One had the full attention of the group. The conference room was quiet. The offices below had emptied earlier that evening. The dense glass window kept the Friday-night sounds at bay.

"First, our former leader," One started, referring to Parker Brown.

"As you all know, our hand was forced. It appears, from what we have been able to piece together, that Brown had planned to use the Lyford trial as a means to expose us. He was going to attempt to manipulate Lyford and his attorney in some way."

Heads around the room nodded. The other three had been briefed on the operation, after it had taken place. Two made no effort to contain the smile on his face. He had argued for a more immediate, violent removal of Brown. He was the most aggressive of the four.

"No evidence has linked the murder to our asset. It appears she made a clean hit. I think that part of our problem is finished." There were more nods of approval around the conference table. This was not the first time Gloria Augusteel had delivered for the Lexington League.

"Noah Augusteel." One embarked on the second update. "We traced him through an email to a meeting he attended at the Portico Café. It is a small café on the second-story of the National Portrait gallery."

Two and Three studied their drinks. One could see Four raise her head. One assumed they all recognized the name of the café from the newspaper coverage. Until now, One had not connected Noah Augusteel to the gunfight.

"Unfortunately, he managed to escape. As I understand it, the timing of the situation required a rapid deployment, and we were not able to plan for every potential contingency."

Three raised his head, hesitated for a moment, then spoke toward no-one in particular. "This situation is spinning out of control." His was the veteran voice at the table. Regardless, his comment earned an abrasive look from One.

And a firm rebuttal: "No. The situation is under control."

Three hesitated again. He lowered his drink onto the conference table and turned to face One. "My counsel is that we escalate our search for Noah Augusteel. We should increase the assets and resources we have on that project."

He looked toward Two, then toward Four. "If my recollection is correct, we believe Mr. Augusteel is in possession of one of the two remaining vials of the substance. It is very likely that he could pose a substantial threat."

Two echoed the comments. "He poses a threat. Period. He was one of our best field operatives."

One's frustration was growing. "Your counsel and advice will be taken into consideration." One stared at Three. "For now, we'll maintain our current allocation of resources." The voice indicated that the discussion of Noah Augusteel had ended. "He'll come to us, and we'll be ready when he does. We can't exhaust our efforts on Noah Augusteel when we have other problems that require our resources."

One rotated toward the communication console and removed a small remote control. The television screen flickered to life. The other three watched as the face of Gloria Augusteel appeared over One's head. They simultaneously appreciated how rare it was for anyone other than the five to participate, in any way, in a meeting. Three appeared instantly uncomfortable, regardless of the assurances about the technology. Augusteel could not see them, they had been told. She could hear their voices, but the voices would be severely disguised. The people in the conference room, however, would be able to clearly see and hear Gloria Augusteel.

"Ms. Augusteel." One had rotated to face the screen. "Please tell us about Luke Lyford."

Over the next few minutes Gloria recounted the events of the past week, starting with the phone call from Mark Ellis and ending with the death of Luke Lyford. For the most part she proceeded without interruption. Yet, as she described the brief responses Lyford had given after ingesting the substance, members of the five broke into her story.

"Ms. Augusteel, there was no doubt that Luke Lyford knew information about our organization?"

"No," she answered into what appeared to her to be an empty room of distorted voices. "There is no doubt."

Two followed with another question. "And it is your opinion that Mr. Lyford received this information through Mark Ellis? So Ellis would have it too, correct?"

"Yes. I agree with that conclusion." The room was quiet. So was Gloria Augusteel.

One offered the last question. "And Luke Lyford indicated to you that he had the Madison letter? The one we've been looking for?"

"Yes."

One turned toward the table, searching the faces of the other three for additional questions. There were none. "Thank you, Ms. Augusteel. We'll be in touch." The television screen faded to black above One's head.

Three broke the silence. He lifted his nearly empty glass from the table. The coaster clung to the bottom of it, then slipped back, falling the few inches onto the conference table. Three moved toward the bar as he spoke. "It appears I was wrong earlier. Noah Augusteel does not have one of the remaining vials. He has *the remaining vial*."

The comment circled in the silent room. One watched the faces of the two still at the table. He knew Two would support the decision. Four would be on the fence. Three, to the right, slowly dropped fresh ice cubes into his glass. The dark back of his suit was to the conference table. *He'll oppose it*, One thought. *But I'll move forward without him.*

"It has to be done." One's voice was unyielding, harder than the stained wood of the antique conference table.

"There is another option," Three responded without turning away from the bar. "You could wait. See what happens. Lyford is dead. There is not going to be a trial. Brown is dead, and you said yourself that the police have no solid evidence."

Three turned and was walking back, passing under the portrait of Madison. One watched his movement, and the drink in his hand. It was another reminder of William Iredell. *How many problems did that letter cause?* he asked himself. *William Iredell. The historian in North Carolina. Parker Brown. Luke Lyford.*

Mark Ellis.

Three would be allowed to voice his opinion, but One had already decided. The discussion was simply to let the others feel involved. *They would go to Mark Ellis. Noah Augusteel would eventually come to them. The last two loose ends would be tied up.*

Three had returned to his seat and was addressing the other three. His white hair pivoted between the other sides of the table. "What is Mark Ellis going to do? Go to the police? He's the obvious link between Lyford and Brown. The police are already looking at him. We can keep the pressure on him. The press is all over him too."

Four was listening. Two was simply acting like he was listening.

"I say we wait. Let him make a mistake. My guess is that he'll sit on the Madison letter. He won't want to draw any more attention to himself. He may go home to North Carolina. There is nothing keeping him here." Three looked around the table to assess whether he was making progress. He looked disappointed. The old gentleman regrouped, retrenching himself in a fall-back position. "If we do . . . ," he started. "If we do go after him, let's wait until the press backs off. We're watching him, right? Let's just keep watching him. When the heat cools down, then we can see if it makes sense to go after him."

One let the other man finish.

"Thank you for your advice. It is always thoughtful and welcome." The empty comment fooled no-one in the room. They had known One too long.

Three searched the faces of Two and Four. If he was going to change One's mind he would need the support of the other two. He could tell from their faces that he didn't have it.

One continued. "I'm going to send Gloria Augusteel after Mark Ellis. I agree . . . ." One looked at Three, the gaze that accompanied the words softening in an effort to ease the tension, now that the decision had been announced. ". . . that the media will complicate this operation. It may take time, but it has to be a priority. Mark Ellis knows too much."

One looked around the room. Four was quiet. Three swirled his glass, rotating the ice cubes in the brown liquid.

"And I want that letter."

Two was smiling again. The same smile that had crossed his face during their discussion of Parker Brown's death. "Hear, hear," he quietly offered to the open air above the middle of the table.

One's arm was extended, drink in hand, and raised toward the center of the table. The dull hum of the electronic equipment vibrated into the space. The dark night watched from the left, blanketing the long panel of windows like a shadow.

"To the Republic."

Three other drinks rose. In unison, they responded. "To the Republic."

Chapter Twenty-Nine

Washington, DC
July 2, 2010

It had been a long twenty-four hours for Mark Ellis. It had been almost exactly one day since he had convinced himself that the Lexington League had murdered William Iredell, and was probably responsible for the murder of Parker Brown and Claire Ellis.

He desperately wanted to keep Luke Lyford's name off that list. However, it had been more than two days since he had last spoken to Luke – since Luke had visited the Echo office instead of Mark – and a desperate prayer was more-or-less all that remained.

As the Friday-afternoon sun climbed over the buildings opposite Luke's apartment, Mark had found that his restlessness increased as his momentum decreased. He could feel his effort stalling, slowing down after he had allowed himself to believe that the Lexington League – a group that he had once considered a simple legal advocacy organization – had much deeper roots in much darker soil.

His slide from action into agitation was interrupted by his cell phone. It was his assistant from North Carolina. After the last three weeks, after Parker Brown, after Luke seemingly dropping from the face of the earth, he felt like there was nothing left that could shock him.

He was wrong.

John Baker had called his office. *John Baker.* "He said it was about your mother," his assistant informed him. "He says it's urgent."

Mark tried to imagine what John Baker might want to discuss, and what it would feel like to hear Baker's voice again, the voice of the man who closed the book on the investigation into his mother's death. He ended the call with his assistant and methodically entered Baker's cell number into his phone.

Minutes later, he and John Baker had spoken and planned to meet the following morning.

He knew the media circus would follow him. He knew John Baker had not considered the media surrounding Mark when he proposed a meeting at a public restaurant. And he knew the last thing David Baker wanted, on the Saturday before he was to be confirmed by the Judiciary Committee, was to be asked questions about why his son was meeting with Parker Brown's attorney – with a traitor's attorney, as the press would, without a doubt, emphasize in the news accounts.

But that is not really my problem, is it? Mark thought. In fact, it was more of a bonus. If the media was going to hound him, he might as well put it to good use.

Hours passed as the sun eased toward the horizon. Mark watched night creep into the city from one of the small chairs in Luke's living area. The press lined the street below and approached – sometimes encircled, always harassed – every person that left Luke's building. He watched the reporters and cameramen scurry, dashing across the pavement every time the apartment building's front door opened.

The kitchen light was the only light on in the apartment. It barely reached the chair Mark had chosen. The darkness of the apartment had a calming effect. The traffic along Massachusetts had slowed. The grinding, constant noise of rush hour had been replaced by the periodic passing of a handful of cars. Downtown Washington had reached the weekend, and its office buildings and parking garages had emptied like water draining from a pool, its people flowing out of the city until there was little left but quiet and vacant street corners.

While the darkness had calmed him, the solitude pressed him toward a decision. *To stay or to go?* His role as Luke Lyford's attorney was likely irrelevant. Parker Brown was dead. *It may be time to go home*, he thought, studying the lifeless furniture in the apartment. *I'll see what John Baker wants and then there will be nothing left for me here.*

The confidence – the aggression – he had felt the night before was fading. *I may believe the Lexington League was involved in each of these murders, but I can't come close to proving it – or doing anything about it.* His thoughts tacked toward Noah Augusteel. With Lyford and Brown gone, Augusteel was the only person left who seemed to be working against the Lexington League. The Portico Café had made that clear. But it was another dead-end. According to Augusteel, Mark was being watched. It certainly was not the other way around: he had no idea how to contact Noah Augusteel. He had no idea whether he was still in DC. Or whether he was still alive.

The oppressive solitude grew around him. *You either beat them at their own game or you lose.* That is what Augusteel had told him.

Was it even possible to imagine that he could fight this group alone? Would he even know how? They had killed a future Supreme Court Justice. They killed Parker Brown *while he was in federal custody.*

Could Noah Augusteel go it alone? Mark crafted the most positive version of reality that he could muster. Augusteel had contacted him. He had survived the shootout in the café and escaped. Augusteel wasn't without resources, Mark reasoned. And he seemed to know enough about the Lexington League to expose it. What had he told Mark? That his family had been a part of the group since the American Revolution?

Mark pulled the small chair closer to the coffee table in the center of the room and turned on the small reading lamp he had moved onto the coffee table. The switch was on the black base. The thin silver neck of the lamp ran from the base to the tiny bulb in the lamp's head. He had angled the flexible neck so that the light fell directly on the documents below.

As evening had set in, Mark had been working with the critical papers that he had collected over the last few weeks, repeatedly reading through them and trying to find something, anything that he could use. Both toxicology reports were on the table: the official report that had been distributed by Carol Cushing and the anonymous report that had been emailed. Next to them was the letter and information from the chemist he had hired to examine the Madison letter.

Mark dug through the remainder of the documents until he found the original email from Noah Augusteel. The date caught his eye. It had been eight days since he had received the anonymous email. The line he remembered was in the second paragraph: *My family and I have served the league since the Revolution.*

Something in that sentence suspended his thinking. Mark couldn't quite put his finger on it, but something had flashed through his mind. Was it something in the rest of the email? He re-read the text. Nothing sparked.

Mark read the sentence aloud, filling the barren apartment. "My family and I have served the league since the Revolution."

It flashed again.

He rose from the chair, reading the same line aloud.

Another flash. It was a memory. It was Luke. It was their first meeting.

Luke was explaining James Wilson's biography. He could hear Luke's voice. He was describing Wilson's role at the Constitutional Convention. He was telling Mark about the relationship between James Madison and James Wilson; about how they had, together, laid the foundation for the Constitution.

Mark closed his eyes. The kitchen light vanished. The reading lamp on the table vanished. Luke was there, in his recollection. They were talking. Mark was leaving. Luke was yelling down the hall, finishing the story: James Wilson had died at James Iredell's house in North Carolina.

Luke had emphasized the ending. He had thought it was important because it linked the Madison letter to William Iredell. He had guessed that the letter had travelled from Madison to Wilson, then from Wilson to the Iredell family, and been eventually passed to William Iredell.

Mark opened his eyes. *But there was more to the James Wilson story.*

The letter. Mark brushed aside the toxicology documents until he found it. *I've been reading this wrong*, he thought. *I've been reading this wrong the whole time.*

He turned to the third page and angled the reading lamp over the copied paper. Under the intense light of the lamp, the writing in the margin was blacker, thicker than the hand-written text.

Mark stared at the scrawled lettering. His first thought – weeks ago, when he had held the letter to the light of Luke's large window – had been that the writing in the margin was a more recent addition to the document, and was therefore darker. *We assumed this was from William Iredell. We assumed it was a message to Luke.*

Their rough translations ran through his memory: *sing office, ring office. An office shaped like a ring?*

But the translation changes if we change our assumptions, he thought.

Mark focused on the writing, tracing each individual letter with the plastic top of his pen. He reorganized his thinking as he followed the curves. His mind worked backwards, straining to recall his conversation with Noah Augusteel at the Portico Café. *James Wilson*. The words had stuck in Mark's mind at the time. *The "family legend". Augusteel's claim that the Lexington League had murdered James Wilson.*

He tried to fit what Augusteel had told him with the hard history Luke had discovered. *If James Wilson had this letter with him when he died . . . and the Lexington League was actually involved with his death . . .*

Could this be a note from James Wilson?

Mark examined the letters in the margin. He imagined an old quill and ink set, the uneven distribution of the black ink causing the writing to take on a different level of darkness.

He returned to where he had been seconds before: the translation changes if the author changes. *If this is a note from James Wilson and not a note from William Iredell, then we have been reading it all wrong.* James Wilson, obviously, would not have written a message to Luke Lyford. *That means what we thought was an "ll" is not Luke's initials.*

He narrowed his attention to the first two letters.

It came to Mark immediately.

Lexington League, not Luke Lyford.

Mark scrutinized the second part. He traced the letters again, trying to put himself in James Wilson's place. He tried to envision Wilson's hand. *What had he been thinking?* He retraced the letters.

He lowered the document to the coffee table and leaned back in the chair. Removing William Iredell as the author changed the entire message. No longer was he constantly returning to the idea that Iredell had been trying to communicate with Luke Lyford, or had jotted this short note about Luke.

Now it was James Wilson.

Maybe.

I'm pushing the limit of speculation here, he thought, trying to balance his assessment. *Probably pushing it too far.*

Sing office. Out of habit, his mind was returning to their original interpretation. Mark tried to push the thought away. *Ring office.* He needed a new approach, a new idea.

He let the speculation run.

If Wilson had been killed by the Lexington League, how did it happen?

The rational part of his mind fought into the foreground. He had no evidence. None. He was just grasping at straws.

In the dark window to his left, he could see his reflection. He could barely see his mother's campaign sign in the dim, reflected distance over his shoulder. In the few watts emitted from the kitchen's single light bulb, the sign looked like it was faded.

Noah Augusteel's voice. *The Iredell hit fits the league's MO – its modus operandi. You know, how we get stuff done. Someone high-profile like Iredell can't just disappear.*

Someone high-profile.

It was Parker Brown this time. From a different memory. He could see his face through the glass divider. He was explaining how he knew the contents of the poison that killed William Iredell. He was explaining how the Lexington League had been using the same poison since the Revolutionary War.

The same poison.

The same poison yields the same reaction.

Twenty-four hours ago Mark had convinced himself that the Lexington League had poisoned William Iredell. Yet, William Iredell had called Luke Lyford's office on the morning of his death. If he had been poisoned on Thursday night, but alive enough to make a phone call on Friday morning . . .

There must be some kind of delayed effect.

Mark watched his frozen reflection in the window. Footsteps passed the door of the apartment along the hard, concrete hallway. He could hear the elevator chime in the hall. Then the doors opening. Closing.

Luke was in his memory now, jokingly mocking him for his weak grasp on legal history. *Come on, Mark. Chisholm versus Georgia? The first big Supreme Court case? There were only five Supreme Court Justices back then, including some Revolutionary giants. Wilson was on the Court; John Jay was the Chief Justice. James Iredell was also on the Court at this point.*

James Iredell was also on the Court at this point. The sentence repeated in his mind.

If there was a similar delay between Wilson's poisoning and his death, would Wilson have tried to get a message to Iredell?

Mark knew he had allowed himself to desperately wander down the speculation trail. It was all he had left. He felt untethered, far from any tangible piece of evidence. Leaning forward in the chair, he reached for the letter. *Sing office.* The same old thoughts were pressing back.

Mark tried to hold them off, to remain focused on his imagined version of James Wilson's final day. He recalled his last thought: *If there was a similar delay between Wilson's poisoning and his death, would Wilson have tried to get a message to Iredell?*

Ring office. Again, the same old translation of the scrawled words. He shoved it away.

What would Wilson try to tell James Iredell?

Mark leaned closer to the coffee table. The thought repeated like a drum. *What would Wilson try to tell James Iredell?*

Ring of . . . . No, he thought. *Focus.*
He stopped. He looked again.

ll ring office

Ring of . . .
"Ring of," he read aloud.
"Ring of . . . what?"

Mark adjusted the small reading lamp. In the tiny spot-light, the focal point of the room shrank instantly to the black letters, bold against the white copy paper.

Fil . . . e? File? Mark asked himself, re-examining the last word – or two words – or three words. *Fin . . . e? Fine?* He worked his way through the alphabet, trying to slow himself to a deliberate pace.

Fir . . . e? Fire?

Ring of fire? He stopped at "r." It meant nothing to him. Another dead-end.

Mark rubbed his eyes in the silent apartment and shoved the head of the small lamp. *Another dead-end.* The flexible neck bent sideways and illuminated the couch. The documents on the table fell back into near-darkness.

Mark pushed off the coffee table and rose to his feet. It was over. He could feel it now.

He leaned against the great window, holding himself up with outstretched arms. Slowly flexing his arms and lowering his head, he allowed his body to tilt toward the window until his head, facing downward, rested against the glass.

He had tried to resuscitate a two-hundred year old – most likely imaginary – murder, without any actual evidence. It had been a desperation heave, a flailing attempt. *More like a failed attempt*, he reflected. What had it earned him? "Ring of fire" and a trip down the alphabet? Sluggishly, he extended his elbows, lifting his head and his body back to a vertical angle. His palms pressed against the cool glass. His fingers spread along the pane.

Ring of fire. F. I. R. E.

"R," he said aloud.

He lifted his thumb slightly off the glass. *This is where I started with that letter.* He lowered his thumb.

"S," he called into Luke's empty apartment.

He raised his index finger and lowered it back to the glass. "T." It was like a countdown he could no longer even hope to stop.

"U." *This window is where it started. This is where it will end.* He raised and lowered his middle finger. The black night on the opposite side of the window had replaced the bright sunlight that had beamed into Luke's apartment during Mark's first visit.

Mark elevated the fourth finger of his hand off the glass.

"V." His voice echoed off the exposed pipe in the ceiling and down the short hallway. His ring finger remained in the air, hovering barely off the window. *V?*

Fiv . . . e? Five?

Ring of five?

❧

The image landed and lodged deep in the tired tissue of Mark Ellis's brain: Parker Brown's ring. He could see him rotating it as they talked through the glass divider. The ring had distinct, flat sides; yet, the sides had seemed too short for a square. *There must be five sides. A ring of five?* He could see Brown's hand, dangling, lifeless and loose, through the bars of the courthouse holding cell. The ring had been missing from his finger.

Mark spun and leaned his back against the window. He stared into the dark apartment. His mind was picking up speed, feeling for a sure step on the firm ground of actual evidence – things he had seen, held. Places. People.

Mark had assumed Gloria Augusteel had taken the ring at the time of the murder. It seemed like the only reasonable conclusion. But the conclusion had fluttered into and out of his thoughts as he was being dragged from the cell. In the confusion of the courthouse hallway it had seemed insignificant; in his rush to contact Luke and meet Noah Augusteel it had been lost.

He considered it anew: Gloria Augusteel could not have had more than a few minutes – maybe less – in that holding room. *And yet she took the time to remove his ring?*

He made another assumption: *It must mean something. Have some value. To her or to the person who sent her. Otherwise, she would not have risked the extra time in the holding room.*

Mark was passing through the living area now. He rubbed the small of his back as he thought. Something was in the recesses of his mind. He stopped walking and tried to reach for it. It floated away.

Go at it another way, he told himself, returning to the idea of Gloria Augusteel taking Brown's ring. "The ring was important to the Lexington League," he whispered to himself as he paced in the confined apartment. "Parker Brown was an important member of the Lexington League.

"Therefore . . . other important members might want it back?" he asked the still air.

Maybe.

He whispered a second idea. "Therefore . . . Parker Brown might have had other important items?"

Maybe, but she didn't take anything else, so far as I know. And everything else was stored at the prison or with his family.

A third idea: "Therefore . . . other important members might have the same ring?"

The fleeting thought was back, lurking slightly out of his grasp. There was something he knew. Something he had seen. It felt like his fingers could touch it. If he just reached out his hand . . .

Cushing. Carol Cushing.

It was the name that had circled his life since he had been face-to-face with her on the steps of Luke's apartment building. The catalogue of what he knew opened like a file folder, spilling its contents on the apartment's hardwood floor.

Cushing had prosecuted Parker Brown. She had secured the death sentence.

Cushing was leading the prosecution against Luke Lyford. He could still see her walking down the short hall of Luke's apartment, directing the federal agents. Handing him the false toxicology report.

The illusive thought fell toward him. Mark reached to pull it into the foreground of his mind.

Cushing had been in the courthouse for the Brown hearing. She was the only person other than the judge who knew Brown would be there. She would have known how the U.S. Marshals planned to transport him. She was talking to one when Brown was killed.

The thought was in his palm. He tried to close his fingers.

Mark Ellis stood alone in Luke Lyford's apartment. The door to the exterior hallway was a foot or two behind him. The kitchen and small dining area to his right, the living area to his left. The short hallway was directly ahead of him.

The thought was slipping through his fingers.

Carol Cushing does not wear any rings.

Mark could see Carol Cushing walking in front of him in the hallway. Her condescending voice was overpowering the sound of the FBI searching and seizing its way through Luke's apartment. She was lecturing Mark like some first-year law student. *Means, motive, opportunity.* She was unfurling her fingers directly in front of him as she laid out her case against Luke. Her fingers were right in front of his face. *There were no rings.*

If it wasn't Carol Cushing, who was it?

The thought was still there. Hovering. Something he had seen. But something he could not recall.

Who else could have known Brown was going to be at the courthouse on that date and at that time? Who else would have accessed the protection protocol for a federal courthouse? Who could have altered it?

Who could have set up the flawless federal prosecution of Parker Brown?

Mark reached for the thought again. His fingertips could feel its wispy border.

Who else was in a position to coordinate the creation of false toxicology report by the Washington, DC medical examiner's office?

He stretched for it.

Who else was in a position to know which FBI agent would be willing to plant the Phenobarbital in this apartment?

It was right there. He was touching it, but couldn't . . .

Mark stepped back toward the documents on the coffee table. *Was it something in here? Something he had read in the toxicology report? Something in his Phenobarbital research? Something having to do with a ring like Parker Brown's?*

His right hand seized the base of the small reading lamp and followed the flexible neck to the light at the head. Mark stopped shuffling through the papers and glanced up at the lamp to adjust its light back to its original position, back from where it had turned when he shoved it.

He froze.

The thought was in his hand. He carefully, delicately closed his fingers around it. The beam of the small reading light ran horizontally off the coffee table, away from Mark. His laptop lay on Luke's couch. Directly in the beam. *That is it*, he knew. *That is where I've seen the same ring.*

Nearly hurdling the corner, he rounded the table and reached the couch. In seconds he found the electronic folder and the video file. Silently, he thanked Luke for sending him the video.

He pushed the small triangle along the bar at the bottom of the screen. The images spun past. *It is near the end*, he recalled. He stopped. He could see the white coat of the young medical examiner. Mark paused it again. The white coat was replaced by the dark suit of the Capitol Police. He recalled the name of the police chief directing the press conference: *Evanston.*

The camera had zoomed closer as Chief Evanston had tried to end the press conference. The podium was out of the picture and the image had settled on a close-up view of his upper body. Mark could see the stress in his eyes as he stood before the world and announced the death of William Iredell.

There were only a few minutes left on the video, but Mark saw what he wanted. It was his memory. The same image. The small flicker. The light. The reflection.

The same ring.

United States Attorney General Edwin Carter. Still, paused on his laptop screen. Carol Cushing's boss. The chief law enforcement officer of the United States. He controlled the Justice Department, and under it the FBI and the U.S. Marshal's office. And the Bureau of Federal Prisons.

He would have known Brown's transportation and protection plan, and could have adjusted it.

He could have ordered Luke's release from federal custody.

The stage lights of the small briefing room were reflecting off the shoulder straps of Evanston's police uniform. The metal bars glowed in the harsh light, just to the left of the Attorney General's hand. Next to the shimmering straps he could see it in the bright stage lights. In the close-up view of Evanston's upper body, he could see it distinctly.

Mark Ellis could see two of the flat silver surfaces of Edwin Carter's ring.

The same five-sided ring. The same ring of five.

Chapter Thirty

Washington, DC
July 3, 2010

He had fled with the scattering mass of people outside the Portico Café and his mental machinery had slowed with each departing step. His first clear thought had been typically human: *I am alive.*

Noah Augusteel had spent the rest of Thursday on the run, shifting and hiding, picking his way through the city until nightfall. He believed he had avoided detection, but he had taken no chances. Friday morning found him carefully working his way toward his rental car – the same one he and his sister had rented for their operation in North Carolina. By now it had certainly been reported as stolen. Noah had changed the license plate multiple times, and it was by no means the only navy-blue Toyota Camry in DC. Nevertheless, he knew, it eventually would be discovered.

He didn't need it forever. He just needed to buy enough time.

After convincing himself that there were no Echo agents watching the car, he had approached the vehicle. Augusteel had swung into the driver's seat and driven exactly three miles, making a series of unsignaled turns. He had reversed course twice. Satisfied that he had not been followed, Noah left downtown Washington and drove directly to a suburban shopping center. The license plate was switched again. A few more miles down the road, Noah had stopped at a fast-food restaurant to reassess his tactical situation. Somewhere in the back of his mind, he could feel his window of opportunity closing; he could feel time running out.

Since his initial approach at the western gate of the White House, Noah Augusteel had made two more attempts, two more one-man operations solely focused on earning a clear shot at his target. Both had failed. And both had failed for the same reason: his sister had encased Attorney General Edwin Carter in a nearly impenetrable cocoon of protection.

Before the man stepped into public, anti-sniper patrols were watching the nearby rooftops. In some cases, he had even seen patrols on the roofs themselves. The patrols meant nothing to Noah Augusteel since acquiring a sniper rifle was out of the question given his limited funds. His would have to be a close-range assault, with his Luger or with his hands.

Or with the substance.

He knew it and she knew it.

And she had planned on it. His approaches had quickly broken on the walls of her defense. She had set up essentially a double-layer of protection around Carter. The traditional federal agents formed one wall. And within this wall – or around it, or woven into it – Gloria had set her Echo perimeter: plain-clothed assets, armed to the teeth and watching for

Noah in particular. Noah had wondered whether the federal agents could even see the Echo assets moving around them.

Noah could, but he knew what to look for. And what he saw was far too much protection to clandestinely penetrate. Just a couple of days before the Portico Café, he had made his most recent attempt. Through the window of a nearby office-building, he had studied the assets and memorized their pattern. He had watched how they rotated, how they paired-up and decoupled as part of his sister's protective web.

Noah knew he could work along the border of her system. *I can get to one or two without a problem. But by the time I take them out, Carter will have moved. She isn't letting him stay in one public place for more time than is absolutely necessary.* One asset might be able to be "off the grid" for a few minutes, but any longer and the other assets would recognize his absence and close ranks around Carter.

Gloria had left him one option: a suicide attempt. Once in the cocoon he might be able to get to the Attorney General, but Noah knew he would never make it out alive.

He wasn't prepared to consider that as an option. Yet.

Edwin Carter was his target, the only member of the five that he knew. Carter had been the one giving his sister direction. He was the one who had sent them after the Madison letter. Whether Carter was *the one* – the one at the top – Noah had no idea. *He may be passing directives through, a middleman between the top and my sister.*

What he knew with certainty was that there were four others, and if he ever learned their identity, he would visit them once he was finished with Attorney General Edwin Carter.

༚

Slightly more than a day after he had left Mark Ellis on the floor of the Portico Café, Noah Augusteel found Ellis exactly where he expected the attorney to be: holed up inside Luke Lyford's apartment.

Augusteel reached Massachusetts Avenue late Friday afternoon. After driving past the line of media vans, he worked his way through the surrounding streets until he located Mark Ellis's red truck. Even in the crowded, downtown street, the rusty metal was easy to spot. Noah waited nearly an hour for a parking spot on the same block, but as the work-week ended, the parking spaces slowly started to open up. Finally, he backed the rental car into one on the opposite side of the street, only a few spaces down from the pick-up.

Night fell, and Augusteel took up a position on the black rooftop of a CVS pharmacy, down the street from Lyford's apartment. From there he could watch the media as they watched the door. His reconnaissance soon located another player prowling the blocks around the apartment entrance. Two men had appeared far too frequently on the same street. *The league is watching too.* He maintained his vigil through most of Friday night, eyeing Massachusetts Avenue, peering over the edge of the two story building like a groundhog checking his shadow – or rather, a groundhog checking *the* shadows, looking for any movement in the dark.

Augusteel allowed himself a couple of hours of sleep as the morning approached. When he woke – stiff and possibly even more tired – on the black-tarred roof of the pharmacy, he could see the beginning stages of a farmers' market coming to life on the opposite end of the street. The stalls were being set up. Some of the produce was arriving, piled in the beds of small trucks and trailers.

The media remained. He rechecked the order of the vans. It was identical to the earlier configuration, indicating that Ellis had not left the apartment during the few hours Augusteel had slept. He watched the street for another hour and a half. There was no sign of the two Echo agents. *Maybe they are relying on their contacts in the press. Maybe they're counting on the media to track Ellis for them.*

Sensing an opening, Noah Augusteel quietly lowered himself into the alley behind the pharmacy. The rubber soles of his tennis shoes landed silently on the broken concrete. He walked away from the apartment building, strolled two blocks to the east, purchased a cup of coffee, and slowly moved in the direction of the farmers' market, circling back toward Mark Ellis.

᠙

It is 08:15. It is Saturday morning. I am following a couple as they exit the building. 450 Massachusetts Avenue Northwest, Washington, DC. I am . . .

Someone bumped into his shoulder, from the left. He spun, pivoting in response and swinging his backpack over his shoulder as he turned. His right hand dove for the zipper as his right leg stepped back. His knees and torso crouched into a firing position. His train of thought was interrupted.

It was nothing. Just someone in the crowd. She apologized and disappeared past him, into the building.

I am at the exit of the building.

I am on the street. I am in the outdoor market.

The crowd was nearly shoulder-to-shoulder in the outdoor farmers' market. Children were moving between the makeshift wooden stalls. Summer tourists and downtown residents blended among the smells of produce and fresh fruit. Noah waded into the mix, carefully searching the faces, looking for any that repeated.

Inventory (on person): $496.57, binoculars, Echo Industrial 9mm Luger handgun, two ammunition clips, one screwdriver, personal 9mm Luger with full ammunition clip, detachable silencer, one change of clothes, water bottle.

Inventory (in vehicle): $2908.73, laptop and battery, first aid kit, hammer, wrench, two screwdrivers, hair dye, scissors, towels, water, Gatorade, additional clothes, my sister's change of clothes, one vial of the substance.

Hat pulled tight and low over his blond hair, Noah Augusteel swayed in the tight crowd of Saturday morning market-goers. Less than a block from his position, he could see the front of 425 Massachusetts. It was Luke Lyford's apartment building and the location to which he had tracked Mark Ellis.

Awkwardly parked press vans lined the block, frustrating the vendors and patrons of the farmers' market. They had little recourse; the vans had been parked in the same spaces for days. The press was both friend and foe to Noah Augusteel. Their constant vigilance and ready cameras offered a level of publicity that would certainly complicate – if not prevent – his sister from executing a straightforward assault on the downtown apartment. Between the networks, newspapers, and other media outlets, the press had effectively surrounded the building. They approached everyone that moved. They watched for the slightest signal that Mark Ellis might leave the building or that someone might enter the building to meet with Ellis.

Of course, there was no exception for Noah Augusteel. If he had tried to enter the building, the media would have swarmed him – and certainly called the attention of any Echo asset assigned to monitor the apartment building's door.

He bought an apple from one of the vendors and studied the long street through the open back of the farmer's stall. He could move safely in the crowd. It was as close as he had come to the apartment. Taking another bite of his apple as he passed down the line of stalls, his eyes scanned the faces in the crowd then turned back toward the apartment building. Noah repeated this pattern as he worked his way through the market, the smell of the fresh vegetables coming and going as he automatically recorded the faces in his memory.

He took the last bite of the apple and saw movement toward the apartment. First it was two men sprinting across Massachusetts. It looked like a reporter, trailed by a cameraman. Augusteel paused, trying to determine whether this was what he had watched all Friday afternoon: overreaction triggered by the appearance of someone entirely unrelated to Mark Ellis.

Two more reporters were following the first. Then another cameraman. Now two more were following. Noah noticed that the first two hadn't backed off. He tried to focus on their subject, but it was too far down the street, and the media had closed off his line of sight. *It has to be Ellis.* He saw one of the vans start to pull out from the parking space directly across from the apartment. *They wouldn't give up that space to chase anyone other than Mark Ellis.*

Noah broke into a jog, weaving past a couple in the market and side-stepping their leashed dog. He tossed the apple core into a dumpster as he reached the edge of the stalls.

Cover reduced.

Running would call attention. *I have to get there before Ellis.* He was between two buildings now. His stride lengthened as he ran down the alley. Slipping the second strap of his backpack over his free shoulder, Noah locked the belt-strap, and cinched it around his waist. His stride had reached its full length by the time he left the alley. Gravel skidded under his shoes as he turned right on I Street. It was nearly empty on a Saturday morning. *I have to get past Fourth before they reach the corner.* Ellis's truck was parked on I Street, one block from where Noah was running and on the opposite side of Fourth Street.

His mind calculated the pace at which Ellis had been moving after the press reached him. He subtracted some speed on account of the press serving as an obstacle; the imaginary Mark Ellis moving along his mental map of DC slowed again. Noah assumed that Mark would have known the press would follow him and would not have left the apartment – much less, left during the day – unless he was willing to be surrounded. *I should be able to beat them to the vehicles.* He accelerated.

Noah reached Fourth Street and looked right. The mob was down the street. He crossed Fourth and passed the red truck. His blue Camry was half a block down. He reached it in seconds, after sprinting across I Street. Augusteel surveyed the scene around him, pausing to look for any unexpected movement. There was none. He ducked into his car as Mark Ellis rounded the corner in front of him.

The blue Camry pulled into the string of trailing media vans. Ahead of him Noah could see the taillights of Ellis's truck. There were three media vans between them. At least two more were in the traffic behind Noah. The vans jockeyed for position, ignoring Augusteel and the other cars surrounding them as they moved up Massachusetts Avenue toward Dupont Circle. For a minute or two he lost sight of Ellis, but the line of vans continued straight down Massachusetts. Noah stayed with the vans.

His concentration shifted from the snaking line of vans to a dark green SUV hovering in his rear-view mirror, lagging like a vulture behind the slow-moving caravan. It had been with them for the last few minutes. On the straightway, it was impossible to assess the vehicle. It could be following Ellis; it could just be another car traveling in downtown DC.

Noah dropped his Camry back a few car-lengths, allowing two vans to pass him. He shifted into the other lane and dropped behind the green SUV. As it passed him, he noticed the tinted windows. He shadowed it in the right lane, now thirty feet off its rear bumper. He could see the North Carolina license plate.

Ahead of him, he calculated, Ellis was reaching Dupont Circle, the large traffic circle that connected the DC streets of Massachusetts, Connecticut, and New Hampshire. The traffic around them increased as they approached the huge, circular intersection.

The vans were entering the traffic circle. He followed them as they rounded to the right. The green SUV was positioned between Noah and the line of media. Taking the fourth exit, the vans moved onto Connecticut and headed northwest. Noah watched as the SUV followed. Then he steered his rental car onto the same exit.

A few miles up Connecticut the processional reached its final destination. With nearly ten media vans chasing a pick-up truck, being followed by a green SUV and a Camry, the street in front of the Open City restaurant was suddenly awash in turn signals, brake lights, and illegal parking maneuvers. Noah slowed once he saw the vans pulling to the side ahead of him. He shifted into the center lane and passed the commotion.

Two blocks. Then he doubled back. He slowed to ensure that he would be caught by the traffic light in front of the open-air restaurant. The light switched to red ahead of him. Reporters were running in front of his car. His rear-view mirrors displayed four cameramen behind him, flooding from the open side doors of their vans. To his right, he could see that Ellis had reached the iron gate of the patio and was speaking to the hostess.

The green SUV turned in front of his rental car. Noah watched it make a left turn from the side street, creep past the hood of his stopped car, and slow in front of the restaurant. Through the open driver's window he could see that there were two men in the car. The driver was talking on a cell phone, looking over the roof of Augusteel's navy sedan and watching Mark Ellis enter the patio. The passenger was reaching into the back seat. The tinted rear window concealed everything above his shoulders.

The light changed. Noah pulled his car forward into the intersection, now watching the SUV through his side mirror as the distance grew between the vehicles. The passenger jumped out as the SUV slowed. The man landed awkwardly on the pavement, balancing himself with only his left arm extended. His right hand remained in the front pocket of a light jacket.

If Noah had any doubt, this erased it. *Echo. They're going in. Now.*

Noah swung his car into an open disabled parking space, grabbed his backpack, and leapt from the car. He immediately glanced up and assessed the spectacle ahead of him. The Open City patio ran parallel to Connecticut, the road on which he had parked. The patio was a rectangle, stretching away from Noah Augusteel. The side street he had crossed stood between them.

Ellis had taken a table at the far side of the outdoor area. Strangely, it looked to Noah like he was inviting the media attention, even if he was not speaking to the reporters. Camera crews lined the sidewalk next to the restaurant, taking up every inch of public property and calling over the iron railing toward Ellis's table. Ellis was sitting alone.

The man who had leapt from the SUV was young and he kept his eyes on Ellis. *Inexperienced*, was Augusteel's first thought. *They think this asset's expendable*, was his second.

It is 08:39. I am on Connecticut Avenue Northwest in Washington, DC. I am armed. One threat, thirty yards north from my position. Threat is armed with handgun. Additional threat identified. Location of additional threat unknown.

Noah took a step backward, slightly concealing himself behind his car. So long as Ellis kept that outdoor seat, the media would stay along the restaurant's fence. They would form a solid wall between Ellis and the Echo asset. He scanned the street for the SUV. Reinforcements were coming. Noah was sure of that.

Echo was in play. The news cameras were literally feet from Mark Ellis. Ellis was contained within the fenced-in outdoor restaurant, and seemed to be content sitting alone at the table. Noah weighed his options. *If I move toward Ellis I'll be identified by the Echo asset and attract the attention of the media. But if I wait, additional assets will arrive and the situation will become more perilous – for both of us.*

I need to get Ellis to move.

He studied the Echo asset again. He had moved slightly down the street and was sitting on a small brick wall, a few feet back from the line of cars parked along the curb. The asset was still staring at Mark Ellis.

Throw a variable into the equation.

Noah opened the passenger door. Unlocking the glove compartment, he reached for the stack of papers inside. The car's rental agreement was inside and Noah flipped it onto the floorboard. The complementary map of Washington, DC followed. On the bottom of the stack he found what he was looking for: the map of North Carolina he had picked up when they rented the car. He quickly opened it and tore out what he needed.

The shouted questions were drawing everyone's attention to the far side of the restaurant. Open City's manager was yelling at the cameramen. The cameramen and reporters were firing back. The other tables on the patio watched the media; the noise was drawing their eyes and ears. "Where is Luke Lyford?" "How long did you represent Parker Brown?"

The Echo asset had been joined by the driver of the SUV. The armed pair watched the scene as they waited.

Mark Ellis sat quietly, drinking coffee in the midst of the hurricane. He was looking away from the cameras, toward the door leading to the restaurant's interior dining room.

Noah examined Ellis as he approached the opposite end of the narrow, rectangle-shaped patio. He watched his eyes. *He's waiting on someone? Someone is going to join him for breakfast in the middle of this?*

With one eye on the Echo assets, Noah lingered near the iron fence. He caught the attention of the nearest waitress and quietly whispered a few words in her ear. Noah handed a twenty-dollar bill and a piece of the North Carolina map through the gray bars of the fence. He adjusted his baseball hat, pulling it lower over his hair as he crossed back over the side street. He glanced over his shoulder and saw the woman walking into the hurricane, toward Mark Ellis.

꩜

Mark watched as the woman approached him. He could see the small piece of paper in her hand. *A message from John Baker?* The newly-minted U.S. Attorney was now more than ten minutes late.

"Mr. Ellis?"

"Yes."

She handed him the ripped out section of the map. He could see the colored outline of a small town along the blue of the Atlantic Ocean. In bold red letters above the town, he read the town's name. *Edenton.*

"What is this?" he asked as he looked up at her.

The press had noticed her, and noticed that their interaction seemed to be more than the normal waitress-customer conversation. Some grew quiet as they strained to hear her speak to Mark.

The waitress leaned in close to his ear. "Your friend from the Portico Café says they are watching. You are not safe. He says to get back to the apartment and keep the media close."

Mark's eyes darted upward; his head swiveled as he searched unsuccessfully for Noah Augusteel.

∽

From the front seat of his car, Noah Augusteel waited as Ellis's red truck retraced its path back down Connecticut. He estimated its speed as being a few miles-per-hour slower than the legal limit. Two of the press vans hovered next to the truck in the second southbound lane. The remainder closely followed. He watched as the green SUV reclaimed its position at the end of the chain of vehicles.

His dashboard clock read 8:43. Ellis had understood his warning and immediately left Open City, slowly covering the half-block back to his truck under the dense blanket of media personnel.

The man Noah was waiting to see arrived within a minute. Noah crossed to the other side of the street and casually strolled back toward the restaurant patio. He had a clear view of the man now. He was standing near the sidewalk entrance that Ellis had used moments before, speaking to the hostess and searching the restaurant's tables.

It is 08:44. I am on Connecticut Avenue Northwest in Washington, DC.

Augusteel scrolled through mental images, like a rolodex spinning through faces he had committed to memory. He had seen this man before.

The spinning images returned a hit: the man from the White House, from the Rose Garden. Noah had recognized him as he had watched the nomination ceremony conclude. The tall, brown-haired man had been standing with the President and David Baker.

David Baker. Another hit from his memory, but the connection was not immediately obvious. Noah had seen the man's face in newspaper pictures, in stories about David Baker's nomination. The confusion cleared. Like sunlight piercing through a break in a shifting bank of clouds, the connection locked into place. *John Baker*, he thought. *David Baker's son.*

The rolodex spun again. *John Baker.* The name brought back a deeper memory. He analyzed it as he watched John Baker speak once more to the waitress and then walk back down the sidewalk. The memory was from years ago. From North Carolina. *He was leading the Claire Ellis investigation.*

From the opposite sidewalk, Noah Augusteel watched as John Baker reached the intersection. Baker hailed a cab and quickly entered the rear seat.

Augusteel's eyes were on the brake lights of the departing taxi, but his mind had already left the DC street. The idea came suddenly, an unannounced and unexpected visitor – yet he welcomed it with open arms: Noah Augusteel now knew how he could get close to Edwin Carter.

Chapter Thirty-One

Washington, DC
July 3, 2010

Saturday was his on-call shift, his time to manage the intake of whatever corpses the city coughed up over his lonely twenty-four hour watch. It was the weekend. That meant more bodies and more work. It also meant quiet, as only a skeleton crew manned the Office of the Chief Medical Examiner.

The few others lucky enough to be at work on a summer Saturday morning were on the floors above him. Sam Ortiz was alone in the basement examination room, plodding through the early stages of the examination procedure, his body working almost entirely from muscle memory as he processed the first dead body of the morning. The woman's body had been placed on Examination Table Two, the middle workspace of the three tables in the room. The first and the third tables remained empty. Two people, without a doubt, had reservations, but neither party had arrived.

Working around the center table, Ortiz had conducted the preliminary physical inspection and had removed the dead woman's clothes and jewelry. He had emptied her pockets and stored the few items he found in marked Ziplock Freezer Bags. The bags rested in a plastic bin, balanced on top of her folded clothes – all of which sat on a small, stainless-steel table next to the body.

Step one was to catalogue the potential evidence. Each body was, initially, treated like a victim, not just a corpse. For Dr. Ortiz that meant he was required to start what would become a closely guarded chain of custody, a detailed recording of what he found on – and sometimes in – the body. Each item would be tagged, bagged, or otherwise marked with his initials. If he was ever called to testify in court, he could refer back to his markings and match the physical evidence with the body.

After removing the clothing, step two began. Identification. Sometimes it was as easy as finding a driver's license in the wallet. In other cases, the physician would simply find himself staring at a naked, unidentifiable body. In those cases, responsibility was handed back to the police – usually to the same unit or division that had delivered the corpse in the first place.

The woman on Table Two had been an example of an easy case. Her recently renewed driver's license had been stuffed in the front pocket of her tight-fitting jeans. Sam had added her name to his evidence log and was preparing to draw blood for the standard toxicological scan when the second body of the morning arrived.

"White male. Thirty-ish," the young police officer pushing the stretcher called toward Ortiz, as the wheels of the stretcher wobbled over the sloped basement floor. "Maybe forty-ish. Not really sure. No ID."

"Great," Ortiz responded sarcastically, toward the quickly departing back of the young cop. "I'll be in touch." The physician laid his instruments across the legs of the woman on the center table and crossed toward the new delivery.

The body bag, like always, was colder than Sam Ortiz expected. He could feel the wide, hard teeth of the metal zipper and the rubbery plastic surrounding the body. *Dead weight*, he thought, as he shouldered the body onto the examination table and kicked the stretcher back toward the double doors of the entrance.

With both hands gripping one side of the dense plastic, Ortiz shifted the unidentified body closer to the top of the metal table. He collected, and then positioned, a small side-table – one that could hold the clothing he expected to find on the person inside the body bag. His right hand found the switch on top of the flexible overhead lights. He mindlessly flicked it on and adjusted the angle of the reflective, silver circle so that the powerful lamp focused on the still-concealed face of the dead man. His scrubs were covered by a full-body, disposable, plastic gown. Through the gown, and his gloves and mask, Sam could already feel the heat of the light.

His left hand, meanwhile, had located the zipper pull and was running it down toward the chest. Sam Ortiz peeled open the two sides of the partially opened body bag. The lamp brought the bloodless face into full view.

෨

It took the deputy medical examiner only a matter of minutes to reach his office. He was sweating, even though he had discarded his protective gear and was nowhere near the intensity of the examination lamps.

In his mind's eye the lamps had been replaced by a rack of stage lights. If he was right, there might be another press conference looming in his near future. *Maybe Paul will send someone else this time.* The thought of his boss brought back the memory of the file room. Paul Sorenson had seen him with the William Iredell autopsy folder . . . and yet nothing had happened. No questions. No discussion. Nothing. It seemed as though it never happened; the entire interaction had simply vanished.

His internet browser was open. He immediately found exactly what he was looking for: the picture of Luke Lyford that had been plastered all over Washington for weeks. Lyford in the William Iredell hearings, questioning the then-nominee from the raised bench. A full-on, frontal image of his face.

It was the same face he had just seen in the body bag.

In his deserted office, Ortiz reclined his cheap, government-issue office chair. The plastic hinge bowed as it reached the limit of its flexibility. There was no doubt in his mind. This was Luke Lyford. Dead, ghost-pale, and – according to the articles returned by his search query – recently released from federal custody without a word of explanation. Sam Ortiz checked a few more pictures. He found a better one – more color, a higher quality image. He scanned the remainder of the search results. There were a few images of Lyford being ushered out of his DC apartment. He matched those to his memory of the face in the body bag.

It is him, he concluded, banishing any remaining doubt. Nevertheless, proposing a positive identification based on the similarity between the face of the dead man and a few pictures from the *Washington Post* would be an unorthodox approach.

The office didn't look too kindly on physicians that strayed from the pre-approved procedural line. It wanted consistency. As a potential witness for the prosecution, he needed to be able to take the witness stand and proclaim that he had a procedure, and that he had followed it to the last letter. Holding a printed copy of an old news photo next to a dead man's face would certainly be considered a departure from the standard procedure. His boss – not to mention the prosecutor's office – would want more. As with most "no ID" bodies, they would want a family member or close friend to make the ultimate, official identification.

Sam Ortiz scrolled back through the article open on his monitor. *Mark Ellis.* Ortiz read the name of Lyford's attorney a few lines into the first paragraph. *He can make this official.*

❦

One phone call and twenty minutes later a photocopied version of the William Iredell file sat open on his desk. It was, he guessed, far simpler to request a copy of the file than to ask the FBI's part-time, weekend secretary to dig through the documents in search of Mark Ellis's cell number. And this couldn't wait until the full staff arrived on Monday.

Compared to some of the other investigation files Sam had reviewed, Iredell's seemed rather thin. It was two inches thick, at most. The bulk of it was comprised of an index of the materials that had been seized in the initial search of Luke Lyford's apartment, a laundry list of what was taken and whether it had been returned. Behind the large index was a smaller one providing the name of each potential witness, the date on which the FBI had interviewed the witness, and whether an electronic transcript was stored in the FBI's database.

Behind the smaller index there was a photocopied image of a file tab. The person who had made the copies, he assumed, had inserted it to mark the beginning of an internal file. On the copied image he could read the name of the internal file: Poison, Phenobarbital. It looked to be a copy of whatever notes the FBI had collected concerning the chemical that, they believed, had killed William Iredell.

The pages spun in his hands as he returned to the beginning. As he had hoped, the agents working the case had set up a communal contact list. *Mark Ellis (Lyford attorney) – cell 919-659-0765*, he read.

Curiosity, as it sometimes did, reached its hand into Sam Ortiz before his own hand could dial Mark Ellis's number. He thumbed back past the indices until he reached the copy of the "Poison, Phenobarbital" folder. On the first page behind the copied file tab he found what he was looking for: the toxicology report that had been distributed by his office, the one that laid the blame directly at the chemical feet of Phenobarbital.

Sam remained uncertain. He had no idea why Phenobarbital had been identified in the fake report. He knew it was incorrect, but was it there to cover something up? Was it there to redirect the attention of the investigators, to point them down the wrong trail? Or was it there to help the investigators point the press and the public down the wrong trail?

There were a handful of additional pages underneath the one-page toxicology report and Sam Ortiz mindlessly turned to the first of them as he pondered the false report. His eyes scanned the document, a handwritten list of names. Notes from some agent, he guessed. Along the top of the document the same hand had titled the list: "Prescriptions in Lyford Apartment."

Ortiz recalled the articles he had scanned moments before. They remained open on the monitor to his right. The FBI had located a number of bottles of Phenobarbital in Luke Lyford's apartment, along with a collection of loose pills. If the press was to be believed, none of the prescriptions were in Lyford's name. The names on the list in his hands, he therefore assumed, must be the names from those bottles.

From the lack of other notes and the position of the "Poison" file in the rear of investigation folder, he gathered the investigators had not spent much time looking into the prescriptions. He had read Carol Cushing's explanation in the *Post*: the FBI had its man, and its man had the poison. The defendant possessed the murder weapon. *If you believe it, there is no need to dig much deeper*, Sam concluded.

The next page was in his hand now. He flipped it over and scanned the pages that followed. Each of the remaining six or seven pages looked similar. They were copies of the prescription labels. Someone had attempted to remove the labels from the brown, plastic bottles, and then tried to copy the curved paper. By the blurred text, Sam could tell they had reached a less-than-optimal level of success. The blurred names on the copies followed the earlier list; for each name on the list, there was a copied page. It looked as though someone had simply taken the time to transfer the names into a more user-friendly format and had then dropped the list and the copies into this small, forgotten folder.

Sam had reached the final page. His mind was already thinking about how to convince Mark Ellis to travel down to the medical examiner's office on a weekend.

Something caught his eye as he raised the reversed pile of copies on his left, preparing to flip them back onto the single remaining page on his right.

Two letters and seven numerical digits. He stared at the blurred image, the characters running along the bottom line of the prescription label on the final copied page. It was the number assigned by the Drug Enforcement Agency. The DEA. Sam instantly reversed to the previous page. The same number. One page back. Then another. The same number. He checked each copied, blurred prescription label. Some were more legible than others, but with some effort, he could make out the DEA number on each rough copy.

The DEA number was unique. Every physician in the country had a different number. It was assigned by the federal agency and used, among other purposes, to record and track the distribution of controlled substances. The number was used to match the prescribed narcotic with the doctor writing the prescription.

Sam Ortiz double-checked each label. Once he had an idea of what number to expect, the blurred text became easy to read. *They are all the same number.* However, it wasn't the similarity that was causing Ortiz to panic. It was the number itself. *They are all assigned to my number.* Each prescription label contained his DEA number. Each prescription that had been found in Luke Lyford's apartment had been, according to the FBI's investigative file, written by Samuel Ortiz, MD.

∾

The ring filled the cab of his truck and briefly distracted Mark Ellis. The news van to his left hovered dangerously close to his side-view mirror. It ventured back-and-forth across the dividing line of Connecticut Avenue, wobbling down the stripe like it was a balance beam, as the group crept back toward Dupont Circle.

Mark patted the front pockets of his pants with his right hand as he searched for his phone. He kept his left firmly planted on the sun-faded steering wheel. His eyes alternated between the van to his left and the road ahead. He had taken Noah Augusteel's suggestion and was keeping his speed at a quite-manageable thirty miles-per-hour – slow enough for the press to easily keep him within arm's reach.

The sound of the phone filled the cab again. This time he caught the location; it was to his right somewhere. His briefcase was in the seat next to him. He flipped it over, digging for the phone. Another ring. Some loose documents were in the seat under the briefcase. He saw the corner of his phone and reached for it as the news van bumped the silver border of his mirror.

"Hello," he called into the receiver, glaring in the direction of the scrawny, thinly mustachioed face of the cameraman behind the wheel, and doing his best to ignore the gorgeous female reporter dangling from the open window of the passenger door.

"Mr. Ellis? Mark Ellis?" the voice on the phone asked.

He had hoped for Noah Augusteel. Things were moving quickly around him and he could use some clarity after the cryptic message he had just received from the waitress. "Yes. This is Mark Ellis."

It was not Noah Augusteel's voice.

"Mr. Ellis, my name is Sam Ortiz. I am one of the deputy medical examiners for DC."

Mark glanced at the vans crowding his rear view. They were blocking both lanes behind him. At his slow pace, they were stalling the entire flow of southbound traffic on Connecticut.

The voice on the phone continued as Mark drove. He had instantly recognized the name of the medical examiner from the William Iredell press conference. He had re-watched the video last night and the image of Ortiz was fresh in his mind. "Mr. Ellis, I hope you don't mind me contacting you by cell phone instead of calling your office. The FBI had the number in its investigative file."

"No problem." His voice was a mix of interest and cautious hesitation. Surprises, these days, were unwelcome. "What can I do for you, Doctor?"

"I'm hoping you can find some time – preferably today – to stop by my office. I'm at 1910 Massachusetts." There was a pause in his speech. For a brief second, Mark heard something in the voice on the other end. Nervousness? Unease? Ellis waited for the other man to resume. He used his left shoulder to balance his phone against his ear as he searched for something to write with.

"Some beat cops found a body this morning. Early this morning. The ambulance brought it here. Our office stores the bodies until identification can be made," the physician continued. "I'm the on-call medical examiner this weekend, so I took possession of the body.

"I think it might be your client, Luke Lyford. I need you to come by and make the official identification."

༄

Sam Ortiz stepped through the swinging, double-doors leading back into the autopsy room. He had controlled his voice as best he could on the phone with Mark Ellis and thanked God that he had avoided the dozen other employees rattling around the otherwise empty office building. His hands were shaking and he tried to stabilize them on the metal of Examination Table Three. The overhead lamp was still on. Leaning in, over the face of Luke Lyford, he could feel the heat on the back of his neck, the circle of warm radiance an oasis in the chilled, underground room.

Mark Ellis was on his way. Ortiz had to find something to take his mind off the photocopied prescription labels. *They must have overlooked the numbers. Or the agent copied the prescription labels and made the list of names – and then someone substituted in new, false prescription labels.*

He had never written the prescriptions. That much was a fact. Yet, there they were, sitting in the official investigation file like a landmine – just waiting for an FBI agent to tread close enough to trigger detonation.

Ortiz understood how easily it could have been accomplished. Numerous assistants had his DEA number. And – now that he thought about it – whoever had falsified the prescriptions would not have even needed help from one of the office's assistants. If someone had access to the DEA system, they could have simply searched the federal database. DEA numbers were not closely guarded federal secrets. And once they had the number, it would have been straightforward: type a new label, stick it on a bottle to create an authentic bend in the paper, pull it off, make a blurry copy, put it in the folder.

His hands were as busy as his brain. Years of practice guided them through the procedure. Unzip the body bag and open the thick plastic. Roll the body left. Move the bag. Roll it right and pull the bag from under the body.

Ortiz had removed Luke Lyford's clothing before he really started to focus on the body on the table. Systematically, he began the process. First, he searched the single pocket of his dress shirt. Then he moved to the pockets of his pants. Out of habit, he started with the rear pockets – just in case the police had somehow overlooked his wallet. It was missing; the pocket was empty, as the officer had noted. His hands travelled to the front pockets and, for the first time, found something in the dead man's clothing.

Sam Ortiz felt the shape through the thin fabric of Luke Lyford's dress pants and immediately knew what was about to crest the rim of the pocket. The white top of the prescription bottle preceded the light brown of the bottle itself. He rotated the light plastic in his hands. The bottle was empty. His heart braced for impact as the label came into view. *One more prescription I didn't write*, he thought.

But Sam Ortiz was wrong. The barbiturate listed on the label had not been prescribed *by* Ortiz. It had been prescribed *for* Sam Ortiz.

Chapter Thirty-Two

Washington, DC
July 3, 2010

*N*oah Augusteel drove forward, out of the parking space, and into the Saturday morning traffic on Connecticut. The cluster of media following Mark Ellis was far ahead. The four-cylinder engine of his Camry revved as he merged into the left lane, swerving smoothly past the rear bumper of a car that had stopped in front of him.

John Baker, he thought. His mind methodically worked through the database of his memory, pulling and collecting each random fact he knew about John Baker, and Baker's father, Supreme Court-nominee David Baker. He was compiling the operational file. Aspects of his plan were falling into place, locking together in front of him and unfolding like the stretch of Connecticut Avenue passing under his tires. They both were leading him straight into the heart of Washington, DC.

Augusteel reached Dupont Circle. He stayed in the far right lane. Rounding the traffic circle he could see the fountain in the center, water trickling over the sides of the stone bowl resting atop the single, ornate pillar of the monument. He accelerated as he took the exit onto Massachusetts Avenue and steered his rental car back toward Luke Lyford's apartment.

~

Mark Ellis had scratched directions to the Office of the Chief Medical Examiner on the back of an old legal brief that had been sliding around his passenger seat. He was following those directions now, leading the news vans on a slow-speed chase past the White House and across the southern part of the city. He could see the Anacostia River on his right as he reached the southeastern quadrant of DC. The vans hovered near. Mark made a left onto 19th Street. The intersection between Massachusetts and 19th was directly ahead of him. Outside his passenger window he could see the squared brick structures of the DC General Hospital complex rising on his right.

Ellis rechecked the instructions from Dr. Ortiz and scanned his windshield for the entrance to the underground parking lot. *Let's see them follow me down there*, he thought. He knew losing the media would run counter to Augusteel's suggestion, but Mark was prepared to take that chance if it meant losing whoever else was watching him. He passed the metro station that Ortiz had given as a landmark and then hooked his truck into the underground entrance. The slope ended at a guarded gate. Behind him, a few of the news vans followed him down the ramp. Others peeled off and stayed on the surface street.

Mark handed his driver's license to the guard, who matched it to the list on his clipboard and waved Ellis through. The vans didn't make it past the guard post. As Mark turned right into the parking levels he glanced one final time into his rear-view mirror. He could see the frustrated guard trying to untangle the line of media vans clogging the entrance ramp.

His tires squealed on the pavement of the empty parking deck. Selecting a spot near the entrance to the medical examiner's office, Mark stepped out of his truck. He instantly recognized Sam Ortiz as the physician stepped through the exterior door, and into the parking garage.

"Mr. Ellis?"

"Yes. Dr. Ortiz?"

"Please call me Sam." Ortiz turned and led Mark toward a set of double-doors, and away from the entrance to the medical examiner's office. "Our examination room is on this basement level. I thought it might be a little more private if we went straight there."

Ortiz swiped his identification card on the reader attached to the white cinder-block wall. "As I mentioned on the phone," he said, as Mark followed a step behind him, "today is my on-call day. Whenever the cops find a body, they bring it to us. This one had no ID. They found it in a deserted area of Stanton Park. Just a few blocks from here."

Ellis could hear the double-doors unlock. Ortiz pushed through one. They entered a sterile white hallway. The doctor led him past a closed elevator door on their right.

Ortiz waved his card across another electronic reader. A second-set of double-doors unlocked, ahead of them in the passageway. This set opened automatically, swinging toward the men as they moved down the empty hall.

"When I got down here to examine the body, I thought he looked familiar. The cops had no idea who he was – and still don't. They just dropped him off and left. I compared his picture to a couple on the internet and thought I would give you a call."

They were in the examination room now. Mark could feel the gentle slope of the floor, angling toward the drains under each table. He noticed some sort of file room off to his right. The cold black hands of the clock on the wall marked 9:10 a.m. Another door was on the far side, past the tables. The word "Laboratory" had been painted above it.

Of the three examination tables stretched out before them, the first was empty. The woman's body on the middle table lay covered under a white sheet, the autopsy unfinished. Ortiz had already reached the third. Mark could see that the face had been partially exposed by the folded sheet. Ortiz pulled it back farther, exposing the entire head and face of the dead man. He pulled the sheet back onto the chest of the body and stepped to the side, allowing Mark to approach.

Mark looked into the lifeless eyes of his friend. "That's him. That's Luke." The feeling was nothing short of pain.

෬๑

The block was dead. So much so that it made him nervous.

I am at 425 Massachusetts Avenue Northwest, Washington, DC. It is 09:15. I am travelling at twenty-five miles-per-hour. There is no evidence of a threat.

There were no media vans. There was no sign of Ellis's truck.

Noah had travelled the simple path back to the apartment. Down Connecticut, turn on Massachusetts. One turn. *What happened to Mark Ellis?* There had been absolutely no sign of any sort of assault on the short stretch of road between the restaurant and the apartment.

He circled the block. *Nothing.* It was like the entire caravan had disappeared into Dupont Circle. His blue Toyota parked in an open space one block from the apartment. Noah cautiously stepped from the car and scanned the environment around him. The farmers' market was still active and the noise from the market stalls filtered down the street. The spaces where the vans had been parked had been filled by families visiting the open-air market.

Opportunity. Move. Now.

Augusteel slung his backpack over his shoulder, locked his car, and quickly walked toward the front door of Luke Lyford's apartment building.

❧

"Have you identified the cause of death?"

"No," Sam Ortiz answered. "I've drawn some blood and started the analytical process." He nodded his head toward the laboratory door.

405

"It will likely be a few days. I quickly looked over the body and there was no obvious evidence of physical trauma."

Mark was listening, but had not taken his eyes off of his friend's face. It was expected, of course. But it was still devastating to see Luke on the cold examination table, frozen under the white sheet. He wanted to see him back at his apartment. He wanted to tell him about Edwin Carter, about the five-sided ring.

Thinking about the press conference brought him quickly back to the present. He recalled Sam Ortiz's explanation about how blood pools at the lower portions of the body, and how the color of the blood can be an initial indicator of poisoning. "Did you see the same type of coloring that you saw in William Iredell?" Mark asked. "Any of the pink coloring?"

"I noticed a slight amount. Not as strong as with Iredell; not enough to make the same conclusion – yet." Ortiz knew what Mark was driving at. "I can't say for sure that he was poisoned, but the slight discoloration does indicate that might turn out to be the cause of death."

Mark instinctively reached for his friends arm, laying his hand on the towel covering Luke's bicep.

"Maybe he was given Amobarbital, too," Sam quietly mumbled.

Mark started to respond. Then paused. His eyes remained on his hand, holding Luke's arm through the sheet. The sterile examination room was silent. They could hear the clock ticking on the wall above them. Ellis was the first to speak. He raised his eyes and looked into the dark brown eyes of Sam Ortiz. "You sent the email?"

Ortiz opened his mouth to respond, but Mark spoke first, cutting the medical examiner off. "I've confirmed what was in the email. I don't see the need to get you involved in this, if you want to stay out of it."

Sam looked back at Mark. His eyes followed Mark's arm toward the dead body on the table. It was the same table that had held William Iredell. Someone was out there poisoning these people. "I think I'm involved, whether I want to be or not," Sam said. "Let me show you something."

Ortiz stepped away from the table holding Luke's body. He had placed the copy of the FBI file on the first examination table, the empty one on the other side of the chamber. He returned, flipping through the pages until he found the photocopied prescription labels supposedly collected from Lyford's apartment. Ortiz handed the documents to Mark and directed the attorney's attention to the DEA numbers on the documents. As he passed the papers to Mark, Ortiz explained what a DEA number was and that this repeating number was his own.

"I take it you did not write these prescriptions?"

"I can't remember the last prescription I wrote." He motioned toward the other autopsy tables. "They don't do my patients much good. And I'm absolutely sure I didn't write these." Ortiz tapped his index finger on the copied pages as he spoke.

"I'm not sure what . . . ," Mark Ellis began in response.

Ortiz interrupted him and turned toward the small table holding Luke Lyford's clothes. "Let me show you one more thing." He found the empty prescription bottle he had removed from Luke Lyford's pocket and tossed it to Mark.

Mark turned the brown plastic until he could read Sam's name on the label.

Amobarbital? He had expected Phenobarbital. He had expected it to match the other prescriptions. Below the name of the drug he read the instructions: "Take one pill, as necessary, to relieve insomnia."

Sam was watching him. Their eyes met again as Mark looked up from the bottle. "Check the DEA number."

Mark read it and then compared it with the number in the FBI file. "It's different. Whose is it?"

"Paul Sorenson's. My boss."

"Why would he . . . ." Mark trailed off. The look in Sam's eyes indicated he already knew the question and already had the answer.

In the empty examination room, his voice sounded louder than the quiet discussion he intended. He started at the beginning and explained everything he knew about William Iredell's autopsy and everything he had done after taking the tube of blood from the rack of Iredell blood samples. Mark listened intently as Sam finished. "What do you think this means, Mr. Ellis?"

"I think it means they have you in check, Dr. Ortiz. And they're only one move away from checkmate." Mark lifted the FBI documents as he spoke. "There is going to be an investigation into Luke's death. I think we can reasonably expect that Luke's blood is going to be loaded with Amobarbital."

He raised the brown, plastic bottle with his other hand. "Eventually, the FBI is going to look at this prescription. Even if you destroy this bottle someone will tip them off and they'll find the record of your boss writing the prescription."

"Then Sorenson will take the stand and offer some sad story about how you couldn't sleep because of all the pressure from the Iredell case. So – since he is such a great doctor and an even better friend – he wrote you a prescription for a sleep aid: Amobarbital."

"But why would I kill Luke Lyford? I didn't even know the man."

Mark could feel the confusion and pain in Sam's voice. He had heard the same in Luke's. It was the unknown, the loss of control. "Sam," he gently shook the FBI file as he spoke. "According to the DEA, you did know him. You prescribed the drugs – all of the drugs – that were found in Luke's apartment. It looks like there was a strong connection between you and the man accused of killing William Iredell. The prosecution is going to say that you helped Luke get the poison."

Mark stalled, then continued with a question. "Do you know what they call a doctor that provides the murder weapon to the killer?"

"No," Sam responded.

"A co-conspirator."

The words and their implication filled the basement room. They seemed to echo off the one empty table and surround Sam Ortiz. His regret – regret that he had come to this room to check the hard copy of Iredell's record, regret that he had taken and tested a sample of his blood – was growing. Whatever sense of pride he had felt at knowing that he stood on the right side of this investigation now had emotional competition.

"The prosecution is going to argue that you killed Luke to cut off the investigation into Iredell's death," Mark said. "They are going to say you wanted it to end before someone noticed these DEA numbers. You needed Luke to die before someone figured out you were involved.

"You're being . . . ," Mark continued. Then he stopped and corrected himself. "No, *you've been* set up, Doctor. Someone has lined you up perfectly to take the fall. I'd wager that you're about one anonymous phone call away from being arrested for the murder of Luke Lyford *and* for conspiring to murder William Iredell."

❦

The media had been waiting on Mark Ellis to leave the underground parking garage and swarmed his truck as soon as he exited, as he hoped they would. It wasn't hard to pick his long tail of vans back up. It was rather easy to spot his truck, especially on the empty Saturday-morning streets. He throttled the truck back under the speed limit. Again, the media had no problem keeping up. A parking spot was available near the apartment. Mark cautiously stepped from his truck and allowed himself to be followed to the front steps of the apartment. He knew they would go no further; there was no point in following him into the narrow entry way or through the tight hallways.

His hand was on the silver handlebar of the building's main door and he turned to face the cameras. The reporters were shouting questions. "Why did you go to the morgue?" One toppled over another as they clamored for an answer. "Where is Luke Lyford?"

Just in case Echo Industrial was watching, Mark Ellis lied. "I needed to pick up some paperwork related to Parker Brown's death. I'm sure a copy will be released to the public soon."

Chapter Thirty-Three

The elevator doors parted and deposited Mark on the seventh floor of the apartment building. The image of Luke Lyford flared in front of him. There was a certain finality to seeing his body. It was conclusively over. His feet felt heavy, like his soles were having difficulty separating from the hard, hallway floor. His shoulders ached. He had felt tired plenty of times since his arrival in the nation's capital, but this was different. This was exhaustion. This was grief. Luke's death was bringing everything down around him.

There had always been hope. Hope that he could clear Luke's name. Hope that he could determine who killed his mother. Hope that he could unwind the last two years of his life and start fresh, that he could turn south and drive away from this town in better shape than when he arrived. Now those hopes were zipped in a body-bag and stored in the Medical Examiner's basement refrigerator.

As he pulled his key-ring from his pocket, Mark thought about what would happen next. He should contact someone. But he had no idea who to call. He had never known Luke to be close to his family. In fact, he had never even heard Luke mention his family.

He approached the apartment door. It had been coming for days, but Mark had finally reached the point where knowledge becomes truth: his friend was dead. Nothing could change that. The empty hallway seemed emptier, like he was alone in it for the first time.

He picked through the keys on his ring, sorting through them for Luke's spare. As he fingered the jagged, metal teeth, it seemed appropriate that he had this key. He had become Luke's spare key – unnecessary on a daily basis, but useful in an emergency. Where had the two years gone? How had he let their friendship go ignored for two whole years? They were irrelevant questions, the attorney in him knew, but he couldn't stop himself from asking.

Mark slipped the spare key into the deadbolt. He heard the same mechanical, retracting sound he recalled from the day he arrived. *Luke should be behind this door. But he's not.* His hand slipped toward the doorknob. In his peripheral vision, he saw the window at the far end of the hall darken. Something blocked the light that normally shone through from the sunlit stairwell. *Something or someone*, Mark thought, recalling Augusteel's warnings.

The feeling of panic was instantaneous. He briefly fumbled with the knob as he opened the door. Glancing down the hall, he saw the stairwell door opening. His mental image of Luke Lyford had been replaced by the image of the executed Parker Brown.

"Ellis. Wait." The voice echoed in the hall. It was familiar. Mark had crossed the threshold and was spinning to slam the door behind him. He stopped and carefully stepped back into the doorway, angling his head around the frame.

Noah Augusteel had covered half the distance between Mark and the stairwell. He was jogging toward the door, his footfalls loud against the concrete floor.

Mark was the first to speak. "What did you see? Who is out there?"

"Echo. Two assets. They followed you to the restaurant and were watching from across the street."

Mark held the side of the door in his right hand. His left was on the frame and his body blocked the opening. "I never saw them."

"How could you, with all those cameras surrounding you?" Noah responded, looking farther down the hall, toward the elevators. "May I come in?"

Like a sentry, Mark stood in silence, contemplating the request. Seeing Luke's body had crystallized the feeling that he was gone. Mark was no longer just using the apartment while Luke was locked up. He fought the urge to step into the hall and close the door behind him, to leave the apartment forever.

"Mr. Ellis, I need your help. And you need mine. It would be better if we talked in private." Augusteel nodded toward the interior of the apartment.

Mark Ellis slowly stepped backward and watched Augusteel step onto the smooth, bamboo floor. He could see Noah's eyes, scanning the room, seemingly absorbing the images surrounding him.

"May I check the other rooms? Just to make sure we're alone."

"Be my guest." Mark lifted his right arm in a sweeping gesture toward the remainder of the apartment and watched as Noah drew a handgun from his backpack. His words brought back the vision of Luke. It was Mark who was actually the "guest" here.

Moments later Noah returned to the living area and laid the silver Luger on the coffee table. He dropped his backpack on the couch and took a seat next to it. A baseball hat covered his cropped, blond hair. He removed it and dropped it on top of the bag. "I followed the vans to the restaurant. Smart move, keeping them close."

"Is Echo out there now?" Mark glanced toward the window.

"I'm not sure. We should assume so."

Mark strode toward the glass and searched the street, although he had no idea what – or who – to look for.

Noah spoke to his turned back. "John Baker arrived shortly after you left the restaurant. I believe he was looking for you."

This comment caught Mark Ellis by surprise. He opened his mouth to ask how Noah had known to wait for Baker to arrive, but Noah continued speaking. "I need you to get in touch with Baker and have him come here, to this apartment."

"Why? What does he have to do with this?"

"Baker has to come here. It is the only way to meet with him in private. You saw what happened when you left this morning. You can't move without the press trailing every step you take." Augusteel paused.

Mark had rotated back to face the room and was watching him, waiting for him to finish his explanation. He was tempted to waive off the request, tempted to say "let's turn those cameras on John Baker and see what happens to his father's nomination."

"We just have to hope that Baker doesn't know about the press outside," Augusteel continued. "He arrived after they left the restaurant, so he didn't see them. Hopefully, he won't know what is waiting outside until he gets here."

Mark took one of the seats opposite Augusteel. "How does Baker fit into this Lexington League situation?" His suspicion was peaking. Baker had only told him that he had new information related to Mark's mother's death, and that he was planning to re-open the investigation – this time from his federal office. He had not mentioned anything about William Iredell, Parker Brown, or the Lexington League.

As he had explained to Mark over the phone, Baker was in Washington this weekend because of his father's confirmation hearings. They were expected to conclude on Monday – two days from now. John Baker had brought his wife and family back to the Capitol in anticipation of Monday's vote to confirm David Baker as the next Supreme Court Justice. "I've got some free time on Saturday, if you can meet then," he had told Mark.

In the tense apartment, Augusteel was answering his question, depicting how Baker fit into their current situation. "In simple terms: Baker is the key. John Baker can convince David Baker to help. And I need David Baker. The Lexington League endorsed his nomination to the Supreme Court – although my guess is that Senator Baker probably only considers them a legal advocacy organization, just a powerful conservative group that agrees with his view of the legal world. I doubt he knows the truth about the Lexington League, but he can get close to them."

"You mean close to Edwin Carter?" It was the first time Mark Ellis had spoken the words to another person.

Noah searched Mark's face. This time he was the one surprised by how much the other person knew. "Yes," he acknowledged. "And John Baker has to be a part of this.

We need him on board." Noah emphasized the "we" in the sentence.

This was a new concept for Mark Ellis. He had only briefly considered the idea that he might be going after the Lexington League; it had been more of a vague notion, a dream. Despite all that he had seen, he had instinctively continued to envision some sort of public, legal battle – not some kind of head-on collision.

Noah Augusteel, apparently, saw things differently.

"If you've included me in this," Mark responded. "Tell me what you plan to do. And don't limit it to 'simple terms.'"

Mark Ellis listened as Noah laid out the plan he had been developing over the last hour. It wasn't entirely complete; it was more of a thorough draft. Mark asked few questions. He could tell that there were multiple moving parts, plenty of things that would have to break their way.

But it was possible. He admitted that much to himself. And it was far better than anything Mark had thought of. Slowly, he felt himself wading into deeper waters. He wasn't comfortable, and it showed. *I am being asked to participate in a conspiracy*, Mark considered. And the objective was the potential assassination of the United States Attorney General. Guilty or not, Lexington League or not, responsible for his mother's death or not, the man was still one of the highest-ranking public officials in the country. He could feel the sweat balling along his temples.

Augusteel must have read the look on his face. "Force must be met with force," Augusteel argued, trying to keep Mark involved, and reiterating what he had said in the café. "You know the truth about the league. You've seen what they can do.

"And you know what they have done," the blond man added. That struck a chord. His family. Luke. Mark could see the image of Luke's body, covered by the sheet and spread on the examination table. He could smell the charred wreckage of his mother's plane.

"And you know what they *will do*." Noah extended his right arm and pointed toward the large window at the end of the room. "They are out there right now. They are waiting on you."

Mark retrieved his cell phone from his pocket and found the notepad on which he had written John Baker's phone number. He reached Baker on the second ring. After a brief apology for his absence at the restaurant, Mark explained that he was available, right now, if Baker had time to meet with him. He gave him Luke's address and ended the call.

"He's on his way."

∾

Noah Augusteel and Mark Ellis monitored the street below through Luke Lyford's seventh-story window. They could see the top of the yellow cab as it arrived at the front steps, and could see John Baker's long leg step from the cab as it pulled to a stop. From the apartment window, Mark could also see a couple of the reporters, moving like small toy soldiers across the pavement and nearing the taxi. Baker must have seen them too, as he quickly spun toward the front door in an effort to avoid the cameras. He mounted the steps in two loping strides and entered the apartment building.

Mark crossed toward the apartment's door. Noah returned to his place on the couch. Most of Mark's paperwork – the chemical test results, the toxicology reports, the copy of the letter from James Madison – remained spread on the coffee table. Noah's Luger was next to them. It was constantly reminding Mark of the escalation. The investigative semi-speculation he had worked through during the last few days had morphed into a very real world over the course of the morning.

While they had waited on John Baker, Noah had walked through his plan for the second time. This time Mark asked more questions, probing some of Noah's assumptions and challenging some of his designs. Together, they made a few adjustments and one addition.

They had spent the last ten minutes watching a panel of journalists discuss the David Baker hearings on one of the weekend news shows. The video footage showed Senator Baker in the familiar Senate hearing room, sitting at the center table. A series of Anderson administration officials rotated through the witness seat next to Baker. They were there to support his nomination and to be "questioned" by the Senate committee.

With the result of the hearing a foregone conclusion, the Senators never considered using their allotted time to question the witnesses. Instead each used his or her fifteen minutes of public attention to offer speeches praising their fellow Senator. The few liberal Senators that were opposed to Baker's confirmation passed on the opportunity to question the witnesses, or were simply absent.

The witnesses watched and listened. Senator Baker watched and listened.

And the clock ticked toward Monday's final vote.

ᕉᘏ

The knock was swift, a firecracker in the apartment hallway. Noah silenced the television and Mark reached for the door handle. For a split second all he could do was look at John Baker. The last time he had laid eyes on the prosecutor was the day Baker had closed the investigation into his mother's death. "John," Mark said, the cold tone of his voice more formal than welcoming. Re-opened investigation or not, Baker still had a lot to prove to Mark Ellis.

"Thank you for calling me, Mark. I'm sorry we missed each other this morning and I appreciate you meeting with me on a weekend." Taller than Mark and well-dressed in a short-sleeved polo shirt and tailored dress pants, Baker stood in the hall, waiting for his fellow North Carolinian to let him cross the threshold into the apartment. "I come bearing good news."

John Baker understood Mark's anger. *I'd feel the same way if it was my family*, John thought. He tried to keep his voice positive, open. They would be on the same side of the re-opened Claire Ellis investigation and he knew he wanted to work with the victim's son, not against him. *Ellis will come around*, he told himself. *Give him time. He needs to see the video from Johansson's speech. He just needs to see the face I found in the video.*

As Baker spoke, Mark noticed the laptop carrying-case under Baker's arm. He stepped back, mirroring the motion he had made with Augusteel, and invited someone he barely knew into an apartment he didn't own.

Baker stepped past Mark, speaking as he walked into the apartment. "Mark, I'll get right to the point: I think the man from the airport has turned up again. We caught him on a video . . . ." He froze, unable to move farther.

"The man from the airport? The water-bottle guy?" Suddenly, Mark's attention was focused on John Baker, leaving everything else behind. He had been expecting something much less significant. He had expected Baker to tell him how advances in technology would enable them to do more with the tissue samples they had saved from the crash site. Or how the federal aviation safety agency was going to take another shot at accident reconstruction.

He had not expected anything related to the unidentified man at the airport.

Baker ignored the questions. His eyes were locked on Noah Augusteel. The blond man's right hand lowered the remote control onto the couch. The voiceless images of the reporters flickered on the television screen, as though it was the images watching the scene in the apartment unfold, not the other way around.

"Well?" asked Mark, watching Baker. Baker had strangely stopped moving. Even his left hand, which had been reaching for the laptop case under his right arm, was stalled in mid-air. Mark followed the prosecutor's eyes. They moved from Noah's head to the coffee table. Then back to Noah.

"John, this is Noah . . ."

The silver shone in the morning sunlight. It was lightning-quick.

"Close the door, Mark." Noah had the Luger in his hand, pointing it at John Baker. Then at Mark. "Close the door and have a seat."

Confusion engulfed Mark Ellis. He could see the hallway through the half-open door. His hand was inches from the handle. For a brief second he contemplated running. But where would he go? Run outside, into the arms of the media? Into the waiting arms of Echo Industrial?

The image of Parker Brown appeared in his memory again. Bloodied and leaning against the holding-cell door.

Noah slowly rose to his feet, like a statue come to life. "Mark." His voice was calm. It was the same voice he heard at the Portico Café. He moved closer to Mark, ignoring John Baker. "Listen to me Mark. We are on the same team here. Let's talk this out."

"It's him," Baker whispered, as much in amazement as for Mark's benefit.

Noah Augusteel closed toward them. He was working his way along the side of the coffee table, shortening the distance between himself and the door. His arm shifted. It looked mechanical, automatic. The barrel locked on John Baker's chest.

Recognition plowed into Mark Ellis. His memory was the same as John Baker's. But he had never looked at Noah Augusteel with this perspective. Every time his mind noticed the familiarity in Noah's face, he had attributed the thought to his resemblance to Gloria Augusteel. But he could see it clearly now. The face and hair. The same as the video. *Noah Augusteel killed my mother*. The idea overwhelmed everything else.

Mark Ellis stepped toward Augusteel. They were close now.

The barrel of the weapon swung back toward him.

He was close enough to see Noah's finger on the trigger. Still. His hand steady. The barrel began a straight line that extended the two feet between its tip and the skin of Mark Ellis's forehead.

"Easy, Mark. We'll work this out."

Mark stopped, his eyes locked on the Luger, his ears barely registering Noah's balanced voice. Noah had shuffled past the coffee table. He took one more step and gently kicked the door from where Mark had left it standing. It closed against the frame. Mark and John stepped back, toward the bedroom hallway and away from Noah.

Noah studied Mark's eyes as he circled between the two men and the door. "Mr. Baker, please move my backpack and hat to the chair." Noah directed the other man with a tilt of his head, pointing in the direction of the chair nearest the door.

With the couch now empty, Augusteel instructed Baker and Ellis to take a seat. Augusteel hooked his foot around of the chair that now held his backpack and slid it closer to the door. He lowered himself on the front of the seat cushion; he was directly between the couch and the only exit. The gun tilted down, its barrel now aiming toward the floor. His hand remained around the grip, but he rested it on his lap.

"He's right. I killed Claire Ellis." The admission thickened the tension in the room and faded into heavy silence. Both men were staring at Noah. He could see the fear in John Baker's eyes. *Understandable*, he thought. *He has no idea what he stepped into this morning.* He saw nothing but hate in Mark Ellis's eyes.

"We both know why I did it, and *we both know who I was working for.*" Noah was now speaking directly to Mark, and he emphasized the end of the sentence to ensure his message would cut through Mark's rising emotion.

Then he turned to John. "Save the taxpayers some money and keep the investigation closed, Mr. Baker. I disappear in forty-eight hours." His eyes pivoted between the two men on the couch. "It is time to make some choices, gentlemen.

"You first, Mr. Ellis." Noah continued, addressing the blood-red eyes of Mark Ellis. "This is our opportunity, our window. It may be our *only* window. But you can walk away. Right now. Just say the word and we'll call this off.

"However – before you choose – think about where you'll be when that door closes behind me. Edwin Carter will be alive, and he'll be looking to sweep up the last pieces of this Iredell mess. Iredell, the old man in North Carolina, your friend Luke. Even Parker Brown. They're gone. *Who does that leave?*

"My sister will still be looking for you." He flicked his wrist and pointed his gun at the window. "She's got a couple of guys out there right now. Are you willing to bet your life on the media shielding you? Every day? How long do you think you can keep that up?

"I'm offering you a chance to strike a blow – not only against the people chasing you, but against the people that sent me to poison your mother."

Mark Ellis was quiet.

"True," Noah offered, rolling his wrist, responding to an unasked question. The Luger pointed in the opposite direction. "The Lexington League isn't going to go away just because Edwin Carter dies." He glanced at John Baker. He could see Baker's fear was mixing with incomprehension.

"But, if we take out the one man who has been calling the shots – who has been tearing your life apart – maybe whoever takes his place has a different view of the situation. Maybe it pulls those assets off the street. Face it: it's the best shot you have left. *I'm the best shot you have left.*"

Noah slowed his pace. "Your best option," he restarted. His voice remained calm. "Is for us to move forward, together – and leave the past in the past."

John Baker turned his head to the left and watched Mark Ellis. Ellis was stationary, statuesque, offering no response to Noah Augusteel.

"But you can throw that option away . . . if you would rather go it alone. Think about that, while *we* talk to Mr. Baker." Noah shifted his attention to John Baker, toggling his focus like a switch. "You don't know it yet, sir; but you also have a choice to make."

Baker's response was immediate, cutting off Augusteel. "Whatever you're planning, I don't want any part of it."

"Fair enough. But hear us out." Noah swung the barrel of the handgun back-and-forth between himself and Mark Ellis as he said "us." "Mr. Ellis, would you mind bringing Mr. Baker up to speed?"

Mark Ellis breathed. It seemed like the first breath he had taken in an hour. His eyes remained fixed on Noah Augusteel for a fleeting moment. Then he turned toward John Baker. For the next twenty minutes, Mark walked John Baker through everything that had happened over the past few weeks. Baker, of course, already knew some of the story – but he remained silently attentive as Ellis covered the entire ordeal.

He told him about the press conference and about the phone call from Luke Lyford. He told him about the first time he and Luke met in this apartment. Mark picked up the copy of the James Madison letter, quickly described its contents, and showed John Baker the stained corner and the scrawled handwriting in the margin.

Ellis explained how Parker Brown had become involved. He talked about their conversations. "Those conversations were the first time that I actually started to believe," he explained. Then he talked about how Brown had linked the Lexington League to William Iredell's murder and to Claire Ellis's death.

At the mention of Claire Ellis, John Baker looked toward Noah Augusteel. Augusteel nodded in agreement.

Mark Ellis had his head down as he spoke. His voice was soft, nearly trembling, but in the hushed apartment, Baker was able to follow the narrative. Ellis shifted gears to the chemical tests that had been run on the copy of the Madison letter. He explained how the tests matched what Parker Brown had told him about the Lexington League, and matched the unauthorized toxicology test performed by Sam Ortiz.

Then Mark talked about Luke Lyford. His voice took on a softness, like fresh-picked cotton, but the tick-tock cadence of his speech gave his words a numbness that seemed to grow as the account of the last couple weeks progressed. Mark spoke about how he had asked Luke to meet with Gloria Augusteel and about how Luke had turned up dead earlier that morning. He quietly spoke about seeing Luke's body at the medical examiner's office and about how it looked like he also may have been poisoned.

Ellis laid the chemical-test results back on the coffee table. Reclining back on the couch, he turned toward the federal prosecutor. The numbness had reached his eyes. Lastly, Mark explained how he had reached his final conclusion about the Lexington League. It had the means: the poison matched. It had the motive: covering up the Madison letter. It had the opportunity: the last witness to see Iredell alive placed the judge near the Lexington League offices.

Mark could see Baker following his explanation, silently assessing the evidence that had led Mark to this point. The monologue turned to Attorney General Edwin Carter. Ellis started with Gloria Augusteel, explaining how she had been in the courtroom. Then he turned to Parker Brown's death and his missing ring. He opened his laptop and showed the video of the press conference to John Baker. He paused the video as the five-sided ring came into view.

At last, he laid out the case against Edwin Carter. His ability to orchestrate the Brown trial. His ability to control the security around Parker Brown. He added in what he had learned from Noah: Carter was the person directing Gloria Augusteel. He had sent both twins to Edenton to retrieve the letter.

"That directly ties him to the death of Everett Johansson," Baker interjected, thinking of his investigation. He broke from Mark's explanation and eyed Noah Augusteel.

"That one wasn't me," Augusteel responded. "If he's dead, it was my sister."

"It also directly ties him to the letter," Mark added, reaching for the copy of the Madison letter on the table in front of him. "The poison that killed Iredell is on this copy. That means the letter was with William Iredell when he was poisoned. We may never know if Carter was the one that actually poisoned Iredell, but we do know that he sent Noah and Gloria Augusteel to North Carolina – *on the night before William Iredell died.* Either he used the poison to get the truth out of Iredell, or someone else did, and that someone quickly reported back the results," Mark said.

John Baker held up an open palm, signaling for Mark to stop. "What do you mean, used the poison 'to get the truth out of him?'"

Mark looked across the small room to Noah. Noah pulled a bound roll of cloth from his backpack. As he unfurled it, a small, glass vial rolled out of the cloth and into his hand. He shook the white powder as he lifted it for Baker to see. "This is one of the last doses that exists – maybe the last dose, period," he said. "All I know is that it has some short-term truth-serum effects . . . right before it delivers a lethal amount of Amobarbital."

The apartment was noiseless. Each eye was on the vial in Noah Augusteel's raised hand. "This is where you come in, Mr. Baker."

More images of the David Baker hearings flickered on the television. Noah laid the final dose of the substance on Luke Lyford's coffee table, the white of the powder bright in the sunlight and stark against the dark wood. He began to explain his plan anew. This time he concentrated on John Baker.

⤳

The initial fear in John Baker's eyes had given way to incomprehension. As Mark Ellis had relayed the story of the past few weeks, the incomprehension had given way to disbelief. *The Lexington League? Have they lost their minds? Edwin Carter?*

Noah Augusteel was leaning forward now, slowly laying out a plan to murder the Attorney General of the United States. Baker had listened, enthralled with Mark Ellis's story. *Maybe it was true*, he allowed. But if so, Carter should be arrested, not killed. *But arrested based on what evidence? A missing ring?*

What witnesses? Parker Brown is dead. Noah Augusteel is not going to allow himself within a mile of a courtroom.

John Baker picked up some of the documents. As Noah spoke, he flipped through the pages, thinking back over the story Mark Ellis had told. *Maybe the toxicology results were fake. Maybe Iredell was poisoned by something other than Phenobarbital. But without testimony from either Noah or Gloria Augusteel – assuming she was involved – no-one could prove that Carter was involved in the murder.*

While Baker was thinking, Noah was approaching his conclusion. "You have a choice, Mr. Baker. In or out? You can get out and try your luck in federal court. Rest assured, however, that you won't have any more luck than you did in the Claire Ellis case.

"In," Augusteel continued, "and you can help us bring justice to Edwin Carter." He watched the federal prosecutor assess the options laid before him. Noah Augusteel had explained most of his plan. As the quiet lingered among the three men, he explained the final stage. "And that is where your father comes in to this."

The mention of his father abruptly altered the course of Baker's thoughts. John Baker looked at the documents in his hands. The copy of the letter from Madison was on top. He glanced at Noah. Then he searched the hardened features of Mark Ellis's face. *He really believes of all this,* Baker thought.

His analysis flowed in a new direction. *If Carter is guilty, but there is not enough evidence to convict him . . .*

Could this be true? Could the Lexington League truly be what these two believe it is? Could Edwin Carter – and Parker Brown before him – and others before Parker Brown – have led this sort of subversive organization?

There were unavoidable hard facts, he had to admit.

William Iredell had a copy of the Madison letter. He was dead.

William Iredell had sent that copy to Luke Lyford. Lyford was killed.

Everett Johansson had possessed the original copy of the Madison letter. He was murdered.

The letter links these murders. Baker was trying to stay detached, to look at this from an objective, prosecutorial perspective. *And the letter could undo much of what the Lexington League has worked for.*

Could this be true? He allowed himself to ask again. *Could these people have been killed to cover up this letter?* Baker remained unconvinced, but the same idea returned: *if Carter is guilty, but there is not enough evidence to convict him . . .*

He could see Augusteel and Ellis. They were watching for his response.

Out! The thought screamed in his head. *Get out!*

Maybe there is some conspiracy. Maybe, God forbid, Edwin Carter is involved in this, he thought. But there was little hard evidence. There was nothing that Baker could use in court, nothing that resonated with his prosecutorial thinking. No solid, certain proof – nothing of the sort he would need to even consider joining this type of orchestrated plot.

But without more – without some kind of proof of Carter's guilt – he simply couldn't go along with the plan Augusteel had laid before him.

John Baker prepared himself to decline Augusteel's gunpoint invitation and to deal with whatever consequences followed. He reached to drop the copy of Madison's letter on the table. His knuckles touched the top of the other documents, but his grip held the letter.

One final thought crashed through, barreling in under the wire: It wasn't that there was no hard evidence; it was just that it pointed to a much more limited conclusion than the one Augusteel was trying to sell.

William Iredell, Luke Lyford, and Everett Johansson all were connected to the letter. They were all dead. If someone – not necessarily Edwin Carter, but someone – was trying to suppress this letter, then anyone who has a copy is not safe.

And anyone who has the original is certainly a target.

Fear had given way to incomprehension. Incomprehension had given way to disbelief. And now disbelief had yielded to hesitation. The letter hung in his hand, hovering over the other documents.

Mark Ellis spoke in the silent room. Through the tone in his voice John could tell that Mark had decided to go forward with Augusteel's plan – and he was making an attempt to convince John to do the same. "There is a failsafe, John. One way to know, before we get too deep, whether Carter is truly involved or not." As Baker listened, Mark Ellis offered a few more words of explanation.

John Baker glanced one more time at the Madison letter. Again, the thought ran through his mind: *anyone who has the original is a target.*

Mark had completed his explanation of the plan's failsafe and Noah added one final sentence. "We simply cannot do this without you and your father, John."

"If I get in – and I'm not sure that I will," Baker said, barely believing that he had travelled this far. "If I get in, I have a price." John Baker stared into the cool, cobalt eyes of Noah Augusteel. The face. The one he had chased.

The one he had found.

"You've killed at least one person. Probably more, I would guess."

His voice challenged Augusteel, rising in strength as he spoke. "Killing Edwin Carter won't wash the blood from your hands. It might be revenge for you." He stopped and looked to his left at Mark. "It might be revenge for Mark. But this is not justice. Don't confuse what you have proposed with justice. This is vengeance. Pure and simple vengeance. "When this is over, you're going to turn yourself in, Mr. Augusteel. You're going to walk through the front door of the state prosecutor's office in Edenton and tell them that you killed Claire Ellis." Baker paused and examined the expression on Noah's face. It remained unchanged, but he could tell he had the blond man's full attention. "Then you're going to plead guilty and stand before a jury, and then they'll decide your fate." The implication was unspoken, but clearly understood by the three men: the death penalty.

Mark Ellis listened as Baker spoke. He watched the light in Noah Augusteel's eyes waver, flicker like the images on the television. Slowly, Ellis nodded his head in support, seconding the harsh price John Baker had affixed on his participation. "Blood must be paid with blood," he added when Baker was through. "That is what you said at the Portico Café. It's my price, too."

Noah Augusteel felt the weight of the Luger in his right hand. He had collected the vial from the table in front of him and he felt its smooth glass in his left. Never had he held such lethality, yet felt so weak. He thought about his life, about the things he had done. About all the regret.

He thought about his sister and her dedication to the league. He thought about the protective net she had cast over Edwin Carter. It would be impossible to reach him any other way. He could feel his time running short. He knew she hunted him.

He knew that John Baker and Mark Ellis were not the only two people with a choice: he had to make one too. Noah could not hide forever. Eventually the clock would expire. "It always comes down to a choice," his Echo instructor had drilled into his young mind. Augusteel knew he had made more than his share of poor ones. Some had been voluntary; some under pressure. But they had always been his – his choices.

Noah hadn't lied to Mark Ellis. This was his window. Maybe his *only* window. This was the *only* way.

He made his decision. He would have his revenge, but at a very steep cost – maybe the steepest. "I will. When this is over, I'll stand before the jury," Noah Augusteel promised.

Their attempt at misdirection was rudimentary, but effective. Mark Ellis left first and slowly allowed the media to flock toward him. He then walked the half-block to the CVS store on the corner, bought a few groceries, and returned to the apartment. Augusteel and Baker borrowed some of Luke's clothes and departed as soon as they saw the cameras follow Mark away from the front door. It only needed to buy them enough time to catch a cab, and it did.

Mark Ellis had returned to the apartment, media in tow. Alone. Again. *Forty-eight hours.* He wondered whether it was safe to trust John Baker, whether it was safe to trust Noah Augusteel. *Will Baker's nerve hold up until Monday? Will mine?*

The first step in their plan was his. He pulled his cell phone from his pocket, found the number he had entered into his contact list, and dialed.

༄

"Sam Ortiz," the wavering voice on the other end answered.

"Sam, its Mark Ellis."

The other end of the line seemed empty. Again, he thought of Luke, of the call that had pulled him off of his deck in Whispering Pines. He could feel the pressure on the other end – newly discovered and smothering.

"Have you told anyone that you have Luke's body?"

"No," Ortiz answered. "I've started the toxicology scan, but there are no results yet."

"Good. Can you keep this quiet until Monday morning? Can you make sure no-one discovers that Luke's body is down there?"

"Yeah, I would think so. It'll be quiet all weekend and it usually takes a couple of days to ID a body anyway. You mind telling me why I would need to do that?"

Ellis paused as he ventured into the more important part of the conversation. Mark slowly detailed part of Noah Augusteel's plan. It wasn't the entire plan, but it was enough to give Sam Ortiz an idea about where the plan led, and whom it targeted.

Sam Ortiz quickly responded. "I can handle that. Count me in."

Ellis prepared to end the conversation. "I'll be in touch on Monday."

"I'd like to add something to Monday's schedule," Ortiz interjected before Mark could pull the phone from his ear. Now that he was on board, his voice seemed to be gaining strength. The train was pulling away from the station and building momentum. "I kept a test tube of William Iredell's blood . . . ."

Part Six

Chapter Thirty-Four

Washington, DC
July 5, 2010

Independence Day, a Sunday, was spent in rainy seclusion. As a summer thunderstorm pounded against the apartment building, Mark had reflected on his conversation with Noah Augusteel and John Baker. By nightfall, it felt like a dream. Like something so foreign to his day-to-day experience that it was difficult to believe it was real. Yet the impatient energy balled in the pit of his stomach reminded him that it was not a dream. It was quite real.

Sleep was difficult to come by on Luke's couch, despite the fact that he had been sleeping on it for over a week. His charcoal suit was stretched across Luke's bed. He would need it in the morning. Everything else he would need waited patiently on a chair next to the bed. His other clothes had been packed; his papers shuffled back into his briefcase. His suitcase and briefcase waited for him by the door. He had done his level best to clean the apartment – and to set it back to how he had found it three weeks ago.

The alarm clock was wailing on the floor next to the couch. Mark Ellis woke to bright sunlight streaming into the room.

It was Monday morning. It was time.

❧

The hallways were quiet as she passed through. To her right, she could hear the low sounds of movement in one of the communication rooms. Electronic equipment hummed through the door. *There was an operation in Bahrain last night*, she recalled. She passed the closed door and continued down the hall.

Gloria Augusteel swiped her identification card along the wall and listened as the smoked-glass door unlocked. She stepped onto the carpeted floor of her office. Already deep in contemplation, she crossed to her desk and passed her palm over the identification reader. The drawers clicked open.

The storm that had torn through the Washington night had passed. Behind her, a humid sun was climbing over the street below. Steam was already rising from the wet pavement. She checked the clock on the wall across from her desk. Six forty-five. Carter would be here soon.

❧

United States Senator David Baker applied his best poker-face as he pushed through the tall, wooden door of his Senate office. His staff grinned through their efforts to suppress their smiles. The reception area was silent as he walked over the standard, congressional-blue carpet. The office telephone was ringing, unanswered. A Blackberry buzzed against a pile of papers on the desk of his legislative aide.

Today was the day – the day he would be confirmed to the United States Supreme Court. His staff knew the rule. They had been through too many elections with him to forget. *No celebration until the votes are counted.*

He checked his watch as he closed the door of his private office. Seven a.m. on the nose. Two hours until the hearing started. Senator Baker breathed in the solitude and allowed himself to think about cleaning out his desk.

❧

Hannah Baker scrambled past her husband as she tracked their daughter around their hotel suite. Her daughter's white dress flapped in her hand. "John, it is 7:30. We are supposed to be at your father's office in fifteen minutes," she called over her shoulder as she rounded the corner into the bedroom of the suite. "Can you make sure Grant is ready?"

John Baker took one absentminded look at his son. He was ten feet away, watching cartoons on the couch and pulling at the collar of his dress shirt. "He's ready," he yelled back.

At the small table in the corner of the suite's kitchenette, John Baker closed his eyes and prayed.

༄

It is 07:45. I am walking west on Constitution Avenue. There are six police cars lined in front of the Dirksen Senate Office Building. Two officers are marking off an area in the lane farthest from my position. One is sweating. The area is fifteen feet wide and forty feet long. There is a similar-sized area on the opposite side of the street, near my immediate position.

Inventory (on person): $350, binoculars, Echo Industrial 9mm Luger handgun, two ammunition clips, personal 9mm Luger with full ammunition clip, detachable silencer, one vial of the substance, Mark Ellis's Blackberry.

Everything else that remained in his possession had been stowed in his rental car. Much earlier this morning, Noah Augusteel had left the car where he planned – where he hoped – he would need it the most.

A black town car was pulling into the area cordoned off by the Capitol Police. It splashed the remainder of a small puddle into the left lane of Constitution as it came to a stop. He could see John Baker's tall frame extending over the shimmering roof of the car. His wife stepped from the rear, driver's-side seat. Baker opened the other rear door and helped his children from the car.

Noah watched the town car pull forward, wait for a break in the traffic, and circle into the oncoming lane. It parked in the area that had previously been blocked off by the police.

It parked directly in front of Noah Augusteel. As they had for each day of the hearings, the Capitol Police had blocked a lane of Constitution Avenue and used it to manage the arrival of witnesses. They used the area on the opposite side of the street as a parking area for the witnesses' vehicles.

Augusteel watched as John Baker and his family climbed the stone steps of the Dirksen Senate Office Building – the family of the king, come to watch the coronation. He tightened the straps of his backpack and lowered the brim of his hat to conceal more of his face.

It is 07:47. I am walking west on Constitution Avenue.

At exactly eight o'clock on Monday morning, Mark Ellis stepped into the painfully bright sunlight dousing the front steps of Luke Lyford's apartment building. He shielded his eyes against the sun and waited for the swarm to arrive. One-by-one they ventured from their vans, bleary-eyed and tired. He could see the looks of recognition, followed shortly by a charge across the street.

Mark waited until each reporter had arrived. Cameramen trailed behind, and took up their usual position behind their respective reporter. The assembled group formed a semi-circle around Mark.

"I was recently contacted by the Office of the Chief Medical Examiner. My understanding is that a body was discovered and has been preliminarily identified as Luke Lyford." His voice was choppy.

A few reporters shouted questions toward him. Mark ignored them and proceeded with his prepared statement. "At ten o'clock this morning I am scheduled to visit the medical examiner's office. I have been asked to officially identify the body."

More questions were lobbed at him.

"After I have identified the body I will be holding a press conference at 464 New York Avenue, Northwest. It is near the corner of L Street and New York. I will be making a major announcement concerning the William Iredell murder."

Questions flew past him, launched from the twelve or thirteen mouths at the foot of the stairs. Mark Ellis turned his back to the crowd and reached for the handle of the apartment building's front door.

∽

"I am scheduled to testify at nine," Edwin Carter said. His dark-blue coat was draped over the shoulder of the chair next to him. Dressed in a white shirt and red tie, he reclined and watched Gloria Augusteel reviewing the map on her desk.

"We'll put assets here, here . . . and two more over here." She was pointing to an image of the Dirksen Senate Office Building. "We'll have two more posted along the rear of the building." She glanced up at the Attorney General. "The police have blocked off an area for your driver. Have him drop you off directly in front of the building. He will then park on the opposite side of the street, in the area the police have designated. I'll trail you in one of our SUVs.

"We'll have the six assets in place before you arrive. Plus your driver. Plus me, and my driver. We'll have nine on the ground while you testify." She looked over his head at the clock. It was a few minutes after eight. "The advance assets should be arriving soon. I'll coordinate the protection from my vehicle. When you conclude your testimony, I'll notify your driver to move back into the pick-up area near the door. We should be able to minimize your time on the street."

Edwin Carter was only vaguely listening to her explanation. He had long ago tired of this sort of operational detail. Instead, he was thinking of David Baker. Carter would be the last witness brought forward in support of Baker's nomination. As the Attorney General he was the highest-ranking spokesman on legal issues in the administration. His testimony would officially represent the opinion of the President of the United States.

He was looking forward to watching the committee vote on David Baker. It was a lock. Baker had more support than he needed to get past the committee. And from there, official confirmation by the whole Senate was a mere formality. Baker was going to be a strong, conservative voice on the Supreme Court. He would have rather had Iredell – Iredell, before he discovered that letter, of course – but David Baker was a close second.

The thought of William Iredell brought other images to mind. *The substance.* Gloria had used their last vial on Luke Lyford. But her brother – they assumed – still had one, the last one. *I'd kill to have that last vial.* He paused, smiling at the words that had formed in his mind. *I'd find whoever took that Madison letter and rip the location right out of them.*

That damn letter, he thought. *Why did Iredell have to find that letter?*

And where is it now?

Edwin Carter rose from his chair and found the small refrigerator enclosed in the bookcase behind his seat. He opened a bottle of water. The sound of the plastic safety ring tearing from the cap was comforting. Until they could put their hands on the last vial of the substance – or Noah Augusteel – he wasn't taking any chances.

The cell phone on Gloria Augusteel's desk sounded a two-note ring. She reached for it and read the face of the phone. "The assets watching Ellis," she explained to Carter before she stood to activate the signal-masking device in the book-shelf to her left.

"Augusteel," she answered. She listened for a few moments, the look of concern growing on her face.

"What?!" She interrupted the explanation coming over the phone.

Carter stopped examining the titles on her bookshelf and turned back toward Augusteel. She was standing near the expansive window behind her desk.

"Are you sure that is what he said?" she asked into the phone.

Another thirty seconds from the other side of the conversation. Augusteel ended the call.

"What did they say?" Carter demanded, now entirely focused on Gloria.

"Ellis made some sort of an announcement a few minutes ago. He's going to identify Luke Lyford's body at ten this morning."

"OK. We knew that would happen."

"Then," she responded, "Ellis is coming here. To hold some sort of press conference about William Iredell."

"'Here?' What do you mean 'here?'"

"Here. To this office. He told the press he was going to hold his press conference at 464 New York Avenue. That's here – that's our office." She pointed out the window. "That corner, right there."

Carter had stepped next to her. Together they watched the rush-hour traffic flow into downtown DC. "Ellis can't make it to this office. You have to get to him before that press conference."

"What about your testimony at the Baker hearing?"

"Leave a few assets on me. Take a few with you. Stopping Mark Ellis has to be the top priority now."

Chapter Thirty-Five

Washington, DC
July 5, 2010

With a deliberate and smooth effort, United States Attorney General Edwin Carter rose from his front-row seat. The deep navy of his suit blended with the dark-blue leather of the chairs in the Senate hearing room. Behind him, each seat was filled. The eyes of the crowd followed him as he stepped forward, toward the center table. Ahead of him, David Baker turned. Baker was already seated in the well of the room, at the witness table – the focal point of the half-circle of Senators that made up the Judiciary Committee. He rose from his seat as Carter, his long-time fellow-traveler in conservative politics, approached the polished oak of the witness table.

Beyond Baker, the media had been allowed to momentarily fill the open space between the witness table and the raised seats of the committee. Their cameras faced away from the Senators, back toward the witness table. Some filmed the

Attorney General as he approached. Flashes from the cameras lit the room behind Carter.

Slowing his pace to a near crawl, Carter enjoyed the attention of the media. He stopped as he reached the seat next to Baker. Shoulder-to-shoulder, they stood and waited for the Chairman of the committee – Baker's chestnut hair, blue tie, and gray suit; Carter's salt-and-pepper hair, red tie, and blue suit. Against the backdrop of the wood-paneled hearing room, the image was one of strength, invincibility. The packed rows of spectators filling the chairs behind them watched in impressed silence.

"Please raise your right hand, Mr. Attorney General."

Carter followed the instructions and listened to the oath as it was read by the Chairman. With an "I do" he acknowledged his obligation to tell the truth. His right hand lingered in the air for a brief moment after he finished. More flashes from the cameras. Mirroring the lenses in front of him, Edwin Carter flashed a smile at David Baker as they took their seats. "Let's finish this, Senator. It's time to get you on the Court."

With the exception of one, each seat in front of Carter was filled. He could see staff members – one or two for each Senator – seated along the rear wall, escorting their respective Senator like royal guards. In the left corner, an American flag overlooked the hearing room, standing next to a door leading toward the Senators' offices. Near the right corner, a large clock hung on the ornate wall. It was now a few minutes after nine.

The Chairman held his gavel aloft, but had turned his chair to whisper something to one of his aides. Carter slowly moved his eyes along the panel of Senators as he waited for the gavel to fall, and for the hearing to start. Even the liberals had decided to appear for this last witness.

The Chairman – a Democrat, but one who had already announced his support for David Baker – had released a rough schedule over the weekend. Carter would testify for the next hour or so, then David Baker would give a final statement before the committee. There would be a break for lunch and then the Judiciary Committee would reassemble for the final vote in the early afternoon.

Carter heard the press re-taking their assigned positions behind him. Most sat along the floor. Some stood along the walls to his left and right. Their cameras now aimed over his shoulder, toward the members of the committee. He examined the single empty seat almost directly in front of him. Senator David Baker's seat – to the Chairman's right, on the raised dais. As the top-ranking Republican on the committee, Baker held the seat closest to the center. As the subject of the confirmation hearing, the Senator had escaped that seat and taken the one at the center table.

The gavel banged. And the questioning started.

The shortest-tenured Senator opened the questioning. A newly-elected Democrat from Maine, she sat in the farthest-left seat along the dais. She sat so far to his right that Carter had to adjust his chair to see her directly. He could hear the media shuffling behind him, angling to film the Senator as she addressed the witness.

As expected, her fifteen minutes were filled with long-winded questions that – if they actually ended in a question mark – called for a simple 'yes' or 'no'. This was the game, and Edwin Carter knew the rules. He listened attentively, provided answers when they were necessary, and reiterated the talking-points the White House had provided.

The Chairman notified the Senator that her time had expired and passed control of the witness to the Republican seated on the far right, the most recently elected member of his party. His questions were of the same sort: lengthy, scripted, and closer to a speech than a question. Where the liberal Senator from Maine had offered praise for Baker as a person, but criticized the conservative philosophy he might take to the Supreme Court, the Republican Senator offered nothing less than glowing support.

And so it continued for nearly an hour. The Chairman directed the hearing. The questioning alternated between the parties and narrowed toward the center of the panel. Each Senator relished his or her fifteen minutes of undivided attention. The media dutifully provided that attention. Carter, again, reiterated his talking points.

And Senator David Baker took small step after small step toward becoming Supreme Court Justice David Baker.

∽

At precisely 9:30, Mark Ellis emerged from Luke Lyford's apartment building. He had locked the apartment door behind him and left the spare key with the doorman. His charcoal-colored suit was a furnace in the sweltering sun.

Mark lowered his suitcase and briefcase onto the stone entrance area. The media was in place; they had gathered near the front entrance as ten o'clock approached, eager to tail him toward Luke's body and follow him to the press conference. It looked to Mark like they had doubled – maybe tripled – in number. It was a nice side-effect of his announcement. *More cover*, he thought, recalling Noah Augusteel's advice.

He gave them a minute to collect their cameras. Some of the reinforcements had brought extendable microphone poles and were stretching them toward Ellis, dangling the black plastic bars over the front steps. Mark lifted his briefcase and suitcase, and with one in each hand he slowly began to walk toward his truck. He only needed to cover a block on Massachusetts, but it took him nearly ten minutes. As he walked – following the plan he and Noah had worked out on Saturday – he spoke to the media, restating what he had already announced that morning.

Hand-held recorders pushed closer to his mouth. The extendable poles swung overhead, their microphones dipping low toward Ellis. Cameramen moved ahead of him, leapfrogging each other to film Mark. Encased in the crowd of reporters, he slowly meandered down the street.

Mark reached the driver's side door of his truck and tossed his suitcase into the rusty bed of the old vehicle. Reaching into the cab, he dropped his briefcase on the passenger seat. He climbed into the cab and closed the door. Two news vans were blocking traffic behind him. *They are going to follow me every foot of the way.* Pleased, he cranked the old engine to life.

It was a straight-shot down Massachusetts to the Office of the Medical Examiner. As he had during his last trip, he slowed his pace below the speed limit and allowed the media to stay close. He worked his way around Stanton Park. *This is where they found Luke's body*, Mark recalled from his first conversation with Sam Ortiz. He checked his rear-view mirror again. The vans were directly behind him. It was 9:49 according to his small dashboard clock. Rush hour was over and his rusty, red truck was easy to track on the nearly open road. *So far, so good*, he thought.

Massachusetts Avenue dead-ended into 19th Street. He could see the intersection one block ahead of him as he turned right on 17th Street. One block later he was turning left on Potomac, copying his path from Saturday morning and following the path dictated by DC's one-way streets. Mark could see the Metro station he had used as a landmark to his right. The entrance to the underground parking area was just past the station. This time the media knew what was coming and stopped short of the entrance, lining the sidewalk of 19th with their vans. Mark watched as he left them behind, the sun reflecting off the small satellite dishes attached to their roofs.

He gripped the cracked leather on the top of his steering wheel and guided his truck downward on the ramp leading into the parking area. The reflection of the sun disappeared. As his eyes adjusted to the dark, he passed his driver's license to the guard at the gate.

❧

It didn't take Gloria Augusteel's considerable talents at urban reconnaissance to track a cloud of media vans and a creaking pick-up truck, travelling at a snail's pace, through Washington – especially since the convoy had spent nearly the entire route on one street. Edwin Carter had left her office after she received the call from the assets monitoring Ellis. She had departed shortly thereafter and positioned herself between Mark Ellis and the medical examiner's office. She parked one block off the route she expected Ellis to take. She waited, a spider concealed in the concrete grass of downtown DC.

From the passenger seat of the black Yukon, she had roughed in an assault protocol. She had what she needed: two specific locations and one specific point in time. He would be at the Office of the Medical Examiner at ten and would proceed from there to the corner outside the Echo Industrial office. The intercept would happen between those two locations.

Target moving.

They watched his truck pass on Massachusetts and then followed – well behind the column of vans, but within striking distance should the opportunity arise. Gloria Augusteel dislodged the ammunition clip from the handgun she had taken from the Echo cache, examined the weapon for any flaws, and re-inserted the clip. It cleanly locked into place.

∽

At one minute before ten o'clock, Mark Ellis steered his truck into an open parking place in the underground lot. The empty parking area from Saturday was nearing capacity on Monday morning, and he had to walk a short way to reach the door to the medical examiner's office.

Sam Ortiz was waiting for him inside the door, his white coat folded over his arm. The entrance area from the garage was not air conditioned and the heat baked the windless corridor. Ortiz wiped a drop of sweat from his forehead.

"Let's get this show on the road, Dr. Ortiz," Mark said as he approached. The two men followed the same pathway as they had on Saturday, except this time Paul Sorenson met them at the double-doors of the examination room. Sam could feel the slight hesitation in Mark's step. As they reached the Chief Medical Examiner, Ortiz introduced the attorney and recounted for his boss how the body had arrived on Saturday, but it had taken until late Sunday before Sam had noticed the resemblance between the unidentified, white male and the pictures of Luke Lyford in the newspaper.

"I tracked down Mr. Ellis as soon as I made the connection, and he was willing to come down to make the identification this morning."

Paul nodded and followed the other two men into the examination room. The official identification required only a quick look at the body. It was over in minutes. Paul Sorenson offered his thanks and shook Mark's hand. Eager to end the charade, Sam quickly ushered Mark down the hallway, back toward the parking garage.

Sorenson watched the two men leave and pressed the call button next to the panel of elevator doors. As he waited, he pulled his cell phone from his pocket. "He's coming your way."

"Thank you." The voice was covered in static – a product of both the underground basement hallway and the portable Echo Industrial signal-masking device Gloria Augusteel had initiated before answering the call.

The line went dead. The Chief Medical Examiner for Washington, DC returned his phone to the pocket of his white coat and stepped into the elevator.

∽

Gloria Augusteel saw the red truck exit the parking garage, turn right, and stop. The media flocked again. The light changed and the truck led the caravan back onto Massachusetts.

I am on Massachusetts Avenue. There are five vans ahead of me and three behind me. Tracking team (two assets) is thirty yards behind me in a green SUV. Alpha team (two assets) is on Constitution Avenue. Beta team (two assets) is on Sixth Street. Three additional assets are securing the engagement area.

She checked her map again as they trailed the line of press vans.

One shot. I have one shot to get this right, she reasoned. *Control the environment. Anticipate the variables. Move the pieces on the board.* Ahead of her she could see the truck circling Lincoln Park. *He's taking East Capitol Street, as expected.*

She adjusted the signal-masking device in the console, and contacted the two teams ahead of her and the three assets waiting at the target's expected arrival site. Ellis was right on schedule and following the path she had anticipated.

They turned onto Constitution. The Dirksen Senate Office Building was on their right. The red truck slowed for a red light, giving her a brief opportunity to check in on the morning's other operation. To her left, Gloria could see Edwin Carter's vehicle parked on the opposite side of the street. The Attorney General's town car sat in the blocked-off parking area. His driver – an Echo-trained asset – manned the front seat like a guard dog.

She adjusted the small radio system at her waist and spoke into the wrist-microphone. She was in-range now and could tap directly into the channel on which the team assigned to Carter was communicating. There were no problems, they informed her. Carter appeared to be nearing the end of his testimony. He was being questioned by the Democratic Chairman, the final Senator scheduled to question the witness before a recess.

Ahead of the line of vehicles, the light changed. She watched the brake lights of the vans darken. Gloria Augusteel switched her radio system back to its original channel and reviewed the map. She was prepared. Ellis remained on the expected route.

Ahead of her a team of Echo assets merged onto Constitution, much closer to the target than her Yukon. Alpha team was in play. The first strand of the web was in place.

Noah Augusteel's eyes trailed the man as he exited the side door of the building and swiftly jogged down 19th Street. From his vantage point he could only see the white medical coat moving through the light mid-morning crowd. The street formed the eastern border of the DC General Hospital campus, and the white coat soon became one of a handful moving along the sidewalk.

Augusteel raised his field binoculars to his eyes, lifting the brim of his hat slightly up as he held the hard-plastic frame. One of the white coats turned into the Metro station and disappeared down the underground stairs.

He checked his watch as he flagged down a cab. It was 10:20.

Chapter Thirty-Six

"Mr. Carter," the southern drawl of the Democratic Chairman filled the hearing room. "I'd like to thank you for your time today, sir – on behalf of myself and my good friend, the ranking Republican of this committee." The heavyset Chairman pointed his gavel at David Baker. "With that, sir, I believe your time with us is at an end."

The Chairman looked down at his watch, and then swiveled his head in order to eye both sides of the curved bench. "We'll take a short break – ten minutes. Then we'll hear from the Senator from North Carolina." He tapped his gavel on the wooden plate in front of him and reclined in his chair to whisper toward his assistant.

Below him, in the well of the great room, Carter collected his notes and backed his chair away from the table. "Good luck, Senator. Expect the President to be in touch this evening. He'll make some sort of statement after the vote."

David Baker rose from his seat, shook Carter's extended hand, and measured the eyes of the Attorney General. "I appreciate the support, Edwin." He forced a smile. "I know I wouldn't be here without you."

Carter turned away from the table. The cameras flashed around him as they targeted both the Attorney General and the Senator. There was other movement in the room as spectators and staff members left their seats during the recess. One of the Chairman's assistants was making his way behind the committee seats, refilling each Senator's water glass. Another refilled the glass pitcher on the witness table and set new, empty glasses in front of the two chairs.

David Baker was a few steps behind Carter and made his way toward his family. He lifted his granddaughter out of her front-row seat and held her in his left arm as he quietly spoke to John. After a minute or two, he handed the young girl to her father. He shook the hands of a few other supporters in the front row and returned to the witness table. Sitting alone, he reviewed the notes he was planning to use in his final speech before the committee.

Edwin Carter returned to the open chair in the front row and settled in to watch David Baker give his final remarks.

ᕯᔦ

John Baker studied the back of his father's head. It was slightly bowed toward his lap as he read the notes in front of him. The cameras had turned away; the media was also taking advantage of the break in the hearing. The noise of the room swirled around him, but it was muted, like white noise lost in the background.

His wife returned from escorting their son to the water fountain in the hall. John squeezed her hand as they took their assigned seats on the front row. *Let this be the right thing to do.*

He had wavered over the weekend, but in the end he had decided to talk to his father. It had been an uncomfortable and awkward conversation. John Baker was passing along a weighty accusation, one that accused the sitting Attorney General of not only murder, but also manipulating and undermining the American government. And, as if that wasn't enough, he relayed to his father what he had been told about the Lexington League: that the simple, conservative, advocacy organization that had supported Senator David Baker throughout his political career was just the public face of a much more insidious outfit.

Finally, he had discussed what he considered to be the hard evidence: the connection between the Madison letter and the three dead bodies. There was a trail – a clear, discernable trail that linked the Madison letter to the murders of Luke Lyford, William Iredell, and Everett Johansson.

John Baker knew that if anyone, other than John, would have brought this information and this allegation to David Baker's office, the Senator would have immediately summoned a swarm of U.S. Capitol police. Yet, he had listened as John spoke.

"What if we're wrong?" David Baker had asked.

"There's a failsafe, dad," John had responded. "If we are wrong, if he has nothing to do with this, then our plan will fall apart before it goes too far."

In the warm confines of his ceremonial office, David Baker had rocked back in his desk chair. His eyes had focused on the aging, white ceiling above him. "And — even worse, John — what if we're right?" the Senator had asked his son. "And if we are right, is this the just outcome? Is this plan, this plot, something our family should be involved with? Is there no other way?"

In response, John Baker had simply risen from his seat and removed the soldered Samuel Adams quote from his father's wall. The ancient piece of the stagecoach was a near replica of the one sitting on John's office credenza, back along the North Carolina coast.

He had read the quote aloud. His words were muddy hooves, pounding on cobblestone.

The liberties of our country, the freedom of our civil Constitution, are worth defending at all hazards; and it is our duty to defend them against all attacks . . .

His pace had accelerated. It was Samuel Adams, on horseback, charging with a ragtag regiment of rebels.

. . . It will bring an everlasting mark of infamy on the present generation, enlightened as it is, if we should suffer them to be wrested from us by violence without a struggle . . .

David Baker's eyes had remained locked on the ceiling. His chair had tilted as far back as it would reach. His voice had joined his son's for the final phrase.

. . . or to be cheated out of them by the artifices of false and designing men.

John Baker was still holding his wife's hand when he heard the Chairman gavel the committee meeting back to order. The three strikes of the gavel drew the eyes of the room to David Baker, sitting alone at the witness table.

John Baker, however, had his eyes on the door in the left corner.

❧

"Thank you, Mr. Chairman. And I would also like to say 'thank you' to the committee. I appreciate the time each Senator has taken over these last couple of weeks. This is a long process, but an important one for our country." David Baker's strong voice was the only sound in the room.

He paused. Behind him, the video cameras were filming each move he made. "Mr. Chairman," David Baker began, "while I have prepared some final remarks and am looking forward to sharing them with my colleagues, I believe it would be technically out of order for me to offer them at this time."

The Chairman was caught off-guard. For a brief moment, the heavyset man looked confused; then he instantly regained the appearance of composure. His deep voice was friendly, but he disliked surprises in his committee. "Senator, I'm not sure I'm following you. We've completed the questioning of each witness. This committee has nothing left on its schedule except for your final comments and then the vote on your confirmation."

"That is just it, Mr. Chairman — we have not actually completed the questioning of each witness."

The Chairman's confusion rippled into the crowd. A brief murmur; then it was quiet again.

David Baker continued. "Until I'm confirmed by the Senate, I'm not a member of the Supreme Court – I'm still a Senator. And, so long as I'm a Senator, I'm a member of this committee." The open seat next to the Chairman suddenly seemed larger. Some cameras quickly spun to film the golden-edged name plate in front of the empty chair that would normally have been filled by David Baker. "And, so long as I'm a member of this committee, I believe I have a right to question the witnesses that have been called before this committee. Would you agree, Mr. Chairman?"

For what felt like a longer moment than it actually was, the Chairman made no move to answer. He studied the nominee, not sure where Baker was leading him. He responded, the words drawn out as they slowly left his mouth. "I believe you are correct, Senator Baker."

"In that case, Mr. Chairman, I'd like to pose some questions to the Attorney General."

The ripple passed through the crowd again, but this time the voices were less restrained. The Chairman rocked back in his chair and swung to the side to address one of his aides. Baker, along with the crowd, watched the side of the old man's face as he and the aide whispered to each other. After the hushed, short discussion with the member of his staff, he returned his chair to face the hearing room. "Mr. Attorney General, it seems your testimony is not complete. Please come back on up to the witness table."

Edwin Carter had watched the conversation between Baker and the Chairman with growing confusion, then concern. The smile was gone from his face as he rose from his seat and strode toward the seat next to Baker. His eyes scanned the room, then the back of Baker's head, then the side of his face. He searched for any clue indicating what was happening — and what would happen next.

The deep voice of the Chairman boomed into the well of the room. "Mr. Attorney General, my staff instructs me that I'll need to swear you in again. Will you please stand and raise your right hand?"

Carter rose from his seat, pushing the cushioned chair slightly back as he stood before the oak table. David Baker stole a glance upward, and to the left, eyeing Carter's raised, right hand. *The five-sided ring*, he thought. *He's wearing it.*

"Do you swear to tell the truth . . . ." The Chairman's voice echoed over the heads of the media. Each camera was trained on Carter and Baker.

Baker reached for the water pitcher on the table in front of him. The empty glasses had been set out during the recess; one was in front of Carter's seat, the other in front of Baker's. He lifted the pitcher with his right hand and reached for his empty glass.

Carter's eyes shifted downward. He watched Baker tilt the pitcher.

". . . the whole truth . . . ." The Chairman's voice rang out.

Baker had filled his own glass. He leaned closer to Carter's waist, shifting toward him as Carter stood in front of the table. David Baker reached under Carter's uplifted right arm and pulled back the empty glass from Carter's side of the table.

" . . . and nothing but the truth . . . ."

Baker filled Carter's glass and placed it back in front of the witness.

". . . so help you God?" the Chairman finished the oath.

"I do," the Attorney General responded, and took his seat next to Baker. He reached for the water glass as he whispered to Baker. "David, what the hell are you doing?"

Baker looked at the man in the chair next to him, opening his mouth to respond. Before he could speak, he was interrupted by the voice of Chairman. "Senator Baker, are you planning to take your seat up here while you question this witness?"

Baker glanced to his left. Carter had taken his seat and was quietly sipping the water, waiting for Baker to respond to the Chairman.

"No. I'll keep my seat down here, Mr. Chairman."

৽৽

Mark Ellis's red truck led the caravan up Sixth Street, toward New York Avenue. A parking structure rose on the right as the truck approached the intersection. Ahead, the light changed to yellow.

Gloria Augusteel's ear piece came to life. Beta team reported in. On schedule: 10:31. The leader of the three-man team stationed inside the parking structure spoke into the open channel. They were also in position, he reported, and awaiting the arrival of the truck.

She checked her watch again, then glanced at the traffic ahead of her. The two assets assigned to the Beta team were on-foot and approaching the target. From her position she couldn't see the red truck. The media remained between her and the target. She knew New York Avenue loomed in front of her, roughly perpendicular to the street she was on. One final turn and the truck would be in sight of her office.

Her wrist rose toward her mouth. Her voice was even, distributing instructions like an assembly line. "Alpha team. Go. Now." Two blocks ahead of her, the black SUV had worked its way directly in front of the slow-moving red truck. The driver heard her instructions through his ear piece and slammed on his brakes, bringing his vehicle to a jerky stop near the intersection.

Behind him, the red truck did the same, its front bumper stopping just shy of the shining chrome of the SUV. The news van behind the red truck didn't react in time to avoid the collision. At the slow speeds it was little more than a slight bump.

Beta team reported to Gloria Augusteel. The two plain-clothed assets were engaging. "Keep your channel open," she instructed, her voice steady.

"Turn right," Augusteel commanded the young asset at the wheel of her vehicle. The SUV turned onto K Street, one block short of where the red truck had been barricaded. To her left, she could see the other side of the same parking structure. It occupied the entire city block and, at its opposite corner, touched the intersection of Sixth and New York. She issued a second command. "There. Take that entrance."

They entered the lower level of the parking garage. The Yukon initially slowed as it turned onto the sloped ramp, but then accelerated as it crossed the cleared-out lower level of the structure. Its wet wheels squealed on the old pavement. Headlights spotted the concrete columns as the vehicle wove between the thick poles.

Opposite her entry point, on the surface street, her two plain-clothed assets reached the target. One moved toward the rear of the truck. The other reached for the passenger door. It was unlocked. The asset at the passenger door drew his weapon as he leapt into the cab. Papers spilled under his feet and out the open door.

The second asset had reached the rear of the truck. He casually crossed into the small space between the first van and the truck's tailgate. His assignment was to delay the media vehicles as long as possible. His partner, the asset in passenger seat, was to direct the driver to follow the black SUV stopped directly in front of the truck.

Alpha team, in the SUV ahead of the truck, waited for the signal.

Below ground level, Gloria Augusteel had reached the team of Echo assets waiting in the parking garage. Deployed in an open semi-circle they had surrounded the open garage door through which the truck would be forced. Their eyes transfixed on the open space, they waited for the appearance of the rust-covered front bumper.

Inside the truck, the asset had his weapon at the temple of the driver. He was shouting instructions. The driver's face turned toward the weapon, gently pushing the circular end of the steel. In the intensity of the moment, the driver seemed, to the asset, to be moving exceptionally slow.

The asset's wrist was at his mouth. The "go" command surging through his throat.

The word stopped before it reached his mouth.

He could see the face of the driver. The asset had expected a look of panic. But the panic was absent.

∽

Gloria Augusteel paced behind the semi-circle of Echo assets. Their guns drawn; their legs bent, offset in a firing stance. *I will have you surrounded.* Her Luger was drawn, loaded, ready.

The first sentence passing through her ear piece seemed directed at someone else. "Who the hell are you?!"

She fired back into the open channel. "What? Who is this?! Identify yourself!"

The voice of the asset inside the truck responded. "Asset Beta check One," he answered, providing his team assignment and individual asset number. Despite his training, his steadiness was collapsing. She could hear the strain in the tone of his voice. She knew something was wrong.

"It's not him."

"What?!"

"It's not him!" The asset's voice was now near a yelling volume. Behind his voice she could hear the growing noise of car horns. She envisioned the media vans, breaking free from their momentary containment and surrounding the truck. Her design would delay them for only a few seconds, only long enough for the asset to force the driver to follow his instructions. That time had expired.

She responded, the volume of her voice climbing. "Not him?! Who is it?"

"Unknown."

"Unknown?"

In the cab of the truck, the asset's training broke completely. "I don't know!" he yelled.

She could hear dull thuds over the communication channel.

"It's some Mexican guy! It's not Ellis. Not Ellis!"

The channel was suddenly awash in noise. Multiple voices. Car horns, now definite and louder. One of the voices saw the asset's gun and was screaming.

Someone had opened one of doors of the truck. The media had surrounded the vehicle. Gloria could hear the asset, pushing his way through the crowd and shouting into the open channel. "Beta check One. Abort!" He repeated the panicked announcement, calling twice into his microphone. The sound of his voice was punctuated by his footsteps. He was running, escaping the red truck.

"Fall back!" She yelled as she pivoted toward her vehicle. She was waving the surrounding assets away. "Fall back, now!"

She was running too. Towards her vehicle. She could feel it. The variable. The sand in the gears. The destruction, the failure of her plan.

It was Noah. This was his work.

It was Edenton. It was the Iredell Family House again. It was a choice. *Noah or the historian?*

Investigate the Latino man in the truck or retreat toward Edwin Carter?

Her driver saw her coming, her silhouette growing in the beams of the headlights. The engine roared to life as she swung into the passenger seat. "Dirksen Senate Office Building. Don't stop for anything." Gloria Augusteel reached for her cell phone as the wet wheels squealed back across the pavement toward the opposite entrance. She checked the clock on her phone. It was 10:40.

Each ear in the Senate Judiciary Committee hearing room strained to hear David Baker, as though his microphone had suddenly failed and left his voice lost in the massive space. He reiterated his last comment. "Mr. Chairman, while I will always appreciate the invitation to return to my old seat, I would prefer to stay here during the questioning. One of my staff members – a new legal counsel I've recently hired – will handle the questioning for me."

The Chairman's eyes remained on Baker. While it was not unusual for a Senator to turn over routine questioning to a staff member, it was rare to see it done during such a high-profile hearing. The departures from his expectation were growing in number, and the Chairman's unease was growing along with them.

To the Chairman's right, the door along the wood-paneled wall opened. Cameras and eyes swung toward the corner. A charcoal-colored suit entered through the door, passing the American flag and brushing against the hanging stripes.

Mark Ellis made his way behind the seated Senators, trying to avoid their spinning chairs as they rotated to watch him. The staff members seated along the wall managed to contain their shock long enough to inch their chairs from his path. Flashbulbs lit the room, breaking the fundamental rule of the hearing. The Chairman ignored them as he joined the crowd and watched the face that had graced the front pages of each DC newspaper for the better part of a month work its way toward David Baker's open seat.

If Edwin Carter's mind could have registered anything other than sheer dread, he most likely would have been quite frustrated by the image of Claire Ellis's son taking David Baker's Senate seat. But thoughts like that were a luxury he didn't have at the moment.

Before him, Mark Ellis pulled back the chair and locked eyes with the Attorney General. It felt like they were the only two people in the room.

❧

John Baker released his wife's hand.

Mark Ellis had entered exactly on cue and the crowd behind him exploded into more sound than the stoic walls of the committee room had heard in years, maybe ever. The Chairman hammered his gavel. Once. Again. It had no effect. The flashes from the cameras continued.

Noah Augusteel was out there. *He said he could get the one he needed*, John Baker thought. *He said he could work around the edge, around the border of whatever protection was in place.* He checked the clock along the right side of the wall. It was a couple of minutes past 10:30.

Edwin Carter was only a few feet from him. Augusteel had told John Baker what to say. He, in turn, had provided the phrase to his father. It was time for his father to pass it to Carter.

The failsafe, he considered. *If he runs, he's our man. It will confirm everything they've told me. If not . . .*

❧

Noah held Mark Ellis's Blackberry to his ear. The hearing was being webcast. He heard Baker speak and then nothing but crowd noise. He rounded the corner and advanced toward his target.

Target is twelve feet ahead. It is 10:32. I am on Constitution Avenue in Washington, DC. Two civilians have passed me. They are fifty yards behind me. Three others are forty yards ahead. Four threats, one hundred yards ahead on right: police officers monitoring the unloading area.

The sound will be completely muffled if pure contact is made. It will not reach the three civilians ahead of me.

Target window: now.

I am tapping on the window with the silencer extension. The door is opening. I am holding his wrist. I am firing downward into his ribs. I am moving the body onto the floorboard.

Time until his absence is noticed: three to four minutes.

❧

The falling gavel finally had its intended effect. The silence was sudden and hit Edwin Carter harder than the abrupt noise. The Chairman was speaking to Mark Ellis. He could see the Chairman's lips moving. The room came into immediate focus. Carter could feel the heat of the lights for the first time. The red lights of the cameras bored into his back. Everything was moving slowly around him.

Mark Ellis was leaning forward, hovering behind David Baker's nameplate. He adjusted, and then spoke into, the small microphone. "I'd like to ask the Attorney General some questions about the federal protection provided to Parker Brown."

Carter was reeling. *How could this happen?* The crowd stirred behind him, anxious but cowed by the Chairman's gavel.

David Baker's hand was on his forearm, bending toward him. He was close to Carter. He was whispering something.

"To the Republic."

David Baker lifted his own glass of water. He tilted it toward the Attorney General, as though he was responding to an offered toast.

Then he lifted it higher, straightened his back, and poured the glass back into the pitcher.

Edwin Carter's panicked eyes had been watching Mark Ellis. They instinctively recalibrated, focusing on the water splashing back into the glass pitcher. It sloshed into the unpoured water, washing against the sides.

He looked at his glass. He realized it was too late.

Attorney General Edwin Carter pushed away from the table. He could feel his blood-pressure climbing. His eyes spun from Baker, to the half-empty glass in front of his seat at the witness table, to Mark Ellis. His chair fell backward as he stood. *My God. Baker? Here? When did he get it into the pitcher?* The chair clamored to the ground, sending two cameras spilling away from him.

The first two steps quickly picked his way through the remaining cameramen squatting on the floor behind the witness table. Every other stride was a dead sprint, up the corridor that divided the hearing-room seats and out the front door of the Dirksen Senate Office Building.

Chapter Thirty-Seven

Washington, DC
July 5, 2010

There's no time.

Edwin Carter was searching. *Where is the damn car?* His mind raced, but was being outpaced by his heart. It pounded against his ribs like a caged animal. He splashed through a puddle as he turned onto the concrete sidewalk.

One of the police officers assigned to the unloading area recognized him and took a step in his direction, but Carter was already sprinting again, twisting through traffic as he crossed Constitution toward the holding area for his car. A delivery van screeched to a stop as he stumbled in front of it.

Black and shining, his town car was already idling when he reached it. He dove in the back seat. "DC General!" He screamed toward the front seat. "Now! Now!" He clutched his chest and willed himself to take deeper breaths.

The powerful engine pushed the car into traffic. Carter could hear the sound of the motor as it increased; he could feel the vibration through the seat. The car changed lanes, then shifted back into its original lane. He could see the architecture of the large gray buildings blurring through the tinted windows. Speed increased as they shot across the intersection.

Carter sat upright in the soft leather seat. He had loosened his tie. His jacket was off one arm. *This is wrong*, he felt. *Something is wrong.*

It was at that moment that Edwin Carter heard the locking mechanisms engage to his left and right. The driver's right hand moved toward the communication console imbedded in the dashboard. *He's jamming my cell signal*, Carter knew.

❧

Noah Augusteel planted his foot against the pedal of the town car. After driving the four cylinders of his rental car for the past three weeks, he relished the feel of the power. He checked his watch before he spoke to his passenger. It was 10:37. "Calm down, Mr. Attorney General. You have not been poisoned."

Augusteel smiled into the rear-view mirror and lifted his Luger over the edge of the front seat, into Carter's line of sight. With the tip of the handgun, he pressed a plastic button on the control panel affixed to the ceiling of the car. A soundproof and heavily-tinted glass divider crawled upward from the back of the front seat.

Noah watched as its top edge climbed. In the rear-view mirror, he could see the graying hair of the Attorney General disappear behind the pane of glass. He relaxed his foot, dropping the town car into the same pace as the other traffic. They were alone.

෨ා

Ten minutes after she left the parking garage, Gloria Augusteel could see the Dirksen Senate Office building. *In sight, in range*, she recalled from the early months of her Echo training. Her right hand held her cell phone and was repeatedly dialing Edwin Carter. She was getting transferred straight to his voicemail. Her left hand was tucked along her belt, adjusting the channel on her tactical radio.

She clicked the knob forward two notches and heard nothing but confused chatter, a rainstorm of voices, the winds gusting left and right as new assets joined the alarmed conversation. Her wrist was at her mouth. She shouted into the radio, trying to cut through the overlapping voices of the detail she had assigned to the Attorney General.

Pointing her driver toward the marked-off section near the front steps of the office building, Gloria continued to try to break through the noise. She could see two of her assets now, standing, exposed and obvious, near the stone steps. Gloria Augusteel leapt onto the curb as the SUV slowed. "Talk." She pointed at the closest asset, his eyes growing wide as he noticed her closing on him.

"He just ran out. In the middle of the questioning."

Augusteel noticed the cameramen for the first time. There were two on the steps, filming the police officers and the sidewalk. And her assets. "Walk." She directed the assets away from the cameras. "He just ran out?"

"Yes, ma'am. By the time we made it out here, he was gone. His car is gone too. We haven't been able to raise the asset assigned to his car over the radio."

Her eyes were steel. She could feel the energy building, but there was no outlet, no direction. Traffic flowed past her as she stood on the corner of First and Constitution. The two assets watched her. She spun in a complete circle, searching the top of the buildings in the Capitol complex. Gloria looked for patterns in the pedestrian traffic. She searched windows, street venders, faces, sewer grates, cars as they sped past. There was nothing.

Noah has him.
She knew it and he knew it.

༄

Edwin Carter's town car eased into the covered parking area behind the building. A moment later the Luger escorted him from the rear seat. It pressed against his back as he walked down the alley and toward the private entrance. Before the security camera could lower its inquisitive eye, Augusteel forced the Attorney General's palm across the electronic reader. The side door automatically clicked open.

Carter needed a perfect reaction, an instant reaction from the guard. He knew it wouldn't happen. And it didn't. The guard hesitated as they entered. Carter stepped through first, with Augusteel clearly visible but shielded behind the taller Attorney General.

The hesitation cost the guard his life. Two soft sounds of metal-on-metal contact rang from Carter's right. It was the Luger. Augusteel had stepped to his side as they entered and his well-trained right arm had buried a bullet in the guard's chest and another in his forehead.

The weapon returned to Carter's ribcage. The elevator doors opened. Edwin Carter and Noah Augusteel climbed toward the ninth-floor conference room above the Lexington League headquarters.

❧

Noah Augusteel used the muzzle of the silencer to push his prisoner toward the ornate bar in the corner. "Fix us a couple of drinks, Mr. Carter." He kept the barrel pointed at the Attorney General as he assessed the room. The James Madison portrait hung on the wall to his immediate left. Augusteel looked over the five-sided conference table to his right, examining the wall of clear glass that divided the room from the city. The elevator doors were at his back, closed.

The liquid hit the glasses ahead of him as the Attorney General followed his instruction. Noah's eyes scanned the table of communication equipment to the man's right. "Have a seat," Augusteel commanded.

"This is my conference room. I'll make the invitation."

The handgun was a blur, swinging until his arm locked at the elbow. His extended arm was a straight line, angling slightly upward from his shoulder to the face of his captive. "Have a seat." Noah's voice was calm, almost unnaturally so.

This time there was no reply.

Carter placed one of the drinks near Augusteel and kept the other in his hand. He chose a seat on the opposite side of the room, placing the thick table between Augusteel and himself. Augusteel followed him halfway around the conference table, stopping at the communication console to locate the remote control for the television. Then he backtracked, moving closer to the elevator doors and lowering himself into the nearest leather chair. His right hand remained aimed toward Carter. With his left, he turned on the television mounted over the communication console.

The voice of the Fox News anchor filled the conference room, floating down on the two men from speakers imbedded in the ceiling above. A still photo of Carol Cushing spread across the screen. She was standing near the front of a bulky, melancholy building. It was clearly a government structure – virtually indistinguishable from many other buildings in downtown DC, but the name above the revolving doors gave away its identity: Office of the Chief Medical Examiner.

Augusteel and Carter both watched, their drinks momentarily forgotten. The anchor had turned the coverage over to a reporter. She stood before the medical examiner's office. Her blonde hair now took up half the split-screen. She brushed it behind her ear as she rotated her head toward the building, and then back toward the camera, turning her face between the subject of her report and the camera filming her, like she had seen so many other aspiring blonde reporters do before her. "Paul Sorenson, the chief medical examiner for DC, was taken into federal custody moments ago in connection with the William Iredell murder."

Augusteel rose from his chair and advanced toward Carter.

"According to sources from the federal prosecutor's office," the reporter continued, "a blood sample was delivered sometime over the weekend. Independent testing confirmed that the DNA in that blood sample matched William Iredell's."

Noah reached Carter's seat and the older man turned from the television. His attention shifted to the Echo Industrial asset holding a loaded weapon to his head. Augusteel held the gun against the older man's temple for a brief moment and then slowly moved the weapon toward the table. As the barrel of the Luger reached Carter's glass, the gun rotated in Augusteel's wrist and hooked around the glass. Using the barrel, he began to slide the liquor away from the Attorney General.

Noah knew where this confrontation was heading, and he wanted Carter's attention directed toward the weapon and the liquor. Carefully, dramatically, Augusteel slid the glass along the smooth conference table, drawing Carter's eyes directly toward the two objects. Returning to his seat, he settled Carter's drink next to his own.

The reporter's voice continued to be the only sound in the room. "Blood tests run over the weekend revealed an entirely different combination of drugs than the combination that had been reported by Dr. Paul Sorenson. The federal prosecutor for DC addressed the press moments ago," the reporter announced in her flat, Midwestern voice.

The screen shifted to a video of Carol Cushing speaking near the door of the building. "My office was notified over the weekend that Dr. Sorenson had engaged in a deliberate effort to conceal the true toxicology results from the prosecution. He has been detained under suspicion that he lied to federal investigators and obstructed the justice process."

From off-camera, the voice of a reporter had been picked up on the video. "Joshua Michaels, *Washington Times*," the male voice announced. "Who contacted your office?"

"The call came from a concerned citizen with specific information about the test results." Carol Cushing smiled. "The source was the very helpful, anonymous kind." The video ended and the reporter's face returned to the screen.

Noah Augusteel muted the television, and again the conference room sounded like a tomb. He laid the Echo-issued handgun on the polished surface of the conference table. His left hand held the small vial. *The last one*, he thought. With his right, he removed the small cap that had sealed in the white powder.

Carter watched. His eyes locked on Augusteel.

He glanced at Carter before he poured it – just to make sure his captive was paying close attention. The powder shifted in the vial as he tilted the tube. It blended into Carter's drink, briefly clouding the liquor before disappearing entirely. Augusteel clamped the rims of the glasses together with the thumb and index finger of his left hand. He lifted both in the air as he re-trained the gun on Edwin Carter. Three steps later he reached the older man and set the two glasses before him. "In case it's been a while since you've reviewed the Echo Industrial interrogation techniques, this is how it works: You've got a choice." He waved the Luger at the two glasses.

Carter glared past the weapon, toward the man holding it. "How dare you dictate to me? If you're going to shoot me, shoot me and get it over with." Carter leaned to his left and rested his temple against the end of the handgun, taunting the younger, blond-haired man.

"You have a choice," Augusteel reiterated. "You choose the clean one – the one without the poison – and, yes, I'm going to shoot you. And then I'm going to go after your family."

Noah let the threat linger in the room. He pushed Carter's head off his weapon and backed away. "You recall that, don't you, Edwin? It's a classic Echo tactic. Day-One stuff. 'Find the target's weak point and apply pressure,'" he quoted. Augusteel nodded toward the glasses on the table. Their amber liquor shimmered in the overhead light. "You take the other one – the substance – and I leave your family alone."

Carter made no move toward the glasses. He continued to glare at Augusteel.

"You'll just have to trust me on that," Noah replied in response to the glare. "You really have no other move here, Mr. Carter. That is, if you want to give your children, at least, a chance at safety. Make a choice. *Make the right choice.*"

Augusteel retreated to his chair and picked up the television remote, restarting the audio on the broadcast. "I'll give you a minute to think it over." He smiled mockingly at his prey.

Fox News had shifted its coverage back to the David Baker confirmation hearing. The news anchor was explaining that the Judiciary Committee had been called back to order after the strange and abrupt departure of the Attorney General. David Baker was alone at the witness table. Augusteel watched, glancing periodically at Carter. The other man stared at the glasses, seemingly unaware of anything else in the world.

"Choose, Edwin. Choose, or I'll choose for you." Augusteel tapped the butt of his weapon against the table.

He rotated his chair toward Carter. His patience was disappearing, fading toward invisibility just as the powder had in the scotch.

"No. I won't." The words crept out of Carter's mouth and seeped into the room.

The bullet sailed behind the Attorney General's head, shattering the central pane of the floor-to-ceiling window. Air rushed into the conference room. Jagged pieces of the window were plummeting toward the ground nine floors below. Carter leapt to his feet. It was more of a reflex: flight, not fight.

"Choose. Or the next one ends this little game." The voice was tranquil, cool. Behind the voice, however, Augusteel's internal clock began its countdown as the shards of glass rained onto the street below.

Carter took one step toward the table, shoving his chair to the side. He lifted the poisoned glass to his lips, hesitated, and looked over the rim at Noah Augusteel. Tipping the glass toward his mouth, the Attorney General threw his head back and consumed the scotch in one swallow.

Then he hurled the glass against the wall, shattering it against James Madison's chest.

Noah closed toward him.

෬

Edwin Carter could feel it now. It was nothing like the panic attack in the hearing room. *This is real*, he thought. *This one is not a bluff.* The pain was deepening. It was slowly growing from his stomach, spreading toward his throat. The sound of the television blasted through him. He reached for his ears, confident blood must be flowing from them. He fell to his knees. David Baker's voice packed into his mind. He could hear him at the witness table. He could envision him, testifying alone in the well of the hearing room.

"This letter," Baker was saying, through the speakers above Carter's head, "has been buried in the vault of history for generations. My friend – our friend – William Iredell uncovered it as he prepared to sit before this committee."

Augusteel was looming over him now. "Tell me the names of the five," he commanded.

No.

Carter knew it was futile. He could feel the air from the open window brushing over his shoulders. He stumbled to his feet. The pain was unbearable and he doubled over as he turned toward the opening behind him.

Baker's voice again, ringing out from the speakers. It was magnified, tearing through his body. "Judge Iredell called me the morning of his death. He knew I was travelling to Edenton after his confirmation hearings concluded. He asked me to visit his family's collection of documents and retrieve the original version of this letter."

Augusteel's hand was on his shoulder, holding him back. *Forward*, he urged his legs, trying to outrace the effect of the poison. *If I can get to the window . . . .* Augusteel kicked the back of his knee. Carter could feel himself buckling, no longer able to hold his weight.

"The names. Give me the names."

Augusteel had rolled him over on his back and was kneeling next to his chest. He could see the television over Augusteel's shoulder. *David Baker has the letter. He's giving it to them*. The voice from the hearing cut through the pain, bringing its own suffering along with it. "My recommendation is that a full-scale effort be made to authenticate this letter."

Edwin Carter realized it was nearly over. The fire was overwhelming. He fought to hold it in, to fight it off. If he could just get to the window. He kicked his legs, propelling the burning skin of his back across the hardwood floor of the conference room. Augusteel caught the other man's shirt as Carter launched himself toward the opening. The Attorney General was over the threshold now, the shattered edge of the window cutting into his spine.

"The names." Augusteel pulled him into a sitting position. Air swirled into the room through the open window, gusting around him. He could feel the heat of the summer air. It was warm and was replacing the coolness of the Lexington League conference room.

Carter could hold it no more. It was barely a whisper, but it was enough for Noah Augusteel. And too much for Edwin Carter. "There are only four, right now." He coughed the names in order, starting with Four and climbing toward the top. "And I am number one," he finished.

Edwin Carter expected a smile from the face in front of him, but it never came. The cold blue eyes were steadfast, unchanging. He hated those eyes. Those traitorous eyes. Those outlaw eyes.

Augusteel released his shirt, and Carter fell back onto the open window frame. His head rolled backward. For a moment, he could see only sky. Then he tilted his chin toward his chest. He could see back into the room. He could also feel the empty space beneath his shoulders. Augusteel was standing above his feet, holding onto the window frame. The room darkened behind the former asset's blond hair. James

Madison fell from view. The five-sided table slid into darkness. David Baker's image was erased, his voice surrendering into the shadow.

Edwin Carter thought of William Iredell. He could see Iredell's body, crossing the threshold of the elevator as he lay on the same conference room floor.

Augusteel was all he could see now, standing against the black curtain. Augusteel's voice thundered down over Carter. "You mean you *were* number one. "I'd say 'For the Republic' – like the league trained me to – but this one's for me."

Bracing his body with his left hand, Augusteel used his right foot to lift the Attorney General's legs, flipping them back toward his torso. The shift in position unsettled Carter's balance along the window edge. He toppled into the open air.

∽

Noah Augusteel turned toward the television. David Baker was reading the James Madison letter aloud. He watched the Senator stall, partially through the text. David Baker lifted his eyes from the letter and looked at the Chairman. Augusteel watched as the Senator's head carefully turned. He was making eye contact with each Senator, summoning their absolute attention.

"And this is the key phrase," Baker said, pointing to the letter. "To each generation, its own interpretation."

Augusteel felt the weight of the gun in his hand. It was nothing compared to the weight of the promise he had made to John Baker and Mark Ellis. He could see John Baker sitting in that apartment. He could hear him: *Don't confuse what you have proposed with justice. This is vengeance.*

He could see himself standing in front of the jury, his death on their lips. One word and they could kill him.

His whole life. The Lexington League had trained him, used him, controlled him. The faces of so many flooded from the recesses of his mind. Claire Ellis came last. He could see her as the images replayed in his memory. In the memory he could feel himself turning, looking over his shoulder as Ellis carried the poisoned water into the cockpit of her plane.

Blood must be paid with blood. Mark Ellis had quoted Augusteel back to himself. He and Baker had set the terms of their participation: Noah must pay for the death of Claire Ellis by turning himself in for her murder and by throwing his fate at the feet of twelve citizens from eastern North Carolina. Noah Augusteel had agreed, promised.

It had been a cost he was willing to pay.

The heft of the Luger strained against his arm. For the first time that he could remember, the lethality felt foreign. The steel no longer felt like an extension of his body. It was separate, distinct, threatening. Death was coming for him now.

If he kept his promise.

Wind rushed through the shattered window, carrying the sound of approaching sirens.

Edwin Carter is dead.

But there are three more. And now I have their names.

To be continued . . .

Epilogue

Arlington, Virginia
July 10, 2010

The dull sound of the helicopter blades was increasing behind her. It cut through the humid, summer air. She could feel the wind accelerating as the engine of the military-style helicopter prepared to lift off the landing platform.

Four was shaking her hand. He had sworn his loyalty moments before she had. She could feel the heavy metal of his ring as she gripped his hand. "Welcome, I'm looking forward to working with you," he yelled over the growing noise in the background.

It had gone unstated, but she knew Noah was the reason she had been forced to join as the second new addition, instead of the first. Despite her longer tenure and her new position at the head of Echo Industrial, she entered as the new Five, rather than the new Four. Her generations-long bloodline now had a blemish. *My twin brother, the traitor*, she thought.

"Thank you. I'm honored and am looking forward to serving," she called back to Four. "I think the council is going to greatly benefit from someone with your military background." She swung her arms out wide and smiled, gesturing toward the landing platform. Her long, blonde hair whipped around her face. "We already have."

They were five stories off the ground. As she turned and walked toward the open door of the helicopter, she twisted her hair into a single braid.

It is 19:30. I am boarding an MD 530F.

Arlington Cemetery stretched to her right. She could see rolling lines of white tombstones from the rooftop. The sun was dropping toward horizon. Her hands finished the thick braid and shielded her eyes. The Potomac was to her left, the water looked still in the dying light.

MD 530F. Capacity: five. Engine: Allison 250-C20. Rotor Diameter: twenty-seven feet, four inches. Maximum Speed: 152 knots. I am seven steps from the door.

Three waited for her in the open door of the helicopter and tossed her a helmet as she approached.

I am Five.

Gloria Augusteel caught the black helmet and deftly slipped it on as she reached the roaring blades of the MD 530F. Her left hand gripped the side bar as she pulled herself through the wind stream and into the helicopter. As she settled into her seat, she wrenched the door closed beside her, latching it shut as the connection between the helicopter and the landing platform severed.

It was lifting, rising above the rooftop landing area. Gloria Augusteel studied the ring on her finger as she felt the helicopter tip forward and gather speed. *Five sides*, she thought, spinning the silver pentagon and tracing the edges of the five-sided star carved into each face. *She had worked for this. She had earned this*, she told herself. It was, now, only to be worn for ceremonial purposes. But that had little effect on her pride.

She had reviewed every second of available footage from the David Baker confirmation hearing. She had watched as Baker had intently studied Edwin Carter's ring before he whispered in his ear. "It could be a coincidence," she had explained, two days after the hearing. "But we can't be sure." After hearing her analysis, the remaining three had removed their rings and One had declared his first order as the new leader of the Lexington League: the five were no longer allowed to wear the rings in a public setting.

The helicopter was turning, tilting left and circling away from the landing platform. She could see the building below from her window.

Five floors above ground, she thought. *Each floor has a main corridor that traces the shape of the building.*

Gloria rotated her five-sided ring and thought about her new seat among the five, her new seat at the top of the Lexington League.

A five-acre, open-air central plaza that is the same shape as the five-sided building.

A perfectly constructed ring of five.

The helicopter completed its turn and leveled out. The Pentagon disappeared from her view.

Gloria Augusteel slipped the ring from her finger and thought about the future.